THE DISTRACTION

SPRINGBROOK HILLS SERIES
BOOK 1

MORGAN ELIZABETH

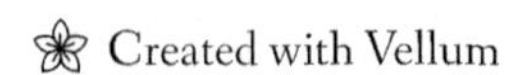
Created with Vellum

For my husband, who has supported all of my crazy dreams since day one.

A NOTE TO READERS

Dear Reader,

I can't tell you how much it means to me that you chose to grab my book off of your to-be-read list and spend some time with my characters. The Distraction was my first book, and writing it scared me, but changed my life. Thank you from the bottom of my heart for making my dreams come true.

The Distraction contains mentions of alcohol abuse, verbal abuse, infidelity, family estrangement, and parent illness. Please always put yourself first when reading—it's meant to be our happy place.

Love always,
Morgan

PLAYLIST

Trouble—Cage the Elephant
Bohemian Rhapsody—Queen
Detours—Jordan Davis
Body—Megan thee Stallion
Living—Dierks Bentley
Good 4 u—Olivia Rodrigo
Love Story—Taylor Swift

PROLOGUE

-HUNTER-

My hands grasp onto generous hips, fingers digging into the flesh as the curvy brunette rides me, her bare, tan back blanketed by a fall of dark hair. Guiding her as she moves, I marvel at the sight of that hair touching my abs, her head tipping back with a moan.

"God, Hunter, so good," she says as her movements become frantic, rhythm no longer a concern as she bucks on my cock, the feel of her tight pussy milking me.

"You like that, baby?" I ask, bucking my hips to drive deeper. Her voice rises to a scream as she clenches tight around me.

"God, yeah, I'm close!" I smile, knowing I'm going to fall right behind her.

The sound of a cell phone ringing shakes me from my dream and into reality. Sprawled in my king-sized bed in my penthouse apartment, I wake to the sound of my phone blaring and a raging hard-on.

I need to get fucking laid, I think as I run a hand over my face, reaching across the empty bed to grab the ringing cell, mentally calculating the months since that blonde I met on a business trip.

Too many.

Autumn, my phone reads.

Shit. What time is it?

5:17

Fuck. No call at five a.m. is ever a good thing. Sitting up, I swipe and put the phone to my ear as silken sheets puddle around me.

"Autumn. What's up, what's wrong?"

"You need to come home." Her voice is fragile, nervous, and cold. It reminds me of when we were kids, and I'd crawl into her bed, upset about mom. How she'd try to be the strong one, the big sister, but she was scared too.

"What's going on?"

"The test results were uploaded into the portal. They aren't good. You need to come home." Ice hits my veins, and my stomach drops to the mattress.

Part of me expects to see it resting outside my body when I look down.

"They weren't supposed to be in until Friday when he meets with the doctor."

"Yeah, well, I guess they processed them early. I don't know. I woke up and checked it like I do every damn morning. It's a lot of medical jargon, I don't understand all of it. But I know the numbers we're looking for. They're worse than expected. I know I shouldn't have Googled it, but—"

"Shit, Aut. I've been telling you not to search for that shit. It's never a good idea."

"Fuck off, Hunter, I know. But I did, and even in the best case, it's not great."

"What about the clinical they were talking about?"

"He might be more likely to qualify now, but it's still experimental. Who knows what will happen? You need to come home. Stay in Springbrook Hills. You need to be close."

"Autumn, I can't—"

"Your project is here, anyway." It's clear she's prepared for this, ready with solutions to whatever objections I have. "You can be close to monitor it. Stay at Dad's, work from home, and commute when you need to. It's only a couple of hours away." Absolutely not. I can't stay in that house, I can't... I don't deserve to be there.

"I'm not staying at Dad's. I... I'll stay at the motel." The motel in my hometown is small, dingy, and basically from the set of a slasher flick, but there's no way I'm staying in my childhood home. Not after everything that happened.

"Hunter, don't be stupid."

"Seriously, it's fine. I don't want to stay there. Plus, it's too big for one person."

"Then stay with me," my sister says. "The kids will love it. School ends for the summer Friday, but they have camp so it won't be too crazy. Plus, we have Hannah when they're home. The guest bedroom is set up with an office."

I want to say no. I want to run through excuses why I can't be in the town that I grew up in after the biggest mistake of my life. But unfortunately, my older sister is nearly always right. Not that I'd ever admit that to her.

If something happens to our father, which is seeming more and more likely by the moment, and I don't make it there in time, I'll never forgive myself. It will weigh on me until the day I die. And she's right—I'm finally working on the Springbrook Hills location, finally making amends, so it makes sense to be nearby.

"Fine. I have to go to the office this morning, grab files, and sort things with Gina, but I'll head out this afternoon."

Silence fills the phone line.

"Autumn?"

"I'm here. You're coming?"

"Yeah, I'll be there tonight. Not sure how long I can stay, a week, maybe two. Just long enough to make sure everything is okay." Which it *has to be.*

"Yeah. Okay. Okay, Hunt. I'll have Hannah set up the room for you. Text me when you're on your way, okay?"

With a sigh, I agree and then hang up. As I do, my morning alarm blares, and I roll out of bed to start my day, pack up and head back to my hometown to make sure I'm nearby in case my sick father takes a turn.

ONE
-HUNTER-

The huge, old colonial house used to belong to the Coles, an older couple whose kids moved away long before I left town. But when my sister settled in our hometown after marrying her college sweetheart, the home not two blocks from where we grew up became hers. With nothing but white wood siding and large expanses of red brick, it makes you want to drive a little slower when you pass by to take in its features.

Immediately it's clear that Autumn and Steve aren't home—neither of their vehicles is in the drive, but this is something I already knew. Autumn warned me that she wouldn't be home until later.

You can hear the loud music from the street as I grab my suitcase from the trunk of my dad's old Bronco I picked up earlier before slamming the door shut. My feet make their way up the pathway made of meticulously placed and cared-for paver stones, creating an intricate pattern.

When I reach the door, I press the doorbell before realizing the sound is coming from inside Autumn's house. Queen, I think. There's no answer, which isn't a surprise considering the noise inside. The music is loud enough that you can feel the bass vibrating on the front door. Next time I ring the bell while knocking against the dark wood. Again, nothing but the music comes through. Except for... laughter and—is that singing?

Sounds are drifting through the cracked windows, telling me whoever is home won't be answering the door. My hand reached for the doorknob, which turns with ease.

"Hello?" My voice echoes through the open door as I step in. As I look around, it's clear the foyer hasn't changed since Christmas two years ago.

God, was it really that long?

The walls are a cream color, with photos in matching wood frames perfectly hung on the walls. The effect is like an art gallery you'd find in downtown NYC, but it's a gallery of family. Looking around, the contrast between Autumn's welcoming, warm home and my cold, stark one is clear. While everything in my space is top of the line, chosen without care for budget, it has never actually felt like home.

"Hello?" I shout again, closing the door behind me. It's so much louder with the solid oak door closed and creating a sound buffer. Inside, it's clear the music is coming from the back of the house.

I hum along to the song playing as I make my way toward the noise. Autumn's house is much more cluttered than my apartment in the city. There, everything is clean and modern, perfectly kept by a team that comes in twice a week. Nothing is ever out of place, the minimalistic style curated by the designer my assistant hired creates structure and precision.

Instead of complete order, toys are strewn about, a scooter leaning against a wall in the foyer. On a table in the hall, a giant leather purse has tipped over with items falling out.

A pack of gum, a toy car, a bright pink wallet. A set of keys with an array of colorful keychains on the floor.

Bending forward to grab the keys, a flash of tan skin makes me freeze in motion. The silhouette of a curvy, petite woman can be seen through the kitchen archway. A ridiculously delicious, obscenely gorgeous woman.

I stare at the entryway for what seems like an eternity. Long, golden legs covered only in running shorts lead to full, curvy hips. Next comes a thin, loose white tank top that, when the light hits just right, reveals a perfectly curved body. Long, wavy, dark hair sits in a messy pile on top of her head, and she's holding hands with my oldest niece, dancing and singing into a whisk. My youngest niece, Rosie, stands on a chair with a wooden spoon to her lips, singing as well.

Lost in what's in front of me, my mind wanders.

Is her face as devilishly angelic as the rest of her?

Sweet, sultry, and tempting all in one package.

I'm finding it impossible to look away from her, bouncing around and screaming the lyrics into a silver whisk. Her voice isn't that of a woman singing like no one's listening. It's the voice attracting me most to her, enamoring me to her. It's smokey and sexy with a hint of goofiness sewn in there. As she sings about thunderbolts and poor families in a voice meant to make my nieces giggle, her voice is beautiful.

Leaning a shoulder against the hallway wall, I try not to make a noise. I don't want to interrupt just yet and end the show. My arms cross my chest, followed by my ankles as I get comfortable, watching as she sways her full hips left and right. All of it makes for such an alluring package.

But when she falls to her knees to perform an air guitar solo, the combination of seeing her drop to her knees and the terribly inappropriate thoughts that immediately enter my mind snaps me out of my reverie.

This needs to end before my mind goes too far. But also, my desire to see her face is unbearable. An overwhelming need to see if her face matches her body floods through me.

When the song ends, but before it transitions into another loud song, I clear my throat to let her know of my presence. She jumps and turns around, shock and horror on her face.

I was wrong. The face isn't angelic at all.

It's downright illegal.

Yes, her face is gorgeous—perfect, tanned olive skin, a light sprinkling of freckles across the bridge of her small nose, and high cheekbones with a flush from her kitchen workout. She's the girl next door, the gorgeous, perfect prom queen, but...

But she is sex. Beneath the freckles and the flush are full pink lips, wide blue eyes, and long, long lashes, which make me wonder what they would look like half closed on the edge of orgasm. Paired with her knockout body of soft curves, she should be illegal.

Her face sparks something in my mind, but it takes a moment to place her. The nanny. Hannah, the nanny. When Autumn signed on to Beaten Path, she had demanded to work from home to stay with her growing family. Knowing my sister better than anyone, Steve knew she would need help while working from home, and they hired Hannah. I'm sure I've met her over the years, but nothing left a lasting impression of the woman. But fuck, is she making an impression now.

She's also terrified. Her eyes are wide, bright blue eyes glazed with fear. One hand tipped in pale pink polish lies on her chest, which is rising and falling in subdued panic.

"Uh, I'm sorry, can I help you?" She tries to seem confident when she speaks, but her voice wavers in a way telling me she is not at all comfortable with me. Keeping her eyes on me, she takes a step to the side, moving to hide my nieces behind her before darting her eyes to the door, seeking an exit.

So, she's protective. Something about the move makes me like her more. I like that she's not giving in, she'd be willing to go down swinging.

"UNCLE HUNTER!" Rosie screams from behind Hannah, dropping her spoon with a clatter before jumping off the chair to tackle me.

"Hey, Rosie girl!" I say, lifting her into the air and twirling her. The sweetest giggle falls from her lips as her strawberry blonde hair flings behind her in a cascade of soft waves. When we stop moving, I turn to the nanny and smile, putting my hand out for her to shake. "Hey, I'm Hunter—Autumn's brother. We've met before, I think. I tried knocking, but the music must have been too loud to hear. The door was open. I let myself in."

Still dazed but gaining some color back, Hannah shakes her head as if trying to clear it. She puts her hand in mine to shake it, and I marvel at how tiny and soft it is. A zing of recognition jolts from her hands and through my arm. An electric charge like I've never felt before, the moment our skin touches. I wonder if she felt it, too.

"Oh, gosh, of course! Of course, Autumn told me you were coming soon. I just didn't expect you today. Oh, gosh, please, come, sit!" she babbles, scrambling to turn off the music, which has changed to a slower, quieter song. "Can I get you anything, Mr. Hutchins? Water, soda, a drink? Driving from the city is the worst. You must want to relax." Before I can even take a breath and put her out of her misery, she keeps talking.

"I can show you to the guest room I think you'll be in, but it hasn't been made up for you yet. I'm so sorry, it's been a crazy afternoon, and—" I cut her off before she runs out of air.

"No, thank you, I'm fine." She's flouncing around, panic clear on her face, and not comfortable with the change to her day. Her hands are wiping and cleaning and clearing the kitchen as she talks, the opposite of a dreadful tornado. It's unclear if she's nervous I'm here, or if it's because she's surprised. When I spot a plate of cookies cooling on a rack, my hand reaches out and grabs one, popping it into my mouth. The taste of brown sugar, vanilla, and melty chocolate chips explodes on my tongue, making me groan out loud. Holy shit, did she make these?

"Those are for—uh, never mind. Are you sure? About the room. It's not a problem. I'm sure you'd like to unwind. Gosh, this is so embarrassing. I'm sorry I didn't answer the door. It's been a rough day around here. I always say a quick kitchen dance party can cure just about any sour mood. Sara chose the song, and I can never resist the crazy amazing sound system in—"

"Please sit down and stop talking before you faint." Grabbing another cookie off the rack, my ass drops into the chair next to Sara, and I use the toe of my boots to push out another chair, motioning her to sit. My keys hit the marble countertop with a satisfying clink right before my boots are on Autumn's kitchen counter.

"Oh, no, I'm fine, thank you. I need to get dinner finished," she says, facing the stove with her back to me before she looks over her shoulder. "Can I make you a plate, Mr. Hutchins?"

"Hunter, please. You're family, right? Or so Autumn tells me. You do watch my favorite girls day in and day out," I ask, plucking a cookie crumb from my shirt. I throw a smile her way, loving how my teasing turns her cheeks a light pink.

She smiles a gorgeous smile that lights up the room. "Okay, Hunter. Will you be having spaghetti and meatballs with us tonight?"

In hindsight, it's clear that was it. That was the moment I fell head over heels for Hannah Marie Keller.

TWO
-HANNAH-

Shit, shit, shit, shit. When I turn my back to the gorgeous man lounging at the kitchen table, I focus on forcing air into my lungs as deeply as possible to calm myself. Whenever something like this happens, panic creeps in like an old, unwelcome friend. Like always, I use the technique which got me through my hardest days as a kid.

But today, the air just won't get deep enough into my lungs, the anxiety a brick wall keeping out the fresh air and mental clarity.

But to embarrass myself in front of this man, this unbearably handsome man? It's just not fair.

Of course, it's important to note this is not the first time we've met. Hunter's been at family gatherings, and we've been introduced in passing. But this is not the same man. No way in hell.

When he walked in, I was sure Hunter was an intruder planning to rob us. Or maybe some crazy drifter, looking to kidnap and use us as ransom. Scenes and schemes ran through my mind with strategies to get the kids out safely and call 911. Until Rosie ran to the man, calling him "Uncle Hunter".

The man I've met in the past was tailored to perfection. A suit, Italian leather shoes, cleanly shaven, neatly cut hair styled perfectly.

That's who I expected to walk in the door when my boss told me her brother would come to stay here while he worked on a local project.

This man—he's... rugged. Unpredictable. The structured, closed-off executive is nowhere to be seen standing in front of me. Hunter is wearing a worn-in flannel, unbuttoned over top a fitted white t-shirt.

Beat-up brown boots sit right below khaki-colored cargos which have seen better days. His dark hair, which I've only seen perfectly groomed and styled, has grown unruly,A!q2 like he's just washed his hair and let it dry after he toweled it off. His face sports a thick layer of dark scruff. Scruff, which inevitably dropped panties at every stop he made along his way here.

With an uneasy smile, my head bobs to acknowledge his request to call him Hunter before turning back around and cleaning up the dinnertime disaster zone without looking too flustered. This man. This man walks in unexpectedly and completely rocks my world.

Change and I are not friends. Predictability, consistency, and schedule are. My best friend Sadie calls it "safe and boring," but those are things I never had. Feelings I work hard to get as an adult. The smallest hiccup—a feverish kid or a rainstorm on park day—can completely ruin my day. It also can make me... dumb.

Consistency and predictability were non-existent growing up. My mom was neglectful, leaving me constantly grasping at straws to keep my sister and me safe. My entire adult life, I have spent structuring every moment to know exactly what is coming next. This just blew every shard of comfort to smithereens.

"So you're the uncle the kids gush about, huh?" *Dumb, dumb, dumb, Hannah! Of course, he's the uncle—Autumn only has one, and you've* met *the man before!* My cheeks flare with heat.

"Do you gush about me, Sar Bear?" he asks, standing and grabbing *yet another cookie* before ruffling the hair on her head. Then, in a move so swift and unbearably sexy, he leans back against the kitchen island with his palms and presses, swinging himself to sit on top.

"Hannah says counters aren't for butts!" Rosie yells, pointing a small finger at her uncle.

"Is that right?"

"Well... yes. It's unhygienic to sit on a kitchen counter where we make food." And really, it is. Chairs are to be sat on. Tables and kitchen counters? Not so much.

"Ahh, well, we're all family," he says, sending a wink my way. My lips purse, biting back the response I want to give and the urge to tell him to get his ass down. *This is your boss's brother, Hannah. Leave it be.*

"Did you bring us anything?" Sara's nine years seem like 16 these days, and she brings the attitude to match.

"Sara Elizabeth!"

In response, Hunter gasps and clutches his chest in faux horror. "Do you think I would come to see my favorite girls in the entire world without bringing you guys presents?"

"PRESENTS!" screams Rosie, making a beeline for the front door to grab whatever Hunter brought them from his car. I grab the little girl by her waist and plop her on my hip. Although she's four, she's small for her age, so lifting her is easy.

"While I'm sure you're excited to see what fun things your uncle brought you guys, I think he would agree we should fill our bellies first!" I say, tickling said belly and making her squeal. My eyes shoot a pleading glare toward the intruder.

"Of course, as long as you've got enough for one more."

"It's nothing special, but my helpers and I made plenty. Do you like spaghetti and meatballs?"

"Uncle Hunter, you're gonna *lose it* when you try Hannah's meatballs! They're the best ever. And I helped her make them, which makes them extra tasty." Rosie yells, her voice at a perpetual volume of seven out of five.

"And I made the sauce!" yells Sara, still wearing a sauce-covered apron. Right then, the egg timer I set to remember to dump the pasta goes off.

"Well, I have to try this famous sauce from my little chef," Hunter tells Sara before hopping down and walking to the fridge. "What can I get to help? Cheese? Drinks?"

He's good with the girls. It's surprising—Autumn always made him sound like a standoffish workaholic. Someone who would never enjoy a simple meal or joke around with kids. While she loves her brother, it's also clear she secretly wishes he'd settle down. Something she's told me isn't in his plan.

"I've got the cheese out and grated and drinks for the kids already. But you can grab yourself a drink." I shake the pasta around in the colander, draining the water out.

I fill the girls' bowls with saucy noodles before each gets a few meatballs, cutting Rosie's up into smaller pieces before putting them on the table in front of the hungry kiddos. I promised I would let them dole out their own Parmesan cheese, and just watching Rosie dump three large spoonfuls on top is making me regret my decision instantly.

My back goes to them in an attempt to ignore the mess being made, and I focus on making Hunter a plate. Grabbing a pasta bowl from the cabinet, I turn to him. "How hungry are you?"

"I can do it," He says, coming my way with one of Steve's fancy craft beers in his hand. He raises it, silently asking if I want one.

"No, I'm good. I don't drink when I'm watching the kids," I say as he grabs the pasta bowl from my hands. His hip gently brushes against my own, moving me out of the way. Even through layers of clothes, where we touch my skin is on fire, a slow burn from my hip and spreading outwards.

My feet step back, moving me to a safer distance as I attempt to get myself together while he serves himself before grabbing another bowl from the cabinet. He looks my way, asking what I want on my plate.

"I, uh, I can do it. You sit, I'm sure you had a long drive here." He stares at me for a second, staring through me as if he knows what I'm thinking, what I'm feeling. *Why is he so unnerving?* Instead of arguing, he hands over the bowl with a wink that makes chills run down my spine. Hunter smirks before heading to the table to grab a seat.

Get your shit together, Hannah! My inner voice chides. *He is your boss's brother. A conceited, stuck-up brother, from what Autumn has said.* While she's never said a truly *bad* word against her brother, Autumn complains to me occasionally about her brother and boss in the way sisters do.

On my way to the table, I grab my phone, and sending a message to Autumn.

Hey! Your brother just got here. Did he text you? Do you have a room you want me to prepare for him?

Oh, God, what a dick. I told him to call me when he was on his way! I'm so sorry, Hannah, I would have warned you had I known!

Totally fine, which room should I get ready?

While chatting with Autumn, Hunter's phone buzzes. He looks at it, then up at me with a smirk. Crap. She definitely texted him. Why does it feel like she's outed me for something?

Don't worry about a room, I'll handle it. Do you mind staying through bedtime before you head out? We're running a bit late, but Hunt's never done bedtime.

Got it! You know I love tucking those boogers in.

With my plate piled high with pasta, my phone goes into my pocket before sitting next to Sara at the big farmhouse-style table in the kitchen. Rosie is sitting next to her Uncle Hunter, who is unfortunately right across from me.

Sara catches us up on how her school day went, gushing about how excited she is for her last day before summer break tomorrow. Once the girls have caught us up on their busy little kid lives, they move on to stories about Uncle Hunter from the many family vacations they've taken together.

"One time, we went to the beach. And Uncle Hunter took me out on the water in a *kayak*! It was so fun! We saw a boat and a fish and a turtle!"

"I was sad I didn't win anything on the boardwalk, and then he spent, like, a billion dollars until I won the giant stuffed dolphin. You know, the one in my room?"

"At Emmy's wedding, Uncle Hunter danced with me allllllll night, even though I stepped on his feet!"

It goes on like this; the girls give me a glimpse into how they see him. He's a good uncle. It's clear that even though they don't tell me all about him often, he's a superhero of sorts in their little minds, doing all the cool uncle things. I love hearing all the stories, but soon enough, they move on to talking about me, and I can't help but cringe at the attention.

"She made my costume all by herself last Halloween!"

"Hannah makes *the best* cupcakes for birthdays, but if you ask really nice, she'll make them for normal days too. You should totally ask her."

"Once I was sick, and we cuddled in bed *all* day. She even sang all the princess songs with me!"

"Doesn't Hannah have the prettiest hair ever, Uncle Hunter?"

While it's heartwarming to know they adore me as much as I love them, each example makes my face burn hotter and hotter. Listening to them gush about me in front of this man is my personal version of hell.

As soon as they're done eating, I clean up plates, getting a small reprieve from the intense stare of Hunter across from me. With each story, his chocolate brown eyes focus on me more and more, until it's almost impossible not to squirm.

"Okay, you hooligans! Mom's coming home late tonight and told me to get you guys in bed on time. Get in jammies and clean your rooms quickly and I'll let you have a cookie and milk before bed!" I say over my shoulder as I load the dishwasher. The sound of little feet running up the carpeted stairs comes through the walls instantly, and I chuckle at how easy they are sometimes.

"You can't blame them. Those cookies are amazing," Hunter says, popping himself up onto the kitchen counter again. Doing so makes the veins in his forearms bulge in the sexiest show of subtle strength. I can't decide if I should chastise him for sitting on the counter or swoon.

"They're the results of months and months of research and trials. Sara is my little baking friend, and last winter, we tested all the top recipes online until we concocted our own."

"Whatever it is, it worked. My compliments to the chef," he says with a knowing and teasing smirk, making me blush. "So are you—" he starts, but the sound of Rosie yelling at Sara from upstairs stops him.

Sighing, my mouth opens to call them down and negotiate, but Hunter puts his hand up. "I'll go up there, straighten them out," he says, hopping off the counter.

"Are you sure? They can be... intense."

"Ah, trust me, I grew up with their mother. I know how to handle them." He winks before walking toward the stairs.

And fuck me, but I can't help but stare at his ass in those cargos as he walks off.

What feels like hours later, I get the girls tucked in and on their way to dreamland, and I make my way downstairs. Hunter sits on the cozy cream couch, scrolling through messages on his phone. When he sees me, he stands and pockets his phone, gesturing up the stairs.

"They asleep?"

"For the most part. Sara takes a bit to settle. She'll read a book for a while, but they shouldn't bother you. Autumn should be home soon, too." My bag is on the hook near the door. My feet guide me at the request of common sense and self-preservation.

"Wanna stay for a drink?" he asks, stopping me short. It doesn't sound like he's trying something on. It sounds pretty genuine, maybe even lonely. I hesitate.

Autumn isn't just my boss. She's also a friend. We've talked before about how frustrated she is with his womanizing ways. He's a brilliant entrepreneur, a solid uncle, and a loving brother, but Autumn can't help but wish he would set it all aside for someone in his life.

After seeing what happens when people don't marry for love, true, soul-deep love, I vowed to never date a man who isn't looking for everything.

Because I want *everything*.

I want the wedding and the golden marriage. I want the kids and the loving family. I want to be the class mom and watch my husband take our girls to daddy-daughter dances. I want to feel loved and cherished and valued until I'm old and grey, then tell our grandchildren about the magical day we met. I want it all and won't settle for less. No matter how handsome and tempting, Hunter Hutchins will never be that. And he's not worth risking the job and relationships I love.

"Oh, gosh, I—uh—I shouldn't. I've got to get up early tomorrow." Guilt eats at me a bit, but the cause is cloudy. Setting aside the fact that it's a bad idea, I have tons to do before bed tonight.

His face flashes, showing disappointment, then interest, followed by resignation and settling on a challenge in the blink of an eye. "Another time," he says, flashing a megawatt smile identical to his sister's, but manly and sexy, and *holy crap, I need to get out of here.*

"Yeah, maybe," I say with a strained smile, grabbing my bag and reaching for the door. "Later, Hunter. It was nice meeting you."

Hunter stands at the door, making sure the front light is on to light my way even though it's still light out. While I refuse to turn and check, his eyes leave their imprint on me, watching until I'm out of sight. Only then does the door shut with a light thump.

Walking around to the cottage, my gut quivering and my heart racing, I have only one thought running through my mind.

I am so fucked.

THREE
-HUNTER-

"Hey, asshole, thanks for telling me you were on your way. I hear you gave Hannah a friggin' heart attack," my sister, the queen ball-buster, says as soon as she walks in the front door and sees me sitting on the large couch in her living room. I have a beer in my hand and my feet propped on the wooden coffee table. A coffee table Autumn spent buckets of money on to look old and weathered rather than fresh from the factory.

Hannah was right. Autumn arrived 20 minutes after I watched her gorgeous heart-shaped ass walk away.

"Sorry, it's been a crazy week. Spent most of the drive on Bluetooth taking and rescheduling meetings." With the Springbrook Hills project starting soon, I had planned to come to town late next month to oversee the final stages of the build and make sure things go according to plan. Until I received the call from Autumn to come home earlier, just in case.

Just in case.

Just in case our father dies. I shake the thought from my mind.

"Yeah, yeah. Was the drive okay?" she asks, proving although I'm

a pain in her ass little brother, I'm *her* pain in the ass little brother, who she loves and worries about.

"Yeah, sis, thanks," I say with a smile. We shoot the shit for a bit, covering the kids and work before she starts in on me.

"When are you going to see Dad?" *Ah, there it is.*

"God, Aut, I just got here. Give me a break,"

"I know what you're doing. Don't play it off. You can't avoid this forever."

I sigh, rubbing my new beard, a result of stress-working, thus missing all of my appointments with my barber. "I'm not sure yet. I need time, with everything going on." *Time to make sure I can report successes to our father.*

Autumn stares at me the way I imagine a good, attentive mom does when she's checking for truth in her kids. Not that I would know. It's a face she perfected years ago, long before she had kids of her own. She sighs. "Okay, Hunt. So, what's with the beard? Have you become a lumberjack since I last saw you?" she says, quirking an eyebrow.

I smile, thankful for the distraction. "I've been too busy to keep up with the shaves. I kind of like it, though. I think it's what made your nanny think I was an intruder, though."

"Shut up. She thought you were an intruder?! But she's met you before!" Autumn said with a guilty giggle. "Oh god, I feel terrible for not warning her."

"Yeah, I came in and she immediately hid the kids behind her. I look a lot different from any of the other times I've met her." And, while I know we've been introduced before, I can't remember actually meeting her. Maybe it was the same for her.

"Well, good to know she'd put herself in danger to save the kids, I guess."

"So, what's up with her? What's her story?"

"Oh, no you don't. Keep it in your pants. I love you, but you're a dog with women. If I have to lose the woman my children adore and I trust with my life because you fuck around with her, I will literally castrate you," Autumn threatens with a glare.

"Hey! I'm not a dog," I say with a smile, denying what we both know holds a kernel of truth.

I've had my fair share of ladies in my bed, but none have stayed for long. As much as I'm intrigued and enamored by the fair Hannah Keller, Autumn's sanity and my nieces' happiness come first. Not to mention, pretty distractions are not on the agenda.

"You know I wouldn't do that to you." I stand, stretching my arms over my head. "Okay, I'm off to bed, I'm beat." Leaning down, my lips hit her cheek. "Love you Autie."

"Love you, Hunt. Glad you're here," she says as I head for the room she pointed to. My body is at the brink of exhaustion and I'm sure I'll pass out the second my head hits the pillows. But instead, I find myself thinking about the gorgeous nanny and what her dark hair would look like spread across them.

FOUR
-HANNAH-

I'm eight, holding my five-year-old sister Abbie's hand. Once again, mom forgot to pick us up. The guidance counselor is calling her while attempting to comfort me. She tells us mom is probably running late, but we both know the truth: my mom forgot.

Embarrassment floods my system as Mrs. Tate comes driving up in her old blue minivan. The Tates are our next-door neighbors, and Sadie Tate is my best friend in the whole wide world. Mrs. Tate is also our emergency contact, thanks to me. I secretly wrote her down on the beginning of the year paperwork mom forgot to fill out. She's been called a few times since and never asked why.

"Hi, Mrs. Tate," I say, keeping my eyes down. Abbie jumps in the minivan behind me, and we buckle up. I wave hi to Sadie in the front seat, and Mrs. Tate looks back at us with a sad smile. She knows the truth, too. A lot of grown-ups give us that smile, filled with pity and a dash of anger.

When we get home, I say 'no thank you' to Mrs. Tate when she offers to have us over for an after-school snack. Just like momma would want. "We ain't freeloaders," she'd say to us, though she's always bumming money from boyfriends.

The dingy grey front door of our small, neglected home with the overgrown lawn is unlocked as usual.

"Nothing but junk in here to steal anyway," Momma always says. I get my sister settled at the old weathered kitchen table with mismatched chairs Daddy found on the side of the road years ago. Pulling the chair with the sturdiest legs over to the cabinets helps me reach the last silver package of Pop-Tarts. We split the packet of stale pastries, hoping it will tide us over until mom makes dinner.

Abs needs help with her kindergarten homework, so we do it together while I work through my math. Next, it's time for us to neaten up our room. After making our beds, Abbie does a puzzle while I organize all of our hand-me-down dolls, making sure I dress each doll and brush her hair before putting her away. Each one perfectly cared for.

"I'm hungry, Hannah," my sister says at 7:30 when we're sitting on the couch. It's her turn to choose, so we're watching The Little Mermaid for the millionth time while we wait for our mom. I stand with a sigh, knowing Mom probably won't be home until late.

After I heat up a can of SpaghettiOs, we eat dinner, giggling over the worn magazine of boy bands we crush on that Sadie gave me when she finished reading it. Before we go to sleep, I'll hide it back under my mattress so momma doesn't find it and throw it away.

We shower and I brush Abbie's long, dark hair before braiding it. We get to bed in the tiny room we share, but not before I lock the doors, keeping the front light on for Momma.

Hours later, I hear banging and scramble out of bed.

No key, *I think. The clock on the cable box blinks bright red numbers, telling me it's long past midnight.*

"Lazy piece of shit," my mom murmurs between loud smacks of her hand on the front door. She knows not to yell too loud. Wouldn't want the neighbors to come asking questions.

"Sorry, Momma." I unlock the door, letting her in and closing it behind her.

"Why'd you lock it?" she snaps. She's wearing a small red dress, the strap falling off her shoulder. The heels she's wearing are too high,

and she trips over nothing as she walks through our small living room. Her eyes cut to me, full of anger and resentment. "I left my key at Jeff's and couldn't get in." I don't know who Jeff is, but it doesn't matter. He'll be done with her as soon as he realizes she's quietly stealing from his wallet before she leaves at night.

"Sorry, Momma," I murmur. Experience tells me this is the safest response to my mom.

"Where're the leftovers?" Cold washes through my gut.

"Leftovers?"

"Yes, you smartass. Leftovers. You fed your sister, didn't you? Or is it just that you really are good for nothin'?"

"Abbie and I just shared a can of SpaghettiOs... There wasn't any extra." I say to her, shuffling my sock-clad feet nervously. There's a hole in the left one, my big toe peeking out.

"Selfish, ungrateful brat. Didn't you think your Momma would want dinner?"

FIVE
-HANNAH-

My phone on the kitchen island buzzes, blaring an alarm and a notification. The sound knocks me out of the past and into the present.

3:15 pm—Last reminder: start walking to the bus stop for Sara.

Shit. A quick glance around shows me the chaos that has grown exponentially in the last hour. I resign myself to the fact it just has to be sorted out after picking up the kids. The bottles of cleaner are placed back in their homes so no one can get into them before grabbing my bag and keys.

Closing the door behind me, the scents of summer hit my nose as the sound of the mailman greeting my neighbors drifts by. *It's almost time for sunscreen and sprinklers and melting popsicles*, I think with a smile. The kids aren't the only ones who are excited. It's my favorite time of year, too.

With the weather so gorgeous, it's hard not to grin again as I pass Mrs. Connor's path that she lines with bright flowers each year.

Eventually, the sign for the bus stop is in view, and I slow to a stop.

When I check the time on my phone, it shows 3:19. The bus

should be here in exactly one minute. Being late for anything makes me itchy, but being late to pick the kids up is unacceptable.

My mother couldn't be counted on to be where we needed her when we needed her as kids. Late for school pick-ups, no show at dance recitals, forgotten lunch money, and field trip waivers. I couldn't even tell you how many times we woke up to an empty house, having to get fed and ready for school ourselves.

The occasional weekends at my dad's place weren't much better. A revolving door of new girlfriends, who ranged from "new mommy" to "why are your children stealing my attention"

I should be thankful things weren't worse. We were always fed and clothed, and neither parent ever laid a hand on us. But when you're told from the age of seven you ruined your mom's life by being born or having your father tell your mother is a whore, it leaves its own invisible scars.

My childhood left a greasy, sad stain across my memories, forcing me to dedicate my life to counteracting the ugliness I experienced. The kids in my care will always feel nothing but happiness, love, and safety.

The sound of the big yellow bus travels three blocks, signaling they're near. It's not the noise of the engine, but the kids giggling and yelling through the open windows. It rolls to a stop before letting out a loud squeak as the doors open. Sara hops out first, followed by her sister who goes to half-day Pre-K, coming home on the same bus.

Sara is tall for her age, nine years old, with long, gangly legs that point to her being tall and lean like her mom when she grows into them. This morning she meticulously pulled her hair into a messy bun, a style we laughingly spent an entire rainy afternoon learning how to "effortlessly" achieve.

"Hey, guys!" I wave, directing them back to the house.

"Hey, Hannah." Sara pulls her book out from the side pocket of her bag. The girl's nose is always in a book. She can famously walk home reading, barely looking up once.

"Guess what!?" yells Rosie.

"What!?" I yell back, making her giggle.

"Only one more day left of school! Did you finish our shirts?" Her five-year-old self is practically skipping down the sidewalk, scuffing her brand-new sneakers in her excitement. The kid goes through a pair a month because of it.

"Slow it down, bud. If you put a hole in your shoe this quick, your mom is going to flip." She slows, but barely. "Yes, I'm almost done with your last-day shirts. You wanted green, right?" I say, flicking one of her pigtails.

Rosie is the easiest kid ever to punk, which becomes clear quickly when she stops in place. She turns to me, almost making all three of us collide. "What? No way! I wanted PINK!"

"I'm just kidding, you goober. Do you think I don't know your favorite color?" She sighs with relief, and I can't help but laugh.

As always, once we walk in the door, Rosie has a million and seven stories to tell me, from what the little boy told her on the playground to what her teacher was wearing today to what she had for lunch (as if I wasn't the person to pack it) to wondering what her Uncle Hunter did all day while she was gone.

For that last one, I can't help but wonder the same thing. The Bronco had stayed in the drive all day, and the door to his room stayed shut. I'm not even sure if he ate today.

One thing I know for certain: I'm glad he's not my boss. More than once, while I was running around the house to grab things or straighten up, I heard him yelling at someone on the phone. A few times, it was loud enough to hear downstairs, the frustration in his voice palpable. I know from Autumn, the company has grown quickly over the last ten years, and there have been more than enough growing pains and headaches. But it seems like Mr. Hutchins isn't as patient with the errors as his sister.

Either way, with practice and ease, learned from years of changing topics, I push the conversation back to school, and Rosie happily follows my lead.

The after-school rush can be stressful for some, but for me, it's calming and soothing to have all of the chaos to handle. We get home, and the girls run upstairs to inevitably make a mess while I get a snack together, clean up, and prep dinner for the Sutters.

Autumn walks in not long after, a stylish laptop bag in one hand, a bunch of grocery bags in the other, and a phone to her ear. Her long auburn hair is tangled between the black straps of the oversized tote she carries everywhere. It's impossible not to laugh at her when, after the call ends, she's still stuck with her head cocked to the side.

"Need a hand over there?" I ask, pulling the phone from her ear as she drops the laptop bag and begins untangling her locks.

"I swear to God, I do not know what I'd do without you." She collapses into the taupe love chair closest to the front door. Her head falls back, and her eyes close. "You will not believe the day I've had."

Normally, Autumn works upstairs while I watch the kids. My job is to keep the kids happy and fed, get them to school or activities on time, and keep them out of her hair.

When Sara was three, Hunter begged her to sign on as head of PR and Marketing. His outdoor adventure chain, Beaten Path, was quickly growing, and Autumn is damn good at what she does. She laid out her demands, including that she works from home at least 80% of the time, and he accepted. The Sutter's hired me not long after to keep the kids occupied, safe, and loved during working hours.

Some days, like today, heading into the Beaten Path corporate office in NYC is simply unavoidable. Thankfully, it's not too far from home, but it can be quite the trek if there's traffic.

"Let me get you a glass of wine, and then you can vent, okay?" I say, heading to the kitchen.

"Only if you have one too!" she says to my back, her eyes still closed.

"I'm on the clock, Aut!" Rolling to tiptoes, I reach high to grab two wine glasses.

"Shut up and grab a glass for yourself." We do this a lot. Technically, there are no set hours, so I'm always off or always on the clock, depending on how you see it. Steve and Autumn pay me a generous salary, plus room and board in the cottage out behind their house, and, in exchange, I'm here when they need me.

It works out perfectly for me since I get to work with the kids whenever needed but also has time to work part-time at the Center, my true passion.

Filled glasses in hand, I make my way back to Autumn, handing one to her before plopping onto the adjacent couch. The living room, like the rest of the house, is decorated clean and modern, but comfy as can be. It's clear to anyone walking in the Sutter's are looking for comfort over style when decorating their home. But they nailed both.

"Okay, lay it on me," I say, taking a sip of the fruity white wine and propping my bare feet up on the coffee table. My toes are a multi-colored mess after letting the girls paint them.

She sighs, looking to see if any kids are nearby. "They're all upstairs playing," I reassure her.

"Dad's declining." My heart drops to my gut. Ron Hutchins is the sweetest, most amazing grandpa on the planet. He spoils the kids like crazy, tells the best dad jokes of all time, and will stop by for a late-night bedtime story anytime Rosie asks.

Six months ago, he found an odd mole on the back of his neck, which was immediately diagnosed as an aggressively spreading form of melanoma. He went into treatment and they've been monitoring his progress since, but the road is still long.

For the past three months, he's been in an around-the-clock care facility, receiving treatment but still thriving. The decision to leave the home he raised Autumn and her brother in was a tough one all around, and Autumn fought tooth and nail to have him move into her home. He still owns the family home, refusing to sell it and believing he'll be back there any day.

Since moving to the facility, he's been relatively stable. Last week was to be one of the big milestones for determining how things are progressing and how he's responding to treatment.

"Oh, God, Autumn, no." Tears well in my lower lashes instantly, threatening to fall. Ron is the closest thing I have to a father figure in my life and a man I cherish deeply.

"We still have a few weeks to get more information on next steps, and the doctors said he might qualify for a new clinical trial, but it's not looking great."

"I'm so sorry. What can I do to help?" This family has shown me so much kindness, love, and grace over the years. Knowing there's not much I can do to ease their pain kills me a bit.

"You're doing it, Hannah. Giving the kids the best sense of normalcy, visiting Dad every week, giving him those cookies even though he totally does not share them, no matter what he says." She gives me a fake chiding look. "It's why Hunter's here."

"I thought it was because of the new project in town?"

"That was how I convinced him to come. But he needs to be close. Who knows what will happen in the next few weeks? I know Hunter. If something happened and he was too far away to get here in time... His assistant is more than capable of handling the day-to-day stuff and forwarding everything to him. Most meetings can be done virtually. But being in the city right now is just too far. Things can change in a moment, and it took me four hours to get home today."

"So, why isn't he staying at your dad's? Not that I care, just seems like it would be easier to work from an empty house."

Another sigh comes from Autumn. "He has some... hesitation with staying there and I'm not gonna push it. It won't be any extra work for you, I promise. He'll just lock himself in his room and live his workaholic lifestyle from there."

"Autumn, that's the least of my worries. Whatever you guys need, just let me know. You're family to me."

Just then, the sound of kids screaming and fighting hits us, making Autumn groan, the back of her head resting on the couch while her eyes close.

"You sit, enjoy your wine, I've got this." I stand, patting her shoulder.

"Are you sure?" she asks with hope and exhaustion in her eyes.

"Totally. Pretend to come home in like, ten minutes. Just relax for a bit."

Walking out of the room and in the direction of the ruckus, a yell loud enough for me to hear but quiet enough not to tip off the kids comes from Autumn. "You're the best!"

Once Autumn has completely unwound after work and is mentally ready to handle her hooligans, I head out to my cottage.

The cottage is a small, cozy detached mother-in-law suite right behind the Sutter's house. You need to walk through a maze of flowers I've planted along a brick pathway to get to the bright blue front door of my tiny white home. I call it my fairy walk, and in the back is my secret fairy garden. Gardening brings me peace and comfort, something which is evident when you look at the little house.

Autumn and Steve gave me free rein to decorate and make it my own. It's not much bigger than a studio apartment, but it has a small kitchen-slash-dining room-slash-living room space, a tiny bathroom with a shower, and a perfectly sized bedroom. It's the perfect size for a single woman who spends most of her time in the "big house."

The entryway and living area are painted a calming, light sage green that makes me want to take up yoga or something. As soon as I unlock the door and walk in, my stress level decreases by at least ten each time.

When you enter my bedroom, the walls are covered in vintage floral wallpaper I fell in love with as soon as I saw it. The room is frilly and girly, complete with a white canopy over my bed and a dusty blush pink duvet cover.

It's safe to assume I've never brought a man back to this room. I go for the manly man types, as Sadie calls it, and I'm pretty sure this frothy princess room would make all masculinity shrivel up and die.

Locking the door behind me, I turn on the TV to watch reruns of my favorite show, *The Office,* while I finish up the t-shirts for the kids' last day of school before finalizing the schedule for the Center's summer camp program.

Although my bones are aching with exhaustion, it's these things I get utter joy from. Making the kids something I know will leave a lasting memory, knowing they're going to flip when they see them—it gives me all the feels.

Summer camp at the Springbrook Hills Community Center, where I work part-time, starts in two weeks, and completing this schedule ASAP is vital.

Little do I know that tomorrow everything is going to change, for better or worse.

SIX
-HANNAH-

"Cocoa Puffs!" Rosie yells, slamming her spoon on the table as I place her bowl of yogurt and berries in front of her. Obviously, my girlfriend has opinions about what should fuel her little body first thing in the morning.

"Nope, yogurt today. Maybe another morning." On each birthday, Autumn and Steve let the kids pick out a single box of junk cereal. They typically pack the house with healthier options, but birthdays are sacred sugar fests. The littlest Sutter's birthday was nearly two months ago, but she's still salivating over the chocolatey cereal. Can't blame the girl.

She harrumphs, knowing that arguing will get her nowhere with me. Her spoon digs into her yogurt, but the gears in her mind are almost visible, planning and scheming how she can get her beloved cereal again.

Turning with a smile on my face at the fierce little girl, the mug of coffee nearly goes flying out of my hands when a drowsy Hunter strolls in wearing baggy grey sweatpants and a white tee. He stops in the doorway, arms stretching overhead and yawning in what can only be described as a humorous caricature of a tired person, but on him, it looks unbearably sexy. Like a hot, tired guy from a rom-com.

God, why do you hate me so?

His slightly overlong hair is a mess, and one corner on top is sticking straight up, begging for a brush. The raised arms cause his tee to lift, showing a stretch of golden skin above his low-slung sweats.

I have to remind myself not to pant at the toned stomach, tanned skin, and a slight happy trail leading into the gray fabric, clearly lacking any kind of underwear. *Holy. Fuck.*

"Good... uh, good morning, Mr.—uh, Hunter. Can I get you something for breakfast?" God, please give me something to keep me busy, so I'm not tempted to stare at this man all morning. Please.

"Is this a thing with you? Always trying to feed and take care of others when you're already busy?" The fuzz around the edges of my vision that was forming at the mere sight of him fades immediately.

"I'm just asking if you want me to make you something. No need to be rude." Turning on my heel, I start cleaning up breakfast. That's one way to kill my interest in him. No wonder he's always arguing on the phone. He clearly has terrible personal skills. Grabbing the spray cleaner, I start to wipe down the marble counters, collecting the juice and drips of honey from making the girls' breakfast.

"Not being rude, just asking a question."

"So, that's a no. You don't want breakfast," I say, looking at him over my shoulder, and putting the orange juice away. This man is such an ass.

"That's a no. I don't really eat breakfast. But I'll take a coffee if you've got it."

I'm tempted to tell him to get it himself, but decide to play nice instead. I have no idea how long he'll be staying here. For all we know, it could be quite some time. "Hot or iced?"

"Hot, please."

"Ah, I see you do have *some* manners," I say as I reach up to grab a mug. He chuckles, and the sound goes through me like a ray of warm sunshine. I pour the brew into the mug before moving a hand over to the sweeteners.

"How do you like it?" Immediately, my cheeks redden, because I'm a 12-year-old and my hormones are unhinged. God, save me. My brain and body get into a tug-of-war, but *this man is not it, body.* Move on and stop looking. Not even close.

With a knowing smirk, he quirks an eyebrow, and my cheeks hit summer-in-August levels of heat before he answers. "Cream and one sugar."

Handing him over the warm mug, he lifts it in thanks before taking a sip and sitting next to Sara. Instinctively, my entire body tenses in a slight panic.

The thing about Sara is she is *not* a morning person. She's the kind of person who you just feed and leave alone until at least an hour after waking. If you don't treat her with extreme ease, it can put her in a foul mood for the entire day. I've seen it play out time and time again, and I'm not ashamed to admit I've taken some extreme measures to accomplish this feat.

Leaning over to look into her bowl, he grabs a raspberry off the top of her yogurt, lifting it to pop it in his mouth.

"Stop it! I was saving that!" Sara yells in a way only a cranky, not-quite-tween can. The voice is already reminiscent of not only anger and frustration but exhausted preteen emotional baggage.

"Hey, quit it, she just woke up," I say, wading in to avoid catastrophe while throwing daggers at Hunter with my eyes.

By the grace of God, he drops the berry and raises his hands in a placating manner. Crisis averted. "My bad, I didn't realize you were so cranky in the morning, Sar Bear." My eyes roll to the ceiling, silently begging for strength and patience.

"She's always cranky in the morning," Rosie pipes in, and my head whips to her with angry, warning eyes.

"Am not!" I sigh, looking at her, knowing it's about to go bad quickly and something needs to be done, ASAP.

"Hey, Sara, babe, you're almost done. Why don't you finish up and then watch a show for a few minutes in the family room, yeah?" This must be done carefully, like defusing a ticking time bomb. A pre-teen time bomb, full of over-inflated emotions and hormones galore.

Thoughts and emotions fly past her eyes before she settles on acceptance. She nods and takes her last bite before rinsing her bowl and heading into the family room.

"Seriously, is that necessary? It's her last day of school." I glare at the other *adult* in the room. Because while I'm annoyed with Rosie, who *knows better*, Hunter is an adult who shouldn't be picking on a 9-year-old little girl first thing in the morning.

"Oh, chill out, it's not that big of a deal. Right, Rosie? She was just a crank pot." Thank God Sara is out of earshot because it's the kind of thing that would set her off in a second. Where Rosie is the drama queen of the two, Sara is usually super easygoing. But awful mornings can really mess with that vibe.

"You know what, how about you let me do my job, and you can do the fun uncle shtick when I'm not around, okay?" His eyebrow quirks in a challenge, seemingly shocked I would say anything like that. To be fair, I also am utterly shocked.

Instead of dwelling, I turn to the instigator. "Rosie, that wasn't kind. You know how she is in the morning." Rosie looks a little guilty, while Hunter looks confused. Officially not in the mood to banter, my hands clap together when his mouth opens, cutting him off. "Okay, come on, finish up so we can get ready for the last day of school!"

Little hands excitedly shovel food into her mouth before running upstairs to go get ready while I turn my back and fully ignore Mr. Hutchins. But his gaze burns on my back as he sips his coffee, trying to figure me out.

Good luck with that.

SEVEN
-HANNAH-

With my charges dressed in their last-day-of-school shirts, I grab lunch boxes and backpacks, rushing them out of the door to get to the bus stop. Turning to grab my bag and keys, I'm stopped by Mr. Button Pusher himself. Honestly, I've already had enough of him, and to make sure he doesn't go complaining to Autumn, I've decided ignoring is the best way to handle him.

"Excuse me." I attempt to go around him, still ignoring the asshole.

"Hey, wait." He grabs my bicep as I pass. "Sorry for bugging Sara this morning," Some of my frustration melts away. He doesn't have kids of his own, and one can assume he doesn't spend much time with them. He has no clue about the ins and outs of dealing with little personalities. "But you really can't baby her. She's just like how Autumn used to be in the mornings, she eventually grew out of it." Annnndd my frustration is back again, but times five.

"Except Sara being in a bad mood doesn't just impact Sara. It brings the entire morning to a standstill, and on the kid's last day, it's not what we're going for. But thanks for telling me how to do my job." It's easy to see my tone is bothering him, but I don't care.

"I wasn't telling you how to do your job. I was just giving you some friendly advice. Sara is just like my sister, and I grew up with her. I'm an expert at dealing with it," he says, still blocking my way. The girls are standing on the grass in the yard, waiting for me to walk them to the bus stop. I shoot them a smile before looking at Hunter with a painfully fake smile.

"Great, thanks, noted. Can you please move out of the way? I need to get the kids to the bus stop, so they're not late." Once again, I try to get past him, but now his arm is around my waist, pulling me close to him. In his eyes is a fire whose source I can't quite pinpoint. Is it anger? Or something...

"Babe, calm down. It won't kill them to be late." His voice is soft and sultry. How does this man both give me tingles and infuriate me beyond belief?

"It's important for kids to be on time to school." He thankfully releases me and lets me move so I can walk past. "Thank you. Bye, Hunter." I make it down one concrete step, almost free, but he grabs my wrist, stopping me again.

"Lighten up, it's the last day of school, who cares. You're not their mom, no need to get all worked up about it when you're just the nanny."

Target hit. The pain of his words shocks me, a sharp lance to my gut, knowing he's right, of course. I'm not their mom. I never *want* to be their mom—they have a great one. But it doesn't mean what he says, what I hear whispered from strangers with cruel intent when I'm out with the girls, doesn't kill. I love these girls with my all, and the snide remarks dig deep.

I yank on my arm, tugging my wrist free from his grip with sharp pain, looking him in the eye. He immediately recognizes his mistake, but I do not fucking care. "Shit, Han—"

"Got it. I'll be sure to take your advice to heart. I have to go be the nanny and get the girls to the bus," I say, cutting him off as I stomp down the stairs, gathering the kids and walking to the bus stop.

"He's such a fucking dick, Sadie." My lifelong bestie sets an iced Americano in front of me, made the exact way I like it. Extra ice, a pump of vanilla, a splash of cream.

It's after the bus drop off, and I'm sitting at the coffee shop workspace Sadie opened four years ago. It has a traditional barista bar with a selection of pastries from the bakery downtown on one side. On the other side are half a dozen cubicles customers can sit in using their monthly membership cards to work in privacy with all the benefits of an office.

The space is a mix of natural dark wood, an homage to the woods surrounding our little town, bright white paint, and large open windows which let in tons of natural light. On the counter next to the register, Sadie creates a beautiful display of delicious treats each morning, each item on gorgeous, unique cake stands and platters we've found over the years at thrift shops.

After seeing the kids on the bus, I hopped right into my car, not going back into the house as I usually do. Thank God I had my keys and wallet with me, a sheer brush of luck since I never bring more than my cell with me.

"Yeah, that blows. Everyone knows you love those nuggets to death, and you know Autumn and Steve see you like family, not just the nanny."

If there's anyone on this earth I can bitch to unabashedly and without judgment, it's Sadie. She's more sister than a friend, and we've seen each other through every up and down life has thrown our way.

"I know. It just hit me differently. I don't know why I let it bother me. It's not the first time I've heard it. And, while he's Autumn's brother, it's not like he's involved with them or knows what it takes day-to-day."

"Is he hot?" Sadie asks, making my head whip up to her.

"What? Sadie! That is totally irrelevant. He's a jerk."

"Oh, it's relevant. And the blush you've got going right now gives me alllll the answers I need." Hands to my burning cheeks, I glare at her.

"Sadie, stop. He's not hot. He's my boss's brother, for God's sake."

"Shut up, you know Autumn is more of a sister than she is a boss."

"So then he's like *my* brother? That's creepy."

"Don't change the subject. Hold on, let me Google him, I'll get the final say." Out comes her phone, and she taps on the screen with purpose.

I'm not sure what comes over me when my hands shoot out over the barista bar to grab her phone. "This is insane. Stop, Sadie." Unfortunately, she steps back past my reach, and stares at me, still holding that cursed phone.

"Han, the fact you're so fluttered just by my *Googling* this man says it all. He must be..." Search complete, Sadie looks at her phone. She looks at me. Then back at her phone. Then back at me. "Holy shit, Han, he is a fucking god among men!"

Realizing defeat, my head meets the reclaimed wood bar we refinished by hand when Sadie opened the cafe and workspace. It took us four whole days to do, and while I cursed her the entire time, it came out gorgeous. I bang my head a few extra times for good measure before she slips a coaster between my head and the bar. Mumbled words slip from my mouth.

"What was that?" She laughs at my misery. My head is still down when I mumble another response. "I can't hear you, babe."

I lift my head. "I said, he's got a beard now." Once again, my head hits the bar, but not before seeing Sadie throw her head back and cackle, long, blonde curls tumbling backward. She knows where my weaknesses land, and a masculine, lumberjack-esque, smokin' hot guy is just my type.

"Oh God, this is *priceless*. The brother is your fucking hot guy dream man. Utter perfection." She wipes her eyes once her laughter dies down. Not only is frustration burning through me, but now everyone in the cafe is staring at me. Crippling embarrassment has entered the chat.

"Sadie, shut up, you're making a scene," I say through gritted teeth. "This is not funny."

"Oh, it is. Trust me. It's hilarious. I can't wait to call Abbie and tell her."

"Sadie, I swear, if you call my sister, I will cut holes in your vintage Stones tee."

"You wouldn't." Her eyes are wide with horror, knowing damn well I will do it if she crosses me. We found the t-shirt while thrifting shopping, and she wears it at least once a week. It's her lucky shirt, and it even got her onstage during a Fall Out Boy concert a few years back.

"Try me bitch." She rolls her hazel eyes before handing me a large to-go cup with my second dose of iced Americano and tea for Maggie.

"Yeah, but who would supply you with your fix, for free?" A smirk is on her pretty, full lips before her voice gentles. "Look, I know what he said was harsh, especially coming from a practical stranger. But you have made Sara and Rosie your world. Maybe it's time to figure out why."

"They're not my whole life. I have the Center. I have you and Luna, I have Abs. And I'm happy with my life the way it is."

"Babe, you know what I mean. The Center doesn't count since you've finagled your schedule so that any time you're not with Autumn's kids, you're with the kids at the Center. You spend every moment of your life taking care of other people, trying to protect yourself and prove yourself. You need to step back and realize you're already perfect, the way we all do. There's no need to run yourself ragged."

"I love you, Sade, but I'm not doing this today." This is not the first time Sadie has given me this lecture. While it comes from a good place, she knows why I do what I do. She was there through the missed recitals and disappointment and verbal tear-downs. She raises her hands as her white flag.

"Okay, okay, I'm not gonna push it. I'm just sayin', the way I hope you would if the roles were reversed."

"Oh, yeah? You want me to Dr. Phil you next? I'd love to crack open my notes on all of your issues." I laugh, knowing she has her demons she's fighting.

"Alright, that's it, get your ass out of my store before you're late for the Center."

Looking at my watch with a smile, I grab my bag from the floor before leaning over to hug her over the bar. "Love you, Sade, see you soon." There's something to say about a friend who you can throw under the bus one second, and hug the next.

"Love you too. Go bang that man!" Turning without acknowledging her, I flip her the bird as my feet hit the sidewalk, still hearing her laugh as the door shuts behind me.

EIGHT
-HANNAH-

The Center is an old, time-scarred brick building at the center of town. It used to be the old middle school before they rebuilt it across town, and it's seen better days. If you know where to look, you can still see the bomb shelter notices from when it served the town as a haven, just in case. On the side facing the main road, there's a bright and colorful mural with a beach theme I worked on with the kids last summer. The sidewalks are lined with chalk drawings, waiting for a rainy day to leave a fresh, blank canvas.

About twice a year, we host big fundraisers to fund improvements to the structure, but the programs need funding too. I work here part-time, though Maggie is constantly nudging me to go full-time. My involvement started as a volunteer position years ago, right out of high school, and I just never left. Eventually, I was added on as one of the few official year-long employees, and it's a position I hold with passion and pride.

The front lawn is looking overgrown, reminding me to make a call over to Chip's landscaping and ask if they can donate their services again this year. The old yellow bus we use to take campers on the few outings we can fund each summer has peeling paint. Maybe this summer, a bus mural would be a fun project.

Sighing at the long, ever-growing list of to-do's, I jog up the three front steps to the big, red steel doors, pulling the heavy metal back with effort. My foot kicks the chunk of wood we use as a doorstop underneath to prop it open.

"Hiya, hun!" Maggie has the friendliest smile known to man as I turn the corner to her office. The tiny, cluttered room is more closet than the office, with every surface stacked high with papers and folders. On one wall, there's a big Rosie the Riveter poster, and on the desk sits a massive computer monitor Mags refuses to upgrade.

Maggie is in her early seventies and never grew out of her flower child phase. Her dark grey hair is to her mid-back, today braided with a headband Willie Nelson style with small, fresh flowers placed between the pleats. The warm weather has her in a loose, flowery skirt and a flowy top, both outrageously patterned. Her arms are full of bracelets and bangles, a mix of braided friendship threads and beaded masterpieces made by the kids that create a symphony when she moves her arms. She is one of my favorite people in the whole wide world.

"Hey, Mags, how's it going?" I say, walking over and hugging her. She smells like baby powder and lavender, the same scent she held 20 years ago when Abbie and I first started to escape to the Center whenever we could. It's also how we met Luna, who is Maggie's niece. I truly have so much to thank this place for, a debt that will never be fully paid.

"Just peachy! The sun is shining, summer is here, and I haven't gotten an ordinance notice in at least a month!" I can't help but giggle at her, handing over the tea Sadie sent me over with. We occasionally get notices from grumpy neighbors. Our building is an eyesore, the kids are too loud, that kind of thing.

"From Sadie, she sends her love." Her hand reaches out, grabbing the paper cup.

"You girls are too good to this old hag."

"Hush, you're not old, Mags. Or a hag."

"Not in heart, and that's all that matters, Hannah Banana." She has her reading glasses on her nose, the flowered chain hanging behind her neck. In front of her is a stack of papers.

"What's this?" I ask, noticing the logo on top as one of the local businesses that donate shirts to the summer campers each year.

Maggie sighs. "Just a letter from the shirt donors, confirming they won't be able to provide the shirts this year." Setting the letter down, she takes her glasses from her nose, letting them dangle at her chest. "It's been a tough year for businesses."

Doing mental gymnastics, my list of people who might take the spot flits through my head. "That's a bummer. Let me call around and see if we can find a substitute." If it comes down to it, I have my secret savings account for the shirts. Maggie would never accept, of course, so I'll have to be crafty, but those kids deserve everything we can give them.

When Mags first demanded I become a paid employee at the Center, I fought it for years. It just didn't feel right to take money for doing something I love, taking funds away from the kids. What she doesn't know is every penny I've earned here has gone into a savings account. Autumn and Steve pay me beyond a fair wage, and with little to no overhead, I truly don't need the money.

The savings account is for my dream project: a camp to help children of poor circumstances process their trauma in nature. A place where they can learn to open themselves up, survive in the woods, and just be content with life without phones or TV or the internet. The counselors would be therapists, mental health experts, and social workers, all to help kids overcome and learn coping mechanisms.

Just like Mags did for me.

Unfortunately, that account gets used more often than I'd like, since anytime the Center can't afford something, I 'donate' it.

"I'm getting too old for this, Banana," Maggie says, leaning back in her chair. We have this conversation at least once a week. She's been grooming me to take over as director of The Springbrook Hills

Center for Kids and Families. The Center saved me and gave me love that I so desperately needed more times in my childhood than I'd like to acknowledge, but I still have a commitment to Autumn and the girls. Even though Maggie has promised she would work with me on a schedule revolving around being there for the kids, I'm just not ready to take the leap.

"Stop it, you're young at heart, remember? You just told me that." Turning my back to her, I attack the stack of filing folders and papers, attempting some semblance of organization. There's no use—even if it's pristine before leaving, it will be a disaster by morning.

"You know I love this place, but chasing donors, keeping up with maintenance, the planning, the programs, organizing volunteers... I'm tired, girl." The exhaustion in her voice makes me turn and has me looking at her closer. Deeper eye circles, more frazzled hair than normal, and her clothes slightly askew. My heart sinks like a stone, realizing what I've ignored over the past few months. She's exhausted and worn thin, for real this time.

"Are you... are you thinking of retiring?" My stomach pitches, anxious for her answer.

"I'm not sure. I don't think so—who would take over?" she says, giving me a pointed look.

Sighing, I look at her. "You know I can't right now, Mags. The kids... I need to be there for them. I wouldn't want them to feel like they aren't my priority. But this summer, I'll be here as often as possible, and we can get things off your plate more. Get you some time off, a vacation even."

This year the girls are attending the Center's summer program, which means I have more time to spend here during camp.

"I know, sweetheart. Not trying to guilt you, just know you would thrive here. Autumn and Steve would bend over backward to make whatever you wanted happen. Whether it was working here or some other bigger dream of yours." *What is with everyone today telling me my life could be more, bigger, better?*

I'm happy with my life. Really, I am. I love the kids, and love my friends. I love my little house. Could I use some more cuddling? Sure. Would an unassisted orgasm here or there be nice? Of course. But my life is far from falling short. Right?

"We'll figure it out, Maggie. What can I do for you today before I need to get the kiddos?" It's a thinly veiled attempt to change the subject, but she always gives me what I need. Maggie gives me a tired, knowing smile.

"Come on, hun, I'm sure we can find 101 things for you to do around here before you have to pick up those girls."

She leads the way, and, just like I did when I was eight, I follow, eager to learn from her.

I'm getting dinner started later that night while the kids play outside. They're running crazy in circles, playing cops and robbers and giggling, the sound making my soul light. With the giant French doors leading outside, I can watch them while I dump marinade and chicken into a big bag to sit for the grill.

These are the kind of nights that give me a glimpse into the future I dream of. Quiet evenings waiting for my husband to come home, kids giggling and running around while I get dinner together. A simple life filled with love and happiness.

While the life I'm living now isn't quite that, it's a far cry from a disappointment. My head turns to the stairs to see Autumn making her way down from the office.

As always, she's wearing a gorgeous outfit, perfectly tailored cropped tan slacks and a flouncy blush-colored blouse, her hair falling in pin-straight sheets down her back, looking like the perfect business executive.

But like always when she's home, she's barefoot, ditching the sky-high heels she wears into the office. In her hands is a bottle of wine with a piece of green paper taped to it. When she enters the kitchen, she stops in front of the island I'm working on and plops the bottle in front of me with a satisfying clunk and a goofy grin on her face.

"For me? What for?" I ask, picking it up and smiling back at her.

"Yes, for you, but not from me. It's from my brother." She leans on the counter, wiggling her eyebrows. The tag on the bottle, if you can even call it that, is torn construction paper and red crayon stuck there with a princess sticker I recognize from Rosie's stash.

I'm a dick.—H

Well, that's interesting.

"Okay, I need to know. What the fuck happened!? Why was he a dick?" Autumn is now leaning with her chin in her hands, "Tell me everything!" It's impossible not to laugh at her antics. "Do I need to kick my little brother's ass? I swear, if he does anything to upset you, he's out of here."

"Oh God, nothing. It wasn't a big deal. He said something not so nice, and I guess he felt bad. To be honest, I probably overreacted, but it was after narrowly avoiding a Sara morning, so I was already irritable," I explain. After my vent sesh with Sadie and an afternoon at the Center, the whole situation is so much clearer. Hunter is under an incredible amount of pressure with his father sick, and the new location Autumn has told me about. Not to mention, the morning chaos can make my grating perfectionist tendencies come out. It doesn't excuse what he said, but it was clear even then he didn't say it to hurt me.

"Well, he came into my office today and looked like shit. Guilt written all over his face. I've seen that look before. Asked what you drink and came back with this."

"Oh, so you told him I like *your* favorite wine?"

"Hey, I know you like it too, you're just too cheap to buy it yourself. So spill. I need details. It must have been bad, to get him to actually leave the house." Wheels are turning in her mind, wheels that need to find a detour ASAP. I don't want to get him in hot water with his sister over something silly.

Why does he care if he offended me? Is it because he knows he'll be around this summer, so we're going to cross paths? Is he just trying to smooth things out before it gets unbearable? Why disrupt his day to run out and grab me an apology gift? The day before, he was in his office all day long, so it's not like he has free time to kill.

"Seriously, it was just something dumb. He was taunting Sara, not being mean, but you know how she is in the morning."

"Oh, God, did she lose it? Not on her last day!" Autumn's eyes are wide, knowing how her oldest daughter can be first thing in the morning.

"No, crisis averted. But you know how it is—if you've never experienced a Sara morning, you'd never know how bad it could be. He thought I was overreacting and was being an instigator, even got Rosie in on it."

I choose not to tell her about what he said. She doesn't need to know all of my insecurities.

"Ugh, my brother's a dick. I'm so sorry, Hannah, I'll have a talk with him."

"Oh God, please don't. I really don't want to make this awkward." Autumn stares at me, her honed mom senses digging deep to decide if she should push or drop it. Thankfully, she drops it.

"Fine. So, are you gonna pour me a glass?" Her head tips towards the bottle. Rolling my eyes, I grab two glasses and walk out back so we can sit in the sun and watch the kids run around. The patio area was finished two summers ago, and as soon as the weather gets nice, I try to spend as much time as possible out here.

"How are things going?" I ask once we both settle in, deliberately keeping my question general so she can fill in what she's comfortable with. So much is going on between work, her brother, and her dad that I don't want to be another pushy burden on her.

Autumn sighs. "Alright. Dad is stable, Hunter is here, and the kids are headed into another great summer with the world's best nanny." I smile at her, but her return smile looks forced and tired. She's drained.

"You're too sweet, Aut," I say, not pushing the conversation. When she's ready to unload, she will. We sit in comfortable silence for a bit. It's the kind of silence you sit in with someone you've seen almost every day for six years. We've seen each other at our best and at our worst. Because of that, it's easy to know when to push a conversation and when to drop it. I'm not simply the help here. Autumn and I are genuine friends, and Steve is like a big brother to me. I imagine the love I feel for the girls is how an aunt would feel.

Eventually, she breaks the silence. "Look, I know you said it's no big deal, but if anything happens with my brother again, please let me know. You're too polite for your own good, but I have no problem kicking his ass."

I spit out my wine, laughing at the unexpected remark. "Uh, okay, Aut," I laugh, coughing. Autumn is maybe five-foot-two, whereas Hunter is at least six feet tall, so the mental image alone is enough to provoke a giggle.

"Fine, I'll have Steve kick his ass." She laughs, and this I believe. That man would lie in NYC traffic for her if she asked him to, and then go to Rise and Grind to get her a latte. "Seriously, Hannah. I love my brother, but if he causes any issues, having you here for the kids comes first," she says, looking me in the eye.

"Thanks, Autumn. I will, I promise. I'm sure it will be fine. It wasn't a big deal." She looks me in the eye, assessing me with her signature mom glare as if I'm telling the truth, before nodding. A beat of silence passes.

"But he is a major dick," I say, and we both throw our heads back, laughing, while the kids run and giggle, trying to catch the first lightning bugs of the season.

NINE
-HUNTER-

Sitting on the back patio, I'm seated between Rosie and Sara for a Saturday night barbecue dinner. The gorgeous nanny is missing, which is kind of a relief. Just hearing her laugh from my room last night while she sat out here with Autumn made me yearn to drop everything, ignore the unending fires that need putting out, and sit outside with them. Get to know her. A dangerous distraction at its best.

The thing is, I do not get distracted. Not since I was 23, and a distraction almost made me lose everything. That was when I vowed to focus, prove my worth, and show everyone what I could be.

And now, just three days at my sister's place, and I've gotten less done in that time than I normally can in a single day. It's absolutely unacceptable to me.

Something's gotta give.

Fuck, I ran out yesterday to blow $120 on a bottle of wine because *I hurt her feelings* yesterday. Me, the man who once made a top-tier executive at Beaten Path cry in his first five minutes of working in the office with zero remorse.

But here I am, wondering still if the fucking babysitter forgives me for an offhanded remark I didn't even mean.

"So, how does it feel to smell the fresh air and see the sunshine, brother?" Autumn asks from across the table with a smirk. "You've been hiding away in that office, working day and night. Shouldn't you go meet up with friends for a drink or something? Take a hike, grab a coffee out? You know, have a life?"

"I haven't spent more than a day in Springbrook Hills in nearly eight years. No one here wants to meet up with me for a drink." And that's probably the truth. I had friends I was close to in high school, but as soon as Beaten Path got off the ground, I barely spent any time here, or put any effort into those friendships. Eventually, people stop trying when you're a brick wall.

"Well, Gina says you don't go out when you're in the city, either." Fucking Gina and her big mouth. The girl can work harder than any CEO I've ever met and keeps my schedule impeccable, but she's always gossiping with anyone who will listen. Especially my fucking sister. "You work too much. You need to enjoy your life."

"You're one to speak. You work similar hours as I do."

"Except I don't, and you know it. I also work from home most days and have people in my life to handle the day-to-day, so I can balance work and life."

"Ahh, yes, the nanny. Tell me about Hannah." I try to sound cool, but it's clear I just sound... interested. Something I am doing everything in my power to not be and failing miserably at. Autumn looks at me with a skeptical glance, the same one she used when I would tell Dad I was going to hang out with some friends in high school but was really going to a party.

"What about her? She's been working with us for almost six years since I joined Beaten Path. She grew up in town, and never left. Graduated four years after you, so you wouldn't have crossed paths before you fled town."

I ignore her subtle dig. "How'd you find her?"

"She was teaching Mommy and Me swim classes down at the

Center. She volunteered there and works part-time now. I took Sara when she was a baby, and we hit it off. I asked her to be our Nanny once you told me you wanted me to take over the department." Immediately, my mind goes to Hannah in a bathing suit. *Jesus*, what is wrong with me?

The next question is out of my mouth without my brain even approving it. "Does she have a man?" Fuck. Real smooth. Autumn looks at me with a small tilt to her lips, eyes wide with humor, like she knows what's going through my mind.

"She finally dumped that douche bag last month, didn't she, Aut?" Steve asks, before taking a bite of his burger.

"Steven! Mouth!" My sister, who has a worse mouth than an NYC cab driver, chides, making me laugh.

"Jesus, they've heard worse, baby," Steve says.

"And, I mean, he was a douchebag, mom," Sara says, and I lose it once again while Autumn glares at Steve, who is trying not to laugh. It's clear he's going to hear it tonight.

"What's a douche bag?" precious, innocent Rosie asks, making me lean back and howl, a hand on my stomach, my face to the sky.

Autumn puts her face in her hands and mumbles, "Jesus fucking Christ."

"Nothing, baby girl. It's a grown-up word your sister knows better than to use," Steve says, glaring at Sara, who shrugs and goes back to eating her hot dog. The conversation moves on, thankfully, and the pressure I typically feel seems to melt off. It's been a long time since I've felt this weightless and happy feeling that's slowly overtaking me, laughing freely and spending time with my people.

We take family vacations together, but it's embarrassing to admit I'm usually on my Mac in the hotel room, taking calls, wheeling, and dealing instead of spending quality time with them. It feels nice to just... be.

After dinner, Steve and I sit in front of the fire pit and drink another beer. I'm pretty sure he's avoiding my sister, but for me, it's nice to enjoy the warm summer air, to feel good, and spend time with my brother-in-law. We bullshit back and forth, a camaraderie built on knowing each other for some time and both having had to deal with my sister's moods.

By the time he's ready to brave Autumn's wrath and heads inside, I've had three beers. While not quite tipsy, I'm feeling a good light buzz. Instead of heading up after Steve, my feet guide me on a walk around my sister's property. It's well-manicured and large enough to lend itself to a stroll, but not so large you can't find your neighbors. Before long, I find myself in front of a bright blue door on a white cottage I know from talking to Autumn is Hannah's.

Fuck. What am I doing here? This is the last thing I need.

But instead of turning around, my hand is knocking on the front door without my consent.

And... nothing. Knocking again and listening, it's clear she is home, as the sounds of music and singing are softly drifting through the walls to me.

Knowing she probably won't hear me no matter how many times I knock, I turn the knob to find... it turns. Jesus, someone needs to teach this woman to lock a damn door. Briefly fighting with what to do next, I decide to go for it and open her door. Inside is tiny and feminine, kind of like her. It smells like vanilla and honey, probably from the candle burning on the dark wood coffee table, which seems to double as her kitchen table.

Hannah stands at the sink, listening to a country song and singing along as she washes dishes. Her voice is gorgeous, a soft lullaby flowing through my soul, soothing rough edges and coaxing something I've hidden away long ago out.

Wearing a loose tank top and a pair of tight yoga shorts, I can see every tempting, soft curve of her body, and it's a masterpiece to behold. Her chestnut hair is piled high on her head, and she's barefoot with white painted toenails, humming along to the song.

As it ends, it becomes clear this is my cue to let her know I'm being a creepy-as-fuck peeping Tom and knock on the door frame my shoulder is leaning on. It's like a private repeat of the first time I saw her. Not expecting anyone in here with her, she shrieks and jumps; the bubble-coated plate in her hands slipping and falling into the air. We both watch it crash to the floor and break into four pieces, splattering soapy water along with it.

"Oh my God, I'm so sorry, Hannah, I didn't mean to scare you." My eyes are glued to her hands, clutching her chest in terror. *Why am I fucking this up with her so much?*

Bending at the same time she does to clear up the broken ceramic and soap, we're face to face. I freeze, shocked to see up close her blue eyes have rivers of green and hazel hidden in the depths. Another soft country song has started, this one about detours and how they can bring you to a person.

"Sorry I scared you," I say softly, noticing bubbles from the dish soap slowly popping on her cheek. Brushing it away gently, I push a dark strand of hair that fell out of her top knot over her shoulder, marveling at how soft it is and wondering what it would feel like tangled in my hand.

That simple touch seems to knock her out of her daze. She pops up, grabbing a roll of paper towels. I lean forward to grab the shattered pieces, picking them up carefully before placing them into the garbage can in the corner. Avoiding my eye, she cleans up the water and soap, tossing the paper towels before leaning on the counter as far as humanly possible from me.

"How can I help you, Mr. Hutchins?" she asks, crossing her arms on her chest. Her sky-blue eyes look stormy, glaring slightly at me and, once again, guilt washed over me for surprising her. "Or are you just here to give me a heart attack? Seems to be your style."

"We talked about this. Hunter, please call me Hunter." My voice comes out more stern and gruff than intended, a result which can only be blamed on seeing her in those shorts and realizing her top is thin enough to see she is not wearing a bra. At all. The vague outline of rosy nipples is barely visible, but my imagination has always been well-honed. And, fuck, my body is loving the mental vision it's coming up with.

"Fine. What are you doing here, *Hunter*?" She's frustrated. I seem to have that effect on her, scaring her, angering her, and making a total fucking asshole of myself.

"I was just taking a walk and wound up here. To be completely honest, I'm not sure why. Autumn told me you lived in the cottage, and I've been... intrigued ever since. I saw the door and figured I'd stop by." Running my hand down my face, scraping over my beard, I sigh. "I'm not used to being back here. When I'm bored at home, I either work until I pass out or I call an acquaintance and go out. Here... it's been so long since I've been here for longer than a day, and I don't know what to do with myself."

In the city, there is a list of people I can call upon to grab a drink. If I'm not looking for company, there are endless options, from museums to shows to parks. Here... here I'm stuck with my thoughts, and that's not a place I want to be these days.

"That sounds... sad," Hannah says, crossing her arms over her chest. Should I feel offended, disappointed, or relieved? At least she's not screaming and kicking me out. "You don't have any friends?"

"Of course I have friends."

"You called them acquaintances. And you don't have anyone here besides Autumn."

"I have friends, Hannah. I'm not a loser." I've officially settled on being offended.

"Yeah? Name one," she challenges me, a slow smile playing on her lips as she uncrosses her arms and uses them to lean back onto the counter. Fuck, her nipples are back and more beautiful than before. *Concentrate, Hutchins.*

"What? No, I'm not naming my friends."

"Why not, you scared?"

"I'm not scared, I'm just not falling for your ridiculous stunt."

"Because you don't have any." She's standing there with her eyebrow quirked and a devilish tilt to her lips makes me think about kissing it right off.

"Babe, I have friends, but I'm not naming them to you just to prove I have friends." She seems to sit on that before deciding it makes sense. But... my stomach churns a bit when I realize I'm not sure who I *would* have named. "But if you want, we can be friends," I say, taking a step closer to lean a hip against the table, cutting the distance between us in the small kitchen in half.

"Are you a huge dick to your friends, too?" Her adorable eyebrow rises again, her full, pink lips pursing in a serious pout.

"You want to talk about a huge dick?" I ask, a smile on my lips, and I have no idea where that came from. I wouldn't blame her if she slapped me. Instead, she shocks me by throwing her head back and laughing. It's beautiful, the sound like magic twinkling and filling my entire chest with bubbles. "Did Autumn give you my note?"

"Yes. Thank you for the wine."

"Look, apologizing is not something I do well. But calling you out like that was completely out of line, especially for a near stranger. Autumn tells me you have been nothing but a Godsend to her, so I should really thank you for making my nieces a priority." She pauses, taking in my words, and breath catches in my chest, waiting and hoping she sees how sincere I'm being.

"Thank you for that. I appreciate it a lot." She accepts my apology with a sigh, and my body melts, relaxing with relief. "Okay, this is way too awkward for me. You're bored. I don't have to be up at the crack of dawn tomorrow. Do you want a drink out back?"

Smiling, I hold my hand out, gesturing for her to lead the way. She opens her fridge, bending low and showing off her perfect ass before coming back up with two bottles in her hands. Hannah heads to the back door, and, as subtly as possible, I adjust myself in my jeans. How the fuck am I going to make it through this without looking like the creepiest man alive? Even so, this is an opportunity I won't miss out on.

When we get out onto her back patio, it's clear she spends a good deal of time out here. Four comfy but functional chairs sit around a raised fire pit. Surrounding the patio is a mix of fairy lights and more sprays of vibrant blooms, this time wildflowers, making it look like an ethereal space out of a Disney movie. "Wow," I say, turning in a circle to appreciate her handiwork.

"Yeah, this is my happy place." She shrugs, sitting in a chair and popping her feet up on the brick wall surrounding her fireplace before setting the second beer on the bricks for me. Twisting off her cap, she puts it to her lips, gently sipping. Her full lips wrapped around that bottle do terrible things to my self-restraint.

Down, boy, I think, sitting next to her and grabbing my beer. "I can see why. Rosie must be in seventh heaven back here."

"This makes me a terrible person, but she doesn't know about this spot. I love the girl to hell and back, but I know the second she finds out about my fairy garden, she'll beg to come back every day. This is my space." She looks ashamed or embarrassed, but there's no need.

"My office is like that. I keep it the way I like it and only let my assistant in. Autumn has bullied her way in a few times when she was working from the office, but that's kind of her big sister duty, I think. It helps to have a spot untouched from work drama."

Though looking around and thinking of my neatly organized office, I can't help but think about how cold and lifeless it feels in contrast. Clean white walls, dark, boring desk, and windows overlooking Broadway; these were a sign of success needed to prove to the world, to my dad, I know what I'm doing. But now that I have them, they feel... empty. Shaking the thought off, I ask, "So what do *you* do for fun, since you seem to think *my* life is boring and sad."

In the faint glow of the lights, her blush is still visible—she seems to do that a lot. I wonder if it's a Hannah thing or something she does because of me.

"I don't think your life is sad and lonely. You're the one who doesn't have friends." Her eyes twinkle and it's clear she's trying to bait me, but I'm dying to know more about her, so I don't bite. Hannah sighs, giving in. "My best friend Sadie says I make the kids too much of my whole life. But I love kids and making them feel loved, safe, and valued more than anything. I go out with Sadie and sometimes Autumn to Full Moon, the bar in town. A friend owns it. I garden, obviously. I also work over at the Springbrook Hills Center for Kids and Families. Right now, we're working on our summer program, which will start in a week, so my days are pretty packed with the girls and then the Center. I guess I'm not much better in the workaholic category."

"What does that look like? The summer camp."

"Right now, it's just a normal day camp. We have theme weeks and themed days to keep a schedule, but we offer tiered income pricing, so it's affordable to parents. It means we don't have much extra after paying counselors for the fun stuff. But we make it work and make sure the kids have a great summer and are safe and loved when some kids don't have the stability school typically offers. We do all the old-school camp stuff, like big games of red rover and friendship bracelets and chalk drawings. Last year, the kids helped me paint a mural on the building to brighten it up. Things like that."

"I saw the mural when I was driving through town. It's great—kids did that?"

"Yeah, Maggie, the director? She takes time to get to know each and every kid, their strengths, and interests. She tapped the big kids who were most interested in art and invested some love and attention into it. It came out gorgeous."

"That's amazing. So, what's missing? What else could the camp be doing?" When I ask, she lights up. It's easy to see where her heart lies. Thinking about the Center, her sky-blue eyes glitter, and her face glows. Her hands fiddle, excitement overflowing into nervous energy.

"In my perfect world, with the camp we have *right now*, we'd take the kids on weekly field trips—zoos, the beach, amusement parks, the boardwalk—all the fun summer stuff. But when I daydream about taking over, I envision... more. I assume you like the outdoors? Like hiking and stuff?" I have to laugh.

"Yes, Hannah, the man who runs an outdoor recreation equipment company enjoys hiking and stuff." Her hand goes out to playfully slap my arm and laugh. God, this feels good. Too damn good.

"Okay, so most of these kids have never been much further than downtown, never got in the woods or hiking or camping. They've never had that movie-worthy, dirt-and-bugs summer camp, and they just never will. It's not in the cards. These days, camps can cost as much as a semester at college. When a family has more than one kid, which most attending the Center do, it's literally impossible for them to afford it. I'm going to create a camp where we can take the kids and give them the *Bug Juice* classic, carefree summer. These kids... so many of them have seen more than they should have at such young ages, or they've grown up already at a disadvantage and are disillusioned. I want to show them... potential. Potential for a beautiful life," she says, with a dazed, far-off look on her face.

"It's important to you, isn't it? The Center, changing these kids' lives?" I ask, wanting to learn more, and know what makes her tick. She sips her beer, contemplating how much to tell me before she sighs.

"I didn't have the best childhood. My parents were... neglectful, leaving me to take care of my little sister most of the time. When I was about Sara's age, I came to the Center for the summer. I knew with school out, we'd be missing stability and normalcy, and I needed that. I needed to keep Abbie safe and to keep me sane. I met Maggie there, and she showed me there was a group of people in our community who wanted to help us however they could, that a community could lift others and keep them afloat.

"When I was 12, I came to Maggie and I was crying about something or other my mom had said. Honestly, I couldn't even tell you what it was now, but I was heartbroken. She set up Abbie at our neighbor's house for the night, so I wouldn't worry about her, and took me camping. Just for a night. I know it sounds weird, and today, if it were my kid, I'd be worried a stranger was taking her to the woods, but somehow... Maggie knew what I needed." Hannah places her beer onto the ground before looking up into the night sky, bright with constellations like she's looking for answers written there.

"Maggie is a huge hippie. She took me into the woods, we

camped, and she taught me how to give my pain and disappointment to the universe. Showed me how healing nature can be when you let it." She laughs, dropping her head into her hands, slim, elegant fingers tipped now with light blue polish. "God, I probably sound insane."

She doesn't sound crazy. She sounds excited and motivated, but most of all, she sounds genuine. I get it—the healing effect of being out in fresh air, trees all around, and not a soul in sight. There's something so humbling about being surrounded by nature and marveling at what God or whatever you believe in has created, this landscape that is so much larger than you can ever hope to be. To wash away the cuts and scrapes, the bruises and disappointments life hands you.

And I know the feeling of wanting to give that to others.

I reach out and grab her hand, so tiny compared to mine, cradling it in my own. Her head lifts, in shock, I think, but she doesn't pull her hand away. She meets my eyes, those blue depths flickering emotions so quickly I can't catch any of them.

"You don't sound insane."

TEN

-HANNAH-

Hunter is holding my hand and looking into my eyes. *Holy crap, holy crap, holy crap.* His hand is huge compared to mine, engulfing it in his. Surprise hits me with how rough they are, callused and worn as if he uses them often. It's unexpected, knowing how much he works in his office job.

"Oh." It's all that comes to my lips, to my mind, which has frozen in place.

Still holding my hand, Hunter stands, moving so he's right in front of me in my wrought iron patio chair where I'm staring up at him. My mouth hangs open a bit, be it from shock or nerves or confusion, I'll never know. His eyes are twin pools of warm chocolate, playful yet serious, with the longest, darkest lashes framing them. The fairy lights around us let me read his intent before he tugs on my hand, pulling me up and to him.

He's so close now, our hands get pressed between us. The position allows me to feel how, like my own, his heart is racing. I'm not sure why this pleases me so much, the knowledge that we're standing on equal footing.

Looking up at him, I feel tiny, petite, and feminine. Never in my life have my average five foot six inches felt tiny, but his towering frame does just that.

"This is a terrible idea, Hunter." The words fall from my lips even as his arm wraps around my lower back, pressing me into him.

"Trust me, babe, I've made a lot of poor decisions in my life, and this is not one of them." Before I can protest, he lowers his head, brushing his lips gently to mine, the scratch of his beard sending chills down my spine. The kiss is gentle and sweet and everything any girl who has read love stories and watched movies that make your heart flutter dreams of.

And then something snaps, like a dam of tension that's been between us since we met. As if this whole time, our subconscious was waiting for the moment, we let our guard down to take over. His teeth nip, and my mouth opens, letting his demanding tongue come into stroke my own, making me whimper. The hand holding mine between us lets go to trail my side before grabbing my ass, and he groans. If I weren't preoccupied trying to get my body as close to his, I'd smile. But I'm winding my arms around his neck, reaching up onto my tiptoes, needing to be closer.

We're an explosion of heavy breathing, a clashing of teeth and tongues, a white fervent desire expressed so blatantly, I'm immediately damp between my legs. Hunter's arm around my back trails up, tangling in my loosely tied hair. He tugs it back, a slight sting causing an uncontrollable moan to slip past my lips as he trails his lips down my neck, nipping as he goes.

"This fucking ass has been taunting me for days. Jackin' myself every night, thinking about how fucking gorgeous this ass is." His words rumble against my neck, adding fuel to my fire. We're crazed, going from sweet and heart-warming to hot and heavy in moments, but it all feels so exquisitely right. Rough hands slip under my thin shorts, finding I don't wear undies with my bedtime shorts. He groans, palming my ass hard enough that I hope it will leave a mark tomorrow, a reminder this was real. "Jesus, fuck, so fucking hot, babe."

"Oh, God, Hunter." A hand slips into his thick hair, so much softer than expected. My other hand, still pressed between us, trails against the ridges of his abs, dying to feel what I could uncover in my bed, not 20 feet away inside.

"So fucking sexy, dying to do this since I saw you, Han." His wandering tongue makes its way back up to my lips. The salt of my skin, the beer he was drinking earlier, and something so uniquely Hunter is on his tongue, the combination so overwhelming, all I can do is groan.

He's earthy and warm, reminding me of a sunny day in my garden, warm and safe and connected. Hitching my leg onto his hip to get closer still, to melt with him, his hardness brushes my center through thin cotton, and I gasp, loving this, needing this, needing so much more.

"Hunt!" The sound hitting my ears has the same effect as ice dumped over my body; it slams me back into reality in a millisecond. My leg drops, trying to pull back in horror at what happened. I made out and *dry-humped* my boss' brother. Oh, my God. Instead of letting me go, Hunter holds me tighter to him.

"Fuck. Autumn," he says, staying frozen and locking eyes with me.

Heat still simmers in them. My insides are battling, wanting to ignore our intruder and see where it could take us, but also completely horrified over what transpired.

"Hunter, let me go." A suffocating panic wins the battle, rising in my chest as I try to pull away.

"Hunt, where'd you run off to?" Autumn says, but the quieter sound signals she's getting further from my cottage, heading a different way to find her brother. The last thing I need is a complication like this. A complication like *the brother of my boss* and me tangled up behind my cottage, his hands still under my shorts on the skin of my ass.

"You have to go," I say firmly and quietly, pushing on his chest, trying to escape.

"Hannah, we need to talk—"

"Nothing to talk about, a lapse of judgment. In fact, let's pretend it didn't happen. At all. Please."

"If you can forget what happened, I wasn't doing it right." He's smirking and still refusing to let me go. And he's right, of course—he sure as hell was doing it right. Just thinking of it sends a thrill down my spine, making him smile wider. Goddammit, he felt it.

"Seriously, Hunter, you need to go."

"Go out with me. Dinner, drinks, I don't care." He drops the request in my lap, giving me both butterflies and a sinking feeling. I can't. I can't get tangled up in someone like Hunter. I made a vow years ago I would never settle, never let myself get involved with someone who couldn't be mine forever. I've seen what that kind of disappointment can do to a woman. And if there's one thing I know about Hunter Hutchins, it's he is not the forever type.

"No. I can't. This was a huge mistake." He looks into my eyes as I break the news to him. He's assessing, deciding, and calculating, his true business savant shining through. He must see something I've hidden in there because moments later, his eyes fill with cunning determination.

"Okay, fine, I won't convince you. Tonight," he says with a spark of determination. And something tells me there is nothing that will stop Hunter Hutchins from whatever it is he wants. With one last slow but chaste press of his lips to mine, he lets me go and walks towards the big house, leaving me standing there.

I work hard to avoid Hunter after our kiss. The task has been a difficult one, considering he lives where I work. Each day is carefully planned, intending to be as far from him as possible. Sometimes it means taking the kids out, and for others it's simply leaving the room whenever it looks like he might come in.

Yes, I'm a coward. No, I do not care. Self-preservation is the name of this game, and I hate to lose.

I make it a full seven days until that comes crashing down.

ELEVEN
-HANNAH-

"Come on, Ava, let's play tag!" Rosie screams in her shrill little voice. The girl chases Rosie, both giggling hysterically and stopping to dance in the sprinkler.

I *love* summer.

Today, Rosie's friend from preschool is here with her mom, Michelle. Michelle is what I call "movie star" stay-at-home mom style.

Her long, blonde hair pulled up into a perfect ponytail seems immune to the East Coast humidity. Her body is perfectly toned and tanned. I'm not sure I've ever seen her without a Starbucks cup in hand, filled with some kind of fat-free, sugar-free $18 drink and the diaper bag she totes dirty pull-ups in a friggin' Louis Vuitton.

But she's nice enough and treats me like a human rather than a scum of the earth employee like some of the other moms at the wealthy preschool do, so I like her.

"Thanks for inviting us, Hannah. Ava's been non-stop whining about missing school now that it's out, and there's only so many princess movies I can watch," she laughs. I completely empathize with her. With summer vacation in full swing but the Center's camp has not started yet, I have about two weeks of utter peace. Sara has sports camp this week, meaning from 9 to 3 it's just me and Rosie girl. But the princess movies and tea parties and non-stop keeping her entertained can be exhausting.

"Any time! We love having you guys here and it's nice to get a break from being the primary source of play all day long." Plus, it wears Rosie out, which means a good nap is on the horizon this afternoon.

"Hannah! Can you get us watermelon? I told Ava you cut it in stars and she doesn't believe me!" Rosie says, standing in her little pink bikini, her belly out for everyone to see and her hands on her hips. Attitude is coming off her in waves. Jeez, this girl is adorable.

"Sure, buddy, be right back." I stand, asking Michelle if she wants anything from inside. When she declines, I grab my cup and head inside.

The lidded Tupperware filled with pink fruit that was cut with a cookie cutter this morning is sitting on the counter. Quickly, I add more ice and water into my cup before turning around to head out. Except I slam into something, and my water cup goes flying onto me, soaking the front of my white coverup with ice-cold liquid. Immediately, the fabric clings to me, crushed ice cubes falling down my top and into my hair.

"What the fudge?" An ice cube lodges itself into my bikini top, making me shiver, and I fish it out with my soaking hand. It's then I notice him standing there. The man I've been successfully avoiding for a full week, wearing a pair of nice shorts and a button-down shirt, the sleeves cuffed to his elbows. His hair is tousled, his beard slightly thicker than it was just a week ago. He looks perfect. And here I am, looking like a wet t-shirt contestant, alone in the kitchen with him.

"What the fudge?" he says, voice full of laughter as he grabs another chunk of ice out of my hair. His eyes drift to my top, where my fingers are chasing around a slippery cube. God, could this be any more embarrassing? "What does that even mean?"

"I don't like to curse around kids. You know, because I'm a decent human." Trying to step back and escape him, my foam flip-flop catches yet *another* ice cube, making me slip and fall to my ass.

Or I would have, except Hunter catches me around the waist at the last second, pulling me to him so we're face to face. His body is already warming my now freezing front. My soaked coverup is making his shirt just as wet.

"Well, look at that. I haven't seen you in a week, and you're already wet for me," he murmurs in a seductive tone, a quirk on his lips. My hand itches to smack that stupid smirk off his admittedly gorgeous face.

"Excuse me, what? You're seriously going to be a jerk when you spilled water all over me and almost made me fall?" The arrogant asshole. He *would* try to turn this into a come-on.

"Woah, calm down there. You slammed into me when you weren't looking where you were going," he says, letting me go and stepping back. His dark brown shirt shows a perfect outline of my body, specifically where my breasts were pressed to him. The blush on my cheeks nearly hurts, like a bad sunburn.

Looking down, he takes in the mess on his tee, smirking before looking at my body, which is clearly displayed. The thin, soaked light-colored cover-up shows my bright pink halter top bikini with its high-cut bikini bottoms coming up over my hip bones. My generous—maybe *too* generous, thanks to my love affair with cookie batter and pasta—curves feel indecent with the way his eyes are roaming my body, leaving a burning path in their wake.

Without saying a thing, I grab a handful of paper towels and bend over to grab the thankfully unopened watermelon container from the floor. A hiss of air through my teeth tells me it wasn't my best plan, and my entire ass is on display to Hunter. But my stubbornness refuses to acknowledge another faux pas. Refilling my cup, I slam the stack of paper towels into his chest, silently telling him to clean up his spill without a second glance back.

Outside, Michelle has removed her cover-up in the blazing summer sun and is applying tanning oil to her bronzed and toned skin, encased in a black bikini. I swear, if the evidence of her clone wasn't in front of me, you couldn't convince me this woman birthed a child.

"Got a little wet?" Michelle asks, a smile on her face.

"You have no idea," I say under my breath, taking off my soaked cover-up. I call the girls over, opening the container and making sure Rosie has a full cup of water. While she munches away, she gets a fresh blast of sunscreen before I sit. Then I hear it.

"Uncle Hunter!" We all look up to see Hunter in all of his tanned, bearded glory, strolling out onto the patio.

"Well, shit. I think I just got a little wet, too," Michelle says under her breath, and it's all I can do not to groan and hide my head in a pile of pool towels.

TWELVE
-HUNTER-

Once again, Hannah comes crashing into my day, distracting me and sending my mind reeling, this time literally. How she can do it every time, I have no clue, but her clumsiness and adorable PG curse word substitutions are too enticing to ignore. Plus, those curves in that near-fluorescent bathing suit... Jesus.

Walking out onto the back patio, I don't bother changing my shirt which still has the perfect imprint of her tits on my chest. It's hot as fuck outside and the blush it created earlier is too much to resist. As soon as I'm hit with the humid air, my niece in a suit matching her nanny's comes barreling at me, grabbing my legs and screaming my name. Laughing, I pick her up and pop her onto my hip, ignoring sticky hands and a watermelon juice-covered face.

"Hey, princess, how's it going?" I smack a loud kiss to the top of her head, making her giggle. Looking to my right, Hannah is avoiding my eye, sitting in a lounge chair. Her wet coverup is hanging on the railing behind her, leaving nothing between that swimsuit and my eyes.

Lightly tanned olive skin. Absolute miles of it, every inch perfect with the occasional freckle spotted along its expanse. The cut of her bottoms leaves her hips exposed and makes those legs look even longer than they are. Perfect for wrapping around me while... *No, Hunter, stop, this would be an unbearably terrible time to get hard.* My eyes continue down, discovering a soft but flat belly and perfectly round breasts encased in that simple but unbearably attractive swimsuit. Physically, she's my dream woman. Curves and softness and unintentional sex appeal.

Baseball. Taxes. Accounting figures. End-of-year spreadsheets. Steve in a Speedo. It takes everything in my arsenal not to get hard looking at this dream woman while holding my baby niece. Putting Rosie down, I turn to the woman next to her.

"Hey there, I'm Hunter, Rosie's uncle," I say, reaching over to Hannah to shake her hand. It's a move that will undoubtedly piss her off, which makes me smirk. She lays there stiff as a board, making me gently chuckle under my breath.

"Michelle, Ava's mom. The girls are friends from Apple Academy." The woman smiles in a way I am all too familiar with, holding my hand a moment too long for a simple greeting. There's a large rock on her ring finger which tells me everything a man needs to know about her.

Standing straight, Michelle's eyes drift to my chest where the wet mark hasn't dried yet before moving her eyes to Hannah's wet cover-up, and her eyes gently widen. I smirk and wink at her, really playing up the drama. It's then it happens. Hannah's jaw clenches just enough to show me she's annoyed. Not by my saying hi, and not even by the insinuation, but by the hint of flirting.

Game on, I think, moving to confirm my assumption.

Sitting in the chair across from the women, I turn to Michelle. "Your daughter is adorable. Just like her mom. What's her name again?" She flashes a toothpaste ad white smile before answering, but I'm not listening. Instead, I'm watching Hannah's blue eyes flare with anger and even a hint of disappointment before dropping large sunglasses onto the bridge of her nose.

"You got the sprinkler on Rosie? It's so hot. Can I play with you?"

I ask the girls, knowing the answer because my girl loves her Uncle Hunter.

"Yes! SPRINKLER!" she yells, coming over to grab my hand and drag me to the grass. Rather than going upstairs for swim shorts, I say fuck it and unbutton my still-damp shirt, leaving me in my shorts. My shoes are kicked off with the toes of each foot.

Eyes are burning on my back. I turn, and my theory is then confirmed when Hannah turns her head as soon as I face her. But the blush she's sporting tells me what I need to know. Michelle is staring blatantly, not even bothering to hide her cat ate the canary glance.

"Hey, Han, if you're still wet, you should come play." She turns her head to me, lifts her glasses, and gives me a look that gives new meaning to *if looks could kill.* "What about you, Michelle? Interested in getting wet with me?" The blonde gives me a head-to-toe which would be an irresistible invitation to any bachelor if it weren't for her sunbathing companion.

"I'll just watch," the woman says, eye-fucking me before, kid you not, she *licks her lips*. Lord, this woman isn't subtle at all. With another wink for good measure, I walk off to chase the girls, feeling a burst of energy greater than anything I've felt in a week.

"Okay, Uncle Hunter needs a break, ladies." These girls have more energy in their little bodies than I've had in my whole life. An hour of chasing, tackling, tickling, and spraying them in the blazing summer sun and they look no more exhausted than when we started. Collapsing into a chair, my head tilts to the sky, and my eyes close, thankful for the shade of the umbrella.

"You're so good with them," Ava's mom coos, leaning forward to give a glimpse of cleavage. Cleavage, I would bet my business is not natural.

"I love my nieces. Don't get a ton of time with them, but when I do, I make the most of it."

"No kids of your own?"

"Nope, no time. I just borrow my sisters when I get the urge."

"And what about your wife? Do you make time for her?" She asks, looking at my ring finger, which clearly has no ring on it. I look at hers, noting at some point, she discreetly removed her own, leaving a thin tan line. *She's a winner.*

"Nope, no Mrs."

"Oh goodness, how did you manage that? If you lived around here, I would just snatch you up."

"The normal, busy work schedule, minimal social life. Just waiting for the perfect woman to run into me." My eyes drift to Hannah, who, although she seems to ignore us, stiffens at my words.

"I'm sure they're always falling over you, especially in the city, no?"

"Not unless he sneaks up on them," Hannah mumbles under her breath, forcing a laugh from my chest.

"What was that?" Michelle asks, looking over at Hannah, slight annoyance on her face. This woman doesn't like the attention off of her at all.

"Oh, nothing, just thinking out loud. Rosie could use another layer of sunscreen." Ava's mom seems annoyed by the interruption, turning back to me.

"Well, you seem pretty free now, no? Why don't we head inside and chat a bit, get to know each other." Michelle leans forward and places a hand on my knee. Her hand is icy from the drink she set down, immediately reminding me of the stark contrast to Hannah's war m, small hands."I'd love to find out what makes you tick," she says before biting her lip. Fillers, I'm sure. Living in the city, I've seen it all, and this woman has had *it all.*

And laying next to Hannah, 'all' isn't enough.

"What about your daughter? She's still playing in the sprinkler with Rosie," I ask what seems like the obvious question. But she waves her hand, not a care in the world.

"Hannah here can watch her, can't you, Han? That's what her

job is, isn't it?" The woman has balls. Something in me starts to boil, angry someone would say something like that, much less to her face. Hannah's entire body stiffens, looking hurt. Emotion flits through her eyes—emotions I saw the day I told her she was just the nanny. Fuck. She looks away.

"I'll uh..." Hannah starts, moving her hands to push herself up, but I speak first.

"That's not why she's here. Hannah is here to care for Rosie, not to babysit your kid while you go cheat on your husband." All the blood drains from Michelle's perfectly tanned and Botoxed face. Normally it would be a great time to bask in a direct hit, but I'm too focused on Hannah and making sure she's okay.

"Excuse me?" It's clear no one ever puts this woman in her place. It's even more clear she needs it.

"You heard me."

"You can't talk to me like that." She's hurdling past her embarrassment and moving on to indignation.

"No, *you* can't talk to *Hannah* like that. You're obviously a lonely woman or just a super shitty wife. I don't care to find out. But it does not give you the excuse to treat a kind, welcoming person that way. You might look pretty and sculpted on the outside, but your insides are fucking ugly."

I'm not sure where this is coming from. I've seen catty behavior for years and years but never stepped in. But something about the look in Hannah's eyes fueled something in me, making me hungry for blood. "And another thing—quit it with the Botox. I can't even tell if you're angry or upset right now, your face won't even move." Hannah snorts a laugh behind her hand, and I look her way, happy to see the look no longer in her eyes.

"I, uh, I think I should get going." Michelle stands, grabs her cover-up, and throws it on.

"I think that's for the best," I say as she calls her daughter over. Ava resists, wanting to play longer, but her mother all but scoops her up and drags her out the side gate, not even bothering to dry the girl off. We sit in silence for a moment.

"Well, that was an eventful afternoon," I say, sitting back with a sigh, running my hand over my face and through my beard.

Hannah bursts out laughing.

THIRTEEN
-HANNAH-

I hit play on the remote, and that magical sound telling us a Disney movie is about to start comes playing through the surround sound. Somehow Rosie talked us into sitting on the couch with her and watching a movie right before her nap time after lunch in a show of force one can only admire. That being said, I think both Hunter and I were a bit worn from the sun and the drama.

Within minutes, she falls asleep with her head in my lap, and her legs draped across Hunter's, well and fully pinning us in place.

"Does that happen often?" His voice is quiet, mindful of sleeping beauty.

"Does what happen often?"

"Michelle. Or, I guess me, too. People treating you like shit, acting like you don't matter."

I sigh. "It doesn't happen *infrequently*. I've been doing this for six years, I can put the blinders on pretty well. Sometimes it hurts more than others, most of the time, I'm able to ignore it."

Avoiding eye contact with Hunter, my fingers run through Rosie's strawberry-blonde hair. I'm not sure where it came from.

Steve is dark, and Autumn's auburn results from going to see Sandy at the salon in town every six weeks.

"Unless it's the brother of your boss who's acting like a dick. Then it's harder to ignore. I bet that one hit deeper than most."

Staring at the ceiling, I try to find the words to explain it. "I told you about my childhood a bit. We saw my dad and his replaceable girlfriends a few times a month. My mom was bitter over the divorce and convinced her marriage went downhill once I came around. She never hit us. We were always fed, mostly, but that was the extent of her motherly duties. I ended up raising my sister, hiding from CPS, and living to try and make my mother happy, which never worked. Some days she wouldn't come home for two, or three days. Never explained why. It didn't matter, anyway."

Hunter reaches across Rosie and grabs my hand, holding it in his. He stares at it, inspects it, but doesn't pressure me to keep talking. Something about that grace, the permission to take my time, keeps me talking.

"My best friend Sadie lived next door. Her mom was... amazing. Think 1950s sitcom mom. She took us in, and never made us feel like a burden. She cared for us. Let us know what a real mom did. She knew. She knew what was happening, but she never turned us in, just gave us the love and comfort, and... direction we needed. It might sound crazy, but I'm thankful for that. Who knows what our lives would have looked like if we'd gone into the system, you know? She baked us birthday cakes and made my Halloween costume when my mom wouldn't buy one. For years we convinced my sister, Abbie that Santa couldn't come into our house because there was no chimney, and on Christmas morning, we'd go over to Sadie's."

A sad chuckle escapes my lips.

"The thing is, I'm grateful. I'm thankful I had what I did. I've seen what happens to kids who grow up like me but without their own Maggie or Mrs. Tate. It doesn't always have a happy ending. That's why I work at the Center. And working with kids, helping them grow confident and safe and loved? That's all I want. Anyone who has something negative to say about someone who wants to devote their lives to the cause? It's a 'them' problem, not a 'me' problem."

I look at him and smile. "No offense."

He stares at me for what feels like an eternity. From just an hour in the sun, his dark hair has lightened in a few streaks, his cheeks have a slight tint that will probably fade to a golden tan.

"My mom left us when I was five," he whispers before clearing his throat. "Autumn was about Sara's age. I woke up in the middle of the night, not sure why. I came downstairs, and my dad was crying at the kitchen table, and... she was gone. I haven't seen her since."

This isn't new information to me. Autumn revealed it a few years back when I had the girls over for a sleepover in the cottage that ended in tears, soul-baring, and Steve delivering us pizzas and munchies. Rather than telling him this, I stay silent. I want to hear him tell his story without interruption, intuitively knowing this is something he needs to do.

"We were lucky. You've met my dad, I'm sure. He's the best guy in the universe, stepped up when he originally planned on being the cool dad. Became everything to us. I've spent my whole life trying to make it up to him."

"I'm sure he would do it every time, over and over again, no matter what you do or don't prove. But I also know he's incredibly proud of you."

It's true. Ron brags about Hunter almost every time I see him.

"Being a parent isn't about repayment. It's about the kids in your life filling your cup in a way they'll never understand until they're parents themselves. It's about giving and giving and never worrying you'll hit the bottom, leaving nothing for yourself. But you'd do it anyway if you had to, over and over again, without a second thought. Knowing if you run out, you'd hit rock bottom and beg and borrow and steal to fill those kids up with everything they need." I take a deep breath, looking around the room to explain without sounding insane.

"I know I'm not a mom. I know it might sound crazy. But I had to raise my sister, and I love those girls. I'd give everything if their cups weren't filled by Autumn and Steve. I see the kids at the Center, the ones who need someone, and it kills me knowing I can't be everything for them. Sadie gives me shit for it, and says I need to focus on me. But if you didn't live it, you can't know... you can't know what it's like to never be full."

His eyes meet mine, something deep shining in them, knowing we share the knowledge our mothers didn't even try to hit rock bottom for us. A bond forms silently. I feel like I should be embarrassed, should be ashamed for my little soapbox moment, but I'm not.

We stay quiet for a bit, our stare breaking when Rosie shifts but falls back to sleep. Eventually, I forget we were talking, losing myself in the movie. The hand not holding Hunter's starts combing through Rosie's hair again, but I hold tight with my other, refusing to end this connection with him. He's watching his niece while stroking the palm of my hand gently with his thumb.

"You're great with them," he says, breaking the silence. For being the craziest of the two, she's the most peaceful sleeper.

"They're easy to love." At the end of the day, that's what it is. Kids are frustrating and difficult, but these kids hold my whole heart, making caring for them simple.

"Why do you do it? Autumn told me you're crazy smart and have other places begging you to work for them. Why watch my nieces instead and deal with the comments? You could be a teacher or social worker. A therapist specializing in kids, a pediatrician. You could make the same impact, but more."

My gut hesitates, not wanting to let this part go, to reveal my soft spot before it lets me answer. Even after my mini-speech, this feels... different. I'm trying to decide if I want to tell him the normal story, that I tried school, couldn't hack it, and dropped out. That it just wasn't for me, so I found another way. Or if I want to tell him the truth.

For some reason, I go with the truth.

"Because... because all I ever wanted was to be a mom. I didn't have a great one growing up, but I saw what it could do. What a strong, consistent figure could do for a kid. I want to be that. I want to be the class mom and bake the cookies and kiss the boo-boos. Having a job society sees as a 'real job' would lock me into a standard where I couldn't be that person to them, and it would kill me."

"You know you could do both, right? Be successful, have a career, be the class mom."

"No, you can't," I say, bristling, because what on earth does this man who can barely make time to breathe between work meetings know about juggling a career and being a parent? "It's hard. Autumn knows, we've talked about it. Both sides have expectations for her. Work wants her to focus on work 24/7, to be there at the drop of a hat, never miss a day, and always be on the ball. Society wants her life to revolve around her kids 24/7, and to have no other passion than her child.

"So she has to choose. Try to be everything, crash and burn or follow her passion and find solutions to make sure her kids still get everything and more. Make sure she's filling her cup while her kids' stay full. She has to carefully structure her priorities, and make sure it all aligns perfectly. Autumn could be those things, but she has an ambition I don't have. Not every kid needs it all, but I have the opportunity to give these kids the hardworking, beyond-loving mom they already have, and a fun, at their beck and call nanny. I get to be that person for them, and one day I'll be that mom to my kids."

My eyes refuse to meet his as I'm exposing my truth.

"Why not find a man who can give you what you want? Why not skip the nannying, get married, and have babies or whatever? I know you know you're gorgeous. You're sweet and smart and kind. Any guy would jump on that," he says, looking me in the eye like he's trying to decode me. Like I'm a puzzle where the missing piece would tell the whole picture.

"I refuse to make that mistake." The words come quickly. "My parents jumped into getting married, and my sister and I suffered because of it. It was miserable. My dad is basically non-existent, and my mother resents us, blaming us for her relationship ending. I won't do that to kids of my own. When I finally settle down, it will be with someone I know down to my soul I'll be with until we die."

We sit in silence, staring at each other. It's like a game of chicken, waiting for the other person to look away first.

I lose.

Glancing at the wall and feeling embarrassed, I say, "I know it sounds crazy. I don't think life is going to be a perfect fairytale. But I just want to be sure, you know?"

"It doesn't sound crazy at all. I get it. It makes sense. My dad loved my mom so deep he lost himself in it. Loved her to distraction. When my mom left, it broke him. He had to raise us on his own, battle heartbreak, help us heal, and he worked damn hard to make sure none of that left scars."

"That's hard, Hunter. But you're one of the lucky ones, with a parent who could and did do it all to protect you."

"I am," he says, and once again, we both drift off into our thoughts. Once again, I'm the one to break the silence, this time taking the pressure off myself.

"Your dad—have you gone to see him yet?"

Hunter sighs and runs his hand through his hair. "No. I haven't. I—I'm not ready for that. There's so much I want to show him, to thank him for... everything. I'm just not ready to face him, knowing I haven't done that yet. Not when there's always a chance it could be..." The unspoken words hang heavy in the air. *A chance it could be the last time.* At any moment, things could turn bad.

"Do you know I visit him? Every Saturday morning. I bring him a big batch of cookies to bring to bingo." I've been taking Ron weekly cookies for years, but once he was in the home, I started making a morning of it, staying an hour or two to chat with the remarkable man.

"That's where all the cookies go."

"What, did you think I just ate them all?" I laugh, raising my eyebrow. Hunter raises his hand, not holding mine in defense.

"Hey, my sister taught me never to ask a woman about how much she's eating, her weight, or any work she's had done."

I laugh out loud, then freeze, worried I've woken Rosie.

When it looks like we're in the clear, I say, "Good for her."

"Yeah, punched me right in the balls when she was 13 and ate a carton of ice cream by herself. My dad found out and gave her a high five."

"Go, Ron," I add because, really, he proves himself to be more and more awesome each day.

"He raised us right. Both of us." I nod, agreeing. He pauses. "So you've seen him? How is he? Autumn... She tries to sugarcoat everything, and doesn't tell me the truth. But when I do... finally... go, I need to be prepared. Mentally." I want to push it, tell him to go see for himself. But instead, I give him what I feel he needs—reassurance.

"He's in good spirits. He looks like he's sick. I'm not going to lie. But he's the same Ron I've known, joking, laughing. He talks about you a lot. Good things, Hunt. All good."

We're both quiet again. Running my fingers through Rosie's hair, I fight the urge to ask why he's so sure Ron wouldn't see him as successful. But Rosie is showing the signs she's going to wake up soon, her eyes fluttering and squinting.

"Hannah?" Hunter probes, breaking the silence.

"Hmm?"

"Go out with me. To dinner. Or lunch. Or dessert, I'm not picky." He says it with a smile, so irresistible. A million excuses and responses run through my mind, but only one answer flits in and sticks, clear as crystal.

But before I can answer, I look down to see Rosie stretching, waking up, and breaking the moment. She yawns, looks at me, then at her uncle before scrambling to her feet.

"Snack time!" she yells, and then we're off, continuing with the chaos of the day.

The rest of the night goes by quickly, with me casting curious looks at Hunter, trying to figure out what is going through his head. The thing is, we both made our wants and needs clear. He needs no distractions; he needs to make his business his focus. I need to find someone who will be it for me, who I can trust to stick with me through thick and thin.

But, even though I will go down denying it to Sadie, I'm lonely. I miss having someone to wake up with, to text just to say hi. Someone to have a drink with. God, someone to kiss. And damn, is he a worthy companion for that.

Which, of course, has me thinking of what else he might be good at.

When Autumn gets home, Sara in tow, I head out. My list of errands is a mile long, and it needs to get done before I make myself a quick dinner. Kissing the girls on the head and waving to Autumn, I head to the door before Hunter joins me.

"I'll walk you out," he says quietly, grazing his hand against mine. Hunter walks me out the door, gently closing it behind him.

Before I can process what's happening, he has me pressed against the siding of the house, his body on mine. Hunter's lips crash to mine in a kiss that's full of need and want. It's been building since the other night in my secret garden. When I gasp in surprise and contentment, he slips in his tongue, grazing my own.

My arms wrap against his neck, knowing this can't last forever, and deepen the kiss. I want... more. I want him. I want him in ways I refuse to even acknowledge for fear of losing what I've protected my whole life: my heart.

The kiss lasts for what feels like seconds but was probably a few minutes. Too short for my liking. By the soft groan he makes as he presses his forehead to mine, he agrees.

"Yes," I whisper, brushing my lips. "I'll go out with you. But I don't want Autumn or the kids to know." He smiles and nods before brushing his lips to mine once more, stepping back.

"I'll see you soon, Hannah," he says, letting me go and walking back into the house. He leaves me trembling, excited, and terrified out of my mind, knowing this man can destroy me.

FOURTEEN
-HANNAH-

A week later I'm raiding Sadie's freezer where I snag a carton of ice cream before plopping on her couch in sweats and an oversized tee from an old boyfriend.

"No, be my guest, eat my ice cream," she says under her breath, grabbing an extra spoon before sitting next to me to share. I pass it over, tossing my head back onto her couch, spoon in my mouth.

"Why are men like this?!" The spoon doesn't leave my mouth, making the sound muffled by creamy goodness.

"Because they are the inferior species," Sadie speaks the words quickly and without hesitation, getting a large scoop of cookie dough ice cream and popping it in her mouth.

"It's been five days. Five days and nothing. It's not like he doesn't know where to find me. I literally work where he's living."

"Babe, he's a guy. He's also a guy running a multi-million dollar business from his sister's guest room. Give the guy a break." She tucks her feet underneath herself before grabbing her remote, flipping through to find some junk TV to watch. Sadie's apartment is nestled in the very center of downtown, a few blocks from Luna's Full Moon Cafe. It's a small one-bedroom, one bath, but it has a magnificent living room and she has the comfiest pull-out couch, which is perfect for movie marathons and stress eating.

Her apartment itself is an absolute disaster, clothes and discarded packaging thrown around, towers of paperwork and books teetering on every surface. You'd think since her business is kept so pristine, her apartment would be as well, but for as long as I've known her, Sadie cannot keep a room neat for longer than an hour. My wild child best friend thrives in utter chaos.

"Yeah, but he's the guy who was pushing a date. It's not like I'm manipulating a situation in my mind. He asked me *twice*."

"Is this the same woman who is always telling me she doesn't want to go on a date unless he's essentially the guy she's going to marry and make a million sweet babies with?" In response, I throw a pillow at her, hoping to hit her face, but my aim has never been true, and it veers off, landing a good foot from her. "And isn't this the guy you told me Autumn told *you* uses women for a happy fun time and then goes back to hyper-focusing on work like an obsessive gremlin?"

"I take it back. I don't want to vent to you about this." She has a point, but I'm not sure I want to hear it. Why am I hyper-focusing on this? Why does it matter? A date with Hunter Hutchins is a horrible idea. He is not the guy who wants to settle down. I am desperate for nothing less. He lives in the city, and I will never leave Springbrook Hills. And he is *my boss's brother*. Let's let that one sink in for a bit.

"Stop. I see the thoughts churning in your mind. This is a great idea. You need to have fun! To get out there, enjoy a fling. Do something for Hannah. And, no, sitting on my couch eating cookie dough ice cream in sweatpants does not count as 'something for Hannah.'" My eyes roll into my head before snatching back the ice cream container with a huff.

"Fine, we can talk about something else." She steals the carton back after I get a spoonful. "How's the summer program going? How's Mags?"

"The program is going... okay. We lost our shirt sponsor, which is a bummer, so I've been making calls locally all week, trying to secure one. It's been a bust. The kids are excited, though. We've got two field trips planned this year, and I got the craft store downtown to donate a bunch of materials for things like tie-dye shirts and friendship bracelets."

"Aww, just like we used to make. You still haven't found a sponsor for the shirts yet? Doesn't camp start Monday?"

I groan, putting my head in my hands. "Yes, I'm screwed. If I can't find something by tomorrow, I'm going to tell Maggie I found something and pay for them from the savings account. She'd flip if she ever found out, but the kids look forward to them, and it makes team activities so much more fun, with the numbers and last names on the back."

"Not to mention trips. It's so much easier to find a wanderer if they all match." Sadie may or may not have been wrangled into helping more than once. "Don't you live with, like, a billionaire right now?"

"I don't know about a *billionaire*, and I don't technically live *with* him, just on the same property. But either way, there is no way in hell I'm asking him for a donation. That would be so weird and uncomfortable."

"Would it? Don't the girls go to the camp every summer? It would kind of be for them, too, right?"

"In theory, yes," I say carefully, knowing where she's going with this. "But no. Absolutely not." But Sadie is hard at work, typing on her phone with lightning-speed fingers. "What are you doing?" She doesn't reply, instead stares at her phone until it vibrates. "Score!"

"Sadie, what are you doing." Panic flows through me. She reaches for my cell phone left on the coffee table, effortlessly swiping her thumbs across my password keypad, knowing the code. I lunge for her, but she's faster than me, anticipating my every move like only a lifelong friend can.

"Hi, is this Hunter?" she says into my cell with a smile, and I can feel the blood draining from my face as my stomach drops to the floor. That traitor!

"Sadie! Hang up *right now.*" My voice is an angry whisper as I try to catch her while she hops around her apartment to avoid me.

"Great, this is Sadie, Hannah Keller's best friend? Mmhm, I'm actually calling from Hannah's phone, so now you have her number, two birds, one stone." To my horror and also, admittedly, my delight, the sound of his deep chuckle swims through my phone's speaker. My body stills, giving up and knowing even if I got my phone this very second, the damage is done.

"I'm going to murder you." My mouth forms the words without sound as my hands make strangling motions. She smiles and continues talking, grabbing a strand of her hair and twirling it as she does.

"See, my girl was telling me she lost her donor for the kid's camp shirts at the Center. She's told you about the Center, right? Mhm. Well, so I said, girlfriend, you have a billionaire practically living with you, I'm sure he could make things happen." Oh, my God. I'm going to murder her. I'm going to murder my best friend in cold blood and not even feel a speck of remorse.

"Oh, yay! You're the best. You see, camp starts Monday, and our Hannah would hate to let the kids down, as I'm sure you know. She was planning on paying out of pocket if she had to, but that's just insane, don't you agree? Okay, well, great, so glad we had this chat. Can you believe she didn't have your number? I had to text your sister to get it! Well, anyway. Do you want to talk to Han? She's right here. Hannah! Your hunk wants to talk to you!"

Murder. I am going to murder this woman. Glaring at her, I grab my phone.

"Oh my God, Hunter, I am so sorry. She's insane. Please, ignore the entire last five minutes. I know I will spend the next 50 years doing just that. Those 50 years might be spent in prison after I murder her, but it would be worth it, you know?" I say, rambling and still in a panic.

"Hannah, baby, calm down." He's laughing. And swear to God,

that's all it takes. My heartbeat slows, and my breathing regulates. What kind of witchcraft does this man possess?

"I am so sorry. I know you're busy. Autumn told me you're on location or something. I swear Sadie did this on her own accord." Still laughing to herself, she flounces out of the room, literally patting herself on the back as if to congratulate herself on a job well done.

"Does the Center need shirts?"

"I mean, technically? Yeah. But I've got it all figured out." The last thing I need is this man thinking I'm using him for his money.

"By paying for them yourself?" My mouth opens to argue, and it's like he can sense it. "No, Hannah, Beaten Path will sponsor them. We have a non-profit quota we need to hit every year. This won't even touch it. I'll shoot my assistant Gina an email as soon as we're off the phone."

"Oh. Well, that makes sense." I wonder why I didn't think of this before. Of course, I would never have asked Hunter, but maybe Autumn. But the little voice in my head reminds me I would have in no way ever actually asked Autumn. Even Sadie has to beg me each year to tell her what Rise and Grind can donate.

"So, what are you up to?" he asks as if he was just ringing me for a normal, everyday phone conversation and not an ambush by my best friend.

"Uh, what?"

"What are you doing?"

"Uhm, I'm at Sadie's? We're hanging out, watching TV in pajamas?" I ask as if I need him to confirm my whereabouts. Sadie snorts a laugh, and I throw a pillow at her. I'm not even sure when she walked back into the room.

"Oh yeah? What are you wearing?"

"What?! Hunter, that is extremely inappropriate."

"Hannah, my tongue has been in your mouth, my hand on your ass, and I think I've made it extremely clear what other dirty things I want to do with you. Asking what your pajamas look like is as tame as this conversation will get, I assure you. So, tell me."

He has a point. I try to turn my back on Sadie in an attempt at privacy. "Uh, sweatpants and an oversized men's t-shirt?" I say, regretting I didn't have something sexier on or at least the presence of mind to lie about it. Hearing me, Sadie lets out a muted cackle into the discarded pillow.

"You sound like the State Farm guy!" Sending a glare at her, my attention is quickly diverted back to Hunter with his next question.

"Whose shirt is it?" he growls, and crap if it doesn't go straight to my core.

"Uh, an ex?" I say, because, again, I'm a freaking moron who can't figure out how to lie about things.

A growl comes over the phone line, sounding like it's coming from low in his throat, and jeez Louise, that is so damn hot.

"Next time I'm there, I'm going to burn that."

"But... it's comfy." I say because it is. It's worn in all the right places, so incredibly soft after 8000 trips through the wash, and I love it.

"I'll replace it with one of mine."

"Oh," I say, because what do you say to something like that? The call goes muffled and I think he's covered the microphone, calling out something before coming back.

"Look, I gotta go. But I promise I haven't forgotten about our date. Everything has been so crazy with work. I'm actually in the city right now for the day."

"Oh, God, I'm so sorry, I promise I wasn't trying to bother you—"

"I know. But I liked it either way." There's a smile in his voice. "Just give me some time, okay? Don't change your mind on me." I don't tell him even if I was planning on doing that, the tone of his voice would have me saying yes all over again.

"Okay. Go back to work now."

"Kay, bye, baby." Why is it so freaking sexy when he says 'baby'? He clicks off before I can say anything else, and I sit there with my phone in my hand in a lust-filled daze.

"So!?" my best friend shrieks, bounding to me. "Tell me everything!"

And I do. Because when a hot guy starts to break down your barriers and make you feel all gushy inside, the only option is to tell your best friend everything.

FIFTEEN
-HUNTER-
10 YEARS AGO

I'm in my apartment with Chrissy. We're sitting across from each other after our enlightening talk, where she admitted everything. She lied that her uncle could help me with the zoning issue. According to her, I'd been so wrapped up in this venture, and she wanted my time, so she made sure she had it.

My phone rings, and I see the name of the township representative in control of our zoning permits. My stomach sinks, roiling. I feel like I'm going to be sick even though I haven't eaten all day.

"Ignore it." Chrissy's breathy voice cracks, her big eyes puffy from tears. "We need to talk about this, Hunter!" The woman is gorgeous. The reason I let her distract me from my goal, let her put everything in jeopardy. But she's an ugly crier. And seeing her this way after the betrayal she dealt me makes it even uglier.

"I can't ignore this, Chris. You might have rich parents who can pull you out of any problem, but I don't." I'm being an asshole, but right now, my vision is crashing around me. Everything I've planned for and dreamed of is going up in flames because I let a beautiful face and a wet pussy lead me by my dick.

The abandoned park on 40 acres was an oasis to me in high school, a place to go, connect with the world, and center myself. When I found out the location was up for sale, including the hidden waterfall I'd found when I was 15, I invested everything I had and more, even convincing my dad to go all-in with my idea. Now it's all at risk.

My gut told me this was the place, the spot where everything would change. When the closing agent handed me over the paperwork, Chrissy told me her uncle would look over it and let me know if there were any issues.

Turns out, she'd never even brought it to the guy. If she had, he would have told me the town had denied zoning this property twice before.

I've been in talks non-stop with the town, financial advisors, and lawyers, trying to figure out how to make it work. But money is running low, and my dream is falling apart.

Months and months of work, years of dreaming and planning, all down the drain because I was diverted from my dream by a selfish woman. Because I thought with my dick and my heart instead of my mind.

"Oh, come on, Hunter, you know I'll do whatever I can to make this right," she says, her eyes brightening and biting her lip. God, how had I been so fucking stupid? This woman was the distraction that would bring me down.

"Chrissy, you need to leave. This is over. I fucked up letting you get into my head, letting you be a distraction was my biggest mistake." Before I knew it, I'm throwing her things into a bag, ignoring her calls for me to wait, to change my mind.

Over the next few months, I would be faced with many hard decisions, culminating in having to back burner and possibly forever abandon this dream project of mine. But the decision to never again let a woman distract me was the easiest one to make.

"Hello, Hunter, are you there?" my Director of Operations and partner in Beaten Path Enterprises, Jonathan, asks me on our video call. Instead of responding and interacting during our conversation, my eyes have been glued to a picture on my phone. It's from Hannah's friend Sadie, showing Hannah in the pajamas she described on the phone to me not an hour ago.

Oversized grey sweatpants and an oversized men's tee plastered with the logo of a local ski mountain, weathered with many washes. The entire outfit engulfs her slight frame, but it's still the sexiest thing I've ever seen.

Okay, that's a lie.

That pink bikini.

That was the sexiest thing I've ever seen.

My head snaps up to see Jonathan looking at me as if I have three heads.

"Yes, sorry, where were we?" I ask, putting my phone down and shuffling through papers to act like I know what the fuck is going on.

"Are you okay?" His face makes me think I might have something on my face, but when I look at the corner of my screen at my reflection, it's just me.

"Yes, Jonathan, just a lot going on here. As you know, I'm back home rather than in the office because my father is ill." Ahh, there we go, a good old sympathy card to distract him.

"Of course. I want to make sure we're all on the same page since these issues need to be cleared up as soon as possible, ideally before we break ground in two weeks."

Our fourteenth location will begin just outside Springbrook Hills, using the abandoned location bought ten years ago. This project has me coming full circle with this business, back to the failure which made me change directions. Back to the place I *need* to succeed to prove myself worthy of my father's pride and confidence.

"What are the issues?" The week has been filled with nothing but solving problems and cleaning messes. It seems that's all I do lately, solve problems other people come to me with. It's hard not to miss the early days when I could dig into the actual business, and the growth strategies, and get my hands dirty. Lately, it's as if I'm flying full speed toward burnout with no escape hatch.

"It's a permitting issue. As you know, the new location will include a rock-climbing wall, a tank to test diving gear, as well as ten campsites for renting. But the city is telling us this may put us into the jurisdiction of a recreational space versus retail. All of our permits are for retail. We have an emergency meeting on Monday, but if they decide it needs to be zoned as recreation, we'll need a whole new set of permits."

Fuck, that could put us back months. "Who did the initial approval of these permits? Who oversaw the final documentation?"

"Sorry, bro, but it was you. On Monday, you signed off on the final paperwork, which was then brought to the Department of Zoning. Wednesday, we got the call there would be a meeting."

How the fuck had I let that slip by?

But I know how. Because a sexy as fuck woman has been distracting me since the moment I got home, clouding my mind and tempting me.

And this is why I avoid women in any way other than purely physical. A distraction almost made me lose everything ten years ago. Here we are, watching history repeat itself, but the stakes are even higher.

"Is there anything else we can do?" I ask, knowing the answer.

"Not really. The department will decide on the zoning requirements Monday. If it goes through as recreation, we can try to appeal, file, and wait for new permits, or remove the aspects they deem recreational. Which would be all of the new ideas we're testing."

Neither option is an answer. I need this to be big, especially if the news coming from my dad's recent scans is not as positive as Autumn makes the situation out to be.

"So we're fucked."

"There's a good chance we won't be able to stick to your aggressive timeline." But it means the same thing to me. The timeline was in case my father's results come back worse than we thought, and I have less time to meet my goals.

"Okay, well, let me know what I can do, if anything, to sway the department."

"Of course Hunter." He hesitates a moment. "Look, I know you're the big boss man, but I need to know your head is in this. If you want to put these deadlines on the team, we need to make sure that everything is being checked and all speed bumps are seen far in advance."

Annoyance flares, but it's quickly tempered by reality. He's right. In the years we've been building Beaten Path, I've been a force of nature, knocking down adversaries and predicting the next moves. This new location isn't simply a new retail space to expand our territory, but it's an introduction to the idea I had years back. It's a way to prove to myself, to Dad, and to the world that I wasn't wrong all those years ago.

A way to prove to my dad before he potentially leaves us that he was right in believing in me. That I'm not the worthless, stupid kid, I was then.

"You're right, Jonathan. I'll be sure to avoid any such oversight moving forward." We say goodbye before I sign off, rubbing my palm down my face, wondering how the fuck am I going to do this.

That night, I decided to stay at my condo so I can head to the office early for a quick meeting, then I'll head back to Springbrook Hills, hopefully missing the weekend traffic. On a bad day, traffic can take a 90-minute commute and turn it into four hours or more.

Sitting on my couch in my high-rise, I can see the extravagance around me, but I also see the coldness. My mind travels back to Hannah's tiny little cottage, decorated with warmth and comfort. The very first thing that hits me is *I want to be back there with her*. The thought startles me.

Fuck, who am I? When I bought this property, I had it gutted and spent tens of thousands redecorating it.

"High class," I told the designer. That's it. I wanted it to be expensive, and I didn't care about anything else. Now it feels... empty.

Without thinking twice, I grab my phone and hit the call button, dialing the newest number in my contacts.

"Hello?" Her voice is slightly husky but also confused.

"Hey." My body settles into my sofa which I'm now realizing is not that comfortable. Getting back up, I walk to the fridge and open it, hoping to find something. Empty, except for a few bottles of fancy-ass wine. Way in the back, I spot a brown bottle, pulling out a craft beer someone must have brought over during a party. Checking the date, I pop it open and take a sip.

"Are you okay?" Hannah asks as I walk to my bedroom, flopping onto my bed, which is blissfully comfortable. At least something in this condo is.

A sigh slips through my lips. "Yeah, just things aren't going too smoothly with the new location opening."

"Want to talk about it?" I can hear shuffling on her end of the phone.

"Not really. Where are you?"

"Still at Sadie's. We had wine, and she has a killer pullout couch. I'm not working tomorrow. Autumn and Steve are taking the kids to an amusement park."

"Still in that guy's shirt?" I'm not sure why it bothers me so much. She's not mine, but the thought of her in another man's shirt makes me completely feral.

"It's all I brought here." The line goes silent as we both fall into our thoughts. This feels so weird to me, to be into a chick who I barely know, to get jealous. To miss her, even.

"Hey, Hunter?"

"Hmm?" I take another sip of beer. It's not great, but it's not terrible.

"What are we doing?" Something about the way she asks has me stopping in my tracks. *What are we doing?* Fuck if I know. "Because I love my job, Hunter. More than anything else. I won't put that in jeopardy for anyone, no matter what. Those girls come first." Her words remind me why I'm so into this woman. Her love for my nieces, her bravery to speak frankly to me. That she won't take my shit, or let me lead her on.

"Look, Hannah, I'm not going to lie that I'm incredibly attracted to you. Fuck, I can't tell you how many times I've jacked off thinking of you in that pink bikini, bent over in the kitchen." A sexy gasp comes from the other line, bringing a smile to my face. I'm not sure why anytime I tell her how sexy she is, she's shocked, but I love it. "But I can't have a distraction right now. I've worked too hard and put too much on the line to risk it."

"Oookay, so what does that mean?" she asks, again as straightforward as can be,

"It means that I want to come home and take you on a date, I want to kiss you some more. I really fucking want to convince you to spend the night with me. But that's it. It's all I can offer right now, and I have no idea if I'll ever be able to offer more."

Silence is not a good sign when you're having this kind of conversation, but it's what I'm hearing right now. It seems like an eternity passes, but then she speaks.

"Okay. That works for me."

The relief rushing through me is palpable. It's ridiculous. I have some of the hottest women in the northeast programmed into my phone, but this one girl from my hometown is making me all kinds of crazy.

"Good. So, now tell me what you have on under that t-shirt."

"Jesus, Hunter, you're a pig."

"So that's a no to phone sex?"

"Uhh, Sadie is essentially asleep next to me, her walls are so thin. That's a no."

"Okay, so next time you're at the cottage, and I'm here, we'll go for it."

"I would need a gallon of wine for that," she says with a laugh.

"I can make that happen. Order some, and get it delivered in 30 minutes." I'm only half kidding because now I want to talk dirty to her on the phone and listen to her come in that breathy voice. Fuck. This *woman*.

We stay on the phone for a while, talking about random things—turns out, we have a lot more in common than I'm willing to realize when I can get distracted by her. We both love hiking, the sport that inspired Beaten Path. She's never been to my favorite trail near the house, a fact I filed away for later. Her favorite show is the Office, and I make her giggle by quoting Dwight Shrute. It turns out she taught herself how to cook and bake, which amazes me since I can barely even find the takeout menus to get delivery.

Eventually, she yawns a sweet, quiet yawn. For once, something involving Hannah Keller doesn't make my dick twitch and instead makes me yearn to pull her into me. Again, who the fuck am I?

"Alright, baby, you're getting tired. Time for you to go to bed." Exhaustion is taking over me as well.

"No, I'm fine, just a little yawn," she lies, and for fuck's sake, could she be any more adorable.

"Go, bed, now. Or I'm going to tell you all the things I want to do to you when I see you," I say, the threat empty since I know my sweet girl is exhausted.

"Fine, fine, I'll go to bed."

"Okay, baby, I'll see you soon. Take you on that date you owe me."

"Okay, see you soon, honey." The words are slurred and mumbled, and I'm pretty sure she's asleep on the phone, but either way, I go to sleep wondering if maybe a distraction could be worth the risk.

SIXTEEN
-HUNTER-

Walking through the French doors of Autumn's house into the backyard the next morning, I roll my shoulders back and fuss with my shirt. I run a hand through my hair and contemplate a trim. Everything has grown out a bit since life came crashing to a halt with my dad's diagnosis. Things like shaving and haircuts seemed... unimportant. Eventually, I'll need to shape up.

I might keep the beard, though. I kind of like it. I sure as fuck liked it when Hannah touched it the night we kissed behind her house.

I should be exhausted, seeing as my seven a.m. meetings came after staying up too late talking to Hannah. Then I sat in the car for two hours driving back to Springbrook Hills. But everything is humming inside of me. It's that feeling when you need to take a deep breath, but the air can't get deep enough. Where you want to see someone so badly that your body feels electric. Excitement and anticipation course through my veins so fervently, I look down at my forearm to see if it's visible. That's how Hannah makes me feel, regardless of if I want to acknowledge it or not.

This might be a bad idea. Fuck, it probably *is* a bad idea, but

Autumn, Steve, and the kids are still away for the weekend at Six Flags, so it's the perfect time to cash in on my date with Hannah. She's going to pull the whole boss' brother card, I know it. And this is an easy way to test the waters without scaring her too much, considering there will be no reminders around of who I am to her.

Walking up to her house with its friendly blue door, I can hear music. Again. Louder this time and I'm pretty sure the sound isn't coming from inside.

Still, my knuckles meet the door, knocking loudly. Nothing. Rather than trying again, I head around back to where the music is coming from. It's some kind of new hip-hop song that I've heard on the radio, except it's a clip that loops.

When it comes into full view, I stop in my tracks, enamored by what I see. Hannah's standing on the bricks with her back to me, white sneakers on her feet that lead to long tanned legs encased in skin-tight bike shorts that hit her mid-thigh in an aqua color I know matches her eyes perfectly. Next comes more curves and her tanned stomach topped with a matching sports bra. Her long hair is half up in a mess on top of her hair, with the rest reaching her mid-back and cascading over her shoulders.

But the real show stopper is what the body is doing.

I watch for about 30 seconds before I realize she is doing some kind of dance, one that loops the same steps in time with the looping of the music.

A dance that begins with her running her hands down her body and ends in her bending over completely and shaking her perfect, generous ass in a way I've only seen on TV. Her phone is propped on the fire pit, streaming what I see now is a video showing the moves on repeat.

The third time she bends over and shakes, I'm more prepared to give it my whole focus. This time, an uncontrollable, audible groan escapes my lips because Jesus Christ, this woman is a fucking dream.

Unfortunately, this scares her, making her tumble onto the ground with a shriek.

"Jesus, I'm sorry." Scrambling, I come to her side to help her.

"Hunter! You scared the shit out of me!" Slapping my shoulder, she tries to steady her breathing. It makes her chest, which is unfortunately right in my face at the moment, rise deliciously, putting my whole body on high alert.

"I'm so sorry. Are you okay?" She fell pretty hard. Taking her hand in mine, I raise her until she's standing right in front of me, with very little room in between us. Instead of stepping back, I wrap an arm around her bare waist, bringing her closer.

"I guess. My ass took most of the fall, and I've got the padding for it." Blushing, it's clear that she didn't mean to say that last part out loud.

My free hand trails down, rubbing where she hit the ground. "Does rubbing it help?" She breathes deep, brushing her breasts against my chest.

"What are you doing here, Hunter? I thought you were in the city? And why are you always sneaking up on me?" She sounds equal parts confused, annoyed, and intrigued.

"I was in the city. My meeting ended, and I came back. With Autumn away, I figured now was as good a time as any to cash in on my date. And I can't help it if you always have your music so loud you can't hear me coming."

Her expressive face reveals everything when I look at her. First, the annoyance takes dominance, ready to fight me. Then her face clouds, confusion winning for a second before clearing into pure intrigue and maybe even excitement as if she just remembered that she agreed to a date at all. She wraps an arm around my neck and begins playing with my longer hair. Maybe I won't be cutting it any time soon after all. "Oh, yeah."

"Are you free?"

"Free for what?" She's dazed, her eyes glazed over and flitting from my eyes to my lips and then back again. Her fingers continue to twirl in the hair at the nape of my neck, and the gesture sends warmth down my spine.

"A date, baby. Do you have any plans?"

"Plans?" God, this girl is cute.

"Yeah, babe. Can I take you out today? Or do you have something to do?"

"Oh. No. I'm free. Wide-open. Not a thing on my schedule." She's rambling and it's hard not to find it adorable.

"Good, so you're mine for the day."

"All yours." Something about her being all mine sounds so fucking right that I can't help but press my lips to hers gently, basking in having her back in my arms, in tasting her sweet, cherry vanilla taste. As soon as I do, her lips part, giving me full rein as her fingers clench in my hair.

I pull her ass in, pressing her as close to my already hardening cock as I can, knowing she can feel it through her thin clothes. This is confirmed when she gasps into my mouth and I slide my tongue in hers, letting it tangle with hers. Why does this happen every time? I can't seem to keep it chaste with her, the hunger and need burning through me the second she's close.

A whimper from her has me backing off. Any other woman, I'd say fuck it, throw her over my shoulder, and bring her inside to get her out of my system. And, I still might do that, but we're going out first.

"Date, babe. Then I'll take care of you," I say against her lips before smacking her ass and pulling away. Not too far, though. She's dazed and seemingly woozy, making me smile yet again.

"Huh?"

"I'm taking you on a date. Get on shoes you can hike in, and maybe a jacket just in case. It looks clear but you never know."

"Oh. Okay." She's still clearly dazed. Unable to resist, I pull her in one more time, press my lips to hers hard, then release her and let her lead me into her house.

SEVENTEEN
-HANNAH-

Hannah's sitting next to me in my truck, the old Bronco that I worked on with my dad as a kid two summers in a row, restoring it to its perfectly imperfect glory.

The truck is technically still his, but he isn't using it, so rather than get a rental, I've claimed it as my own.

She threw on a faded old denim jacket, a size too big so it swallowed her a bit, but with her skin-tight outfit underneath it works, making her look smaller, more delicate.

"So, what were you doing outside?" I ask, breaking the silence.

"Learning a dance for the girls at the Center."

"I'm sorry, what?" I laugh. "That's not exactly what I'd expect kids to be doing at summer camp." Jesus, if it is, I should talk to Autumn about whether it's the best option for Sara and Rosie.

She giggles, "It's not on the curriculum, don't worry. Rosie won't be coming home shaking her ass." The horror on my face thinking of my nieces dancing like grown women must be visible because she snorts the cutest little laugh.

"Have you ever heard of TikTok? It's a video-based social media, but a lot of it is these dances kids make up and they go viral. Then people learn them and upload their own versions."

"Okay?" I encourage her to keep going, glancing over before putting my eyes back on the road.

"So, with the super famous ones, all the kids learn it, but they need to watch the video over and over to learn it. A lot of the girls are hesitant to talk to the adults. But also, a lot of them don't have a trusted adult in their life. I found that if I learn a dance, then offer to teach it to the girls, it builds trust. Next thing I know they're giggling with me and telling me about boys and dreams and fears and their home life."

"God, you're incredible." The words come out without preamble or warning. Because she really, truly is. How many adults would learn kids' dance on their day off just to earn the trust of some teenagers?

"I just want to help them."

"So you learn these intricate dances in your free time so you can bond with them?"

"Pretty much. In all fairness, they're fun to learn, and they give me a good workout." She smiles.

"Hey, whatever it is, I'm here for it." My mind drifts to remembering her ass moving as she bent over, quickly transferring that into a different kind of daydream. One that has me adjusting myself as I drive. "Let me know the next time you're learning one, I'll watch and give you critiques."

"I'm sure," she says, a smile in her voice. "So where are we going?"

"Hiking."

"Thanks, Captain Obvious. I got that when you told me to put on hiking shoes." She'd traded her pristine white sneakers in for dark leather hiking boots. Not the kind that you wear as a fashion statement or that scream that they were bought and never used, either. No, dirt cakes the soles and the toes are worn down.

"We're going up to the water gap." I'm being intentionally vague, still not sure exactly why I'm doing this as our date, of all things.

"And what are we doing there?"

"Hiking."

"Goodness, you're impossible," she says, rolling her eyes and huffing. I try not to laugh at her dramatics, but I give in all the same.

"There's a place up there I used to go when I lived here. A waterfall. It's quiet, and this time of year when everything goes green it's gorgeous."

"So, is this where you brought all the girls into high school?" I glance at her while driving, trying to read her. She's not offended in that way some women are when you talk about your past. Just curious.

"Nope. I've never brought a soul here."

"No one? Like at all?" Her gaze burns as I drive, pulling into the gravel parking area. The sound of the rocks on tires is loud through the open windows as the truck rocks on the uneven surface.

"Nope. You're the first. This was always my special place. I'd come here to think a lot. In school. Then when I'd come home on breaks, I'd disappear for hours. Plan out businesses and programs that I wanted to create." Eager to end the conversation about me, I turn to her after I put the truck in park. "Ready?"

We walk quietly for a bit. It's not an uncomfortable silence. It's the opposite—a silence that's so perfectly comfortable it should probably scare me.

"You know, when I was in high school, I had one friend I'd go hiking with. He was the kind of kid who was always talking. We'd go hiking and from the second we hit the trail, his mouth would be going. Drove me crazy, but that was just him. Sometimes I go hiking and I still hear him talking nonstop."

"What happened to him?"

"Nothing. He still lives in town. I think he was engaged for a bit right after high school, but we lost touch. He runs his dad's construction company now, from what Autumn tells me."

"You should reach out, add to your long list of acquaintances." She's teasing, bumping her shoulder into mine. The act, her joking with me, making fun of me... warms me through. With my job, being the big boss, no one does this with me. Except Autumn, of course. Everyone is always on their toes, trying to impress me. Not Hannah.

"Yeah, maybe." It's not a bad idea. I could use a friend here if I'll be spending more time in Springbrook Hills. We walk in silence, leaving the trail for a less busy one that will take her to my spot.

"You thought of Beaten Path out here?"

I let out a puff of air. "No, not quite. Beaten Path was actually a project I did in one of my marketing classes in college. It was the responsible, well thought out business plan I needed to follow."

"So, you daydreamed here. Anything good come out of it?"

"My worst idea and my biggest regret came from daydreaming here."

"What was it?"

I sigh, trying to decide how to explain what happened. If I even want to explain it, dredge up the past. "I had this vision. When I was a kid and came out here, it was usually when I was feeling down about my mom or I was feeling less than. Struggling over something internally. Things like that. I'd come here and... it would go away. I could focus, things made sense, I could calm myself. I wanted to build something like that. It wasn't too far from your summer camp idea, but for-profit and not just for kids. For anyone who wanted a space to connect with the world and let their troubles go. Guided activities to assist with that, themed hikes and exercise classes, that kind of thing."

"That's amazing. What happened?"

"I planned it out, made the business plan, found the location. But I didn't have the money to make it happen. I was fresh out of school, and no one would give me a loan to jump-start it. Except... my dad." It's clear my inquisitive Hannah has a million questions but bites her tongue, letting me guide the conversation. "He took out a second mortgage that he couldn't afford. It was my great grandfather's—have you been to it? It's about two blocks from Autumn's."

"Yeah, I've seen it. It's gorgeous. It's my dream house. Gosh, that front porch is amazing."

"My great grandfather built that porch with his two hands for my great grandmother. Renovated nearly every room in that house himself, He asked her to describe what she wanted, and he made it happen."

"Wow."

"Well, I grew up in that house. And I almost made my dad lose it completely." We're quiet again, deep in our thoughts. I haven't talked about what happened in 10 years. It might be catharsis, it might just be her, but as I'm talking about it, the weight I feel from it seems to lighten, a freeness taking its place.

"I was cocky. Thought I knew everything. Bought a plot of land at a location I thought would work great. Didn't read the fine print and it turns out, it needed a bunch of permits and inspections to get the land approved for building. It wasn't zoned for what we needed. But I was distracted, being a big shot, thinking I knew it all and didn't read the fine print. By the time we got the approval, I was out of money. Six months and it was all up in smoke. My dad was working two extra jobs on top of his day job to keep up with the mortgage. He eventually got caught up, but it nearly killed him."

Looking over at her, I expect Hannah to have a look of disgust. Instead, she looks thoughtful. I drop my bomb, ever the glutton for punishment, almost trying to coax that feeling of disgust from her.

"I can't help but wonder if that's what's happening now. It's all caught up to him." Water is rushing ahead, signaling we're almost at our destination. But Hannah stops and grabs my hand, pulling me back, her beautiful face aghast with pain. Pain for me.

"Hunter, no. That has nothing to do with your dad's cancer. You know that."

I sigh, the sound coming out exhausted and full of worry even to my ears. "I do, in theory. But stress like that puts a strain on your body. And after everything... I haven't even been able to walk into that house since. The idea of it makes me sick. I paid him back once Beaten Path got off the ground, but it's not the same. And now he's sick and going to die before I can even prove that his belief in me wasn't off base."

"Honey, your dad is so proud of you. He's told me. Every time I see him, he tells me." She looks so earnest and beautiful, the dappled sunlight coming through the trees and dancing on her face as she looks up at me.

"Of course he says that now. He's a good father. But I could see it then, his regret in believing in me."

"That's just not true, Hunter. And even if you really, truly had to prove something to him then, you would have exceeded that expectation. You founded an incredibly profitable national chain. In less than 10 years. That's amazing. You are amazing." I need to change the topic because I don't enjoy how this one is messing with me.

"Yeah, well, that's my sad story. It's why I can't afford any kind of distraction, anything to get me off my paved path. What's yours? You had a shit childhood. Where was your place?" I walk her forward again, still holding her hand. Hannah, being the incredibly insightful woman she is, sees the diversion for what it is, but allows it.

"Sadie's." The words are soft. "She lived next door my whole life. She was born three weeks before me like we were born to be best friends if we couldn't be sisters. Her family was my lifeline. My sister Abbie and I would go there when my mom started bashing my dad and drinking. Eventually, the Center and Maggie were added to my list of safe places."

Every time she talks to me about her childhood and the shitty parents she had, it all makes a bit more sense. She puts so much pressure on herself to be everything to Sara and Rosie.

"It makes sense, you know. That you want to help all these kids, give them what you were missing."

"Let me guess, you took a psych class at that fancy Ivy League school." I laugh, tipping my head to the clouds. God, this girl. One minute I'm dumping the heaviest parts of me on her plate and the next moment my soul is lighter than air.

"I actually did. But it was to learn how to get into girls' pants."

"Oh yeah? Did it work?" I couldn't have timed it better. Right as she asks, we step into the clearing of our destination—a hidden waterfall dropping into a clear, small pool of water. Trees surround the clearing, tall and incredibly old, full of big green leaves. The waterfall isn't huge, maybe eight feet high, but it splashes down peacefully and in the pool, you can see little minnows scurrying around, Bright wildflowers are growing sporadically, pinks and yellows and purples, reminding me of Hannah's backyard, the fairy oasis she created.

"Don't know. Is it working on you?" Moving behind her, I wrap my arms around her waist. Pulling her into me, I kiss her neck softly, breathing in that innocent cherry vanilla scent.

"Oh my goodness, this is gorgeous, Hunter. Is this our stop?" she asks, and I nod into her neck, scraping my stubble along the soft skin there. She shivers in response.

"How did you find this place?" she asks, marveling at the surrounding beauty. "I've been here before, hiked here. I've never seen signs or heard people talk about it." Her head is still turning in all directions to take it in. While a waterfall in the northeast doesn't hold the decadence one in Hawaii might have, it's a gorgeous sight to see.

"I got lost once. Wound up here, then spent three weeks that summer trying to find it again. I made it here four times before I finally figured out the exact path to get here without getting lost again. I've never seen anyone else here, so I like to think of it as mine."

"And you brought me." She turns in my arms, a sweet, surprised smile on her beautiful face. We're pressed chest to chest. Her arms are around my neck, playing with my hair again. I'm never getting it cut at this rate. My arms wrapped around her waist tighten a bit, pulling her in closer until our bodies are flush.

"And I brought you," I whisper against her lips before pressing my own to them. I've never experienced something like this, where each kiss makes me hungrier for her, adding to it rather than quelling it. Every time I see her, I'm at peace with the world and living in the moment, a feeling I haven't felt in years. But at the same time, I'm already excited for the next time I can see her. Nothing is ever enough with Hannah.

Deepening the kiss, I walk her back until her back presses against a smooth, oversized beech tree. The move presses her closer to me. I can't get close enough to her, barriers of clothes stopping me from what I truly want and need. Her hand in my hair tightens, pulling me closer too. It's as if she's feeling it too, this need to be inside her, to consume her, to be one.

As I trail open-mouthed kisses down her neck, tasting her skin, feeling her pulse under my lips, hearing her small pants, her gasps as she tries to gain control. A smile breaks out onto her soft skin before I trail my tongue up, up, up to her ear, biting the lobe gently. Another gasp, another tug on my hair. She's pulling my face back to her and we're a clash of tongues and teeth and desire.

My hand slides up and around, feeling her skin exposed by her sports bra, dipping to trail the tips of my fingers under the waistband of her tight shorts. A breathy moan escapes her mouth, breathing life and desire into mine. Smiling into the kiss, those fingers trail up once again, this time to the front. My thumb trails the line of her skin right below her bra and another breathy moan slips out.

She shifts slightly, still pressed to me so that her center brushes against my straining cock, sending jolts of pleasure through me, needing this woman right now. After weeks of tension building, we're both at a breaking point. Hand drifting upwards again, fingers meet the thin front of her bra, her breasts swollen with want and need. My thumb finds her hard nipple through the fabric, making her gasp and press into me harder.

Groaning, I let my pointer meet my thumb over her nipple, pinching and rolling.

"Oh, God, Hunter," she pants against my mouth, unable to catch her breath. This fucking woman is irresistible. I've never needed anyone as much as I need her at this moment.

"Yeah, baby," I say, using my other hand to trail to her ass and encourage her hips to grind against my hard cock. I'm so ready for her, it's an actual, physical pain, but each press she makes with her full hips brings the slightest sweet relief. My mouth makes its way down her neck, exploring. She's unable to keep oxygen in her lungs, panting and making small mewling sounds. All that goes through my mind is *I want to make her come. I* need *to make this woman come for me.* Out here, in the open, in the place that's always been mine and mine alone.

The hand on her ass slides down for purchase and then lifts her quickly, forcing her to wrap her legs around my hips. Bingo, cock, meet happy place. I groan loudly and her heat seems to sit right over my dick in my loose athletic shorts.

"Jesus, Hunter." The words come out of her mouth, but they sound like they're swimming in the surrounding air, pants, and mewls drowning out even the loud rushing of the waterfall beside us.

Leaving her nipple, my hand goes down, down, down until I'm at her core, unbearably hot against me. I can feel dampness seeping through her shorts, telling me just how fucking soaked she is. "Jesus fuck, Hannah, I can feel how soaked you are. Are you wet for me, baby?" I ask, pressing over her shorts, teasing her clit, her swollen nub begging me to help, to make her come.

"Yes, Hunter, right there, holy shit," she says in a whimper. She's grinding her hips now, my cock lined up, so it's rubbing against the seam of her shorts. I know that if there were no barriers between us, her slickness would drip down my length, preparing me to slam into her. The thought alone nearly makes me bust right here, right now.

"Are you going to come for me, baby? Out here in the forest, just us, are you going to come on my cock, fully clothed? Jesus, Hannah, I want to fuck you so bad right now. You've got me so crazy, so fucking hard for you." Her frantic movements tell me she's liking this, liking me talking to her, telling her what she's doing to me. Eager to get more from her, I press harder on her clit, she squeals, bucking sharply.

"You're going to come when I tell you, okay, baby?" I ask, stepping back just enough to look between us and watch her hips grind against me, making another groan break from my throat. It's taking everything in me not to turn her around, tear off her little shorts and slam into her, fucking her like the animal I've become out here with her.

"Uh-huh," she says, her eyes glazed and hooded. She's so fucking close, so fucking sexy. I think about slipping my hand beneath her shorts and sliding into her, making her come on my fingers, but instead, I want to see her come like this. Knowing she was so ready and primed for me, that I didn't even have to put an actual finger on her skin. That what we have together is so explosive, so intense, neither of us could wait.

My thumb is rolling and pressing her clit, my hand kneading her ass, my lips whispering how unbearably hot she is. She's grinding down on my cock, but just like I imagined, she's damn perfect, holding off until I tell her she can explode. "Such a good girl, Hannah," I whisper into her ear before biting her lobe. This makes her moan loud and clench her pussy so hard I can feel it through the material. I can't fucking wait to see if it was the nip or calling her my good girl.

Finally, as her mewls and whimpers are becoming desperate, she begs me for it. "Please, Hunter, God, please." She's there, ready to go but, in a purely Hannah move, unwilling to come unless it's what I want. This woman.

My thumb presses hard onto her clit. "Now, baby, come for me." And she comes. She shouts so loud, birds scatter from their perch. She's quaking against the tree as I hold her up, keeping her safe and allowing her to feel her orgasm to its fullest extent. Fucking beautiful. She's unbelievably perfect, panting to catch her breath, eyes closed in rapture as her head leans against the tree. I'm still gently rubbing her, pressing occasionally to watch her tits jolt in an aftershock she can't control.

"Good?" I whisper against her lips.

"Holy shit. I'm not sure I can get back to the truck." I chuckle but stop with a hiss through my teeth as she once more rubs against my achingly hard cock. "Oh, God, Hunter, you! Let me—" she says, unwrapping her legs from my waist, but I hold her tight, not letting her down. Any other girl, I'd let her finish her sentence, then make good on her word. But this woman... for some reason, her offering is enough.

"No, stop, not here. The first time I come for you is going to be in that wet pussy of yours," I whisper in her ear, making her rub into me once again, and I groan. "But, if you could, try not to make that decision a harder one." She giggles, the sound so sweet and night and day from the sex kitten I held just a minute ago.

"Ha, you said hard." She is too much. The perfect woman. I chuckle then let her gently unwrap herself from me, checking her back to make sure that in my haste, we haven't cut it up on the tree. She settles her head on my chest when I pull her to me. It takes everything in me not to groan again when she brushes my erection with her body. "Thank you." It comes out in a soft whisper against my neck.

"Thank *you*," I say before she looks at me, confused. "That was the hottest thing I have ever seen in my life, hands down." A blush erupts on her cheeks and she bites her lip, looking away. This might be my favorite thing to make her do.

Okay, second favorite, now.

We stand there for a while, listening to the water flow, me rubbing a hand up and down her back. It's peaceful. This place has always been a serene retreat for me. Somewhere to collect my thoughts. Somewhere to make sense of things.

Here with her, everything seems crystal clear, in 20/20 vision. Not long after, we feel a few fat raindrops. I look up and see the sky has turned an ominous grey.

"Let's get going before we get soaked," I say, grabbing her hand

and heading back the way we came. It's about a 30-minute hike if we hustle. The drizzle continues until we can see the parking area in front of us. It's then that the sky opens up. The rain comes down in sheets, turning the already damp ground into rivers. I look at Hannah and she throws her head back, laughing before tugging her hand out of mine and making a run for it to the truck. She's got her hands above her head as if she can shield herself from the downpour with her small, delicate hands alone.

Unfortunately for her, the Bronco is old and I locked it when we left. This means that when she gets to the truck and realizes there's no way in, she's stuck standing in the rain.

I should start running. Really, I should. It's kind of mean not to. But she's standing there: hair that five minutes ago showed evidence of my hands in it dripping in long, chunky strands, her already tight clothes leaving nothing to the imagination. The light color of her top shows her small, dark nipples through the fabric, the cold making them peak. So instead, I walk casually. I'm already wet. What's the rush?

"Hunter! I'm getting drenched!" Hannah shouts over the sound of rain hitting the pavement. I keep my pace, smiling at her now. "Hunter, you asshole, come on!" She's laughing now, so I know she's not actually mad, which makes me smile wider.

When I reach her, I turn and pin her back to my truck. My fingers float up the back of her head into her hair, bringing her lips to mine. Kissing her, the rain falling over us, water seeping in between our connection and onto our tongues, it's like the flame has been re-lit. I need her again. Tasting her reminded me. Pushing her into the truck, I thumb her nipple and grind my crotch into her soft belly.

"Let's go back to your place. I need you," I say, pinching the tight bud between my thumb and forefinger and pulling quickly through her bra. I'm desperate for her to agree, desperate for her naked body in a bed with mine.

"God, yes, quick." Her hot tongue licks water off my neck. Rain is dripping off my nose as I stare at her, reaching around to unlock her door. I pick her up once the door is open, placing her in her seat. My hand cups her pussy, pressing my finger to her opening and going in slightly with those skin-tight shorts while rubbing her swollen clit with my thumb. "Oh God, fuck, Hunter. Let's go, please," she begs, her hip moving forward to try to get my finger in deeper. An impossible task. I smile at her but oblige.

After slamming the door, I run around to the driver's seat, putting in the key and starting the truck, my wheels turning before the door even shuts. Pulling out of the parking lot, I look over to see her squirming and biting her swollen and bruised lip, already ready for me again. Never in my life have I been as thankful for a bench seat as I am right now.

One hand firm on the wheel, I lean over, slip my arm between her and the seat, wrapping my arm around her waist and pulling her over until we're thigh to thigh. She's breathing heavily as I move my hand up to her stomach with my intent clear. Hannah leans back, giving me a clear path to slip my hand into the front of her shorts, groaning in a mix of pleasure and pain when I hit the top of her wet slit. "Fucking soaked," I say, running a finger down and up, drawing a long, low moan from my girl.

Slowly, torturing both of us, I press my middle finger into her hole, so wet. It's a mix of her earlier orgasm and her current excitement, so deliriously good we both groan at the feeling. Two shallow thrusts of my fingers later, she says in a whisper, "More," and fuck if I won't oblige. Another finger joins, and then she's in my front seat, riding my fingers and moaning like she's already close. There isn't much room for me to work with, driving and her wet shorts sticking to her body, but that doesn't seem to bother her much.

"Jesus fuck, you're so hot," I groan, glancing at the red light on the deserted road that I'm tempted to drive straight through. She looks over, and her eyes flare before flicking down to my lap, my cock uncomfortable and throbbing. We're about five more minutes out, but that look makes me want to pull over, pull those shorts down and sink into her on the side of the road.

"Don't look at me like that, baby, not if you want to make it to your bed," I warn, thrusting deep with my fingers again. That one makes her lose eye contact with me, rolling hers into the back of her head.

But then she looks at me again, fires in her eyes, and tugs my arm out of her pants, scooting back on the seat.

EIGHTEEN
-HANNAH-

Need engulfs every part of my body in searing flames despite the cold, wet clothes clinging to my body. I stare at Hunter driving, his eyes flicking from me to the road and back again. Air can't seem to get into my lungs fast enough. I'm panting, practically mewling, unable to control my body. It's like an out-of-body experience, primal desire taking over. Staring at him for his reaction, I slide my hand over his thigh, making my intention clear as I grab his stiff cock through his shorts.

"Fuck, Hannah, we're almost there." He grabs my wrist to stop my progress, rough hands caressing my sensitive skin. Instead of words, I simply shake my head gently, moving his hand to the wheel with my own, so both are occupied with driving.

Shimmying his shorts down, I notice he's going commando. Good. Makes my job easier. His hard cock slips out of his shorts, and I take in a sharp breath, marveling at my luck. It's long and thick, the tip glistening and weeping with pre-cum.

God, not a single inch of this man isn't pure perfection. *Made for me,* I think instantly. Nope, don't go there. Shaking the thoughts out, I scoot back in the seat. With one last glance up, I see his eyes have widened. He finally got the hint, realizing exactly what my plan is. I can't help but feel a slight thrill of pride.

Before he can object, I duck under his arms and pop the tip into my mouth, running my tongue around it like it's a decadent lollipop. His salty pre-cum hits my taste buds, making me groan around him before I take him deeper.

"Holy fuck, Hannah," he says, bucking his hips up and going even deeper. His frayed resolve breaks then, giving in to what he really wants and tangling a hand in my hair. I'm out of control, so turned on, I can barely think straight.

As I bob, my free hand slips into my shorts, gently touching my swollen clit, just enough to tease myself. This entire afternoon has me on edge and although the orgasm in the woods was deliriously good, my next will be with him inside me. Not on my own. Still, I moan around him, making his dick vibrate in my other hand that's picking up the slack of what I can't fit comfortably.

Abruptly, I hear gravel, and my body rocks as the truck slams into park. Strong hands go under my armpits, lifting me and placing me so my back is to the wheel and I'm straddling him.

Immediately his mouth is on mine, and I grind on his dick, still out like we're high schoolers trying to get off without going all the way. I'm moaning and whimpering, so close already, even though every fiber of my being is screaming for more. So much more.

Hunter reaches between us, rubbing my clit with a quick, rough swipe, the friction making us both moan. He tucks himself away and opens his door, practically jumping out of the truck. I'm forced to wrap my arms around his neck as he leans back in and snatches my keys off the seat, then stands straight. Wrapping a muscled arm under my ass to keep me secure, he jogs around to my front door, rain still pounding on us both. But I don't feel the cold. All I feel is hot and needy as my lips suck the rainwater from his neck. I'm pinned to my blue front door, the man holding me kissing me like he wants to eat me alive, trying random keys in my lock.

"The cloud one," I say, directing him to the fancy key I paid way too much for to have made. The relief I feel when he gets the key in, the lock clicking, and he turns the knob is laughable, but we're in. He slams the door shut with his foot, taking long strides and taking us to the bedroom I showed him the last time he was here. Once there, he tosses me onto my soft bed, pillows flying off before he strips off his tee. It lands with a loud slap as he tosses it in a wet heap in a corner.

I want to take him in longer—the perfect pecs with small, pink nipples, the smattering of chest hair that points perfectly to exactly where I want to be right now, the gently outlined abs, and telling me working out isn't his whole life, but he still puts in the effort, the honed hip bones like brackets, showing me right where his perfect dick is.

But then his pants are off, and I can't focus on anything but the look in his eyes, hooded and burning straight through me.

"Hannah, take off your top," he demands, crawling up my bed between my spread legs, I cross my arms in front of me, grabbing my bra and struggling to get the damp material off before it falls to the ground with a wet thwack. My eyes are glued to the newly revealed flesh, but his are on my nipples, my own new addition to the festivities.

Without hesitation, he bends forward, taking the left one into his mouth, sucking hard while cupping my other breast in his hand. My neck snaps back, my spine arching as I moan, loud and low, finally free to do so without inhibitions. His warm hand feels absolutely devilish on my cold flesh.

"Just like that, baby, arch that back for me and show off your pretty tits," he says in a growl, and I can feel another rush of wetness between my legs as I whimper and obey. He spends what feels like an eternity at my breasts, sucking and nipping, switching sides, pinching and rolling the nipple his mouth is neglecting with rough fingers. I can't breathe, I can't think or function, except to lift my hips and try to push my wet shorts down in an invitation to speed things up.

Thankfully, he gets the hint and rolls off me to bend and grab his wallet from his shorts, coming back with a condom already between his teeth. My shorts are off, and I'm panting and trembling, but I reach out with shaking hands to grab the condom, doing the honors as I roll it gently down his length, marveling at him.

"Lay back, Han." How is he so calm now when I'm so frantic with needing him? I do what he asks, leaning my back against my mountain of pillows. Putting my feet on the bed, I spread my legs, dying for him to slam into me.

"So pretty, baby," he says, on his knees in front of me and taking me in. His hand lifts, and he strokes his thick shaft. A strangled sound comes out of my throat at the move, something so primal and intimate, my hips shifting to find him.

"Shh," he whispers, lifting a hand and running a finger down my slit, from the top of my clit to my entrance, dipping in, making me cry out. "So fucking wet." The words are spoken for himself, reverence dripping from them as he follows his path back up, collecting my wet and running his finger through my short curls and leaving a trail on my belly.

"Hunter, please, need you, now," I utter nonsense.

"Please what, Hannah?" He leans forward to place his lips to mine, his forearms on either side of my head.

"Fuck me, Hunter." My plea comes out stilted and weak. But it seems to do the job, because the next thing I know, he's slamming into me, making me scream, arching my back, and letting the top of my head meet my pillows.

"God, so tight, so wet, so hot," he moans as he pulls out and reenters me with the same force. It sounds like a prayer in his strangled voice. As he's thrusting in, I'm running my hands up and down his perfect back, digging in nails with each hard pump, I feel myself already, creeping towards an orgasm I know is going to consume me and forever change me. Leaning up, I nip his chin, that irresistible scruff scratching at my lip. His face is still so close to mine, like we both understand that even with the intensity of this first time, we need that connection.

"Hunter, honey, I need..." I mutter, letting him know how close I am. I'm writhing and panting, so fucking close. My eyes drift closed, anticipating the orgasm to end all orgasms. He's grunting each time he enters me, seeming to be as out of control as I am.

"Eyes, baby. I get your eyes when you come for me," he says gruffly, making me clench around him, pulling another groan from him. Then he moves his arm from the bed, trailing down my side until his thumb is positioned right above my clit. I know all I need is one quick press... "Open your eyes, Hannah." It's a clear demand, and my eyes pop open. He presses, and it all crashes on me. It's like an explosion of light from inside, or an avalanche tumbling through me, making my entire body shake as I come harder than I ever have before.

He holds my gaze, watching me scream my release. Moments later, his own comes, making him throw his head back and roar, my name a prayer on his lips. After, he keeps thrusting gently, milking himself, grazing my clit, and making my hips jerk until we both come back to earth.

Instead of rolling off and going to handle the condom, he lays on top of me, his head nestled in my neck, both of us drained and panting. He runs his lips over my neck leisurely and whispers, "beautiful," under his breath.

I'm not sure he meant to say that out loud or for it to reach my ears, but it did.

And in that moment, I feel safer and more adored than I ever have in my entire life.

Four hours later, I'm in Hunter's shirt and a pair of panties, eating my third slice of pizza and arguing about the hierarchy of cookies in front of the fire pit he lit for us.

"Hunter, no, you're wrong. I'm sorry. Raisins and oatmeal are breakfast foods. If you want to put them into a cookie, you'd better be eating them before 11 a.m. Not as a delicious dessert."

"Oatmeal raisin cookies get the third spot. They're popular for a reason."

"Yeah, because old ladies like them. There are lots of old ladies on earth."

We've agreed that chocolate chip is first, followed by sugar with sprinkles. The obvious answer for number three would be peanut butter. But Hunter is fighting me on it.

"Babe, they're a classic."

"Babe," I mock in a fake gravelly voice, "they're gross." Through his dark scruff, which is looking more like a thick beard these days, I see his white smile crack through. I can't help but smile back.

I'm surprised by how easy this is with him. Sitting around, arguing about things that don't matter. Since I've met him, it seems like he loves to push my buttons, but turns out, I kind of like it.

"Well, don't count on me making them for you any time soon," I say, smiling before taking another bite. Hunter follows suit. He's in a shirt and sweats, having snuck back to the main house and come back with provisions, including the frozen pizza I keep on hand for the kids.

As soon as he walked back in my door, he threw one of his tees at me and asked where my ex's was. I laughed, putting the soft, oversized tee with a giant Beaten Path logo on it over my still-naked body.

"Seriously Hannah, get it,"

Laughing again, I walked over to him, wrapping my arms around his neck. "Why don't I go start the oven for that pizza?"

"Baby, get me the tee. Then I'll be starting a fire in your pit and burning it."

I stared at him for a second, trying to figure out if he was, indeed, serious. "Are you serious?"

"Dead."

"You really want to burn a t-shirt because it's some other guy's?"

"Baby, am I not speaking English? Go get the damn shirt." I smiled, kissed him sweetly, and then, you know what? I turned my ass around and got that shirt.

Now he's smiling at me, chewing sub-par frozen pizza on my back patio in my secret garden, arguing about cookies. My ex's tee is long gone, ash in the blazing fire we lit once the rain stopped. I pick at the edge of the shirt, already worn and threadbare in places. I refuse to admit to him that this one is more comfortable.

"Tee looks good on you."

"Why, thank you, Mr. Hutchins. A darling friend gave it to me." I smirk. But clouds roll over his eyes.

"A friend, huh?" He asks.

"Well, you're not my enemy anymore. I think you've graduated. And you're more than an acquaintance. If I hear you call me one, I might lose it, fair warning."

"Do you fuck your friends like you can't get enough of them often?"

"Uh, no. Can't say I do." Laughter bubbles from my chest, a feeling that seems to happen often when he's around.

"That's what I thought."

"Thanks for a great day today, Hunter." I pull my feet up to my chair, wrapping my arms around them after I set my empty plate aside. "It was the best and strangest first date I've ever been on."

"Thanks for agreeing and finally giving me a chance to prove I'm not a total ass."

"Oh, you're an ass, just not a *total* ass."

Placing his pizza down, he says, "I'll show you a total ass." Then he leans forward, grabbing me under my armpits, lifting me with each, and placing me in his lap, straddling him. He slips his hands down the back of my panties, "Now this, this is a total ass."

I giggle. "Do you like my ass, baby?" He almost always seems to stare or touch or talk about it.

"Fuck yeah." His voice is a sexy growl as his hands squeeze my cheeks roughly.

"What else do you like about me, Hunter?" I ask, breathy and already thinking about getting him back into my bed to explore him, slower this time.

But then he surprises me.

"I like your laugh, and how you do it without caring who hears. And I love how sweet you are to my nieces. And how passionate you are about the Center. I like that you can hike a mountain with me without complaining and that a night in with the frozen pizza you bought is the best date. And that you didn't push me when I wanted to burn that fucking shirt."

A smile plays on my lips at his sweet words as I run my thumb through his beard.

"I like how little your hands are, and the tiny ass outfits you wear, even if they make my dick inappropriately hard. I like your hair, and how it's the perfect length to wrap around my fist."

A shiver runs down my spine, thinking of the possibilities. "And I like how you learn crazy dances to make teenage girls open up to you, that you know what you want and won't settle. I like you, Hannah. I like you a lot."

"You know, you're a lot sweeter than your gruff exterior shows." My hand runs through his hair, taking on a mind of its own as I gaze into his warm chocolate eyes.

"Yeah, don't tell anyone."

"Don't worry, I don't want to share you." And even though I'm joking, I'm wondering if I'll have to. It's a dark cloud on an otherwise perfect day.

"Don't want to share you either, babe." The words whisper against my lips before my hips are pulled in closer to his, and he kisses me hard, tongue and teeth clashing. As he carries me to bed, I can't help but hope he meant that the way I think.

The next morning I wake up to a cold bed, rolling over to find... nothing. I'm tucked in, which is weird for my wild woman sleep habits. I usually wake up a few times a night to find I kicked off all the blankets and need to pull them up off the floor. Stretching, I realize I didn't wake up once last night. The warm man sharing my bed could be the reason.

I wander out of my bedroom into the kitchen, making a beeline for the coffeemaker. There I find a note on my flowery stationery with the big letter H on it. It's so pretty, but it cost me way too much, and I usually only end up using it for grocery lists.

Babe—

Left early to avoid questions from A. You sleep like the dead.

Coffee is set, just flip the switch.

Thanks for a great day.

-H

I let out a little squeal that would rival one of Rosie's. The sound is embarrassingly loud, reverberating off the walls of my tiny kitchen. Thankfully, the only people to hear it are me, myself, and I. I flip the switch before checking my phone on the couch. Wrapping myself in the throw I keep there, Hunter's scent envelops me.

After having his way with me once more in my bed after dinner, we migrated to the couch to watch TV. This, of course, led to more fooling around, which led to me bent over the arm of my couch and Hunter behind me. A shiver runs down my spine, and it is not from the morning chill.

My phone is sitting next to the note, so I grab it and tap out a text.

Hannah: Thanks for the coffee

. . .

Hunter: Any time. Had a good day yesterday.

Hannah: Me too. I think you owe me a proper dinner, though.

Hunter: I'll get right on that.

A smile plays on my lips as I fix and sip my coffee. Hunter somehow knew only to make one cup since I usually head to the big house once I'm awake and dressed, where I sip on an enormous glass of iced coffee.

I get dressed in a white oversized off-the-shoulder top with another bike short and sports bra set, this time leopard. You know. In case I see Hunter and need to remind him of anything. When I'm dressed and caffeinated, I walk over to the Sutter's to see if they need any help today, entering through the back sliding glass door to the kitchen.

"Good morning, Sutter family!" I chirp, greeting some of my favorite people in the universe. The girls are in pajamas, still with bedhead, eating bowls of cereal while Autumn is already dressed to take on the day. Steve looks like a mix of the two, a style he seems to have perfected. Sitting at the other end of the table, I spot Hunter with a coffee and the paper. He meets my eyes over the edge and smiles a secret smile.

When his eyes roam my body, his smile turns to a wicked grin that sends an unexpected warmth straight between my legs.

"Hi," says Sara from behind a book.

"*Hannah, I missed you!*" Rosie nearly knocks over her bowl of cereal to get to me. I swing her up into my arms and sit her on my hip.

"I've missed you, Rosie girl!" I tap her nose with a finger, which makes her giggle.

"We went to Six Flags! And I rode teacups and met a big bunny and saw *animals* in our *car*!"

"No way, Jose!"

"Yes, way! We had so, so much fun! Did you have fun while we were gone?"

"I did."

"What did you do, though?" the nosey girl asks, and it takes everything in me not to look at her uncle.

"I hung out with a friend, went on a hike, and had pizza."

"That sounds *awesome*!" The shriek is right at my ear, and I wince.

"It really was, my girl. It was the best." This time I risk a look at Hunter, who winks at me, making me blush. I look around at Steve and Autumn to make sure they didn't see.

Sooner than later, I need to talk to Hunter about his sister. While I want to explore things with him, I will not put my relationship with Autumn or her kids in jeopardy, especially if he's not serious about giving this a go.

Which is fine, I remind myself. *A fling is fun!* A fling is perfect for where I am right now. But flaunting this... whatever in front of the kids will not fly if that's all it is. I can't risk messing with the kids' heads, getting their hopes up, and then it being awkward.

"So what are your plans today, brother?" Autumn asks, looking at Hunter's way.

"I have to head to the city today. I've got some paperwork Gina needs me to sign in person. I'll probably spend the night in the condo," he says, eyes still on his paper *why on earth am I bummed out?*

"You should've told me. I would have grabbed it when I was there."

"It's new, for the zoning issues."

"Oh, got it. Have you been on location recently? Heard your truck was there yesterday," she says, with a glint in her eye.

"Yeah, went there yesterday. Took Hannah to show her around." He looks at me with a smile, knowing he's pushing the limit of what I'm comfortable with. I want to smile and curse him out all at once.

"What'd you think, Han? Autumn asks, her eyes alight with knowledge and understanding. Jesus Christ.

"I didn't know it was where the new location would be, but it's a gorgeous place," I say, leaving out that I came next to the waterfall and humped her brother in the parking lot. Jesus, I hope no one saw us.

"Did you know that's the first place that Hunter invested in?" she asks. Hunter glares at her. But I'm so invested now, knowing Hunter's first investment was a wash.

"No, I didn't. It's a gorgeous spot. Did you retain ownership this whole time?"

"Yes. Now I just need to figure out the zoning issues once and for all, then I can get part of my vision finally realized."

The conversation continues around work stuff and zoning and boring things, but I can't help but understand now. I thought it was another random location that Hunter was creating. But instead, he's using his father's investment, his first faith in Beaten Path, to show Ron that he was right to believe. To make this vision a reality would come full circle, so he could go to his dad if he worsens with his head held high.

Realizing that, I also realize a small but valuable piece of my heart is already his.

Fuck.

NINETEEN
-HANNAH-

"Okay campers! Welcome to Camp Sunburst! We are so excited you all are here to hang out with us this summer!" My voice travels through my cupped hands as I shout across the field at about three dozen kids of various ages. "Now, we know you guys are just as excited, but before we hop into the fun, we need to go over our rules and guidelines to make sure we can keep everyone safe and having a blast."

I spend the next 10 minutes explaining rules and regulations that we expect the campers to follow, then the other counselors and volunteers start working on dividing the kids into the age groups they'll be in through the summer. It's the first day of camp at the Center and even after all these years, it still gives me nervous butterflies.

After a quick wave and smile at Rosie who is sitting excitedly in the grass and waiting for her group, I walk over to Maggie.

"An awesome group this year."

"Yeah, a little bigger than last year. More families can't afford those fancy camps across town this year," Maggie says. I sigh, knowing she's right.

"Going to be our job to give them the best summer we possibly can."

"You mean it's *my* job." Maggie elbows me. "You refuse to accept a proper job here and let this old woman off the hook."

"You know why, Mags. Plus, the girls coming here for free all summer is more than enough." She won that battle last week when I tried to bring in the camp deposit for Sara and Rosie.

"Hush, girl. You know what I'm saying. It's just my job to give you a hard time. Did we ever confirm those shirts for kids?"

"Yes! The donation department of Beaten Path told me they should be delivered today," I say excitedly, relaying the conversation I'd had with Gina, Hunter's assistant via email Friday.

"That was very generous of them." She's baiting me, looking to get more information. Chances are, she gossiped with Sadie this morning, evidenced by the iced Americano she walked in for me.

While my best friend is typically a vault with my secrets, she has no problem sharing with Maggie. Knowing the two of them, they either spent the early morning chatting about how I'm stubborn and need to open myself up or planning my wedding.

"Yes, Maggie, it was very generous. Luckily, I work for Autumn, so I had the in." Evasion is my goal here. Maggie harrumphs, knowing I'm bullshitting her, but smiles at me all the same.

Not much later, the words I've come to associate with butterflies in my belly hit my ears, directing me to look to the parking area.

"*Uncle Hunter*!" A blur of pink and sparkles runs past, going straight for a man with a brown cardboard box under his arm.

Hunter.

I stand there, shock and confusion infusing my system as I take him in. But soon, I'm following in Rosie's footsteps, walking in his direction and trying not to seem too eager to see him. He catches my eye all the same and smiles his knowing smile, an ever-present tease reminding me of his late visit to my cottage last night when he got back from the city. A shiver runs through me, and his smile widens into a toothy grin through the dark of his beard.

"Hey." My voice is breathier than I expect, and his eyes warm in a way I can't quite explain. His hand subtly reaches out, brushing against mine but not grabbing. Rosie is jumping up and down next to him, alternately saying hi and his name.

"Hey, princess! How's my best Rosie?" Hunter drops the box he's holding in favor of picking up his niece.

"I'm your *only* Rosie, Uncle Hunter." She giggles like he's a silly boy who understands nothing.

"Ahh, that's right, I forgot," he says, kissing her hair before putting her back down.

"Whatcha doing here?" I ask, trying to seem uninterested.

"Delivering your shirts. And a few extras. It's all in the truck."

"What extras?" I feel my brows furrow in confusion.

"Just some things for the kids we figured they'd like."

"Do you need help getting them out?" I look into the distance, trying to see where his Bronco is in the parking lot.

"Yeah, I will."

I bend to Rosie. "Why don't you go back to your friends, girly? It looks like they're getting into groups, and you know the rule is to stick with your group." She nods.

"Make sure you say 'bye, okay?" Her stern little face glares at her uncle, a tiny finger waggling in his direction, making us both laugh.

"Got it. Now listen to Hannah and go," he says, pointing to the field with the kids. She skips off, and we both watch her go. I turn to him.

"Really, what are you doing here? Gina said the shirts would be delivered today."

"Yeah, by me. That's why I went to the New York location yesterday after I signed those papers. I had to get a few things."

"Oh. I guess that makes sense." Why does Hunter delivering them personally make me feel all fuzzy and warm inside? Jesus, get it together, Hannah.

"Who's this, Hannah girl?" Maggie says, coming up next to me, smiling because she already knows exactly who this is and wants to make me miserable. "Is this your new fella?"

I could kill her.

"Oh, Mags, n—"

Hunter sticks out his hand and answers before I can finish. "Sure am, ma'am. I'm Hunter, Hannah's man." At the same time, he wraps his arm around my waist in a clear statement.

"Well, isn't this just a lovely surprise? I'm Maggie."

"Nice to finally meet you. Hannah talks extremely highly of you." My face is a five-alarm fire burn, capable of tearing down a forest in a moment. Maggie looks at me with warmth in her eyes.

"Our Hannah does love to see the good in others,"

"I've come to see that," he says, squeezing my waist.

"Okay, enough talking about me like I'm not here. Hunter is dropping off the shirts his company donated. Can you go make sure the kids are listening to the counselors while I go help him?"

"What, are you trying to stop an old woman from gushing and embarrassing you?" Her thin, weathered hand goes to her chest like she's aghast at the idea.

"Yes, now go," I say, pointing to the field. Maggie laughs, throwing her head back, her long grey braids falling down her back.

"Okay, okay, I'll leave you be this time. Hunter, it was great meeting you. Hope you'll be back again soon." She says, walking away with a wave, her floaty skirt trailing behind her.

"Sorry about her. She's a nosy nuisance. You can leave that box here, the kids can help with it later."

"I think she's great." Hunter grabs my hand as we walk toward the lot. Glancing over my shoulder to check if anyone is looking, I see the kids are occupied with an icebreaker.

"Yeah, wonderful. Where's the Bronco?" I ask, scanning the lot and seeing it nowhere.

"Back at Autumn's." My body slows, but his warm hand tugs me toward a big box truck.

"Is this yours?" I'm confused. Less than 100 t-shirts shouldn't need a box truck. Hell, you could probably fit them in two boxes, easily.

"Yup," is all he says before he pulls me around to the other side, facing away from the field. Pulling me in close quickly, he pushes me into the warm metal of the rented truck, boxing me in with his body. He's looking at me, eyes on my lips. We're breathing the same air, warm breaths hitting my lips.

"Hunter, what are you—" Before I can finish asking, his lips are on mine, controlling and possessive. I should push him away, and reminded him there are dozens of children just yards away, but I missed him. Somehow in the twelve hours, since I've seen him last, I missed this confusing and sexy man.

When I woke, he was already gone from my bed, leaving it and me feeling cold and empty.

Instead of pushing away, I roll onto my tiptoes, pressing into him as my mouth opens. Without hesitation, his tongue slips into mine, as domineering and aggressive as the man himself. He tastes of fresh air and sin and a hint of coffee.

He continues to kiss me, slipping his hands to my ass to squeeze as my hands go to his neck to tangle in his hair. We continue like this for what feels like a mix of hours and as quick as seconds. The kiss stops only when, in desperation for more, I grind my hips into Hunter's, making him groan.

"Jesus fuck, woman," he says, pulling away and pressing his forehead to mine. "What are you doing to me?"

"Uh, sorry, honey, but you're the one who professed you were my man to my surrogate grandmother and then pulled me behind a box truck to suck face." I smile at him.

"Suck face?" His face has broken into an easy smile, a beautiful sight to see on his normally serious face.

"Yeah, Suck face, make out, swap spit."

He chuckles, warm breath across my lips before kissing me once more, this time chastely.

"You're doing it to me too, you know. I missed you this morning." I rub a thumb over his beard, feeling the rough texture on the pad.

"You have no idea. Can't think of anything but you for weeks. Distracted at work, when the last fucking thing I need right now is to be distracted. I'm thinking of your sweet laugh and your sweeter pussy all fucking day long, daydreaming during meetings and planning out when I can get to you next." A shiver runs through me, a shiver that grows when he pushes his hips into me, showing me how much I'm affecting him.

"Yeah." It's the same for me. How did things get this confusing this fast? "So you're my man, huh?" I ask with a smile.

"Are we just friends?"

"Well, I hope not. I don't do that thing with my tongue on my fri—" I start, cut off by an utterly feral growl from deep in Hunter's chest that reverberates straight to my core, making me quiver.

"Hannah," he warns.

"I'm just saying."

"Are you fucking anyone else?"

"No, honey. Are you?" My gut drops, scared for the answer.

"No. Are you mine for now?" *For now.* I can't quite verbalize why that cuts a bit, but it does.

"Yeah, I'm yours. For now."

As if he can sense what I'm thinking, his face softens. "Baby, I can't promise you forever right now. Not in that place. I've got too much going on. Don't want to lead you on, but I enjoy spending time with you and I want to explore that more." I can respect that. And if that's what I get from him, if that's what I need to do to *have him,* I'll take it.

"Okay, honey," I whisper, my lips brushing his once again. He looks in my eyes like he's trying to decide if I mean it or if I'm really okay with this. Whatever he sees, he seems to accept it.

"Alright, Hannah, Let's get all this stuff out."

"What stuff? What's in the truck?" I ask, confused. He smiles, then leads me to the back of the truck and opens the door.

Inside are stacks and stacks of boxes.

More boxes than one would need for 100 shirts.

My eyes scan the hand-scrawled words written in black marker, and tears well in my eyes at the realization of what is happening.

Sunscreen

Bug spray.

First aid kits.

And there are fun words written, too.

Soccer balls.

Yard games.

Baseballs and mitts.

T ball stand.

Helmets,

The brown boxes are stacked high in the box truck, all with the Beaten Path logo stamped on them. There are even a few bikes and scooters in various sizes strapped in.

"Hunter, what is this?" I whisper, both in a panic and in awe. These kids... some of whom haven't had much at all, are going to be absolutely spoiled this summer, and it's all because of this man. I step forward to the tailgate of the truck and lean in, grazing a rough brown box with the tips of my fingers. Trying to reassure myself that these are real. This isn't an elaborate dream.

"It's for you."

This is more than four years of fundraising could afford.

"You mean the campers." My head swimming with thoughts and emotions, words that are too dangerous to slip from my tongue.

He laughs. "Yes, the campers, but I'd be lying if I said it wasn't for you, as well."

"Hunter, we can't accept this. It's way too much, a fortune."

"You can, and you will. We have a non-profit budget, a healthy one. I'm actually pretty pissed that you've never talked to Autumn about sponsorship, but we can talk about that later," he says, bending close to my ear, "maybe with my hand on your bare ass."

I shiver, a constant reaction when he's around, before turning to him. "I never wanted to create that expectation. I do things myself, not because I know people." Embarrassment heats my cheeks at the words. At the fact that I feel I need to say that. He spent all of this time and money on... me. No one has ever done something like this for me.

"Well, now, you do them with me."

TWENTY
-HUNTER-

It takes about an hour to unpack all the donations from the truck and bring them into the Center. The entire time Maggie's eyes water with a mix of disbelief and gratitude.

Guilt eats at me a bit since I told Hannah it was completely a donation, but in truth, I paid for at least half of it out of pocket. I couldn't stop myself. Every time I saw something in the catalog, I'd think about how it could be used and utilized to benefit these kids.

Walking back to the truck to return it to the rental store, I'm humming to myself. As I was leaving, Hannah told me to stop by the cottage tonight for her to show her 'gratitude'—her words, not mine—and Jesus fuck if I cannot wait for that.

My phone rings again. Jonathan. Fuck. I have no desire to answer and have him ream me out, but I've missed four calls already from him, and he will not get more friendly with a fifth.

"Hello Jonathan, how are you on this bright, sunny Monday?"

"Don't fuck around with me. Where have you been?"

"Delivering the donations to the camp in Springbrook Hills, helping Beaten Path's image in the community. Why?" I ask because this seems more than a general frustration that I wasn't answering.

"Why? Why?! Are you fucking kidding me? I've been calling *you* since 10 a.m. when the zoning department called *me* to say that one paper you were supposed to have signed yesterday is missing. But you're so busy fucking around with some chick and being Robinhood that we missed the goddamn meeting."

My stomach drops like a rock, knowing how important that meeting was. The paperwork needed to be submitted so when the zoning department had its weekly meeting, they could add our issue to the agenda.

"Fuck!" I shout the words at my windshield. Angry that I missed this call, angry that I missed this meeting. "What now?"

"What now? That's all you have to say? Are you fucking kidding me?"

"What do you want me to say, Jonathan? What's done is done. I can't go back and sign the paper, I can't go back and answer your call." Though I wish I could do just that. Knowing the zoning meeting wasn't so far from where I am, knowing I could have dropped off the paper in person, schmoozed a bit. Fuck, that's what I would have a month ago, even two weeks ago, without having an unsigned document as an excuse. But instead, I was...

"I want your fucking head in the game. You're off fucking around with the hot nanny—yes, I've seen her, Hunter—while we try to make your insane vision happen. I get it, Hunter. I do. But I will not have history repeating itself and this blow up in our face because you're off fucking some hot piece."

He's right, of course. The reason we're even in this position, trying to make this location work, is because 10 years ago, I was so caught up in a woman that I lost sight of common sense. 10 years ago, I let a woman wrap me up so deeply in her charms that I almost lost everything.

But still... anger and a strange protectiveness threaten to suffocate me.

"It's not like that, Jonathan, and I'd appreciate you not talking to me like I'm a fucking child that you have the right to reprimand. I'll remind you who you work for. And I don't appreciate your commentary on my personal life."

"Fuck off, Hunter. If you want to tackle this insanity on your own, have at it. But if you want to succeed, you'll need to listen to me and think with your head, not your cock."

"Send me whatever information you need immediately, and then call Gina to inform her of the next steps." Ignoring his threat, I swipe to end the call before throwing my cell to the floor. I probably just cracked the screen, but I don't fucking care.

Putting my hands in my head, my frustration and confusion consume me, sucking all the oxygen from the parked car. This project is so important—the *most* important, but Hannah is such a delicious distraction right now. I need to focus on what's in front of me. Last I heard, Dad still hasn't improved or entered the clinical trial. The clock is on to get this done.

I can't see my dad yet. Not until I have something to show him. Looking at him like this and knowing that I haven't turned things around isn't an option.

Autumn doesn't get it. Every day she tells me I need to go see him. It's not like I've avoided him for the past 10 years. But it's not about that. It's seeing him like this, sick and vulnerable, knowing that I may have had a hand in this, knowing that any visit could be the last. I can't bear to see the disappointment, the exhaustion, the pain in his eyes and know somewhere deep and hidden, I'm to blame.

Sighing, my hand reaches to turn the key in the ignition, and I'm off to do whatever it takes to make this happen.

TWENTY-ONE
-HANNAH-

"You look wiped, Aut." I'm wiping the kitchen counter after breakfast when she comes downstairs and sits at the island. It's not a camp day, and since it's miserably rainy, the girls are upstairs playing semi-peacefully.

Autumn, who usually stays in her office from 9 to 5 like clockwork, sits with her cup of coffee pushed in front of her, her head on the marble. She lifts it, placing her fingers to her temple, her arm braced on the counter. "Anything I can do to help?"

"Just tired. And drained, physically and emotionally. I saw Dad last night. Mentioned that Hunter still hasn't come by. It's been four weeks, for fuck's sake. He's here to be closer to him, but he's always closed up in that room, working."

"Ron mentioned the same to me last time I dropped off his Bingo cookies," I say, grabbing my cup and standing across the island from her.

"It makes no sense to me. Why come at all?"

"Look, I can't speak to where his mind is, but I was talking to him last week, and he told me a bit about the business your father invested in that went bad. He's got a lot of guilt around it. I think he has some grand plan of proving himself with Beaten Path to make your dad proud."

"What a fucking moron. Even you know Dad is so incredibly proud of what he's done. There's nothing he needs to prove. Fuck, even if he hadn't grown a damn empire, he'd be proud. Hunter's entire adult life has been spent working, never actually enjoying what he's built because he's so busy trying to make up for what he sees as some grave mistake. A mistake that no one holds against him."

"I told him that, but he won't see reason. Autumn, I think he believes on some level Ron being sick is because of the stress he put him through."

"Oh, Hunter. He's always trying to solve problems that aren't there and take care of people without taking care of himself." I nod in agreement. "Like someone else I know." She pokes my arm, and I roll my eyes, but otherwise ignore her accusation.

After a few minutes of quiet, each of us lost in our own thoughts, Autumn breaks the silence. "So, my brother, huh?" she says with a smile. Panicking, my face burns, trying to figure out how to answer.

"What?" I squeak out, "Oh God, no. No Autumn, nothing is happening there. I'm here most of the day, and the girls adore him. We just cross paths a lot. That's all." She looks at me skeptically, a disbelieving light in her eyes. She's using her talent to sort out lies with a simple look on me, a talent I'm sure all wonderful moms have. A long beat passes while she stares at me

"You know I wouldn't care, right Han?" Her voice is soft. "You could be good for him, you know. And he you. If something happened."

"Nothing to care about, Aut. Just had a drink together after the kids went to bed and talked. Went hiking together. Nothing special."

"Alright, Hannah, whatever you say." She's still looking at me, eyes searching, trying to determine where the truth lies with her secret x-ray mom vision. "Okay, I need a change of scenery. I'm headed to Rise and Grind to work from there. My mind is too scrambled today."

"No prob, enjoy! Let me know if you want me to get anything started for dinner, I say, heading upstairs to mediate the brawl I can hear brewing, I'm eager to escape this conversation, making my mind go places that aren't safe for my heart.

Later I'm scooping cookie dough onto baking sheets when muscular arms dusted with dark hair wrap around me from behind. Lips hit my neck, and Hunter's smokey, smooth voice breathes into my hair. "Those look delicious."

The girls are scattered at sleepovers with friends, while Steve takes Autumn to a last-minute overnight in the city to help de-stress her. Nights with no one here aren't common, but when they happen, it's quiet and peaceful. Except, now I'm not alone.

"Hey." I turn my head to meet him for a kiss. It's sweet and soft, a brush of lips as a greeting. Home and comfort, not sex and desire. It's something I can't remember if I've ever felt from another man, making the conversation I had with Autumn this morning whisper in my ear again.

Pulling back, he looks around. "Do you have any finished baking?" I point to the cooling rack where two dozen fresh chocolate chip cookies are sitting.

"Just one, though, I need them for tomorrow." Grabbing my scoop, I get back to filling up the lined trays.

He comes back, a cookie stuffed in his mouth and another in his hand, making me roll my eyes. "Do you ever listen?" A small smile is playing on my lips, though, since I kind of love that he digs my cookies.

"I listen when it benefits me. Like when you're moaning and telling me to—" I slam my hand over his mouth, looking around to make sure there are no little ears around.

"Hunter!" I laugh, remembering that everyone is out for the night. "You're the worst."

"That's not what you said last night." He winks as he reaches for another cookie.

"Stop, you thief!" I slap his hand away with my spatula. "Those are for bingo night! Your dad and the other grumpy old men will kill me if they're short." Hunter puts the cookie down like it burned him and leans on the counter, looking at his feet. A heavy silence hangs between us for a few moments.

"Are... are you mad at me?"

"For taking my dad's cookies? God, I'm not that big of a dick, Hannah. Of course not, my dad deserves all the cookies he can get." His voice highlights the delicate balance he's been keeping.

I smile softly at him, knowing his struggle. "You know, you could come with me tomorrow," I say, looking away and scooping. "I'm sure he'd love to see you."

Deciding to take the shot, I go for the full gusto, remembering how stressed Autumn looked and how Ron clearly misses his son. "Autumn says you haven't gone to see him yet." The words come quieter, like I'm a branch and he's a balloon stuck in a tree. One wrong move, and he'll burst. Turning to look at him, it's clear it was a poor choice. His entire body has locked, jaw tense, teeth grinding.

"Oh, so you're gossiping with my sister about me now? Weren't you the one that insisted my sister can't know about us?" he says, the words coming out like a whip, anger burning in his eyes.

Shock pours over me like a bucket of ice-cold water. It's clear he wasn't excited to talk about his dad. But where is this shit coming from with not telling Autumn—wasn't he cool with that? Hadn't we had the conversation that until we knew for sure, we'd keep her in the dark?

And, shit, isn't he the one who isn't sure? The one who's hesitating, who won't commit to anything more?

"I—I'm sorry, Hunter. I meant nothing by it. I wasn't gossiping, I swear. Autumn brought it up to me the other morning, completely unprompted. It would have been weirder if I *didn't* join the conversation."

"Yeah, and I'm sure you couldn't resist throwing gas on that fire. Fuck, Hannah, I'm getting enough shit from my sister. Even Steve's getting on my ass lately. I don't need it from you, too."

"I said I'm sorry, Hunter. I was just asking if you wanted to come with me. It might be easier. Less stress with a buffer." I'm starting to get annoyed now, the icy shock melting to a warm burn of frustration.

"I don't need anyone worrying about my stress level, Hannah."

"That's not what I meant. I just meant it might be easier to go if you're with an impartial person. I know how hard this is for you—"

"What do you know, Hannah? You roll yourself so thick up in bubble wrap to avoid any kind of conflict, working so hard to make sure everyone is happy at the expense of yourself. How about we analyze that, huh? When was the last time you made yourself happy, not the girls or Sadie or the kids at the Center or my fucking sister?" he says, and now it's clear. There isn't only anger in his voice. Hidden behind it are hurt and fear, frustration, and maybe even a dash of concern. For who? Me?

Either way, there's no excuse for how he's acting.

"Okay, that's unnecessary. You don't need to be mean and spiteful. I genuinely asked a simple question. If you don't want to come, that's fine. I wasn't pressuring you, I made a simple suggestion. I won't stand by and let you make me feel like a pushy bitch." I'm so embarrassed and angry and, worst of all, deep down, hurt. My eyes water, and I need to get out of this room that's suffocating me.

I move to walk away, deciding to finish the cookies later. But before I get far, Hunter grabs my wrist, tugging me back to him and into his arms. A tear falls, and though I refuse to meet his eyes, it drops onto his grey shirt, leaving a dark spot we both stare at.

"Oh, baby, I'm so sorry. God, I'm a dick. I'm so stressed with this new location at work and Autumn busting my balls. I took it out on you, and that's not cool." I'm quiet, not knowing what to say. What am I doing here? What am I doing with this man? I told myself I'd keep my heart out of it, have fun and enjoy whatever he can give me, but fuck, is it too late? I'm in so deep already. Me, the girl who refuses to fall unless it's forever. In deep with the man who can't have a distraction.

"Hannah, baby, look at me. I didn't mean what I said. I get why you're cautious. I get why you don't want to tell Autumn. I can't promise I can give you what you need, and you need to protect yourself from that. *Of course,* you do. And you need to protect Sara and Rosie from that letdown, too." His hand is on my chin, a soft touch with work-roughened fingers. Fingers that I've felt all over my body, fingers that have shown me adoration and pleasure.

"That wasn't nice, Hunter," I mumble, still not looking at him, embarrassment and shame still roiling in my stomach.

"Fuck, I know, Han." He sounds relieved that I spoke, relieved that I haven't run yet. I wonder if he'd let me if I tried. "Work is overwhelming. I got a call today, and things are a shit show. I'm gonna have to leave for a few days to go back to the city, and I know Autumn is going to give me shit. I took it out on you, and that's not okay. Do you hear me? What happened is *not okay.*" I'm looking at him now, seeing the exhaustion and stress on his stricken face. God, this man. I wish he would stop and see what we all see—the success, the drive, the worthiness. Instead, he sees a mistake that needs to be fixed. My heart breaks for him, over and over again.

"You're a dick. And you're right—it was not okay. But I'll forgive you. This time," I say with a small smile and a sniffle, turning so I'm completely engulfed in his arms, cuddling into him. His warmth seeps through our clothes and into my skin, building back that bubble of safety and... home.

"I'm serious. You're allowed to talk to me about things, ask me about what's going on. Accusing you of gossiping with Autumn was wrong—you wouldn't do that. And then to throw it back in your face? That's unacceptable."

"It's fine, I get it. You're stressed."

"Not an excuse."

God, this man. A small part of me is screaming to do whatever I can to keep him, to make him mine, to argue with and makeup with, to grow with forever.

"It isn't, you're right. But you've apologized and recognized the issue."

"How can I make it up to you?" His voice drops an octave, making it warm and seductive. His hand finds a lock of hair that's fallen from my bun and gently tucks it behind my ear.

"I don't know. What do you have in mind?"

"What I'd really like to do is fuck you right on this island." It comes out as a low rumble, and the hand around my waist pulls me in tighter until we're flush against each other.

"Hunter!" I say, laughing because the idea is absurd. Still, as I attempt to pull away and finish my cookies, it's impossible to ignore the clenching of my core at the mental image.

"Or maybe just lay you out on top and eat you out until you scream my name." He's holding tight, making moving away impossible, and staring straight into my eyes. The warmth of his brown eyes is quickly deepening into a full blazing fire, ready to consume me. As his hand on my waist lifts just enough to brush a thumb along the underside of my breast, my breath becomes quiet and thin...

"Hunter, come on." My voice is breathy, so much so I don't recognize it.

"Maybe I should just kiss you and see what happens."

"Hunt—" His lips are on mine before I can finish my protest, but I have no objections. My need for this man is inexhaustible. My body is constantly charged around him, waiting for him to make his move. He kisses me and kisses me until all the breath leaves my lungs. I'm already gasping and writhing, and his hands haven't even touched my skin. Need is bubbling up inside, a need that terrifies me with its intensity.

Hunter's hands go from my waist to under my arms, lifting me up and placing my bottom on the cool marble island. "Hunter, what are you doing?" I ask, panting.

"Hips up, baby," he says, his fingers creeping under the waistband of my leggings at the hips. *Oh God, oh God, oh God!* Leaning back onto the palms of my hands, I do as I'm told, allowing him to slowly peel the tight leggings off my body, hooking his fingers in my lacy panties and dragging them down together.

"Already ready for me," he whispers to himself, dragging one thick finger up my slit and spreading my wetness around my clit. "Guess I'll have to take care of this."

"Yeah," I breathe. His finger is lazily dragging up, down, up, around, over and over, driving me insane. So gentle, never entering, teasing me slowly. And then, without warning, he looks into my eye and thrusts two fingers into my pussy, making me arch my back in sheer pleasure.

"You're so fucking wet. Is this all for me?"

I've learned Hunter has a dirty mouth during sex, and, *God,* I love it. Each word drives me higher, and sometimes I'm convinced I could come from his words alone. I nod, knowing from experience he wants me to answer. His thick fingers continue to piston in and out, faster, then slower, then fast again, occasionally brushing a thumb over my clit and making me whimper.

"Hunter," I moan. "I need more." I'm squirming, already on the edge, so turned on by him, by what he's doing to my body. My hand slips under my shirt and my thin bra, pinching my hard nipple to try and relieve some kind of pressure.

"Okay, baby, I'll take care of you, don't worry." His head drops until he's face to face with my pussy, stroking his nose on my wet, swollen clit. "Jesus, I love this. Such a pretty pussy you have, honey, and it's all mine." His words send another shot down my spine, heat blooming there, already so close.

"All yours, Hunter," I moan, my mind in hyper-drive. His eyes meet mine one last time, the fire flaring, his pupils dilating with hunger.

And then, just like he promised, he devours me. First, with his mouth covering my clit, gentle licks, and soft sucking, and then moving his fingers and replacing them with his tongue. In and out his tongue goes, going deep, tasting me, teasing me. His thumbs pull me, holding me open so his tongue can go even deeper, and his nose can dig into my clit. Dropping to my elbows, my face shoots to the ceiling as I moan loudly, panting and bucking against his tongue.

Hunter moans against my pussy, vibrating up my core, and causing my body to quake. I'm so gloriously close. "This cunt, so fucking sweet, God, Hannah. I'm gonna suck your clit again, and you're going to come in my mouth." He says this, looking up at me, his mouth coated in my wet, eyes hooded. Nodding, I moan again as he puts three fingers in me this time, pumping hard, and then his entire mouth goes over my clit.

One strong suck and a scrape of his teeth and I'm *screaming*, back arched, spasming on his fingers and gushing into his mouth, unable to get air into my lungs. My vision goes black, white stars shooting across, and bolts of pleasure shoot through me. It is the most intense orgasm of my life.

What could be moments or days later, after he continues to lick me, absorbing my aftershocks slowly as I come back to Earth. Hunter steps back to look at his handy work as I shake and shiver, still moaning gently. And it's then I see at some point he undid his pants and is now jacking himself, staring at my exposed body on display. I moan again, already ready for more, already ready for him again.

"Fuuuuck," he groans, watching as I take a finger and circle my clit, then my entrance, begging him silently to give us both what we want. Instead of taking me right there though, he bends, putting a shoulder into my belly, standing and carrying me upstairs, my head facing his back.

"Where are we going?"

"My room so I can get you in my bed." He trails a hand up my inner thigh to play with the wet that's now dripping down my leg.

He opens a door and kicks it shut before placing me on my feet. I immediately drop to my knees, pulling his pants and underwear down, and dive in, taking his entire cock in my mouth without hesitation.

"Jesus, Hannah," he groans, putting his hands in my hair, and gently pressing me forward and back to guide me. Flattening my tongue to rub along the underside, I use a hand to grab his balls gently, teasing and tugging, and he moans incoherently. I'm drooling around his dick, but my pussy is dripping just as much, something I learn when my hand slides down to touch myself.

"Are you—? Fuck, so hot, finger that cunt for me, baby," he says, staring down at me as I look up, his cock in my mouth, my fingers in my pussy. I'm so wet that I start dripping down my fingers as I ride them, moaning around him as he slips into my throat. "Fuuuck." Suddenly, he's gone from my mouth, and I'm tossed on his bed. The sheets smell like his cologne and sweat, but there is no time to take anything else in as I strip off my shirt and bra.

He goes to the bedside table and grabs a condom before crawling up the bed, the wrapper between his teeth. *Fuck, this man is sexy*. He rips it open before stroking the latex onto his cock, his other hand on my tit, pinching and pulling at my nipple.

Without another word, he's slamming into me, making my back arch, and a scream rips out of my throat. He pounds in, grunting with each thrust as my hand trails down, rubbing my swollen clit. "So fucking sexy," he mumbles before pulling out completely.

A whimper escapes me, but then I'm tossed and flipped over onto my belly. I start to get on all fours before he puts pressure between my shoulders until my face is pressed to the mattress, my ass high and raised when he slams in again. The angle is different and extreme, and the way I'm bent means it's tighter and more sensitive. With each thrust, a grunt is escaping my throat, animalistic and low.

Unexpectedly, his thumb is on my asshole, circling the puckered flesh slowly, in contrast to the hard and fast attack that he's executing on the rest of my body. I've never done anything like this, much less wanted it. But now that it's been offered, offered by Hunter, I'm rearing back, silently begging him. He brings this out in me. This crazed, unleashed version.

"Do you want my thumb in your pretty asshole, Hannah?" he

asks, his dirty words sending another shot through me, getting me close again.

"Yes! God, yes!" I shout, taking his assault on my pussy, but needing more. Without hesitation, his thumb is pressing in and out, just the tip, and I *shatter*. I'm wailing, coming so hard, it's like an out-of-body experience, screaming his name, maybe going so far as to speak in another language, I have no clue.

He keeps pumping, growling, slamming into me, and a few moments later, follows me over the edge.

TWENTY-TWO
-HUNTER-

"Okay, open your eyes." When I do, I see Hannah's kneeling on the bed with the biggest, goofiest smile on her gorgeous face, her body covered only in a too-big tee of mine. In her hands is a white plate towering with cookies. "I made you your own batch earlier today."

"Are those oatmeal raisin?" She shrugs, a light blush blooming on her cheeks. "I thought you hate oatmeal raisin cookies?" Something is warming in my chest, something I'm working hard to deny.

"Oh, I do. I felt like I was committing a sin stirring in the raisins. But you like them, so... yeah." God, I'm such a fucking asshole. Not only did I snap at her, bitching at her for bringing my *sick father,* who I *haven't even visited,* cookies, but she made me my own because I told her I like them. Fuck.

"You're sweet, you know." The plate of cookies is quickly set onto my nightstand before I take her arm, tugging her until she's lying chest to chest with me, only my worn tee between us.

"Yeah, I know." She smiles again, bright and blinding, and I'm ignoring the warmth that's burning inside me, slowly taking over my whole being little by little. Each smile makes the feeling ratchet up a notch. Each kindness she shows me, each time she reveals a part of herself, makes herself vulnerable.

"I'm sorry about earlier." My voice is softer than expected, even to my ears. A strand of dark waves has fallen out of her messy bun, and my hand tucks it behind her ear.

"It's fine. You're stressed out. I get it."

"No, it's not. It's not okay. That was not okay." My eyes meet hers, showing her my truth. In hers, bright and blue, I can see shards of hurt still, her guard up a few inches higher than it was hours ago.

"You're right. It wasn't okay. But I get it. Let's move on, okay?" Her little fingers are making shapes on my chest while she avoids my eyes.

"I have a lot going on right now. So much with my dad and work. I can't have any distractions right now." Her finger pauses on my chest for a second, almost imperceptible, before starting again.

"Of course. Plus, you're in the city. I'm here." Normally, a woman accepting an arrangement where we fuck without strings would be cause for celebration. Why does Hannah's agreement that this isn't anything bigger than sex bother me more each time we discuss it?

My fingers dig at her hair tie, watching her long dark hair fall around her shoulders. As I tuck what's fallen into her face behind her ear, I marvel once again at how soft and thick it is. My palm runs down her smooth back until it's on her perfect ass. "When's Autumn coming home?" I drag her naked body until her mouth is right in front of mine.

A distraction. That's what we need right now.

TWENTY-THREE
-HUNTER-

"What can I do for you, Jonathan?"

This week is never-ending. It's been non-stop working as I try to figure out the zoning issue without ruining our original timeline. This is on top of my normal fire-putting-out that has become the entirety of my role at Beaten Path. We've had to move the groundbreaking back one week, but now that it's all ironed out, I can breathe.

Or so I thought.

"We've got an enormous problem." Now, Jonathan can be dramatic. He has been since the beginning, and he will be until he dies. This is a phrase that's been uttered by him at least once a week for as long as I've known him.

"What now?" The wheels of my leather desk chair roll back over the creamy carpet until it's braced against the wall. Why my sister has a white carpet in her home with those two girls is a mystery.

"The construction company is fighting us. The change in schedule doesn't work for them. It overlaps our projected end date with the start of another project and gives them no space for a buffer. They're threatening to drop the account if we can't keep to the original timeline."

Fuuuuuck. This is *not* what we need.

"Okay, so what's the next step?" This is what's gotten me this far. Rather than panicking, we need to accept that there is an issue and immediately find a solution.

"I can't be the only one with solutions, Hunter. I've been trying to figure this out all morning, unlike you, who's doing God knows what in that podunk town. They're unwilling to compromise and start the week later."

"Jesus, Jonathan, maybe the company wants to break the contract because you're such a dickhead."

"I don't have time for niceties." He's pissed at me.

"Okay, let me make some calls and do some schmoozing. I'm sure it's not a big deal, then I'll see what I can do."

"Whatever. You need to call before two, though. The contract gives them leeway from breaking without consequence if done seven days from the agreed-upon start date. They have another contract lined up, one that fits the timeline they need." He hangs up, and the back of my head hits the wall with a thunk.

I don't have time for this shit. My plate is piling up. The stay in Springbrook Hills was to be nearby for meetings and construction regarding the new location, but every day I'm stuck in this room putting out fires, most not even related to this project. Not to mention, I still haven't gotten the balls to see my father.

As soon as we have a solid confirmation on groundbreaking, I tell myself. Then I can tell him.

Tell him how sorry I am. How much guilt I hold for putting him in that position all those years ago. How I've gotten past distractions and poor decisions. How I can finally make him proud.

But right now, being the CEO of this company I built to prove myself is anything but fulfilling. I wanted to start a business to help people, to build services for kids, families, and individuals that would get them into a better headspace, get them active, get them healthy. Now I'm dealing with contracts, employee infighting, zoning issues, and schmoozing investors. It's exhausting. Unfortunately, I don't have time to dwell—I need to figure out this issue immediately.

But instead of getting right into it and calling the construction crew, my feet guide me downstairs, where the light giggling of little girls and the full laugh of Hannah can be heard traveling up to my room.

"Hey there, Hunter," she says when she sees me coming down the stairs, a secret, easy smile on her face. Hitting the kitchen, the marble island is cool beneath my forearms as I lean forward with a sigh.

"Everything okay?"

"Ehh. Just work stuff that never seems to go easy."

"I'm sorry, Anything I can do to help?" Her offer is innocent, but the translation I give it is far from. My eyebrow quirks and a sweet blush fans across her cheeks. "Hush, you." A chiding smile appears on her full lips that I want to kiss freely. Every part of me begs to grab her face in my hands and lay one on her in front of my nieces. let them know she's mi-

Woah. Where did that come from?

Her hands are working, packing things into a cooler while she talks. Seeing her hands on that island brings memories to mind of the last time we were here.

"Where are you guys going?" I ask to get my mind off the topic.

"The park. We need a change of scenery to change the kids' attitudes."

"How long do you think you'll be?"

"An hour, just enough to eat lunch and run around." An hour out of the house sounds perfect. Looking at the clock that says it's barely after ten, I make my decision.

"Mind if I join?" The words fall out of my mouth, and even she looks shocked, like the thought never even crossed her mind. Should that bother me? Probably not. The thought would never have crossed *my* mind, and the request just fell off my tongue as is.

"Uh, no, not at all. Let me make you a sandwich really quick. Any preference?"

"Surprise me." She beams, filling the room with brightness and joy, confirming my choice to be a good one. Tunnel vision sets in. A day at the park with Hannah and my nieces sounds exactly like what I need right now.

Excellent choice, Hunter. Excellent choice.

Driving to the park, the kids are chaotic, but Hannah handles them with precision, kindness, and ease that can only come from practice. When she gets out of the car, Rosie scrapes her knee, and Sara whines that she forgot her softball mitt, but again Hannah calms the potential meltdowns like a pro. Handing Sara the basket, she directs her to set up, and I follow.

"Are you and Hannah like boyfriend and girlfriend?" my niece asks, not bothering to throw any punches. She's quiet most of the time but reminds me so much of my sister.

"You know, you're exactly like your mom when she was a kid. You'd think she was quiet and sweet, nose in a book, but when you got her alone, she wouldn't shut up, and she was a sleuth." This makes her smile, clearly a compliment.

"Okay, but are you?"

"Uh, no? No. We're not?" The words are a jumbled mess in my mouth and brain. We are together, but we're not supposed to be in front of the kids. She's my girl, and I sure as fuck don't want any other man getting that confused, but the kids, well, their confusion bleeds into everything else. But saying it out loud feels like a betrayal.

"Well, I think that would be cool. She'd be like my aunt."

"Uhh..." My entire brain freezes like it has stage fright. Like in third grade, during the spring play when I was supposed to introduce myself as a raindrop. Instead, I blurted, *I water*, and ran off the stage. Autumn has never let me live that one down.

"She's super nice. And pretty. She'd make a good mom. And then we could have cousins!" The panic is rising in my chest, trying to escape in a scream or strangled moan. Looking around for Hannah to save me shows that she's on bended knee, tending to Rosie's boo-boo. Shit.

"She'll be a great mom one day." The words fall out of my mouth without my permission, but it's the truth. Some day, she'll make a man extremely lucky. Why does that make my stomach sour?

"Oh my goodness, you guys are so sweet!" If heart eyes were a thing, they'd be covering Sara's face completely.

"Sara, you need to understand..."

"How's it going, guys? Great job with the blanket, Sare bear!" Hannah saves my ass from the all-consuming panic. During said panic, Sara was able to interrogate me while also setting up the entire picnic. How is that even possible?

"How's your knee, Rosie?" Sara asks, looking at me and winking as if to say, *your secret is safe with me.*

Totally Autumn two-point-oh.

TWENTY-FOUR
-HUNTER-

An hour turns into a relaxing afternoon packed with catch (the mitt was in Hannah's Mary Poppins bag, plus one for me), chasing around the girls, eating a delicious picnic, and lounging, watching clouds float by overhead.

It isn't until hours later, back in the office, that my mistake hits me.

The clock reads 3:13.

And fuck, fuck, fuck me. Another distraction, fucking up this cursed location.

Frantically, my fingers are flying on keys, trying to make the call in time, even though I see an ominous email from Gina in my inbox.

Begging, cajoling, pacing, and arguing are no help. The construction company canceled our contract when they didn't hear from me, leaving us one week from breaking ground with no one to actually break the fucking ground.

A roar breaks from my chest, anger and disappointment freeing themselves. How the fuck has it gotten to this? How have I allowed this to go so far, allow myself to get so far off track? How have I not learned my lesson?

I want to rage, to yell, and throw things. I want to run downstairs and blame Hannah, explain that *this is exactly why* I can't start this shit with her. But it's not her fault. Not even a little.

With a sigh, I pick my phone back up and call my sister.

"You know we're literally in the same house right now, right?"

"Shut up, do you have a second?"

Her eye roll is practically visible through the phone. "I guess. What's up?"

"Who do we know with a construction company that could start on an extensive project next week?"

"I'm sorry, what?"

"The firm that was supposed to start the build next week backed out for scheduling differences. I was supposed to call before they officially ended the contract but I missed the deadline." Shame suffuses my system.

"You missed the deadline? You. Missed the deadline? Why? How? You're Hunter."

"Jesus, Autumn, I really don't want to get into it, but I was distracted. I was stressed, so I went with Hannah and the kids to their park trip and completely lost track of time."

"You missed an important work deadline because you were with my kids and my nanny. At the park." She sounds a mix of confused, entertained, and excited. With my patience running thin, I take a deep breath in an attempt not to shout at my sister.

"Seriously, Autumn, right now is not the time."

"Okay. Well, shit. That blows. But why are you on it? Isn't that Jonathan's job?"

"He put it in my hands, and to be honest, I'm terrified of calling him and telling him I fucked up without a concrete solution." Even though Jonathan is an ass when stressed, he's helped me grow the business faster than I could have ever daydreamed. He's a great business partner, a hard worker, and a fantastic problem solver. But he's right—it's not fair that I put all the problems for this location I've been pushing on his shoulders.

"Huh. Interesting. Well. Let me think." The sound of fingers on keys, typing away to check her contacts, drifts through the speaker.

"Autumn, seriously, I am so fucked if I can't figure this out. The entire project is screwed. We'd have to refile the permits and zoning restrictions again with the new start date and that week would cost more money, not to mention it would mess up opening timelines, everything. We've already sent out marketing materials with the grand opening date."

"I know, I know, trust me, who do you think has been promoting this? Okay, let me look. No... no... no..." My gut drops deeper into the floor with each negative. "Wait, this might work?" Hope springs within me.

"What is it?"

"What about your friend from high school? He owns his dad's construction company now. Maybe they'd have an opening? It's a long shot, but it couldn't hurt."

"Who, Tanner?"

"Yeah, that's his name."

"I didn't know he runs the business now." I'm starting to realize how out of touch I am with... everything.

"Yeah, a couple of years ago, he took over. You should reach out. If only so you have more friends than King Cranky Pants, Jonathan."

A snort comes from my mouth because he really is consistently a cranky guy. Autumn has never really been a fan of him. "Yeah, okay, I'll see if I can reach out to him."

"So. You went out with Hannah and the kids, huh?" My eyes roll to the ceiling as my finger hovers over the disconnect button.

"Shut up, Autumn, I have things to do."

"Just saying, you guys would be a cute couple!" she yells as the call ends, but her tinkling laughter can be heard traveling up the hall.

"I hate to be that guy who talks business when I haven't seen you in a while, but that's where I'm at. Can you help?"

Tanner Coleman is a tall guy with short blonde hair and a broad build. He sits across from me at the pub right outside town, leaning back in his chair with arms crossed over his chest. It's dimly lit, but not too loud like Full Moon gets. Just a quiet din of diners eating, plates clinking, and beer bottles being set on tables.

"Not gonna lie. It was a surprise to hear from you. It's been, what, 10 years? Longer?" he says with a chuckle. Thankfully, he doesn't seem annoyed but entertained. "You never were great at keeping in touch. Hell, in high school, if I wasn't making plans for us, no one would see you for weeks on end."

He's right, of course. People and relationships aren't exactly my strong suit. Tanner was the people pleaser, quarterback, and homecoming king dating the head cheerleader. I was the kid on the team who would disappear into the woods and sit on the sidelines at parties. Somehow we worked back then, but drifting apart was on my end.

"Yeah, probably. In all fairness, I probably wouldn't even remember to keep up with my sister if it wasn't for her calling me regularly."

Tanner laughs, a deep laugh that brings me back to days hiking out in the woods together, talking trash about the assholes at school and the hot girls we lusted after.

"Okay, look. The timing for this is actually pretty great for us. We had a client drop out last month, so we picked up a few minor jobs here and there, but nothing full scale. If you can get your assistant to send me over the complete details of the project, I can get back to you with a quote by end of the day tomorrow."

"Are you serious, man? You'd do that?"

"Well, I'm not doing it for free, so don't get too excited."

"If you quote a reasonable price, you've got my business. My options are limited and you have an excellent reputation around here." Regardless of Tanner being an old friend, I still made some calls around to check his work. In doing so, I got nothing but glowing referrals. I learned the lesson not to trust someone's work just because you know them years ago.

"Alright, well, have them send it over, and we'll figure something out." Pulling out my phone, I tap out a quick email to Gina as Tanner relays his email address to CC him on.

"So you took over, huh?" I ask, slipping my phone back into my pocket and taking a sip of my beer. The warm relief that washes over me, knowing that at least one issue is possibly fixed, is indescribable.

"It was time. Dad was getting old, and the stress of the daily grind was affecting his health. He signed the business over to me six years ago, and it's been growing every day since." His eyes look lackluster and out of focus as he talks about his business.

"What about Courtney? Whatever happened to her?" Courtney was the homecoming queen that we all figured Tanner would marry and have a crew of kids with by now. His eyes sharpen as a cloud passes over.

"That, my friend, is a long as fuck story that requires a lot harder drinks."

"Ahh, I've had one of those as well."

"Yeah? What kind of story are you working on these days?"

"I can't afford distractions right now. Too much going on. You own a business, you know how it goes." For the third time today, I find myself trying to downplay my... whatever with Hannah and feel grimy doing it.

"See, you say that, but the speed you came to that conclusion and the look in your eyes tells me something' else completely." Fuck, he could always read every one he met all too well.

Glaring at him, I tip my beer back and empty it before answering. "I've been seeing Autumn's nanny."

"I'm sorry, what?" Tanner sputters on the sip of beer he took, clearly caught off guard. "Hannah? Hannah Keller?" I pause, unsure of the right answer. "Long dark hair, big bedroom eyes, sexy as fuck curves, works at the Center?" A growl rips through my chest, making him laugh. "Alright, I guess that's my answer. How'd you manage that? She avoids any kind of relationship like the plague."

Interesting.

"Not sure, it didn't seem to be an issue. We're not in a relationship, though. Just seeing each other while I'm in town. As I said, I'm not in the market for anything."

"Uh, sure. Sure, Hunter." His face says it all, but then a look of hesitation crossed his face. A silence sits between us for a few moments. "Look, I don't want to be that guy..."

"Then don't."

"Bro, just listen. She's a good girl. Sweet to everyone she sees, loves those kids a ton. I don't know her whole story, but I know that her childhood was pretty shitty. Just be careful with her. Make sure she knows what's up."

My gut sinks to my feet, having Tanner confirm what's been in my face for weeks. Hannah is a good woman with an enormous heart, and whether I want to admit it, whether I asked for it, that heart is precariously set in my hands.

"And, from what I see, you're not the settling kind of guy. Nothing wrong with that," he says, hands up in the air in defense. "But something to keep in mind. I wouldn't want to see a girl like that broken."

Although it's tempting to fight him on the subject, I don't, because he's right. And fuck if I have any clue what to do with that.

"Yeah, well, neither do I, trust me," I say before clapping my hands to signal a topic change. "Okay, so tell me what's been going on over the past couple of years in your life, Tan." My hand goes up, tipping my empty bottle to the server, asking for another before Tanner fills me in on Springbrook Hills since I've been gone.

TWENTY-FIVE
-HANNAH-

For three years now, every Friday has been a date night for Steve and Autumn. It's something I started, and insisted on after seeing the stress of work and kids strain their relationship. Since then, every Friday for me is dinner, movies, dessert, and utter kid chaos with my two favorite kids.

This week, we have a special guest.

At the kitchen table across from me eating homemade pizza sits Hunter.

He came down not long after Autumn and Steve left, asking how he could help. At the time, I was elbow-deep in pizza dough, Sara stirring sauce and arguing with Rosie over toppings.

Eagerly, I accepted his help and not because I was overwhelmed.

But because my gut has been so unsettled, a gnawing feeling I can't seem to get past. Our argument about his dad brought to light how tenuous our "relationship" is and how invested I am in it. As dangerous as that is for my heart, I can't see any way around it.

This week went by relatively smoothly, with hidden meetings in the cottage and sneaky kisses here and there. But it's also been another week where he's locked upstairs most of the time, working away at the new location and making sure everything goes without a hitch. Each time I see him, he looks more exhausted and more strained, the bags under his eyes that much darker.

When I accepted his help, he jumped in seamlessly, tackling the mini brawl brewing with a suggestion of mini pizzas where everyone could choose their own toppings. Then he came over to Sara and me, helping by cleaning up around us as we cooked, stirred, and kneaded.

Together, we monitored pizza creation before I cleaned up while Hunter and the kids set the table.

Now we're sitting across from each other, the kids babbling on about camp and pizza and who has the best hiding spots in hide and seek.

Like a car with cut brakes hitting a brick wall, uncontrollable, inevitable, and painful, it hits me. I'm falling for this man. I've created a dream in my mind of family dinners with our two-point-five kids, loving them, working side by side to raise them. Staring at each other across a dinner table while they chatter on every night, then watching them grow up and make us proud.

And, fuck, but I don't know how I got here.

Still, I can envision a future that is so beautiful it makes my soul hurt. A future I want to curate and make happen too badly. And I don't know if he'll ever be in the place to give it to me.

"Hannah?" Hunter asks with a strange look on his face.

"Huh?" I shake my head, snapping free of my daydream and nightmare.

"I said, are you okay? You looked... lost."

Lost is a good way to put it.

"Oh, I'm fine, just zoned out for a bit. So what did you do with Ms. Daisy today, Rosie?" I ask the littlest Sutter, knowing exactly what was on the schedule for Daisy's group but desperate for a distraction. Of course, it works, putting Rosie on a tangent that lasts another 10 minutes. 10 minutes where I stubbornly decide I can't let my mind go there anymore. I refuse.

After dinner, the kids head upstairs to play before sundaes while

I clean up what little we missed. Hunter comes alongside me, drying dishes without being asked. We quietly work together, a synchronized work of what I always thought to be fiction. Again, a sharp stab goes through my chest, a mix of immense pleasure and all-consuming pain.

Side by side we finish out the night, getting a sundae bar together, letting the girls go crazy with toppings before they get baths and slip into pajamas. I try to plan messy meals like this for days. They'll get a bath since Rosie is covered from constantly sticking her fingers in chocolate sauce and her sister doesn't look much better.

Jammies, teeth brushing, and bedtime follows. Sara is easy. I get her water, tuck her in and let her be, but Princess Rosie can be a handful. Hunter gets her started while I settle Sara. As I'm walking to her room, I hear a quiet conversation, making me pause.

"And then what happens, Uncle Hunter?" Rosie whispers, her little girl's voice groggy and slow. Peeking in, I see her tucked into her bed, a princess carriage complete with a lacy pink canopy. Next to her, Hunter is sprawled on the floor, looking positively gigantic, surrounded by miniature toys and furniture.

"Well, then the prince went after the dragon and slayed it, making his entire family proud of him. The town realized he wasn't the bad guy after all, and the Princess kissed him. They fell in love and lived happily ever after." Warmth rushes through me with hope trailing it, hearing the end of his story and realizing there could be a kernel of truth in the fiction.

"I like that story." Her little body rolls away from him with a tiny yawn, curling up into a little ball. That ball will expand overnight into a giant starfish at some point, taking over the entire bed and creating a rat's nest on her head that takes 10 minutes to brush.

"Me too, honey." He bends low to kiss her forehead. Before he catches me watching, I tiptoe past the door and downstairs, where I pull out a beer for each of us.

Not long after, his feet are thumping down the stairs, and he collapses into a chair in the family room. Handing his beer to him, I laugh.

"You okay there, Uncle Hunter?"

"Holy shit, how do you do this every day? How does Autumn do it? No wonder she needed to hire you. I'm fucking exhausted." After taking a long pull on his drink, he sets it on the side table before laying his head back and closing his eyes.

"You get used to it," I say, giggling and sipping my own.

"You're good at this." His eyes are still closed and his body still limp.

"You were a good teammate tonight. Thanks for tagging in." Fidgeting, I tug at the label of my bottle, unsure why I'm still so unsettled.

"Seriously though, how do you do this every day? Two hours of it *with expert help* and I'm dead on my feet." He raises his head to look at me, seemingly looking for an honest answer.

"Besides spending a good chunk of my childhood taking care of my sister, Abbie? I don't know. This is all I've ever wanted. I love taking care of people. Making them feel safe and loved? It gives me energy." My fingers run along the soft gray fabric of the couch, hesitating. The lights in the room are dimmed, mid-summer dusk hitting and giving the room a cozy feel, even though it's barely past eight. Unable to see his face too clearly, I go on, more comfortable than I would be in broad daylight.

"All I've ever wanted was to be a mom. These kids... they're everything to me. I know it's weird. Trust me, Sadie tells me daily that I need a life. But until I have kids of my own to take care of and nurture, to make a difference in, I have them. They have amazing parents, but I love knowing that I'm also there, helping to shape these amazing little people."

Silence takes over, making me uncomfortable, hoping I didn't expose myself too much.

"My dad did all that," he says, his voice low and rough. "When my mom left, he took over everything. I can't even imagine doing all of this with two angsty kids, one income, and trying to keep it together. His heart was broken, but that never hit us."

"Your dad's an amazing man."

"Yeah. He always saw the best in us. That's why he invested in me all those years ago. He saw the passion I had, saw my potential."

"You still have the potential. What about the passion?"

He sighs. "I thought I did. I've been working on this new location, using the failed space. It's good. It's huge. The retail hub is almost two times the footprint of our other locations. And the camping aspect is smart. It has areas for classes that will boost sales, then create repeat customers when they need equipment for their newfound hobbies. But I go there, and I just see my original vision." He's staring off, mind in another place.

"Why didn't you tell me when we went hiking where we were? You told me what it meant to you, but left out that you owned it."

"That day wasn't for harping on my failures. It was getting to know you, taking you somewhere that meant something to me without letting you know about the baggage."

"Baggage makes us who we are."

"But what if we don't like what our baggage says about us? What if the baggage makes us a failure, irresponsible?" God, the pain in his voice. It hurts to hear.

"What happened to that location, Hunter?" I ask, curious. No one has explained it to me, though I've never outright asked. Air leaves his lungs in a heavy blast, and the weight of it fills the room, making it feel stagnant.

"I had a vision. I told you about it—the camp for people to get out, connect with nature, and find a passion. I bought the location, but before it was finalized, they gave me the packet to go over, to make sure I didn't see anything worrisome. I was 23. I was a business major, not a lawyer. I should have hired a lawyer. I know. But my ego..."

"Okay..."

"So I was seeing this girl. I thought she had the potential to be it, to be by my side while I built this empire, while I paved my own way. She came from money, and had no idea how much things cost or how much you had to work for things."

Why does his talking about building a future with a woman who is not in his life anymore make me want to stab something?

"The day I was going through the papers, she wanted to go out with friends. I told her to go, but I needed to read this paperwork. She was spoiled. Never heard no from her dad, always got her way. She told me her uncle could look over it. He was a real estate investor who I'd talked to a few times. A smart guy, knew his shit. So I told her if she sent it to him and he agreed to look it over, I'd go out with her."

My gut drops, already knowing where this is going.

"I was so wrapped up in her. A distraction. God, that morning I was looking at rings. I was going to ask her to marry me at the grand opening. A fresh start to a new life full of promise. When I asked her about it the next day, she said he looked at it and said I was getting a great deal. I was so excited—it was my first investment, and knowing this guy thought I was doing it right was a confidence boost.

"Three weeks later, I'm in a planning meeting with the town and find out it wasn't zoned the way we needed it to be, that the specific zoning permit we needed had been denied twice already. I confronted her, and she came clean, crying that she was tired of me not paying attention to her, that she thought it wouldn't be a big deal, and she wanted more time with me. Tried to make it seem like it was my fault that she'd never even give it to her uncle."

"Oh, Hunter," I whisper, horrified that this woman could be so selfish.

"Before we could finish the zoning fix, we were out of money. I tabled the project, I found a deal on a bankrupt sporting goods store and brought it to my financial advisor, Jonathan. I showed him the plan for Beaten Path I created in school, and he backed me personally. Even though he knew it was my fault the previous idea crashed and burned. Financed most of it and helped to secure investors.

"I named it Beaten Path as a reminder that following the Beaten

Path was the safe option. Retail is basic, there's a structure and a proven record. I can work with that. Creating an entirely new concept is too dangerous. That mistake almost made my dad homeless. That's a mistake I can't make again."

"Hunter, you know that none of that was your fault, right? You were young. You were in love—"

"I wasn't in love. I was in lust, listening to my cock instead of my brain."

"Whatever, you know what I mean. You're older and wiser now."

"Yeah, well, ask Jonathan, and he'll disagree."

"What do you mean?"

"I've been fucking up again. I swear this location is cursed. This week I wasn't on top of the paperwork and missed a huge deadline. We're supposed to break ground next week and still don't have the modified permits because of my fuck up."

"But it's getting done, right?"

He sighs. "It's looking positive. But I can't have any more issues or it will all crash."

"And your vision, what you're building right now—it's what you want?"

"What do you mean?" I can see in the dim light his head is twisted toward me and although it's not clear, I can picture his adorably confused face, brows furrowed and mouth tipped down.

"You're putting this stress on yourself, pushing yourself to make this 'failure' a success," I put air quotes and emphasis on failure, letting him know how I feel about that. "But is it what you want?"

"It's what will be a success. I can't see my dad until I have that success." As much as I want to argue, want to ask him *why*, my gut says to leave that one aside. The last time I brought up his dad ended in an amazing orgasm, but before that was harsh words and hurt feelings.

I stay silent, not knowing what else to say.

"What would you do with it?" he asks, looking at me, interested. He doesn't seem offended that I'm questioning him, but I can vaguely see amusement and curiosity playing across his features.

"I don't know. Not a retail store. No offense," I laugh. His chuckle hits my ears, bringing me a bit of relief and giving me the confidence to continue. "That location... It's so gorgeous. A building there and a giant parking lot sounds like a bummer." He lets out an agreeing sound, which eggs me on. "Okay, ever since you told me your first idea, I've been thinking about it non-stop. A summer camp for kids, like the kids at the Center. My dream summer camp with that Bug Juice style camp experience but also teaching them how to connect with nature, how to channel emotions into healthier habits." I'm on a roll, excitement at the mere prospect heating my veins.

"Sadie's family was really into camping when we were kids. They took Abbie and me a few times on their family vacations. We learned so much. Between the Tates and Maggie, I avoided a life drifting or making poor decisions, I think. You could do that for other kids. Teach them skills for outdoor survival, give them something that they can do, a sense of accomplishment. But affordable, so that everyone gets the opportunity. Or pay what you can model. Or a scholarship. I don't know, I'm not a business wiz like you are, but the impact it could have... And then you have an aspect for adults, to possibly offset the cost and have something when kids are in school. Classes teaching them to connect with the world, release stress, and find new outlets. You could offer fitness classes, and since the summer campsites would be empty, even getaways like bachelor parties or girls' weekends..." I fade off, realizing that I've been babbling and word vomiting.

Hunter's eyes are on me, my eyes adjusting to the dip so I can see them gleaming with something new. Admiration or adoration or something in between. His full lips are quirked like he's amused by me, and all of his attention is laser-focused.

"Sorry, I got a little excited," I say, an embarrassed giggle falling from my lips.

"No, no, I love to hear these kinds of things. That's an amazing idea. Maybe one day." He says, with a sigh. "One day when I'm not answering to a board and out to prove... something."

"I hope you get that chance, Hunter. But I also hope that soon you realize there's nothing to prove."

"Yeah, well, we'll see," he says, finishing his beer.

Standing, he reaches out for my hand before pulling me up into his arms, and kissing me on the head. Everything feels... off.

"Are you okay?" I ask softly. He's so much taller than me, which I normally love, but right now, looking up at him, it feels like another wall between us. Glancing at his guarded face confirms that.

"Holding you? How could I be anything but?" His whispered breaths dance on my lips before he drops his head to brush his to mine. Whether it was a line or his truth, I can't tell, and with his mouth on mine, I find it hard to care.

Lifting me from my waist, he forces my legs to wrap around him, deepening the kiss fast, like the stress of our conversation has made him crave a release. Happy to oblige, I rock my hips into his when he sits on the couch, turning my rock into a deep grind that has him groaning.

"We can't do this here," I moan softly as his lips travel from my lips to my neck. He licks and nips the spot he found the other day right under my ear, making my breath hitch as sparks shoot right to my clit.

"I know." He grabs my hips, guiding them to glide along him so I'm grinding against him in a caricature of clothed sex. I gasp, feeling wetness leak from me.

"We need to—"

The front door clicks with the sound of a key entering and turning. I know that in a few seconds, the heavy wooden door will swing open, Autumn will walk in on heels, a little tipsy, and Steve will saunter in after.

Attempting to scramble off Hunter's lap, I nearly fall to the floor and hit my head on the coffee table before he catches me in the nick of time. My legs are still trapped behind his back, pinning me in place. He stands, setting me gently to the ground. Frantically, I step back and start straightening my clothes.

In comes Autumn, who stops in the doorway with a stutter step, staring at Hunter and me.

"Well, well, well, what do we have here?" Autumn mutters, glazed eyes turning me on to the fact that she may have had more than her normal two margaritas. I'm not sure if I should panic or giggle.

"Babe, what—" Steve follows in, looking at us and smiling. "Oh."

"What have you two been—" Autumn starts.

"Okay, Aut, let's get you upstairs." Steve diverts her attention, directing his wife to the stairs. Thank God for Steve.

"Oh, yeah, it's time for the fun part of date night," she mumbles before Steve guides her up the late wooden staircase.

"Have a good night, guys. Thanks, Hannah," he says before disappearing.

"Fuck," I grumble under my breath. "I need to go." I pull away to scramble off in a fit of embarrassment. My wrist is tugged back, though, making the task impossible.

"Hey, it's fine, I promise."

"Yeah, okay. I gotta head back to my house, though."

"I'll be there in a few minutes. I need to get a bag." When he looks into his eyes, it's clear arguing with him on this will be useless. I guess it's time for this talk, anyway.

"Okay. I'll leave the door open for you." When I say that, a flicker of warmth goes through his eyes before he leans down and gently kisses me.

Not long after, I'm sitting on my couch in pajamas—a pair of pink silky shorts and a matching cami—when Hunter enters with a small yet distinguished overnight bag and locks the door behind him.

"Hey." I mumble the words into my wine, praying that it will soothe my ragged nerves.

"Hey." The bag drops next to the door with a thump before he's at my side in two long strides. "You okay?"

"I'm fine."

"No, you're not. Is it Autumn?"

"Yes?" I'm unsure of what the right answer is. Of course, Autumn catching us making out has my stomach roiling, but it's so much more. It's knowing I'm falling for this man with no safety net. I'm drowning.

"Hey, baby, it's fine. I promise."

"I wanted to keep it a secret until..."

"Until what?"

"Until you were sure," I confess, the words falling out of my mouth ineloquently and harshly. But that's the reality of it. I could fall for him and fall hard. But if he's not open to that, if we pull everyone that matters to me into this relationship and it goes bad because we're not both on that page, it could ruin everything.

"Sure of what?"

"Of us? Of this? Of... I don't know. Of what you want? Look, I know you're busy, and you're not in the market for distractions. I don't expect a confession of love or a marriage proposal. But I can't let this get messy and affect my life. Affect the kids and my job." There. I said it. I might puke, but it's out there.

He runs his hand through his beard. "I know. I know. I can't promise you anything. I wish I could, Hannah. I really wish I could because you deserve that certainty. What I can tell you is I love spending time with you. And the thought of you spending time with any other man makes me want to put my fist through a wall. I don't know if I'll ever be ready for anything more than dating. I just don't know if I have that in me. But I can promise I'll never lead you on."

It's not the confession of love I was secretly hoping for, but the ball is in my court now. Do I accept what he can give me? Do I ask for more? Can I keep my heart safe if things change? When things change?

But the bigger question is, can I walk away right now without regret? With that, I have my answer.

"Okay."

"Okay?"

"Okay, Just... be gentle with me," I beg, hoping I'm not making a huge fucking mistake.

"I can be gentle."

Softly. his lips glide along mine in a kiss that's hesitant and filled with something so close to love that it almost breaks me, almost brings burning tears to my eyes. It's a kiss unlike any we've ever shared before.

Gently, as if I'm something precious that he can't bear to harm, he lifts me from the couch, forcing my arms around his neck. He cradles my body close to his, carrying me to my room, where he places me on the bed just as gently, reverently.

A soft swoosh hits my ears as his shirt falls to the ground, followed by the clinking of his belt and pants hitting next. I quickly discard my pajamas, throwing them aside in time for him to crawl up behind me. He places soft kisses along the way, worshiping me like I'm something precious that he can't believe is in front of him.

"Hunter," I breathe as his mouth circles a nipple, sucking gently. My back arches off the bed at the feeling, eager to get my breast further into his mouth, to get more, feel more.

"Shhh," he whispers, using his hand to pinch the nipple on my neglected breast before switching sides.

"Oh, God." His hand is sliding down, down, down until he hits my curls, a rough finger grazing my clit and making my hips jump. He plays in the wetness there, taking his time to tease me, explore me with just the tips of his fingers.

"Hunter, I need..."

"What do you need, baby? Tell me."

"You, I need more. I need you."

"What about this?" He thrusts two fingers inside my pussy and I can hear my wetness on his fingers as he pushes in, making me moan louder.

"Yes, Hunter, God."

"Is that good, Hannah? Do you like my fingers in your beautiful cunt?" The dirty word makes me moan again, biting my lip and nodding as his mouth goes back to work on my nipple.

"I need you," I mumble, my fingers touching, grasping anything I can reach.

"What do you need, Hannah?" he repeats, still fingering me, but now pressing forward with each thrust. Grazing my g-spot. Making me insane.

"Please, honey." He keeps on waiting for me to tell him, to demand it. "I need you inside me, I need your cock," I whisper, too far gone to be embarrassed or shy.

"Okay, baby." I lose his fingers and mouth, making me whimper. This pulls a smug smile to his lips. "Gotta go get a condom," he says, kissing me quickly and pulling away, rolling to the stash in the bedside table on his side of the bed.

But I can't bear it. I can't bear to lose him, to lose his physical touch. If I do, I might lose my mind.

"I have an IUD."

There's nothing but his eyes on mine for a moment before he breathes in sharp. "Are you sure?"

"Yes, God, please. I want to feel you." I'm begging now, out of my mind with need. I need this connection, I need this reassurance.

Before I can even take a breath, he slams into me, making me shout his name in pleasure. The feeling is exquisite, the sweetest pain. I've never done this with a man. Always careful, always calculated, never wanting a surprise. The intimacy of having him in me without a barrier is beyond words. I'm animalistic.

"Holy fuck, Hannah, baby, so wet, so tight. So fucking good." He grunts with each thrust. He feels it, too, I know it. We're looking into each other's eyes, connected as we've never been before. I see everything there. His trust, his fear. His excitement and joy.

And right before I come, his finger pressing perfectly on my clit, I think I see love.

TWENTY-SIX
-HUNTER-

The next morning I wake up to Hannah on my chest, hair a dark mess across it and down my arm. Last night we stayed up talking about everything under the sun. The music we like, movies we've hated, and where to find the best pizza in town. Learning everything there is to know. The minutiae that make up a person.

I learned her sister is a nomad who she sees every few months, and that she hasn't talked to either parent in over three years. From her few childhood stories, I can't blame her. Turns out that she and Rosie share the middle name Marie and it's not a coincidence. The connection between her and my sister is sincere and meaningful to both of them. No wonder she's been so worried about messing that up.

Last night I made a promise that hasn't been forgotten in the light of morning, nor is it a promise I regret making. While I can't predict what will happen in three months or three years, being gentle with her is something I can swear on.

Warmth is radiating from her body onto mine, and in her sleep, she looks so at peace. The weight of her childhood is something that could bring her down, and create a horrible, untrusting person, but

Hannah is the opposite of that. She's open and kind and giving. Never in my life have I encountered someone like her.

Running a hand down her arm, then her bare hip, I remember we fell asleep naked after one last round where I ate her until she screamed, then fucked her hard until we both came, collapsing until the morning. The no condom thing was a new addition to sex for me, and fuck if it wasn't the most amazing experience.

Finally, Hannah stirs, blinking her eyes hazily, and I'm glad I stayed this morning. The look she gives me, full of relief and joy, affirms that it was the right choice. It's not that I ever truly want to leave her when I stay the night, but it was a necessity when staying under wraps.

"Good morning, gorgeous."

"Uh, hey." A small smile graces her lips, making her look innocent and sexy all at once. "You're here."

"Yeah, honey, I'm here."

"I kinda like waking up with you." *So do I.* More than I would have imagined. I haven't spent a full night with a woman since Chrissy, always leaving before the sun comes up to avoid any misunderstandings.

"You want coffee?" My hand pushes her hair back, revealing the full expanse of her naked back, tempting me to stay in bed longer. As if she reads my thoughts, she giggles.

"As much as I love whatever you're thinking, I need to brush my teeth and drink some caffeine." Rolling over, so she's underneath me, I help her change her mind.

"So we're going over there together? Today?"

"Yes. It will be fine, baby. If we need to, I'll talk to her, but I guarantee she already knows, and knowing Autumn, she's ecstatic."

"You think she knows?!" Her voice has now raised an octave and her face shows a mix of horror and nausea. I have to try not to laugh at her.

"Yes, Hannah. And it will be fine. She loves you. Probably more than she loves me." I run my hand down her arm, squeezing when I reach her hand in reassurance.

"Probably? I'm definitely the favorite." There's my feisty girl.

"Do you want to head over there looking thoroughly fucked?" I ask with a smile, silently begging her to say yes.

"Shut up, let's go." Hannah takes my hand and leads me out of the house, but I stop her one last time, pulling her body into mine.

"It will be fine. There's nothing to worry about," I say, pressing my lips gently to her.

"Okay, I trust you." The look in her eyes tells me she means more than simply with this Autumn situation. Right now, she's putting all of her trust in me, hoping I won't fuck it up. As much as the idea of such responsibility scares the fuck out of me, I'm ready.

We stroll up the flower-lined path of her cottage to the main house, Hannah's little hand in mine trembling slightly. The back doors are already open, letting in the cooler morning air and we step into the house, landing us directly in the kitchen. A hungover Autumn is sitting at the island, sipping coffee with her head propped in one of her hands.

"Huh. So that wasn't just a drunken vision." Hannah blanches.

"Fuck off, Autumn." Releasing her hand gently, I grab a mug to make Hannah a cup of coffee, just the way she likes it. Because I'm a whipped son of a bitch. My sister watches me while I do it, taking in that I know exactly how my girl drinks her coffee.

"Huh," she says again, this time the sound is filled with intrigue.

"Look, Autumn, I... I... uh... I..." Hannah starts and stops, stuttering adorably.

"What Hannah's trying to say is we're together. She's super nervous that you'll be mad or that I'll fuck it up. But don't worry, I've reassured her that if I do, your loyalty lies with her, not with me." Leaning against the counter, I pull the stricken Hannah into my arms, telling her with my body that everything is going to be okay.

"Damn straight," Autumn says, looking me dead in the eye. "You fuck this up, I'll fuck you up."

And that's it. Drama over. It seems Hannah gets it, too because her entire body relaxes against mine.

"Who's fucking who?" Steve says as he walks in the door. "Oh, you guys are finally out in the open. Cool. Don't fuck it up, Hunter."

"What? You knew for sure!?" Autumn turns to her husband, annoyed.

"Yeah, babe. We have a video doorbell, and they weren't very sneaky."

Well, fuck. I completely forgot about those. Hannah is back to ghost status, now from embarrassment and trying to hide in my shirt.

"Don't worry, Han, nothing more than PG was recorded."

"I can't believe you didn't tell me!" Autumn says, smacking her husband's arm. I wince at the sound and the knowledge of how hard that woman can hit.

"Didn't think you wanted to know our nanny was doing the nasty with your little brother, babe."

"Oh my God, kill me now."

"You know, Rosie mentioned Hunter asking you out a few weeks ago, but I thought that was all in her little girl la la land. Guess I need to trust her spy senses more often," Autumn says, taking another sip. This does not surprise me. Rosie has the biggest mouth in the universe.

As if summoned by the mere mention of her name, my little niece comes bounding in. She stops in the doorway. Looks at Hannah. Looks at me. Looks at Hannah. Then, at the top of her little lungs, she says, "*I get to be the flower girl!*"

Now it's my turn to blanch and freeze up, but this is Hannah's territory. "Oh, honey, no, that's not happening." Hannah softens the blow with a sweet giggle that vibrates through my chest.

"That's how it works. You fall in love, then you get a ring, then you have a flower girl," my niece says, one hand on her hip, her other counting down the steps on her little fingers. "Ava's uncle got married, and she was a flower girl, and she talked about it alllll the time, so I want to be one now and get a pretty dress and tell Ava all about how I was a better flower girl than her." Ava of the bitchy mom. It doesn't surprise me that her kid would be of the bragging variety.

"Honey, your uncle and I just started dating. Let's not scare him off too soon," she says, winking at her.

Rosie struts closer until she's right in front of me. Her hair is a tangled bedhead mess, and she's wearing a Minnie Mouse nightgown, which makes it even harder to take her seriously. Then she crooks her tiny finger at me, almost tipping me over the edge. I swear this girl is going to give Steve hell one day.

Instead of laughing, I wisely bend so she can be eye-to-eye with me. "Don't mess this up." One tiny finger stabs me in the chest before she's turning on a heel and skipping off. "SARA! *We're gonna be flower girls*!"

"What on earth just happened?" I'm dazed and still bent forward because I think I've been bullied by a five-year-old. In lieu of answering, all three of them crack up.

Autumn insisted that Hannah take the weekend off and "do something young and stupid." I guess to my sister, that meant calling up her best friend and forcing her to go out for drinks. Not five minutes later, as we walked to the cottage, Hannah's phone rang.

"Hello?" There's muffled mumbling on the other end before Hannah rolls her eyes and hits speaker. "You're on speaker, Sade."

"Hi, Sadie," I say.

"Oh, hey, hot stuff. Your sister called me, we're going out. Do you have any friends?" Hannah's best friend is a force of nature, but you need to admire the girl's balls.

"Uhh, yeah?"

"You mean acquaintances?" Hannah giggles under her breath, and I poke her in the side. She giggles more, the sound beautiful and free.

"Okay, good, I don't want to third wheel it, and I don't have, nor do I want a man. Make sure whoever you invite knows that too, 'kay buddy?"

"Uh, sure?" This woman scares me.

"Okay, so I'm thinking Luna's so that we can say hi to her while we're there and because it's walkable from my apartment. That way, if I get slammed, I don't have to pay an Uber. You guys will need to figure out some kind of DD sitch, though." My head is spinning before she's even done talking.

"Sadie, calm down, where and when. I can figure the rest out," Hannah says in the same calming tone I've heard her use on Rosie. She gets the details from her firecracker of a friend before hanging up.

"So I guess we're going out tonight," Hannah mutters.

"She kind of scares me."

"Yeah, me too. But she's like a sister to me, so I have to love her." Hannah shrugs before she opens her door and lets us in.

This brings us to now, sitting on her beyond the comfortable grey couch, waiting for my girl to be done getting ready and getting on the road. We're not going far, and it's not an exclusive or extravagant club, so I'm not sure of the hold-up.

But when she finally walks out of her room, the wait seems inconsequential.

Her feet are strapped into sky-high, bright red heels with straps along the ankles that I can assure you will stay on tonight when I'm fucking her senseless. Trailing my eyes up her bare legs, I see a dark dress that comes to a full hand above her knee with a sweet, dangerous slit up the side and encases her curves to her breasts, where a straight neckline shows curves, but not cleavage. Two small, sweet strings are tied in bows at each shoulder, holding the black masterpiece up and leaving her entire top nearly naked.

Her long dark hair is down and curled, teased out, and messy. Just begging me to tuck my hands in it and grab a handful. Black lines her eyes, making the ocean blue color look even more striking, while her lips are painted a bright red.

I'm immediately hard and wondering how much later we can be without Tanner being scared off by Sadie.

"Jesus, fuck baby. How am I going to keep my hands off you all night?"

"Uh, I don't know, but you'd better. My hair took forever."

"Your hair would look better with my hands in it." Her eyes widen enough to show that I hit my intended target.

"Hunter, we don't have time for this." She tries to step back as I step closer.

"I'll be quick," I promise.

"Hunter." Taking a step back on those heels, she teeters in them before I catch her. holding her steady.

"Hannah," I growl under my breath.

She's pinned against the kitchen counter, her hips between mine, making me realize with those shoes, she's the perfect height to bend over and... I groan right as I put my mouth to her, knowing we'll be late.

It was worth it.

TWENTY-SEVEN
-HANNAH-

"I cannot believe we are so late." I dig through my bag and try to reapply my lipstick in the bumpy truck.

"Baby, we're fifteen minutes late. Not an hour."

"It's rude, Hunter. Being late shows others you don't think their time is valuable." I absolutely loathe being late.

"Did you come?".

A quiver runs through my core. "Yes."

"Did you do it hard?"

"Yes, Hunter. You know that. What's the point."

"My point is, you came hard. You should be more relaxed."

"I would be relaxed if we weren't leaving our friends wondering where the heck we are."

"Oh, one look at you in that dress, those heels, that hair? They'll know exactly why we're late."

"Ugh! You're not helping!" Hunter simply laughs, pulling into the parking lot for Full Moon, the bar our friend Luna owns and operates.

Walking in, I spot Sadie and Hunter's friend, Tanner, at a small table in the corner. I recognize Tanner from around town his company may have even done some work for us at the Center in the past.

He graduated a few years ahead of me, and in theory, he should be the kind of man whose arm I'm on tonight. Steady, down home guy. Homecoming king, the town's golden boy with roots, someone who will be a clear family man. But comparing the two in my mind, he feels... lackluster.

"You fucked her, didn't you?" Sadie asks, taking a sip of her drink, a bright pink concoction in a tall martini glass, the rim showcasing a perfect lipstick pout. Tanner chokes on his beer. Hunter smiles that arrogant smile.

"Sadie! I will kill you!"

"Babe, that dress, those lips, that sex hair? It's obvious." I want to die. Instead, I turn to Hunter. He's laughing with an 'I told you so' look in his eyes.

"Can you grab me a drink?" I ask, my hand barely twitching in the direction of my bag.

"You even think of offering to pay, we're going back in the Bronco, I'm pulling you over my knee and smacking your ass." I'm not sure if that's supposed to be a deterrent or encourage me to pay. I hesitate, and he smiles a grin, white teeth shooting through his now thick, dark beard. He leans in.

"My baby wants me to smack her ass tonight, we can play. But I'm paying for drinks."

"Okay," I whisper, trying to get control of my lady parts as I watch him walk away.

"Holy fuck, I think I just had an orgasm," Sadie says, before bursting out laughing. It's going to be a long night.

Full Moon Cafe is dark and swanky, but also gritty, a weird yin to its own yang. In the far corner, there's a stage where local bands play occasionally, though tonight it hosts a DJ. A handful of relatively well-known bands have played here before they got big, including the well-known band from Springbrook Hills aptly named Hometown Heroes.

The lights are dim, but not so dim that you can't see each other and have a conversation, but it is loud. Always. Even when it's relatively empty, there's always some kind of loud music playing, blaring from one of Luna's millions of playlists.

In the center of the room is an old, cool-as-all-get-out wooden wrap-around bar where bartenders can see and serve all four sides, making it easy to flag someone down and get a drink. Beaten old tables with mismatched tops and chairs are scattered around the room, but on the weekend, they're pushed toward the walls to make room for dancing.

Sadie and I have been coming here since Luna took over, revamping and renaming the joint. About once a month or so, we get dolled up, head out, and dance until we need to crawl back to Sadie's apartment. Sometimes we drink, sometimes we dance, but we always have a good time.

"Shots!" Sadie screams, pointing at the bar, her short light blond hair bouncing. The low back of her dress threatened to reveal too much at any moment. She walks efficiently in her high, black pumps, a skill we learned to master when we were nine, and raided her mom's closet.

"Get ready for a night out with Sadie," I warn Hunter, who is nursing a beer with a smile, before I tug him over to the bar where Luna hugs Sadie.

"Hey, miss thang!" Luna chirps at me, eyeing Hunter. "Finally gave in and caught yourself a hot one."

"Shut up, Luna. This is Hunter, my..." Stalling, I look at Hunter, unsure of what to call him. 'My boyfriend' feels... weird.

"I'm her man." He puts his hand out to shake Luna's, his tan skin contrasting with her pale. Luna is naturally an arctic princess with super fair skin and nearly white blonde hair. "Nice to meet you."

"What can I get you, handsome?"

"Shots!" Sadie screams again.

"I'm good with my beer. I'm driving." He lifts his bottle towards Luna who nods.

"Party pooper."

"Get the girls and Tanner whatever they want, and open a tab. I've got it."

"I take it back, you're a perfectly fun gentleman." Sadie smiles, facing Luna. "I'll take two shots of your finest tequila, wench."

It's going to be a long, wonderful night.

A few hours later, I'm soaked with sweat, plastering my dress to every curve of my body. At some point, Sadie challenges me to an ass-shaking contest, so we request the perfect song before showing each other up. Laughing hysterically, I almost fall on my turn when Sadie comes around and smacks my ass, so hard I'm sure it will leave a mark.

We're completely drunk, cushioned by the comfort of being two women out drinking with two big dudes who are watching our every move at the bar our friend, sister of a bodyguard owns.

Seconds later, while shaking is commencing, Sadie rooting me on, rough calluses catch on the material of my dress, then a warm chest is over my back.

"That's enough of that," Hunter growls in my ear, making me stand straight and turn around.

"What? Why! We were having fun!" I yell over the music, my arms wrapping around his neck regardless of my annoyance. God, he smells good.

"Because every man in this bar, including my friend, has his eyes glued to your ass and, heads up, Han, I am not that guy."

"What?" I shout over the music. He gives Sadie the one-second finger, then pulls me into a corner that's a bit quieter.

"You're mine, yeah? That body, that ass, it's mine. I'm fine with you wearing a tight dress, showing off, knowing I'll be the one to peel it off you later. I'm not okay with anyone seeing how that ass can move and picturing it moving on top of them."

"Oh," I say, a shiver running through me, picturing just that scenario, Hunter peeling off my dress and then moving...

"But I'm leaving on the heels," he adds.

"Oh." My body feels flushed.

"Feel them digging into me when I eat your sweet cunt later."

"Can we go now?" I ask, my breath coming in pants. Never in my life would I have thought calm, cool, and collected Hunter was possessive or jealous. Why would he, when he lived the way he did, looked the way he looks? But seeing that look in his eyes... Holy shit.

With my words, Hunter laughs, throwing his head back, causing another flutter in my belly. "We'll wait. Get you good and riled up. I'm looking forward to fucking my girl drunk."

"Oh,"

He drags me back to Sadie, where he deposits me, telling me to be a good girl—his words!—before walking back to the bar where he's sitting with Tanner, nursing a beer. It's clear Tanner ribs him a bit about something when he sits, but doesn't seem to bother Hunter. Throughout the night I glance over to see the men deep in conversation. Other times I find Hunter's eyes like a laser on my body, sending ribbons of heat radiating through my body.

Sadie and I are dancing, holding hands, giggling, scream-singing the songs we know, and grooving to the ones we don't. There aren't many we don't know, partly because we both love music and partly because Luna knows what we like, so she curates the playlist for us. We've always connected through music. From the days of creating dances to show her mom to going to Hometown Heroes concerts at the football stadium before they were big.

Nothing is quite as freeing as blasting some music and singing with your best friends.

At some point, I look over at Hunter to see him glaring in a corner. I follow his gaze, looking over Sadie's shoulder to see a man in a dark outfit, watching Sadie's every move.

Now, generally speaking, this isn't odd. My best friend is a bombshell, tiny and curvy and beautiful. But any woman will tell you that her intuition can sniff out a creep at a moment's notice and something is off with this man. It seems Hunter knows it, too.

Minutes later, when I look over again, the man is gone, forcing me to sigh internally with relief. We drink more, dance more, sweat more, until we decide it's time to take a break, heading back to the guys. Hunter is still watching me with an intensity that is turning me inside out, reminding me of his promise for tonight. Maybe it's time to head out and get the night started.

-hunter-

Watching my girl dance has been pure torture. She writhes and grinds on her friend, oblivious to the men's gazes on her. I silently glare at each man who is getting a little too interested, telling them with my eyes that I will fuck them up if they even get close.

All I want is to throw her over my shoulder, toss her in my truck, and get her to the cottage away from prying eyes and out of that goddamn dress.

But then it happens. Some fucking asshole comes up behind Sadie, daring to put his hands on her hips when it's been clear all night that men were not on her agenda. She turns, gives him the polite smile and shake women give men when they're not interested, then turns back to my girl with wide eyes.

That would be fine. A guy can shoot his shot. But he doesn't leave. Instead, he chooses to grip her hips tighter, forcing her to turn towards him. Elbowing Tanner, I stand, making my way toward the women. Sadie turns to the creep again, this time frustrated and annoyed, too brave for her own good. There are a few muffled shouts, and it's clear his hand, now on her shoulder, has tightened to a point of hurting her.

I see red.

Racing forward, I move Hannah and Sadie aside, yelling for

Tanner to get them out before cocking my arm back and crashing my fist into the man's face.

"What the fuck!" I grab the collar of his shirt and press him to a wall, ready to go for more.

"The lady said no," I growl in his face, my spit hitting his face in my anger. There isn't much that gets a genuine reaction from me, but displays of men not respecting women are one of them. Probably the curse of my only sibling being a sister.

"She's been a fucking tease all night. Everyone can see she wants some dick."

"If a woman says no, that means no, no matter what the fuck your twisted scum brain tells you."

"Fuck you, man, who the fuck do you think you are."

"A man with fucking restraint, making you a lucky fuck," I say, grinding his face into the wall a bit harder. But common sense is coming back to me, the haze slipping away, and I realize I could probably get away with one hit. More than that could get messy.

"Hunter, the police are on their way," Luna says, her voice soft and strong, and I take a second to realize the music has turned off, a jarring silence all around.

"Sit here, I'll be back," I say, tossing him into a chair before heading to my girl to check on her. "You okay, Sade?" I'm pulling Hannah into my arms, needing to touch her and know she's okay. Her tiny body is shaking, from nerves or adrenaline, I don't know.

"Totally. Thanks. That was kind of hot, like Roadhouse or something." Does anything shake this chick? She smiles and winks at me, making me shake my head. Next, a scuffle is heard from where I left the douche bag.

"Hey, stay there!" Some random guy says, and I see the guy I punched heading out the door.

"Fuck."

"Leave it. I don't want to press charges, and we don't need you getting any attention for this," Sadie says.

She's right, of course. With everything going on, the last thing I need is attention, someone saying I punched a random man at a bar unprovoked or some shit like that. But still. "Are you sure? He hurt you." Glancing at her shoulder shows evidence of how hard he grabbed her, the skin red and already darkening.

"No big deal, just glad I had two big, macho men to protect me." She smiles, putting on a great facade, but I can see underneath she's tweaked.

Either way, I nod and drop the subject. I'm pretty sure she's got a brave face on right now, not willing to show how she's really feeling or how deeply it's affected her. But as someone who buries things myself, I know to respect that and not press it.

"Let's go home," Hannah whispers, still tucked tight under my arm.

"Can you walk me home, handsome?" Sadie asks Tanner, who looks as frustrated as I feel.

"Sure. But Luna called the cops, and I think you should stay, and make a statement."

"They'll be here in five, I talked to Tony myself." The ethereal bar owner comes over. "No offense, but I need you guys to stay. I need to make a note of anything even vaguely violent that happens here to protect my ass."

"Of course, Lune. Can I get a shot, though?" Leave it to Sadie.

"On the house, all of you."

"Not for me, I'm driving." Too many stories have crossed my news feed of people driving home a hair over too drunk and ruining lives. Two beers is my limit.

"Same here, but for the girls," Tanner agrees, directing us to the bar while Luna sets up three shots for Hannah, Sadie, and herself.

The police come and take our statement, and I chat with Officer Tony Garrison, who was another buddy of mine in school. Seems like I have a lot of... friends coming out of the woodwork now. Tony pulls Luna aside, and they talk, the conversation awkward and intriguing, but not my place. Before we head out, I make plans for a drink with

Tony and Tanner, hopefully with less excitement. With everything settled, I'm free to take my girl home.

Hannah is still tipsy, and as the drama from the night settles, the air in the Bronco begins to feel electric, fueled with alcohol, adrenaline, and lust.

Glancing over at a light, I see Hannah watching me, lip between her teeth, rubbing her palms up and down her bare thighs like she doesn't know what to do with them.

"You good, baby?"

"Uh, yeah." I raise an eyebrow at her in question, knowing the source of her jitteriness. "That was so fucking hot," she blurts out, then, in an adorable move, covers her mouth with delicate, pink-tipped hands.

"What was?"

"You, That guy. Punching him?" Her voice is unsure, as if the concept she would find that attractive is strange. "It was hot."

"Oh yeah? Huh."

"Like, really, really hot," she breathes, her chest heaving. There's no bra under that tiny dress, and the evidence of that is clear in her tight, hard nipples showing through the fabric. The light turns green and my foot slams the gas, needing to get home now.

Reaching over, my fingers grasp one end of the bows on her shoulders, holding up the top and tug at it. Thank fuck it's dark as sin out, because one corner of her dress drops, revealing her gorgeous tits. Not too big, not too small, a perfect handful. Her skin is creamy white and covered with a layer of goosebumps. The quick intake of breath tells me it was an unexpected move, but the rubbing of her legs together incessantly tells me not an unwelcome one.

"We really gotta stop doing this shit in cars," I mutter, trying to maneuver my hand to touch her exposed flesh. It's awkward and a strange angle, but she's so fucking hot, so turned on, and the house seems so fucking far.

The squeak she makes when my fingers meet her nipple makes it worth it, and I pinch, the noise getting higher and hotter. "You like that, baby? You like me touching your pretty tits, pinching them?"

"Fuck, Hunter, yes." Every time this woman utters my name, my dick jumps as if she's addressing it personally. My hand leaves her tit to reach down and adjust myself, palming to release a bit of pressure. Hannah watches me, a small groan escaping her throat at the sight. I can't help but smirk. My fucking girl gets off on that, watching me stroke myself.

If she wasn't so eager to have my cock in her at all times, I'm pretty sure she'd just sit and watch me touch myself. That's an idea I file away for the next time I'm out of town.

"You wanna watch me jack off, baby?" She groans again, her tiny hand trailing up to touch her own tit, pinching hard and moaning while she nods. "Fuck Hannah, you're the perfect woman."

As I say that, the Bronco pulls into the gravel drive. Showtime.

TWENTY-EIGHT
-HUNTER-

After throwing a giggling Hannah onto her bed, she works on taking her dress off. My hands land on hers, stopping their progress immediately. Tonight, that's my job—I want to peel it off her, to unwrap my package.

"Let me." I move her soft little hands from the ties before undoing the one shoulder strap left. A quick tug at the strings and the entire front drops forward, revealing tempting nipples begging for my mouth. Of course, I oblige. Bending low, I take one in my mouth, nipping before sucking hard while I tug on the opposite one with my fingers. Her back arches, and her hands are in my hair, pressing my face closer as she moans.

"Holy shit, Hunter." Her hips lift, grinding the air, begging for more, for friction. We work together to tug off her dress, and I find a small hidden zipper on the side before I tear it in my haste. Eventually giving up, I let her take over while I remove my own clothes. I'm desperate to have her skin on mine. This hungry for a woman is so foreign to me, this reckless in my need.

Finally, the tiny dress is off, leaving her in a small scrap of lace parading as panties and nothing else, nothing but miles of olive skin for my mouth and hands to explore and taste. She bends forward to get her shoes off.

"No, Leave them." All night I've been fantasizing about fucking her with those on. With a tipsy smile, she leans back on her bed, her dark hair a mess behind her, eyes glazed with lust. I bend my body towards her, and my finger hooks into the waistband of her tiny, black underwear and yank, dragging them to her knees.

Instead of pulling them over her feet, I leave the panties where they are, a seductive constraint, and dive face-first into her wet pussy. it's already dripping, glistening with her excitement and practically begging for my mouth. Slowly, so fucking slowly, savoring the soft breath that escapes her mouth, I drag my tongue from her entrance to her clit, sucking hard at the swollen nub.

Once again, her back bows off the bed, leaving just the top of her head on the pillows this time as she moans loudly. A groan creeps up my chest and into her pussy as my hands go to her hips. One hand presses to her belly, keeping them down and urging her closer to my mouth, not allowing her any relief.

And then I'm eating her, feasting like a starving man. That's how she makes me feel, anyway. Starving for her, for her body at all times. The slurping sounds my mouth makes against her sopping pussy are explicit and hot, my cock throbbing hard in my boxers. I creep a hand to her entrance before hooking two fingers into her, filling her as I continue to suck.

Hannah screams my name again, those heels digging into my shoulders as she does. Breath pants over her clit as her pussy tightens on my fingers, a fresh wave of liquid soaking my hand. She's close. So fucking close, I can feel it. And I'm dying to make her come on my face.

"Come on my mouth, baby. Gonna eat it all up, then I'm gonna fuck you hard." I pause my mouth only to make my demand, looking into her eyes before returning to her clit. I suck hard, simultaneously pressing hard on her g-spot from inside, and she explodes, liquid gushing on my hand and face. I lick her clean, and by the time my body is coming up on hers, she's squirming again, hot and ready for me.

My lips meet hers, tongues clashing, hot breath mingling. The wetness in my beard is being spread across her face, making it all the more erotic. Removing my boxers and freeing my aching cock, I straighten to sitting, ass to heels. My girl is spread before me, writhing, already needing me again. Two fingers find their way into her, thrust hard a few times before my hands are back at her hips, dragging her up to my cock.

Slowly, I press the head into her, looking into her eyes as I do. Her eyes are hooded and glazed over, lips parted as my cock slides in, then out, then in again, over and over, little by little, until it's seated completely in her.

Then I stop.

"Hunter, what are you—"

My thumb hits her clit while she's full of me, rolling the sensitive nub and her eyes slam shut as she whines. "Hunter, please!" She's begging me to fuck her, her head lolling from left to right in desperation.

"Please what, baby?" I ask in a tease, still rolling her clit.

"God, fuck me, Hunter!"

"You ready for that? Gonna be hard, baby." She groans, and I smile before I give in, pulling back and slamming back in. The feeling is all-consuming, a rightness that shouldn't exist, but here she is. Here we are. *This woman.* With each thrust, I look into her hooded eyes, and watch her take one step closer to the edge. Her tight pussy is squeezing my cock, forcing me to concentrate, and work her to make sure she gets hers again.

"Gotta come, baby, need you to come on my cock." I growl at her, pounding in, still on my knees above her, watching her tits move with each thrust. And then she shatters. Her back bows off the bed, hips grinding into mine, forcing my cock to plant deeper than ever. Feeling her convulse around me has me coming alongside her, exploding as a firework display goes off behind my eyelids. The release, the experience—hell, this woman—is so much more than words can explain.

So much more than I'm ready to admit.

The shrill scream of my phone jolted me out of sleep, and I slap at the side table blindly. Squinting at the bright screen, Autumn's name is flashing alongside the time.

3:54 in the morning.

No good call comes at four in the morning. My stomach drops, making me instantly nauseous.

"Who is it?" Hannah mumbles into my chest.

"Autumn." My finger swipes across the screen. "Hey, what's wrong?" My voice is still rough and groggy with sleep.

"Hunter, you need to come to First Presbyterian. Now. They've just admitted Dad." *They've just admitted Dad.* Shit, shit, shit. I am not ready for this, not at all.

"What do you mean they've admitted him?" My hands press into the bed, pushing my body until I'm sitting straight. Hannah is next to me, scrambling to sit as well, her face white.

"I'm on my way, I'm not sure. They called me, and I didn't get any details. I was going to wake you, but you're not in the guest room, so I figure you're with Hannah."

"God, I'm sorry, Autumn, we went out and..." Another sign of my fuck up. My sister needs me, my dad needs me, and where am I? Naked, sleeping in the nanny's bed.

"Shut up, Hunter, get dressed and head over. Bring Hannah. Steve is with the kids." She hangs up, leaving me sitting cold with the phone to my ear.

"Hunter, what's going on?" Hannah is looking scared and worried. She's close to my dad, but that's not my concern right now. All I care about is getting to the hospital before it's too late.

"My dad's been admitted to First Presbyterian. I need to go."

"I'm coming, let me get some pants on." The urge to argue and force her to stay is strong, but common sense tells me she won't back down, and time is limited.

"Fine, hurry."

We get to the hospital in half the time that it should take, part in thanks to an empty highway at 4 a.m. and the rest because of reckless driving. After parking, we clamber out and into the hospital, where we're directed to the correct floor.

"Oh, thank God you're here," Autumn says as the doors shut behind us, running over to me. Her arms wrap around me tight, and she immediately sobs into my shirt. I try to reassure her, rubbing her back and whispering words of comfort, but it's no good. And I know nothing will help until she knows for sure our father will be okay.

"Autumn, what happened?"

"They went to give him his medication, and he was on the ground, unconscious. Not responding. We're waiting for more information, but that's all I have."

"Who can I talk to? We need answers. We need—" Hannah touches my arm, distracting me from what I was saying. "Go sit, Hannah." My voice comes out more stern and gruff than intended, and I shake her arm off mine. I need space.

Autumn's red eyes are wide, but we have bigger problems to deal with than Hannah's hurt feelings. "Hunter, there's nothing we can do right now. They said when they know anything at all, the doctor will come out with more information. Calling for them now will just take them away from the actual job at hand."

"I want to make sure—"

"Hunter, trust me, I would stand at that nurses' station for hours if I thought it was worthwhile. It's not." She's got her mom voice on, and it irritates me. But it sounds like sound logic, whether or not I like it. "Fine," I say, then sit down next to Hannah, who avoids looking me in the eye.

"Ronald Hutchins?" A doctor comes in through the double doors, calling for attention. The call is unnecessary since we are the only people in the waiting room, and I've been watching the door like a hawk since we sat. Hannah picks her head up from my lap, a crease on her cheek from my pants.

"That's our father," I say, standing and walking towards him. "What do you know?"

"Well, the good news is, your father is doing well and is going to be fine. The bad news is he hit his head pretty hard when he fell. It seems Mr. Hutchins stood to use the bathroom and had a dizzy spell, and fell on the ground. Couldn't have been down for more than a few minutes before the nurses found him. We had to do some surgery because he broke his elbow pretty bad, but other than that and a concussion, he's fine. We're in contact with his oncologist to have them in and do a full evaluation in the morning. He's out from surgery and awake, in good spirits, so you can head back. When you see him, you will notice his head is wrapped from a minor laceration he endured when he fell, and there are many wires and monitors, but those are simply to make sure things go as we foresee."

Relief washes through me, a relief that I didn't even know I needed.

"Can we see him?" Autumn asks, looking both eager and terrified.

"You can, one at a time. I can take one of you back with me, then you can swap out."

"Do you mind if I go first? I can head home after, relieve Steve." Of course, I nod, thanking the doctor and sitting next to Hannah. So much is running through my mind that I don't realize she's talking to me until she places her hand on my arm gently.

"You know, Hunter?" Hannah is looking at me expectantly.

"Hmm?" I'm still half-dazed, trying to come to terms with the fact that my dad is fine—for now. I have no clue what she even said.

"I said that's great news. Ron's going to be fine with little to no side effects."

"Yeah, sure," I say before looking away. She wants me to comfort her and talk with her, but right now, my patience is zero. I just want to be in my head. Hannah seems to get the hint, staying quiet until Autumn comes out, eyes red and puffy but looking relieved all the same.

Walking over to her, my arms are around her in a moment, letting her cry on my shoulder once more. "Oh, Hunter, he looks terrible. He's awake and alive, but the machines, the tubes..."

"Go home, Autumn. Take Hannah with you. I'll be home later," I say, kissing her forehead. She tries to stop me, to talk to me, but I keep walking, following the directions the nurse gave us until reaching door 102.

The brown faux wood door that seems to be in all hospitals is already open, revealing my father lying in a bed, white sheets pulled up to his chin. The man I idolized my whole life, strong and stable and larger than life, looks tiny and frail. His head is wrapped in white gauze, with multiple IVs in his arms. The sight is terrifying—no wonder Autumn took it so hard.

"Hey, Dad." My voice doesn't sound like it comes from my body, both croaky and soft.

"Ahh, the prodigal son arrives!" he says with a smile, but it cuts through my gut all the same. I'm not sure what I expect, but to be honest, him being awake and messing with me is far from it. "Apparently, I had to land in the hospital to convince you to come to see me finally."

"God, I'm sorry. Had a lot going on. How are you feeling?" The guilt is eating at me, acid churning in my stomach and making me sick.

"Shut up about me. I've been waiting a month since you've gotten into town for you to come to see me. Now tell me, what's new?"

"Dad, we can talk about that any time. You just had a medical emergency and surgery. We could have lost you."

"Hunter, I spent 20 minutes listening to your sister hem and haw and cry over me. Give your old man a break from the health shit and tell me what's new." I pause, unsure of what to say, what to tell him about.

"Uh, well, we're finally making use of the Springbrook Hills acreage. Turning it into a retail space with recreational sales components." It sounds like I'm pitching him. Why do I sound like this? The fact that I don't have more to tell him, that I can't tell him we broke ground, that things are concrete, that the project is in motion, is killing me. Had I stuck to my original timeline, had I not gotten distracted and fucked up too much, we'd be a week in. I'd have visited him, told him everything, and made peace already.

"Autumn told me. Sounds great, kid. Are you happy with it?" The question hits me out of nowhere, making me dizzy and weak. What is *wrong* with me?

"It's a great decision for the company. The market in this area is huge for hiking and mountain biking, and the additional campgrounds will be a great beta project for future locations."

"Fuck, boy, are you a robot?"

"I'm sorry?"

"A robot, a robot who's taken over my son's body. You sound like you're reading a damn pamphlet," he says in his distinct, gruff voice.

"Uh, no, just telling you the details of the project. It's a great opportunity,"

"What about that camp?"

"What camp?" I ask, confused.

"The one you planned for originally. Helping people, giving them experiences in nature, helping them cope with things naturally and connect."

"That's not feasible. It's not as profitable an idea as the Beaten Path campgrounds and retail store."

"Who the fuck cares?"

"Well, my advisors, for one."

"That's your company, you own it."

"And?"

"And why aren't you following the passions that brought you here."

"Following those passions is what got me in trouble in the first place." How could he not remember this? The passion I had put me in a position that almost ruined *everything*.

"No, being young and cocky and impatient got you in trouble." His thick grey and black eyebrows are pressed together, bringing the deep lines on his forehead deeper. "Hunter, you're not still tied up with that, are you?"

"Dad, I don't really want to talk about this right now. Can we talk about you?"

"Are you still tied up with everything that happened all those years ago?" His brows are furrowed, concern awash on his face. I sigh, rubbing my hand over my beard.

"Of course I am. Why do you think I'm using this location?"

"Not financially, emotionally. Do you feel some shit about that still? Guilt for that? Or, I don't know, do you think you need to prove something?"

"Look, I'm not here to talk about this. Let's talk about you, let's talk about something else. You collapsed and were unconscious, breaking your fucking elbow." My throat is thick from saying that out loud.

"Fine, we can change the subject, but we're not talking about me. Why don't we talk about Hannah?" There's a twinkle in his eyes of humor, a glimpse at my dad, the man underneath this illness.

"Hannah?" I say, confused. What does she have to do with any of this?

"Yeah, Hannah. Sweet girl, pretty brown hair, gorgeous face, makes amazing cookies?"

"I know who Hannah is, Dad. What does she have to do with anything?"

"Autumn tells me you're dating her. Excellent choice, bud. I'd go after her myself if I was 30 years younger."

"We're not serious." Saying that feels dirty, like a sin that will stain my soul. "We're just having fun while I'm here."

"She doesn't seem like a just having fun kinda girl, son. That woman is the kind you pin down and marry before she gets smart and dumps your ass." And *that* makes my gut sink like a stone, a dense, nervous feeling that's solid, makes something in my soul heavy.

Before I can answer, refute the fact or agree, I'm not sure, a nurse in light pink scrubs comes in, knocking on the door frame. She's in her mid-sixties, pretty and kind looking, with a dark brown, blunt haircut.

"Hello, Ron, who do we have here?" She eyes me skeptically with a smile playing on her lips. "Oh, well, that's obvious. You two look exactly alike. Good to know you looked just as good as a boy," she says with a wink.

Normally anyone calling me a boy would raise my hackles, but something about the combination of the warmth in her brown eyes and the fact she was clearly hitting on my dad doesn't bother me.

"Ahh, I can only hope to look that good when I'm as old as he is," I joke, winking at my dad.

"A flirt, just like your dad, I see." She smiles and tucks a lock of hair behind her ear before looking at my dad. "Well, gotta break up this party, time for Ron to get some sleep." My dad smiles back at her, making me wonder what is going on here.

"Alright, son, you go on, find your girl and get back to your sister's." Rather than argue, I bend to hug my dad, something I don't know the last time I've done. He pats my back in a pleased and relieved way that washes a mix of love and guilt through my bones. I walk through cold, sterile hallways back to the waiting room to leave.

When I arrive back to the waiting room, sitting curled in a ball, her long hair draped over the uncomfortable, hard plastic is Hannah. First, warmth suffuses through me, knowing she fought Autumn tooth and nail to stay here. Staying even knowing she had no other way of getting home because she wanted to be there when I got out, to check my pulse.

Warmth in the knowledge that she was worried for me, so worried about my dad that she stayed to make sure all was well.

And then annoyance that she didn't listen to me. That she *never listens to me.*

Then guilt for feeling that way, followed by frustration because conflicted emotions like this are the absolute last thing I need right now.

"Han, wake up," I say, touching her shoulder. She pops her eyes open and sits too quickly, making her rock unstable on her feet. My hands reach out to grab her arms and steady her, but I take them back once she settles, putting them in my pockets.

"Oh, Hunter, how's your dad?"

"Fine, for now, let's go." Not grabbing her hand or urging her to follow in any way, my feet aim towards the door and start walking, eager to get out of this place, away from the smells and the beeps and claustrophobia.

We get into the truck, quickly heading back to Autumn's in silence. Hannah is gnawing on her lower lip. The tips of her white teeth popping out to grab the pink lip, concern, and confusion in her eyes.

Pulling up to the small drive for the cottage, the Bronco's tires crunch familiarly, and I put the truck in idle, giving a clear indication that she is to get out, but that I am not following.

She turns to me, grabbing my hand. Her face now looks frantic and concerned, like she knows what I'm thinking, knows what's happening. "Come inside, spend the night." Her voice is soft and nervous, pleading.

"I don't think this is a good idea. I'm gonna go back to Autumn's."

"What do you mean? What's not a good idea? Spending the night?"

"Everything. All of it. Spending the night, us. It was all a bad idea." Even to my own ears, I sound cold and cruel. Saying the words leaves a terrible taste in my mouth like my body is revolting to the truth, but it's just that—the truth. This was all a terrible idea.

"What are you trying to say?" A sigh is released from my soul as my hand runs down my beard, frustrated that she's playing this game. We both know what's happening.

"Exactly what I just said. You're a smart girl, Hannah, I don't think I need to spell it out. This is a bad idea. We need to stop."

"Come on, Hunter. You don't mean that. It's been a long day, you're stressed—"

"No, you're not getting it. This is done. You're nothing but a distraction. I came here with two goals, just two fucking things I had to do, and instead, all I've done is fucked around with you."

"Hunter, you're so wrapped up in proving yourself that you're missing the life in front of you. You're not living the dream because you're trying to *chase* the dream. But Hunter. The dream is right here in front of you." Tears are welling in her bright blue eyes, like waves in their ocean depths. Looking away is the only way I can focus, so I stare at the trees in front of us, the light glinting on her cheery blue front door and the morning light breaks through.

"Yeah, I'm going to take my business and life advice from a woman who doesn't even have a real job and uses other people to get her kid fix because she's too scared to have her own." God, I'm a fucking dick, but the only way I'm going to get through to her is to break her heart. Make her hate me. The business needs my entire focus, my dad needs my focus.

She hesitates, her skin blanching another shade to an unfamiliar, pasty white. It looks wrong on her normally beautifully tanned face. "That was mean, Hunter." Her voice cracks with her words, sending a wave of nausea through me. *Just go, Hannah. Get out of the truck. Don't make this worse.*

"No, Hannah, what it was is honest. Everyone uses kid gloves around you because you had it rough, but you need a dose of reality. I'm not going to be that guy to give you the white picket fence and two point-five kids, and I'm sure as fuck not going to be your happily ever after. I have more important shit to figure out, and this—this—fling has gotten me off track even more. My dad is dying, and you're just a distraction. I'm over it."

Looking over at her, it's clear the target was hit, that I broke her, and she's done. Still so strong, still not crying, still more beautiful than I can bear. Her face shutters, reaching for the door handle and fumbling before it catches. Then she drops her parting words.

"You know what, Hunter? You're right, we're done. I don't deserve this. Have a nice life. I hope you figure out how to live it before it's too late."

TWENTY-NINE
-HANNAH-

The noise of the truck door behind me sounds how my heart feels: crushed, destroyed, slammed. Still, not a tear drops as my feet thunk up the brick pathway, lined with cheery flowers that I hate at this moment.

Just a few more steps, I plead with myself. *Come on, girl, you've got this. Get behind the door.*

Reaching into my pocket, the keys feel clunky and confusing in my hands. I'm fumbling, scratching my lock, scratching the blue paint on my door.

"Fuck," I mutter, the words burning my throat that is coated with unshed tears. *Come on, just a few more moments.* He's still in the truck behind me, not pulling out to park in Autumn's drive. *Such a gentleman, waiting until I get inside.*

The key slips in the lock and turns, allowing me to twist the doorknob and whip it open desperately, no longer able to look calm and collected. I'm so close. As the door slams behind me and I slide to the ground, finally allowing the tears to fall, all my heart can say is, *I told you so.*

THIRTY
-HANNAH-

On Monday, I call in sick to the Center.

It's the first time I've done that in four years, so Mags immediately agrees, but not without a good measure of concern in her voice.

After dropping off the kids to camp, I go back to the Sutter's and spend hours and hours cleaning. Stress cleaning is how I process most of the emotions I have ever felt.

Okay, fine, it's how I *avoid* most emotions.

The truth of the matter is that I'm in pieces. Shattered across my tiny cottage are shards of me stuck in memories of us. Memories are embedded in each corner and fiber of my home, everywhere I go, I'm reminded of what we had. And fuck, if this isn't why I avoid men. This is why I've spent my entire life guarded, carefully choosing each person in my life. Vetoing men who didn't meet every single standard, who didn't fit the mold of who I envisioned for myself. Of who I need in my life.

Because when you fall in love, and he breaks your heart, you're broken irreparably.

Thankfully, Hunter's truck hasn't been at the house since

Sunday, meaning I can compulsively clean without fear of an awkward run-in.

On Tuesday, I call out again, this time exhausting myself with yard work even though Steve hires an amazing lawn service that takes care of everything. The need to do something with my hands is overwhelming, and the need to distract myself from the hollow hole in my chest all-consuming. Normally I'd tend to my garden, weeding and taking care of my fabulous fairy garden, but all I see there is him.

Even my sanctuary, my private happy place, is stained with memories of Hunter.

Wednesday, my guilty conscience won't let me miss another day at the Center, so I head into work. Still, I'm very careful to stay as far away from Mags as possible. The woman can read into my soul, pull out the most painful shard, and then get me to talk about it until I'm a bloody mess at her feet. As much as I adore her, I can't emotionally handle that right now. I'm not ready.

By Thursday, I'm pretty sure the girls have noticed what is happening. On Thursdays, the kids stay home from camp, and we do something fun, but we stayed home, watched movies, and ate cookies. The whole time, Sarah kept side-eying me, confusion and worry on her face.

On Friday, my worst fear happens. Exactly what I was trying to avoid from the very beginning.

"Hannah, why are you so sad?" my sweet, sweet crazy Rosie asks as we drive home from camp, more attentive than I give her credit for.

"Me? I'm not sad, bud!" The voice I use is sugary sweet and baked with pep, and it sounds fake as fuck, even to me.

"Yes, you are. I heard Mommy telling Daddy that Uncle Hunter is an asshole for letting you go. Is that why you're so sad?" My emotions are bubbling in a weird mix of hilarity, exhaustion, and heartbreak, but I beat them all down to reprimand her.

"Hey, Rosie, you know that's not a nice word. And haven't we talked about listening in to grown-up conversations?"

"Sorry, Hannah."

"So, did you guys break up?" Sara asks. My eyes meet hers in the rearview, and there's no way I can simply brush them off.

"Yes, we did. But that's fine, we're still friends, and you know friends are the best kind of people!" I say, my voice going up at least an octave.

"I won't be a flower girl?" Rosie sounds absolutely crushed, making me want to crumble alongside her.

"Rosie girl, I promise that whenever I finally get married, you can be my flower girl."

"He's an idiot," Sara grumbles under her breath. This is *exactly* what I was trying to avoid. This is *exactly* why Hunter, of all men, was the worst idea for me. What the fuck was I thinking, getting involved with my boss's brother?

"Sara, stop it. Sometimes people just aren't meant to be together." She looks skeptical, but as I say it, we pull into the drive, and I make a big show of getting everyone out and into the house, effectively changing the subject.

It doesn't come back up all night.

On Saturday, the Bronco is back in the drive, and my heart is in my stomach, making me feel like barfing at every and any creak around the house. I'm jumpy, wondering when he'll come around the corner and when I'll have to finally face him, since Autumn and Steve asked me to watch the girls while they went to a wedding.

Turns out that's at around lunchtime when I'm doling out fruit and sandwiches in the kitchen, and he comes down the stairs looking as handsome as ever.

His hair is a mess, a sign I learned during our short time together means he's been stressed and running his hands through it incessantly. Dark circles line his eyes, a nod to what I assume is his lack of sleep. Under the layers of makeup I've taken to slathering on this week, I have twins to his. He's dressed in a white button-down and black slacks, making this the first time since he came to stay here he's not dressed casually. And fuck if my body forgot that we're not together, instantly drawn to him and craving his touch.

Of course, I remind myself why that's no longer a possibility.

"Hey girls, Hannah," he says, walking past us to the coffeepot. He's reaching high to grab a mug, his shirt stretching against his back to show with definition his beautifully muscled back, and—*No! Hannah, get it together.*

Fuck. This is impossible.

"Hello, Hunter, anything I can help you with?" I'm aiming for a polite and unaffected tone, but I'm afraid I gave off strained and hysterical.

"Nope, just getting some coffee. How are you guys?" Hunter asks the kids.

"Fine," Sara says, the words short, nose staying in her book.

To my horror, Rosie, sweet, sweet Rosie, stares at her uncle, picks up her sandwich, and takes a bite, making it clear she's not talking to him. Shit.

"Uh, Rosie, your uncle asked you something."

"I heard," she says after swallowing. Never in my life has this girl talked back to me, much less any other adult, with such blatant disrespect. Fuck, fuck, *fuck.*

"Rosie! Attitude!" I say, trying to stop this from getting worse. Instead of apologizing, she puts her sandwich down and crosses her arms over her chest. "Sorry. She's... in a mood right now," I say in apology, refusing to meet Hunter's eye and beginning to clean up the lunch mess. "Tired, I think."

"Not your problem." He sounds curt and professional, breaking me all over. How did we get to this place again? This place of short replies and distance.

"She's mad because you broke Hannah's heart," my sweet Sara says quietly. Looking over at her, I see the depths of her soul and the disappointment on her face.

"And I'll never be your flower girl," Rosie says, picking at her sandwich. She looks sad now, too, rather than angry. Hunter looks at me, brows furrowed, confused, as if he doesn't understand what's happening. How does he not get it? Doesn't he see that this is what I was trying to avoid all along, why I resisted, why we were my worst decision ever? *This* is why I fought him as hard as I did. Fought us.

"Girls, why don't you go upstairs and get ready to head to the park," I say, my voice cracked and painful, as I fight to keep myself in check. Both girls quietly clean up their plates, glaring at their uncle as they do so before walking up the stairs.

"Hannah, I—" Hunter starts, but I can't. I can't do this. It's unfair for him to expect it of me, too, here, at my work.

"I might not be a fancy businessman with important projects on the line, with a life that revolves around pleasing investors and making things profitable, but this is still my job. Please respect that." I nod at him, then walk away, refusing to run, refusing to let a single tear fall. That is, not a tear drops before I hit the bathroom, where I cry quietly into a towel until I hear the kids come downstairs for our trip to the park.

"Autumn, we need to talk," I say, popping in after I know the kids are asleep and she's out in the back with Steve. My throat aches with unshed tears, and my body lethargic and ready to collapse. Who knew that doing the bare minimum could be so exhausting?

Her eyes dart to mine, and there's resignation there. She knows what's going on. "Of course, Han, sit. Wine?" she asks, lifting her glass. As much as I want to say, 'Yes, an entire bottle, please,' I need to get this done.

"No, I'm good."

"So, what's up?" she asks. Steve is looking at me, face serious, not saying a word.

"I think it would be best for everyone if I found a new place of employment. Or take a leave or something." I pause, looking at where my fingers are picking at my chipping nail polish. "You know I love working here. Love your kids. But I think my being here is doing more harm than good right now."

It takes everything in me not to break, to realize that I set myself up for this, to let these kids down. But I'm telling the truth. Things have been so tense at the house since Hunter and I ended things. Even Rosie is feeling it, more quiet than usual. While he stays in his room most of the time, the few times we cross paths have been unbearable. The tension, the awkwardness, the heartbreak.

I never thought I'd be the woman to let a man destroy me, always swore up and down to anyone who would listen that I'd never let myself get in so deep without knowing that it was forever.

And I sure as hell swore that I'd never let my heartbreak impact the kids in my care. Yet here I am.

"Absolutely not," Autumn says. "No."

"Autumn, I—"

"No, Hannah. I will not allow this. My brother is a fucking idiot and an asshole. I'm not completely sure what happened, since neither of you has said anything, but I can take a good, educated guess."

"Regardless of that, the effect it's having is my fault. Sara is reserved. Rosie won't even talk to him. They both snapped at him today at lunch. I'm trying my best to keep things normal, but they're smart kids. They deserve better."

"And you think better is you leaving them?" she asks, breaking my heart more. My vision blurs with unshed tears as I sit on the deck, putting my head in my hands. After a few deep breaths, my head comes up, eyes still watering, but my breathing is a bit more regulated. My resolve is stronger.

"I don't know what to do, Autumn. I was an idiot to let things get this far, but I never thought that after a little over a month..." My voice falls off, not willing to admit how hard I'd fallen for her brother, only to be destroyed.

"Here's what we're going to do," Steve says, interrupting before Autumn can say anything. "Autumn is going to talk to Hunter. You're going to give us two weeks. Let shit settle. Things are always the hardest in the beginning, Hannah. Then in two weeks, we'll talk again. You feel like things aren't better, we think the kids are feelin' it, we find a better solution."

This sounded reasonable. It also sounded so much like a Steve Sutter solution. Nevertheless, the kids...

"Steve, I—"

"Kids are resilient, Han. They can deal with adult drama. But right now, they're confused about you and their uncle, confused and worried about their grandfather. Let's not add to that right now by taking you, too."

Crap, he was right. God, this was so fucked up. "Okay. That makes sense." My voice cracks with the words.

Autumn was staring at me, sadness and her own form of heartbreak in her eyes. "He's a good guy, Hannah. He has too much on his plate, puts too much on himself."

"I know, Autumn." It's all I can say. Hunter *is* a good man. The best. I know that in another world where he wasn't forcing himself to prove his worth, we could be together, and it would be *beautiful*. Breathtakingly beautiful. Or maybe if we were in a world where I could overlook it, where I could settle—then we could make things work. But neither of those situations is our reality.

"Two weeks, Hannah," Steve says, grabbing my hand. My eyes meet his, and I see the love I've always felt for the girls' father, like he's my big brother and he feels that tether, the connection that forces him to take care of me as well. He's kind and caring and loyal to a fault.

"Love you, Steve," I whisper.

"You know we love you," Autumn replies because the two are really a unit.

I smile, then sigh, standing up to head back to my cottage and eat another gallon of cookie dough ice cream. "I'll see you guys in the morning."

"Wake up, you lovesick bitch!"

My bed is jolting, and my heart is racing when I crack an eye open to see my best friend's tiny ass sitting on the edge of my bed with a bottle of champagne in one hand and a bottle of tequila in the other. "What the—"

"I called in reinforcements." Autumn walks around the corner into my room with a smile, holding a chocolate cake and a bag of groceries.

"What the fuck?" I ask, sitting up and rubbing my swollen eyes. They feel like sand has taken root in them after I fell asleep crying, leaving me in need of eye drops and a warm shower.

"We're here to have a pity party. Fair warning, it will be the last one, and tomorrow I will expect you to have it out of your system," Sadie says, popping a cork in the champagne. Confusion at being woken by women yelling at me and toting post-breakup goodies consumes me. What in the actual fuck is going on?

"What in the actual fuck is going on?" I ask out loud.

"After we spoke last night, I called up Sadie. We decided you need an intervention. I scheduled a day of food, liquor, and crying," Autumn says with a smile, clearly proud of herself.

"Look, I get it. Hotty McHotterson was a dick and dumped you, and that hurts because you finally let a guy in for once in your damn life, and you feel like it backfired. But you're young and deserve happiness, so fuck that guy." Sadie looks at Autumn. "No offense."

"None taken. My brother is the world's biggest idiot."

Swinging my legs over the side of my bed, I sit up and stretch before looking at my friends. There is no way out of this—Sadie and Autumn are the two most stubborn people I know,

"Fine. Get me a glass." My hand shoots out to steal the champagne bottle and take a swig, Sadie and Autumn cheering.

THIRTY-ONE
-HANNAH-

A bottle of Champagne, several rounds of shots, and a handful of hours later, all three of us are sitting in my secret garden, drinking margaritas Sadie whipped up and eating the chocolate cake straight from the container with forks.

God, I love my friends.

"This place is freaking gorgeous, Hannah," Autumn says. "How did I not know it was back here?"

"Because I hide it from Rosie," I laugh, forking more chocolate goodness into my mouth.

"Makes sense. She would lose her mind if she knew this was here."

"Love the girl, but I need my space on occasion." Autumn lifts her drink, clinking against my own.

"I hear you there."

"Okay, so let's get this over with," Sadie starts. "Tell us everything. Don't leave anything out. We need that catharsis and to over-analyze."

"Uh, please leave out the NC-17 parts, for my sake."

"Are you kidding me, Autumn? That's the only good part." My

two friends bicker back and forth about whether I should be forced to share my sex life before I start.

"I don't know if I'm ready for this."

"Too bad. We're doing it," Sadie says, sitting back, fingers steepled on her toned tummy like she's settling in for a bedtime story.

"Okay. Fine." And then I tell them everything. From the very first day we met, which has them both rolling with laughter, to our first kiss to the day with Michelle and Ava. I tell them about hiking and the falls, leaving out anything raunchy for Autumn's sake. I tell them about taking care of the kids together and how easily I could picture our future. And I tell them about the end.

"And that's it. That's the whirlwind." A tear slides down my cheek, and I sniff like the emotionally drained drunk girl I am.

"Wow," Sadie says, her voice soft and stunned.

"Holy shit," Autumn agrees. "And this was all... my brother? The work-crazed, egomaniac I've known my whole life?"

"As far as I know, unless he has a very convincing doppelgänger. He's... he's not like that with me. I mean. He wasn't. Like that with me."

"Huh."

"Huh, what?" Sadie says what I'm thinking the way she has since we were kids.

"Just... look, I know he's my brother, so I'm biased, but as driven and obnoxious as my brother is, he's a good guy. But he doesn't do romance and love and blah blah. Between what happened with my mom leaving us and then his first real girlfriend fucking him over when he was younger, he avoids relationships at any cost. Women have tried, don't get me wrong."

A knife plunges into my gut.

"But he's always clear about expectations. He doesn't take her hiking to secret spots from his childhood or watch *Tangled* with her and a five-year-old or go donate thousands of dollars of merchandise to her cause. He just... doesn't." Her voice drifts off, contemplative.

"Okay, and?" Again, Sadie is my mouthpiece.

"And... I don't know. It just seems to me that... maybe there's some hope there. Maybe you shouldn't completely give up on him, Han."

"Honestly, Autumn, love you. Love what you're saying, love that you want that for him, for me. But I can't handle having hope right now. It's too exhausting, and I need a sure thing. I've always needed a sure thing."

"Babe," Sadie starts. Her tone is gentle and reluctant. "Sure things don't exist." It's a shock to the system. Our whole lives, I've talked to Sadie about my intention to only marry once, marry for love, and marry forever. Never once has she argued that it wasn't a possibility. "Look, I get it. Your mom got her heartbroken, and it fucked you and Abs up so much. But, babe, that's her problem. You've made it your problem for literally no reason. Are you telling me that if you got your heart broken, you'd abuse your kids, neglect them, let them live the life you lived?" My answer is immediate.

"God, no, but I want—"

"You want your kids to live a fairytale. And, Hannah, not to be that person, but my kids basically live as close to a fairytale life as possible, and it still isn't, perfect. And if something happened to Steve and me, God forbid, you know as well as I do that while they would be emotionally affected, they would *not* live the childhood you did. Your mom is a piece of shit. Your dad just as bad. But that does not mean you need to sacrifice everything so that you can be everything to my kids, the kids at the Center, or your future kids."

She pauses, looking at me with meaning in her eyes. "You can't put your life on hold chasing some ideal."

"Autumn, I'm not sacrificing—"

"I know about the job offer at the Center. I know about your dream camp. Han, it's perfect for you. Taking over Maggie's position would offer you the experience you need to make that dream happen. It would fill your cup up more than my girls ever could. What's stopping you, Hannah? It's meant for you." Shock reverberates through me at this revelation. How does she know about the job? About the camp? And how can she even ask what's stopping me from taking the next step?

"I love my job, Autumn. I need to be free to be there for the kids."

"Oh, shut up, Hannah. You and I both know that's bullshit," Autumn says, looking me dead in the eye. Even though hers are glassy with drink, she's serious as can be.

"I don't understand. Are you... are you telling me to quit working for you?"

"God, no. Don't say that, I need you," she laughs, a hand to her chest in near shock. "But I *am* saying that we can work things out so that you can follow your passion. So that you can help even more kids." I'm so confused. It's like I'm being thrown in a million directions. They came to help me vent and cry over Hunter, but now we're talking about... my dreams? My career?

"Look, Hannah. Rosie starts kindergarten full-time in the fall. And when that happens, what will you do? Clean the house neurotically, as if we don't have a cleaning lady? Bake until your arms fall off?" I giggle, knowing she's right. "I will always need and adore you, but this can't be it forever."

Of course, this has crossed my mind in the past. But it was always a future me problem. A lump forms in my throat.

"Honey, we're not trying to ambush you," Sadie says softly, reaching out to grab my hand and squeeze it.

"Speak for yourself, Sadie. I'm older and wiser than you guys. I'm totally ambushing her." Sadie rolls her eyes. Turns out that when they drink, Sadie becomes Autumn, and Autumn becomes Sadie. Weird. "Hannah, I hate that this happened. I hate that you're not getting that happily ever after with my brother, so I can chain you to my family for now and forever. But maybe it's a sign. Maybe you need to work on yourself, make *you* happy, live life *for you* before you can bring someone else into your life."

There's silence after that mic drop.

"Am I crazy?" I ask. Autumn and Sadie look at each other, trying to decide if they should break it to me. "Okay, yes, I'm a little crazy, I know that. But you realize I don't want the kids to be my life forever? I just... I love your kids, Aut. And having the opportunity to be there for them, to add to their life? It's been amazing."

Drunk and emotional, Autumn's eyes tear up before she's pouncing on me to wrap me up in a bear hug. "I know, Hannah. And I am so thankful for you and what you've been to us. But you need to live for yourself, too. Your mom fucked you up a lot, but you have so much to offer. Take the chance, take a jump."

Breathing in deep, I contemplate my options before nodding. "Okay. I'll talk to Maggie on Monday." The girls whoop in a cheer only drunk women can achieve. "But I'm still working for you, right? I can still live here and be in your life? Take care of the girls?" Why am I so nervous about this next step?

"Hannah, nothing will change. You'll just *actually* work for Maggie and have the ability to do more. They're are at the Center all summer and then in fall, both will be in school. And I've talked to Mags in the past—she's willing to work with us in any way to make sure you're happy and the kids are cared for."

Relief must be clear on my face because Autumn smiles, hugging me again. "The best thing that happened from this broken heart is being able to talk to you about this. It's been weighing on me, Hannah. You do so much for us, but I can't help but feel that we're holding you back from your full potential." Her voice is gritty, unshed tears hidden behind the words.

"Oh, Autumn, no—" I start, but she cuts me off.

"Shut up, I know, I know. But you have so much to offer." We hug once more, and she gets back into her chair after refilling drinks for us all.

"So what about this asshat brother, huh?" Sadie asks, breaking the moment.

"I need to talk to him. Force him to get his damn head on straight before he lets this get too far," Autumn says to Sadie as if I'm not here.

"Uh, no. He made his thoughts clear. We'll be cordial and kind, but that's it, Autumn." I don't need Autumn stepping in and making things more awkward or uncomfortable.

"But, Hannah—"

"No, Autumn. I don't want to delay this and make it worse. The kids are frustrated. I've been a mess for a week, it's too much. It's not meant to be. That's all." Saying that feels like a betrayal, but I stand firm in my decision. Because what's the other option? Hang on to hope that's useless? Continually break my own heart? No, thank you. I saw how that plan played out my entire childhood, and it doesn't end like a rom-com.

"What about—" Autumn starts.

"Leave it be, Autumn," Sadie says, her eyes on me, reading my soul, the gorgeous green eyes I've known my whole life showing compassion and understanding.

"But—"

"No, Autumn. He can decide on his own if he wants, but that's on him. Hannah doesn't need his bullshit, period." I smile at her, grateful for how well she knows me, grateful for that sisterhood we share.

"Thanks, Sade," I say to her, and she smiles back, then looks around.

"Hey, Autumn, can we convince Steve to order us a pizza?"

"Oh, yes, totally," Autumn says, already taking her phone out. The moment is broken. Back to the best feeling of being with your girls and at peace with the world. "And maybe drop off some more snacks and drinks." Taking in my two friends, warmth fills my soul, knowing that I'm going to be okay.

THIRTY-TWO
-HUNTER-

Exhaustion is seeping through my bones in an unprecedented way. Since that night at the hospital, work has been what I eat, drink, and sleep. It's been an incessant cycle, hyper-focused on the end result.

Monday, Tanner's company is set to break ground at 8 a.m., meaning I can confidently go visit my dad at the hospital. He's been moved out of the ER unit he was previously staying in and into the cancer wing, where he's finally been approved for the clinical trial.

While last week's scare should make us feel less optimistic, the doctors tell us that his results are showing the opposite—a few small signs of recovery and remission. Small signs I am hanging all of my hopes on.

As I walk the halls to his room, my gut is churning, acid burning through my stomach and leaking into my exhausted veins, making me feel alive and alert for the first time since... well, never mind, It's finally time to tell my dad everything, everything I've done, everything we've accomplished.

As I enter his room, he's lying on the small hospital bed with machines beeping and monitors with lines going up and down in a rainbow of colors. A printer to his left is constantly spitting out a trail of white paper with a line, what I can only assume are his vitals, until a small pile is collecting on the floor next to him. The television on the wall is showing highlights from last night's Yankees game, but when I enter, he turns it off. A smile breaks his tired, gaunt face.

"Hey, son! Good to see you!" He sounds so genuinely surprised and happy to see me. The acid rises higher, bile creeping into my throat at the thought that I've let him down so much. So much that it's surprising that I would visit when he's so ill.

"Hey, Dad, sorry, I would have come earlier, but we're running on a crazy deadline."

"No problem, Autumn's told me all about the new project."

"So you've heard we're breaking ground on Monday?" I ask, not sure if I should be annoyed or relieved that he knows. My big sister has always had a big mouth, for better or worse.

"Yeah, sounds great. You must be disappointed that the original plan won't be happening, though. Know that was a passion of yours," he says. The words confuse me like they won't sit right in my brain and make a coherent sentence.

"Well, we're working to build the brand and improve profitability," I start my speech, spending the next few minutes telling him all the minutia of the project. It feels like I'm giving a presentation, waiting for approval at the end. Which makes sense, since I rehearsed it on the drive here.

"Sounds nice, son. And what about Hannah?" he asks. Once again, he catches me off guard.

"Hannah?"

"Yeah, Hannah. Are we doing this again?" He chuckles a bit, wincing when the move tweaks something. I stare at the maze of wires and tape and needles, unable to pinpoint the source.

"No, I know who Hannah is, of course."

"And? How is she?"

"I'm not sure," I say, rubbing a hand down my beard. God, that sends another wave of sickness through me when I remember the last time I saw her in Autumn's kitchen. She looked terrible, with dark circles under bloodshot eyes, pale, and she'd probably been eating less since she looked suspiciously thinner. I hated it.

"What do you mean, you're not sure? She's your woman." Where on earth is this coming from? His eyebrows are furrowed, disappointment and confusion clear on his face.

"We broke up not long ago. Well, we weren't really together, but we're no longer seeing each other. I needed to focus more on the project at hand, and she wants a... bigger commitment."

The phrase tastes sour in my mouth, knowing while I'm sure she would love a commitment from me, she never even hinted at trying to force it on me. Over the past 10 years, I've been with enough women to know what that is like, women who I casually dated dropping hints. Leaving toothbrushes at my place, asking about my job, or even straight-up demanding a commitment. Each time, it did not turn out well for them, and I ended the relationship soon after.

"Why would you make an idiot move like that?" He looks angry, his eyebrows form a dark slash across his lined forehead, making his eyes, so much like my own, appear small and squinted.

"Hannah... Hannah was a distraction. Just another poor decision that I've made." My gut twists at the lie, the lie I need to convince myself of to get through this. Nauseated at the mere idea of calling Hannah, beautiful, sweet Hannah who deserves the world, a poor decision.

"The only bad decision I see is you letting that girl slip through your fingers."

"Dad, I have too much to do. The business is... I'm not sure. It's not right, and I'm not going to fix it by fucking around," I sigh, looking toward the ceiling to find the right words. "Hannah, she deserves, well, she *needs* a man who can devote everything to her. I'm not that man. The business comes first." But, God, if I could be that man, if I could be worthy of her while keeping this business going, it would be heaven.

"You know what's wrong with the business? Why you hit so many speed bumps?" My eye shoot to him. "Shut it. Your sister has a big mouth. Tells her old man everything. I know all about the deadlines and the zoning and the construction company. You have such issues, Hunter, because your heart isn't in it. Your heart is with that woman, boy, and you're letting her walk away with it. God, you started workin' on that camp, and you were so passionate, Hunt. What happened to that man?"

"He failed. That's what happened. You believed in me, and I made stupid decisions, got cocky, and almost lost everything for you. I failed, and you had to pay the price for it. And after everything you did for us our whole lives... I can't be that guy again. My head was in the clouds, but I need to stay down here, in the real world."

What doesn't he get? Isn't it clear? Letting my heart lead landed him in near financial demise, everything collapsing around us. Everything he worked for, everything he sacrificed for us over the years. Dust.

My dad is silent for a moment. "Are you telling me that all these years, that's what you've believed? That you failed and I suffered? That you deserved to be punished?" His brows are pinched, and his head has pulled back further into the pillow as if he's been struck. The shock on his face confuses me.

"Dad, you almost lost the house. You had to work double shifts every single day to keep it. You didn't take a day off for five years. After everything you did for us..."

"Jesus, who gives a fuck, Hunter?" My head jerks like he smacked me, my mind spinning, completely at a loss as to what's happening. "It's a house. A house that's just sitting around now, I should add. Yeah, it's been in the family for a while, but who the fuck cares. You know what I care about? That you went for something you believed in. That you tried and you failed, and you *learned*. And look what you've built from that lesson. That's what a father wants to see for his son. The only thing missing is you, enjoying your life."

"I am enjoying my life, Dad."

"Don't bullshit a bullshitter, Hunter. You like what you do, but it's all you've got. That's not living, bud."

"You can't mean that." It's like I'm having an out-of-body experience. My limbs are limp, out of my control, and my head light and spinning.

"For such a smart kid, you're really dumb, Hunter," he says, leaning forward to grab water and take a sip. The action makes him grimace a bit, bringing to mind once again what he's been through.

"Dad, I love you, but this makes no sense. How could you not be frustrated that I fucked up so bad? You worked your ass off to make our childhood amazing after Mom left. Did everything for us, sacrificed so much."

"And I'd do it again, every fuckin' day, if it meant I could see you and your sister live free and happy. If I could see you two live a good life, make mistakes, build a business, build a family." He pauses, staring at me, unspoken words echoing in the room.

"Hunt, one day, I pray to God you have kids of your own and see that I do not give a shit about any of that. All a decent father wants is to see his kids happy. To see them thrive. I don't give a fuck about the business and your revenue and how many locations you have. I was happy to make those sacrifices for you. Honored, even. You've done amazing things with that company, but if it's crushing your soul and you're doing it to prove something to me, then I've failed as a parent."

It's like a switch is flipped. All these years, all those times, he told me he's proud of Beaten Path, of what I've created. Those times Autumn and Steve and even Hannah told me I have nothing to prove. It's all clicking.

"You mean that, don't you?"

"Of course I do, Hunter."

"I've been spending the last 10 years working to make up for that mistake. Working to make you proud." His face softens, a flash of guilt flaring across his eyes. "Not because you didn't show me. You did, I see that now. But all these years, I thought they were nice words because you're a good Dad."

God, I'm a fuckup. This entire time. A wasted life. Building a business that just pulls from me and drains my soul. Being aggressive, consumed by this business, never making connections, working towards some vision of perfection, of success. And now that vision has been flipped on its head. My carefully crafted worlds are imploding around me in this small hospital room with beeping machines all around.

"Fuuuuuccccck," I say, dropping my face into my hands, elbows on my knees. In my mind, a montage of videos and, scenes, and photos from the last month fly past, each one making everything clearer, more painful. Hannah dancing with kids, Hannah with soap bubbles on her nose. Going hiking with her, kissing her in the rain. The oatmeal raisin cookies she hated but made me anyway. Helping to put the kids to bed together, feeling like a well-oiled machine.

Annihilating her when I told her she was a distraction, a mistake.

The look in her eyes the last time I saw her, hollow, empty, and destroyed.

I fucked up.

I fucked up, and I have no clue how to fix it. With a moment to think about it, I turn to the man who has always had the answers I need.

"Dad, I need your help."

Four hours later, Dad's cute, dark-haired nurse walks in again, and his eyes light up.

"Well, hello there, Ron!" she says, smiling huge, the smile genuine and maybe even a little excited.

"Hey, Rhonda, you remember my son, Hunter, right?" Dad's smile matches hers.

"Of course! The handsome, younger version of you!" While I remember her from the ICU, it's easy to notice that she is not the same nurse who has come in to check vitals and give meds while I've been here.

"You off shift?" Dad asks. His back has straightened, and his hands fuss with the blanket and gown covering him before he's patting his hair. He's... nervous.

Holy shit, my dad has a crush on the hot nurse.

"Just got off, but I can come back later, let you visit with your son." She's blushing now, turning to leave.

"No! I was just leaving!" I shout too loud, surprising myself. Looking at Dad, he looks relieved and winks at me. I put my hand out for a fist bump before collecting my computer and the piles of notes I've made since arriving. It feels good to be the wingman.

"Oh, uh, okay," she says, looking a bit confused but also relieved.

"See ya later, Dad. Thanks for... everything," I bend down to kiss him on his cheek. Pulling back, his eyes are wet and filled with meaning. The look gives me another stab to my heart, knowing I spent years avoiding this. Years spent thinking I had something to prove.

"Keep me updated. Go get that girl back and sort out your damned priorities, son," he calls after me as I'm talking out the door to his room, making my laugh boom through the hospital hallways.

That night, my phone rings with a number I vaguely recognize but isn't saved into my phone.

"Hello?"

"You are a dick." The words come through the speaker slightly slurred. I know the voice.

"Sadie?"

"Of course, it's me, you dumb ass."

"Are you okay? Do you need something?"

"I'm fine. You know who's not okay? Hannah. You broke that fucking girl's heart." The acid in my stomach is churning again. "She's a mess." The words break me, knowing I did that to her. To sweet Hannah, who helps everyone.

"I know." It's really all I can say. My fingers pick at the loose white threads falling loose from the comforter on Autumn's guest room bed.

"So what are you going to do about it?"

"I'm sorry, what?"

"You break it, you buy it, bub." Her words are slurring, and I can picture spit flying with each 'b' she overpronounces.

"Wait, what? You want me to fix her? Not leave her alone?" I ask, trying to confirm what she's saying. Sadie's opinion of me doesn't matter, but having her on my side wouldn't hurt my new cause.

"Jesus, you're a dumb one. Of course, I want you to fix her. She deserves the happily ever after. Your sister says you're not as much of a dick as it seems, so I'm gonna trust her on that and trust you with my bestest bestie." She burps after her mini tirade.

I want to laugh. I want to do a fist pump, knowing she's on my team. But I'll never win over Hannah if something happens to her best friend. "Sadie, do you need a ride or something?" If she's out and about this drunk, it's not safe for her.

"Nope, I'm perfectly safe right now. I might as well be in your backyard," she says before she laughs uncontrollably like it's a joke that I haven't been let in on.

"Okay, Sadie. You're in a safe spot?"

"God, I want to not like you, but you're a nice guy, Hunty Hunt. Yes, I'm perfectly safe and will not be getting into any kind of trouble." I really hope that doesn't become a new nickname,

"Tell me more about what I need to do for Hannah. How do I win her back?" I ask, willing to use whatever sources I need to hit my goals.

"Wait, seriously?" Her voice is a squeal of drunken excitement, and it tells me what I need to know: there is still hope with Hannah.

"Yeah, Sadie. Gotta win her back. Can you help?"

"Make her feel like a princess. NO! A queen! She needs to feel loved. And wanted. She needs someone to give her back the love she gives everyone else." Her voice is soft and serious now, like the thought of her best friend not feeling the love she gives brings her low, too.

"I know, Sade."

"Oh, and good sex. Lots of it!" she screams into the phone before cackling and hanging up.

Sitting in bed, I stare at my phone, confused about what the fuck just happened. One thing I do know is there's still hope, and I need all the hope I can get.

When I walk downstairs the next morning, Steve is standing at the stove making pancakes and grumbling to himself.

"Hey, Steve. Where's Autumn?" I ask, pouring a cup of coffee and walking to the fridge to get cream.

"Girls all got hammered at the cottage last night. She spent the night there." He doesn't look up from the Mickey Mouse-shaped pancakes he's making, reminding me that I live in a Mary Poppins movie.

"Uh, Hannah's cottage?" I ask, trying to be nonchalant, a task I'm failing miserably at.

"Yup." He flips a pancake, catching it on the edge of the pan and dripping batter all over onto the burner. "Goddammit." I try not to laugh, knowing that the kitchen is not his domain by any stretch of the imagination. He can grill a mean steak, but pancakes seem to be over his skill level. Though his skill level outranks mine by a mile.

"They got hammered?" I ask, and the pieces fall into place. "Wait, was Sadie there too?"

"Yeah, they ambushed her at noon, stayed in there all day drinking. Had to deliver pizza over there personally, and saw the damage. I don't imagine they'll be up any time soon. And when they do, I'd avoid Autumn." Knowing my sister, I have to agree with him.

"Thanks for the heads up." I sip my coffee at the kitchen island, going over what's on my list for the day while also trying to remember the night Hannah and I had fun on this very island. I need to follow up with Tanner as soon as it's a reasonable hour and make a few other calls. Lots of changes need to be made before the morning.

"Hunter, I gotta talk to you. Man to man," Steve asks abruptly, clicking the heat off the stove and dumping his last misshapen pancake onto the plate.

"Uh, sure." Nerves start in my chest since Steve is a pretty straightforward guy, and 'man-to-man talks' are not his thing. Not *our* thing.

"Look, I know you had a thing with Hannah." I can guess where this is going and try to interrupt, but he raises a hand. "Let me finish. I know you had a thing with Hannah. It ended. I don't want any details or explanations, I don't care. What I care about is that girl who works for us but is really part of our family. And lately, she's been miserable and broken.

"I know you're staying here because your sister loves you and you're working on a project nearby, but I'm putting my foot down. Hannah tried to quit the other day. She didn't say it outright, but it's because of whatever happened with you two." *Fuck. Goddammit, Hannah.* She's always putting others before herself, but this is too far.

"Steve, you can't—"

"I told her no. But I promised that I'd revisit her request in two weeks and reevaluate if things aren't better." That makes sense, at least. Should be enough time. Enough time to fix this mess I made.

"You need to leave." His words are firm, with no questioning or room for arguments. Shocked, my head goes back as I stare at him. Steve has always been a good guy but mostly quiet, following Autumn's lead. "This is not Autumn's decision. This is mine." Even more surprising.

"You're welcome here, but not right now. You need to find somewhere else to stay. My kids come first and foremost, and this is hurting them." My eyes lock on his, seeing the emotion there, the care and love he feels for Hannah.

"You're a good guy, you know that, Steve?" Now it's his turn to look confused and shocked, crossing his arms on his chest with an eyebrow raised. "Always thought that. You don't take shit from Autumn. You let her think she has the lead, which she likes, but we all know who lays down the rules. Always wanted her to find a man who would stick up for her, and do whatever it took to keep her happy. Glad she found it."

"Are you telling me you're not mad? You're going to move out? Just like that?" he asks. Standing, I empty the last of the coffee in my mug before walking it to the sink.

"Was already planning to. Saw Dad last night. Gonna move into his house. Buying it from him."

"I'm sorry, what?" he asks, rightfully confused. I haven't stepped foot into that house in 10 years. "Don't you live in the city?"

"Yup, selling the condo. Moving to Springbrook Hills."

"What the fuck is going on?" Steve asks, but a small smile is playing on his lips. My feet head towards the stairs to get started on my plan.

"I'm restructuring my priorities," I say as I walk out, leaving Steve stunned but smiling big.

THIRTY-THREE
-HANNAH-

"Alright, guys, now go break off into your groups and start brainstorming your creation!" I yell at the crowd in front of me, false enthusiasm coating my words. We're using up the boxes from the Beaten Path donation to create a cardboard village. Each team gets to make its own building and decorate it. Later this week, we'll vote on the winner.

Kids scatter, some yelling, some grabbing boxes they had their eyes on. I made sure the groups have kids of all ages, so it's a fair competition. I love to see the big kids help and support the little ones.

Maggie walks over, and I smile at her.

"Hey, Mags, can I talk to you?" I ask, gesturing to the building her office is in. She's been so busy all week, running around for fundraising and donations, Wednesday is the first time I see her since my night of revelation with the girls. My body and soul are still exhausted, and my heart still a painful ache, but slowly I'm mending.

"Of course, Banana. Let's go to my office."

Grabbing a soda from her mini-fridge, I sit back and look around the tiny space. It's hard not to wish we had something nicer, larger, and more... fitting for her.

"Should I be nervous about this talk, Hannah?" Maggie asks with a smile, grabbing her soda. Mine opens with a sharp hiss before I take a sip, the carbonation burning my nose.

"No, I don't think so." I set the can down with a clink before placing my hands on my lap.

"Then why are your hands shaking?" Looking down, I see that she's right. My hands, painted with bright pink polish, are shaking slightly.

"I want to take the job."

I'm not sure what I expected when envisioning this moment, but the calm and collected, "Good," I get from Maggie is... not it.

Silence settles after that word, and I look at her, expecting more. "Good?"

"Yes, good. About time. This old maid can't do this much longer. You finally talked to Autumn?"

"Well, yeah?"

"I've been telling her for a year straight to talk you into taking this position, that I'd work around your schedules. She said you're as stubborn as I know you to be." Her eyes roll to the ceiling like she's having a private conversation with God about how annoying I am.

She returns to earth. "We'll figure out all the details on pay and schedule next week, once things settle down from the start of camp." Turning her back to me, she shuffles some papers, and it's hard not to be confused. Why is this so... easy?

"That's... it?"

"Well, yeah, honey. Nothin' more to say, I've had the spot ready for you for a year straight. Know you won't negotiate the pay or hours since it's you. We'll figure the rest out later." Her voice is a matter of fact like this is obvious, and I'm slow. I stare at her some more.

"So tell your Aunt Maggie. You fix things with that boy yet?" she asks, and the knife that's been sitting quietly in my chest wakes up and turns at the change in subject.

"Nothin' to fix, Mags. He's not looking for what I'm looking for," Maggie harrumphs in response. "Seriously. It's all fine, though, fun while it lasted." With those words, she looks me in the eye, seeing into my soul, all the pain stuck inside. The same way she could 15 years ago.

"Sometimes you gotta fight, girl. Sometimes you need to sit back and accept things, but sometimes you need to fight, and do it hard." She whispers this, tearing through me, reopening the wounds, and cleaning out the infection I've let simmer in there. God, this woman.

"I know Mags. And sometimes you need to protect yourself. I'm doing what I need to do to survive. Tried to fight, was knocked down and taken out."

Her eyes settle on me for a moment, reading me in a way no one else can. After what feels like minutes, she sighs deeply. "Fine. Just remember, though, Hannah, if you get the hand up off the ground, take it. If that hand feels safe and secure, let it heal you." She stares at me a moment longer. Then she stands, kisses the top of my head, and walks away, her flowing skirt trailing behind her in a train of green and purple magic.

"Well, shit," I whisper under my breath, chugging my drink before heading back out to help with the kids

---

Two weeks later, the girls are loaded in the back seat of my car when my phone rings over Bluetooth. The screen says "Sadie," so I answer, but talk before she can get a word in.

"In the car with tiny ears, you're on speaker."

"Well, fu- I mean, darn. Whatcha up to tonight? Do you have kiddo duty?" She asks, making Sara giggle when she catches the not-quite curse. I wink at her in the rearview mirror.

"Nope, their parents should be done by five, and then I'm free," I say, looking forward to a kid-free evening. These kids are the best, but some days I need to be free of little eyes.

"Alright, we're goin' out, girlfriend," she says.

"Oh, Sade, I don't think I've recovered from the last time," I say, groaning, the thought alone making my already tired bones want to crumble. I want my bed, ice cream, and trash TV.

"Too bad. There's a band coming to Luna's. She's putting up the reserved sign on our stools. We're obligated to go." Luna took ownership of the bar in town not long after we were legal, and since then, we've had our own stools. On nights when it's busy, she makes sure we always have a spot to sit and chat. Whenever a band comes to our small town, Full Moon Cafe gets packed. In all honesty, it's usually a blast.

Even so, I'm tired. "Sade, I want to go. I do! But I'm so tired."

"Too bad. I'll be there at 8, I'll bring you an energy drink. Text me what you're wearing." Then silence. Well, fuck. She had already hung up.

"She told you," Sara laughs, causing me to glare at her as she giggles.

At 7:45, Sadie comes into the cottage, ready to go. She's wearing a short, high-waisted shimmery skirt and a black tank with pretty flat sandals.

"Am I okay like this?" I ask, motioning down my body at my distressed shorts and old band tee I cut, so it's a short, loose crop. I threw my hair up artfully in some kind of 'intentionally a hot mess but also not a slob' look, adding heeled booties for good measure.

"You look hot for a depressed bitch."

"Gee, thanks. Who's driving?" I ask, grabbing my bag and phone.

"I will. If we have to Uber it home, it will be a quick walk to get my car in the morning," she decides, walking to her car and hopping in. Immediately she rolls all of her windows down and cranks the music up, blasting a song about angry breakups. Perfect.

An hour later, Sadie and I are sitting at the bar chatting with Luna while the band sets up. "So, where are they from?" Sadie asks, eyeing the band. Or, more accurately, the lead singer's ass.

Luna giggles the tinkly laugh she's always had, the kind that makes everyone around us turn their head to find the magical noise. "Texas. Austin. They're bar hopping and playing across the country. Not sure how they found me, but they've brought a crowd, so I'm happy."

And they did—the bar was more packed than I've seen it in some time, making me thankful for our special seats. Granted, we've already had a few gross bar flies hitting on us, using our seats as an excuse to try out their worst pickup lines.

"For sure, it's packed tonight," I say, sipping the Dirty Shirley Luna made me, which ends up being 1/3 cherries and more booze than I need.

"Uh, yeah, looks like everyone's here tonight," Sadie says, and when I look at her, she's cringing, panic and guilt in her eyes.

"What?" My stomach drops, but I know. *I know.*

"I'm so sorry, Hannah, I didn't think..." Sadie says, staring across the bar. Following her line of sight, his eyes are right on me, connecting his gaze with mine. A warmth that used to burn for me when we were together is in his eyes, dousing me in a strange mix of burning hot and ice cold.

"Fuck," I mumble, looking away quickly.

"Lune, shots, now," Sadie says, but Luna, having looked behind her to see Hunter, is already lining up three glasses and topping them with tequila.

There goes any hope of leaving here relatively sober.

THIRTY-FOUR
-HUNTER-

As she downs her third shot, Hannah tips back, making the feet of the stool lift slightly, but is thankfully caught by a giggling Sadie. My body jolts her way before reminding me I can't. It's not my place. Not right now. Not yet.

"Jesus fuck." Tanner laughs out loud next to me, witnessing my version of Hell. Earlier tonight, he called to say a band was playing at Full Moon and asking if I want to come to grab a drink. Since I've been incessantly working since talking with my dad, I agreed, deciding one night off wouldn't mess my timeline up too much.

It probably is funny to watch me struggle, watching *my girl* get hammered, knowing I'm most definitely the reason. The need to be next to her, to keep her safe and erase those dark circles under her eyes, the sadness on her face. It's strong and painful. I'm resigned to the fact that I need to wait it out, keep the plan I crafted carefully, and avoid fucking it up.

Except some scumbag catches my eye as he elbows his buddy, points to Hannah, and starts walking her way. When he gets there, he comes up behind her and places a hand on the bare skin between her shirt and shorts.

This fucking guy just put his hands on *my fucking girl.*

"Oh fuck," I hear Tanner say as he stands, but I'm already halfway across the bar. Grabbing the douche by the neck of his shirt, I tug him back.

"What the—"

"Back the fuck off." The words are a feral growl, low and menacing, but he sure as fuck can hear them even over the music.

"Woah, man, chill out, what the fuck?" The preppy douche yells at me. He's a big guy, decent-looking enough, and it's clear he knows it. I've dealt with his kind more times than I can count, and they're all assholes.

"Hands off my girl, asshole," I say, turning my back to him, creating a barrier between the guy and the girls. My chest is pressed against Hannah's side, and feeling her warmth feels like home.

"Hunter, what the—" she starts.

"Hey, man, I was talking to her," the asshole says. Then, proving he has a fucking death wish, pulls my shoulder, so I'm facing him. He pushes my chest like we're in high school. Poor guy doesn't realize that because I was a bitter high schooler, Tanner and I got into our fair share of fistfights as teens. When I see Tanner come up to my side, I know this guy is fucked if he tries something.

"Seriously, bro, walk away," Tanner says in warning, but my eyes are glued to this guy, rage burning deep in my bones, ready to attack.

"Who the fuck are you?" he asks, and I want to laugh at how cliche he is.

"Doesn't matter, just trust me, you don't want to do this." Instead of listening, the guy cocks his arm back, Tanner tensing to react. The hit never lands, though, because his wrist is grabbed by bulky security, who pulls him away. I watch them go, mildly annoyed that the fight I'm itching for won't happen.

But then I feel a small, warm hand low on my back and the sweetest sound ever whispering in my ear. "Honey, let it go." Her front is pressed against my back, my body aching to have her in my arms, dying for her to be mine again.

Staring at the guy one last time, I turn to Hannah, letting professionals handle the interaction. He continues to make a scene, arguing with security, pointing and screaming my way, but I've been dragged back into my girl's stratosphere. He no longer exists to me. "You okay?"

"Uh, yeah?" she asks like I know the answer instead of her. Her eyes are glazed with one drink too many. The look reminds me of the last time we were here, but I know the night will end differently.

I look behind Hannah, seeing Luna's security ushering the guy out. He's screaming that he'll sue, or some other entitled shit. I know his type. Fuck, I've *been* his type. That's all changed now. All thanks to the woman in front of me.

"Let's get you another drink, baby," I say, guiding her back to a seat at the bar that Sadie seems to save for her. Tanner and I pull over two more chairs to where the girls are and spend the next few hours talking and listening to the band, which is pretty decent. The decision to sit furthest from Hannah is one of the hardest things I've done, but I'm determined not to suffocate her. The way her shoulders relax when I do shows she appreciates the gesture.

It's clear I fucked up. I need to fix things with this woman before I lose her forever. When I told Steve I was restructuring my priorities, it was the truth. What I left out was that I'm doing it all for her, the woman who makes me a better person and opened my eyes to what the world really is. What the world could be.

A slow song comes on, soft and sweet, a perfect contrast to the alternative rock that's been blaring all night. Hannah's eyes pick up, meeting mine with glazed hope, and drunken love, and a hint of lingering hurt and hesitation. Instead of replying to her silent question with words, I stand, taking her hand in mine and leading her away from the bar to where people are coupling up to dance.

All night my mind has drifted to thoughts of her small warm body in my arms, the ache in my chest unbearable. Finally, it's happening, and for the first time in a week, I'm whole again.

"You good, baby?" I ask. She's settled her head against my chest after clumsily hooking her arms around my neck. Most of her weight is pressed on me, forcing me to keep us both standing. Not a single moment of it is frustrating or annoying, though.

"Mmmm," she mumbles. While the music is quieter than when the band was playing, it's still too loud to hear something so soft. Instead, I feel the vibration of her chest on mine, making for an easy translation.

"Missed this, honey." She stills, and I can't help but question if I just fucked it all up.

"Not tonight, Hunter." Her body relaxes again like she decided she's not starting the argument, allowing herself to enjoy where she is.

"No, no, not tonight, baby. But soon," I whisper in her hair. Her arms tighten around my neck, and I swear I feel a whisper of a kiss, soft and quick, against my chest where she lays. The moment will be burned in me forever.

An hour later, Sadie and Hannah are done. Looking at them, Tanner and I decide without a word that they need help to get home, and I'm not letting them call a cab.

"Who drove?" I ask them as we stand outside Luna's, music still playing to entertain the few remaining patrons inside the bar.

"Me!" Sadie says, raising her hand like she's in school and knows the right answer. "But I'm close, we're leaving the car here and crashing at my place." Sadie reaches for Hannah's hand, and it takes everything not to growl at her for even thinking about taking her. Hannah is leaning against me with a drunken smile on her face. My arm is wrapped around her middle, keeping her up straight.

"I'll be walking you home," Tanner says, locking eyes with me. "And Hunter is taking Hannah home." Even for two drunk women, his tone has to be unmistakable in its finality. Sadie looks me over like she can't decide if I'm worthy. Looking at the stress and pain, I've put Hannah through. I can't blame her. Until last week, I was sure that nothing I did in life would deserve someone like her. And I still don't, but I'll spend every day of my life trying.

"Works for me," she says, breaking into a smirk. This girl is devious, and I'm sure this was all somehow part of her master plan. Any other woman, and I'd say there's no way she could have orchestrated this entire night. But knowing Sadie, you can never be sure

Hannah opens her mouth to object, but one look at her best friend has her shutting her mouth and nodding. Well, that was easy. We say our goodbyes. Hannah drunkenly hugs her best friend while I tell Tanner I'll call him in the morning and thank him for taking care of Sadie.

Unlocking the truck, my hands go under Hannah's arms, lifting her into the seat. Reaching over to buckle her, she drunkenly giggles, the sound pulling at my heart. I want to always make her sound that happy and carefree.

"What's so funny, Miss?" I ask, putting my hand on the top of the door to close it.

"Your butt looks so good in those shorts." She giggles again. Her eyes are still glazed with drink, but now there's a layer of exhaustion that wasn't there earlier.

"Alright, crazy girl, let's get you home," I say, checking that she's tucked in safe before slamming the door and jogging around to the driver's side.

On the drive home, the temptation to look over at Hannah every second is overwhelming. Street lights light her face up as we drive, making her look angelic and peaceful in her half-asleep state. Her eyes keep drooping shut, then opening as if reminding herself she's not home yet. It doesn't take long for them to settle and stay closed.

The wheels crunching gravel outside of her cottage make her eyes pop open briefly before closing again, a soft snore escaping.

"Hannah, baby, where are your keys?" I ask, gently shaking her thigh. No response. Rather than keep trying to wake her, I walk around the truck and open her door. Her keys are sitting right on top of her bag at her feet. Lifting her out of the seat, she's cradled in my arms with her head on my shoulder when I kick the door shut. The cloud key turns smoothly in her lock with a quiet click before we're in and headed for her bedroom.

"Baby, gonna get you dressed for bed, okay?" I ask, hand on her shoe. The boots are subtly sexy, little dark brown short boots. Just enough heel to show off her legs, but not so much that she'd break an ankle.

"Mm-hmm," she says, lifting the foot my hand is touching as she rolls to her back and splays. Her eyes are still closed but she reaches up to pull out the hair tie, releasing her long dark strands. A waterfall of hair I'm always dying to tangle my fingers in falls free.

Unzipping one and tugging it off, I grab the next boot and follow suit, dropping each with a thunk. Her arms cross over her stomach, grabbing the edges of her band tee and lift, showing nothing but smooth, bare skin and pert nipples. "Jesus fuck," I say under my breath, going for her socks.

"Can we have sex? I miss sex. I miss sex with you." Her words are muffled through the shirt she left over her face. In an effort to distract myself from her perfect tits, I help her tug it over her head.

"No sex tonight, baby," I say, even though it hurts to say it. Not like this, though. The next time I'm in her, everything will be clear, everything will be settled.

"Why?" The word comes out in a whine, forcing a small smile to play on my lips.

This woman.

"Can I help with your shorts?" I ask, my hands pausing over the button. She nods, so my fingers undo the button then pull the zip, revealing tiny, pale pink lace underwear. She wants to kill me. Plain and simple. "What are you wearing to bed tonight, beautiful?" She needs to get something on before I lose my mind.

"Your shirt," she says, eyes still closed, arms over her head. She looks like a perfect pin-up. Begging for my eyes and hands and lips.

"Where is it?" I ask, looking around for the shirt I forced upon her when I burned her exes.

"On you, silly." Her hands reach up, grasping the hem and

tugging.

"Honey, I'm wearing this tee still," I laugh, brushing hair out of her face as my ass hits the edge of her bed.

"Stay."

"Baby, that's not a good—"

"I don't care. Stay. I don't want to be alone." She opens her eyes to look at me, hurt and pain and loneliness there, mirroring my own. Sighing, I nod. It's not a hard decision to make.

"Fine." There's only so much begging from her I can take. I won't stay the whole night, won't risk her regretting it. Especially when my plan is already rolling along, so close to fruition. But I'll give her this.

Give myself this.

"Good," she says, a small, cat-ate-the-canary smile on her lips as her eyes close again. Quick decision-making tells me to leave the jeans on before stripping my shirt off. I toss it at her, silently praying she puts it on and helps me make it through the night without attacking her.

"Smells good," she says, putting the shirt to her nose and sniffing in an adorable and sweet moment. "Miss it," she says again. Again breaking my heart and giving me hope in one moment. Thankfully, she pulls the shirt on over her head, not bothering to remove the hair stuck under the collar. Then she rolls over to her side and pats the bed next to her.

After turning off the lights and checking doors are locked, I make my way back to Hannah. My body lines up perfectly behind hers, the same perfect fit I noticed that first night. Brushing her hair from her neck, my lips touch her there, making her sigh. My arm wraps around her front and her little hand twines its fingers with my own.

"Miss you, Hunter," she mumbles before falling asleep with soft, deep breaths almost immediately.

"Miss you too, baby. I'm gonna fix this." I whisper the promise into her hair before falling asleep myself, secure and content in this tiny bed, in this tiny house, with this woman who holds my whole being in her tiny hands.

THIRTY-FIVE
-HANNAH-

My mouth is dry when the sun hits my eyelids in the morning, waking me. It's a foregone conclusion, proven with many nights of drinking that as soon as they open, a million tiny hammers will start pounding on my brain. Cracking one open to test my theory, I quickly slam it shut when my hypothesis proves correct.

Why do I do this to myself?

Groaning, I roll onto my stomach before throwing a pillow over my head, blocking out the happy birds outside my window.

"Shut up," I grumble into my mattress, but then, my mind remembers the night before. My stomach almost rebels as my body sits up straight in a split second, looking around my room for him.

Nothing. My heart drops, angry with myself for the cruel dream my mind crafted.

Stumbling out of bed, I nearly trip on my booties. As I'm looking down, I notice my shirt—the shirt Hunter was wearing last night. The shirt I ordered him to give me in my drunken state. The shirt that still smells of him.

"So, not a dream." Should I feel bad about that? Embarrassed, maybe? None of those fit. Instead, disappointment crashes into me as

I stumble into the kitchen and don't see him at the table sipping a coffee and waiting for me to wake.

Instead, there's a note.

Take these. Yes, that's an order. Missed sleeping with you, gorgeous. Autumn's got the kids this morning. Talk soon.

-H

Beside the note are a bottle of water and two aspirin. My mind tries to catch up with what's going on, but the fog is blocking any form of reason.

Taking the pills and chugging half the water, my eyes drift to my next stop, the coffeepot. On the black machine is a bright pink note from one of the many post-it pads I keep lying around.

Just flip the switch, coffee is set.

Reading the note, I force myself not to read into it. Instead I go about making my coffee, fixing it the way I like, and sitting with a cup and my phone. A few texts from Sadie, none of which have excessive caps so they can wait, a text from Autumn confirming that she took the day off and will take the kids to the zoo, and... a text from Hunter.

How are you feeling?

How do I reply to that? Do I go with honesty? Or fake nice? And if I choose honesty, do I go for the emotional state or physical state? Or both?

Something tells me that "Nauseous, achey, confused as fuck, and completely heartsick" isn't the right answer.

Thankfully, that reply is delayed when Luna's name flashes on my phone.

"Hey babe," I answer, standing to look through my cabinets for a bland breakfast my stomach won't revolt at.

"How ya feeling', sloppy?" Her voice is cheery, regardless of the early hour and the fact that she works late into the night. She's seriously an alien.

"Shut up. And terrible."

"Girl, I haven't seen you drunk more than once in a year since you turned 21. What in the hell is this man doing to you?" God, if she only knew.

"I have no fucking clue. But this morning reminds me why I don't drink this much anymore." My stomach settles on crackers, and I pull out the sleeve before leaning against my counter and munching.

"That bad, huh? Need me to come by and drop off some pills and essentials?"

"No, funny enough, Hunter left me water, pills, and coffee this morning."

"He spent the night?!?" she shrieks, forcing me to pull my phone from my ear. "I thought you guys were done!" Needles insert themselves into my brain at a high pitch.

"Jeez, Lune, hangover, remember? But yeah, me too. I have no idea what's going on."

"Crap, sorry. I guess it didn't look too over last night. Also, can you guys stop causing a scene every time you're here? Zoe's dad keeps sending Tony over, and it's so awkward." Luna had the biggest crush on Tony Garrison in high school.

He's her big brother Zander's best friend, and something happened at some point to make it weird. She avoids him like the plague, but being the main bar in town, she ends up having to call him more often than she'd like.

"Sorry, totally not my fault, though. The first time was Sadie's fault, the second was Hunter's."

"Yeah, yeah, yeah. Not buying it, you've always been a drama magnet." She's not wrong. Since my childhood, drama seems to trail me no matter how boring of a life I lead. "So the real reason I'm calling, besides making sure you're alive—why did I see your man chatting with Aunt Mags at Rise and Grind this morning?"

"What?" Oh, God, I am too hungover for this much confusion this early.

"Yeah, they were talking at Sadie's, not sure what about? I was there getting coffee and shooting the shit with Sade, but they were sitting in a corner, papers passing back and forth, laughing. Any clue what that was?" I pause, trying to figure out what could be going on. He left early without saying goodbye to go have coffee with... Maggie?

"I mean, he donated a bunch of stuff to the Center a couple of weeks ago. Maybe that's it?" My head is spinning, and not from the hangover, which is mercifully fading into the background. How has my entire life gotten so complicated?

"Yeah, maybe, that would make sense if he needs tax forms for writing it off or something."

"Yeah, tax forms," I say, but I'm not convinced. After that, we catch up, chatting about random things like acts coming to town and if we should plan a girls' beach weekend soon. Eventually, my brain feels less fuzzy and my stomach less tumultuous. We hang up, promising to get together soon.

But my mind won't stop running. Why was Hunter with Mags? What the fuck happened last night? Why was Hunter there? Why did he care so much about some random dude touching me? Hunter was the one that ended everything, and decided it wasn't worth it. Too much of a distraction. Why is he now fucking with my head, getting me to bed safely? Leaving me sweet notes and telling me he misses me.

And most of all, why am I letting my heart build hope again?

THIRTY-SIX
-HANNAH-

By the time my body is fully functioning and over the risk of getting sick, it's a little past noon, and I'm headed to town to check in at the Center.

My new schedule doesn't give me hard and fast hours or days that require me to come in at a specific time, which works great. Maggie forced me into *not* having a set schedule. She explained how, inevitably, I'll be there too much anyway, so why lock me into something?

Which, to be fair, is completely true.

My tires crunch into the gravel parking lot outside the fields, a cloud of dry dust flying up and obscuring the other cars. It's been a dry, hot summer so far. As soon as I step out, the sound of giggles, shouts, and summer fun hits my ears, warming my heart. It's the reminder I need that *this* is why I do this. That sounds of carefree innocence, kids outside, connecting and being, well, kids.

Instead of walking to the fields, I head to the building, pulling open the heavy front doors. The handles are hot from the blazing sun, making my hands burn a bit before entering Maggie's office. And there she sits, same as ever, feet propped on the wobbly desk.

"Hey, Mags, how's it going?" She looks fresher lately, more well-rested, which dumps a bit of guilt onto my soul. Knowing that I could have helped her burden earlier by accepting the position one of the million other times she offered.

"Good, my girl. How are you? Heard you got a little toasty last night?" She laughs her magical, throaty laugh. Spotting her Rise and Grind to-go cup, my eyes roll into my head, knowing Sadie's big mouth has been blabbing.

"Alright, gossip queen, I don't need to hear it from you. I've got a lot going on lately," I say, plopping my butt into the extra chair in her messy office. Which I guess is also my office now. "Anything fun on the schedule today?" While we create a calendar of themed days for camp, sometimes we have people come in for events or to speak to the kids. My hands grab the calendar off the wall, tugging it to bring it close and inspect the date.

"Actually, we do, but it's a last-minute addition, so it's not on there yet," Mags says, looking over at the calendar in my hands. "They're starting a new sleep-away camp for next summer and offering lower-income pricing and scholarships. The founder wanted to come by and talk to the kids here, get them on the waitlist first."

"A sleep-away camp? Here? How have I not heard of this? Is it new?" I look over the calendar at her.

"Yup, some rich city slicker. Came down, found a spot, and is investing in our little town. Cool, huh?"

"Very cool. Do I know the company?" I ask, looking over what else is going on this week distractedly. The calendar is covered in Maggie's frenetic scrawl that is both artsy and a plain mess.

"Don't think so, they're brand new."

"Interesting. So what's this I hear of you meeting Mr. Hutchins at Rise and Grind?" This has been bugging me since Luna's call.

"Did Sadie rat on me?"

"No, your niece," I say, laughing at her annoyed face. "You're not what I'd call discreet, Mags." Pointedly, my eyes travel down her tie-dye maxi dress that would make her stand out at any music festival.

"Ahh, my Moon Goddess Luna. Nosey and secretive. Always was." I snort because it's the truth. Lover of the night and the knower of all secrets. She makes the perfect bar owner. "Mr. Hutchins?" she asks a thin grey eyebrow-raising.

"That's his name, Maggie." My nails interest me now, their chipped polish reminding me to make an appointment for a mani soon. Maybe I'll bring the girls, make a day of it.

"Hmm. I suppose. Yes, I was there. We had to talk business and his contributions." She confirms my thoughts from earlier that they must have had some kind of tax papers to sign. Nodding, my feet hit the floor to stand.

"Okay, well, I'll go out, see if the counselors need anything. Anything you need from me today?" My staff shirt is tugged on over my cami before I spray my face with a quick blast of sunscreen. There's no shade on the field other than a few trees.

"No, ma'am, just remind everyone to be at the bleachers for two. That's when the owner will talk to the kids."

"One-two-three! Eyes on me!" It's an overused phrase, but it usually gets the message across. This is proved when most of the kids immediately quiet down. "Okay, campers, we need you all to be on your best behavior!" I shout through the microphone.

It was one of the few splurges we made this year when we had a budget excess for the first time in years, thanks to the Beaten Path donation. With all the kids, it can be hard to catch their attention, and megaphones get so annoying. Now we can be heard over the kids shouting for announcements or visitors. "We have a special guest here to talk about an opportunity for this winter and next summer."

I still haven't seen this guy, and I'm unsure of opening up the forum to the kids since I can't imagine an entire, brand-new camp being ready any time soon. But Maggie seems on board, and I always trust her opinion.

After handing the mic off to Mags and settling into my seat in the bottom row of the hot metal bleachers that have been out here since I was Rosie's age, she starts. "Today, we have an extra special guest. He reached out to me recently to talk about partnering with the Center to offer a more comprehensive summer and winter program."

Partnering? Didn't she say it's someone opening a new camp? Not a *partnership.*

"While the program is new and won't be open until Winter Break, he's being so generous to offer the waitlist positions to kids here at the Center! Here to tell you more about Camp Sunshine is Hunter Hutchins!"

The blood in my veins goes cold like someone injected them with ice or threw me into an icy lake. My lungs refuse to take in new oxygen, leaving me suffocating and frozen. The skin on my eyes stretches with the size they've opened in surprise. What little air that's leaving my chest is coming through parted lips. My chin dropped as Hunter walks from the door onto the field smiling.

That smile. At first glance, Hunter's smile is all white teeth and Americana good looks. An image consultant's dream. He could be a politician and run on that smile alone. But look at it longer, and you see sincerity and vulnerability. Nerves are dancing at the edges of his eyes as he looks through the bleachers. Searching. Searching... searching for what?

His deep chocolate brown eyes land on me, his nerves melting away and his smile melting into a familiar warmth, more genuine. In that smile, there's hope and joy and pride. *Pride.* It's absolutely beautiful.

God, it breaks my heart and heals it all in one moment.

He takes the mic from Mags, kissing her on the cheek and making her blush. Maggie! Blushing! What kind of witchcraft does this man have? As she sits next to me, it's impossible not to lean over and growl at her. "What the hell, Mags?!" But my eyes never leave Hunter.

"Oh, hush, give the man a chance." Her voice is dancing with laughter and happiness. And then Hunter starts to talk.

"I grew up in Springbrook Hills. Was on the football team—go Dogs," a few of the older kids cheer. "I went to the town street fair every year, jumped from the cliffs at the track into the water. Born and raised here, but what I loved most about this town was the woods." He's scanning the crowd, making eye contact with the teens, and smiling at the littles. "When I was a kid, I loved to go in the woods, gave me a place to collect my thoughts, and handle my emotions." Mags puts an arm around my shoulders, hugging me gently, knowing that's what the woods bring to me as well. Emotion is swelling alongside confusion, feelings creeping from my chest up to my throat in a slow bubble.

"Just like all of you, I had my fair share of struggles in school. Friend issues, girl issues, and parent issues. Going into nature is how I handled that. My whole life, I've wanted to find a way to teach people, kids like you, to use nature to do the same. To connect with the world and forget about your problems.

"My dad's the one who taught me that. I'm sure over the years, a few of you have learned from Maggie as well." Out of the corner of my eye, I see a few kids nod. Kids who I know have gone through tough times, and experienced more than a kid should. Kids I know Maggie helped save. "Years ago, I had the vision to create a space for people to connect with the woods, to learn from it. Learning how to be in nature, make friends with others, sit around a campfire, and let your problems go."

"I hit a speed bump with that program and let it collect dust. Instead, I built a company you probably know but isn't important for what we're talking about. I lost my way, forgot what I wanted to do, and tried to push all of my thoughts and dreams, and disappointments aside to build something great, something that would make those who know me proud.

"In some ways, I succeeded, but in others, I didn't. Recently I had to come home to Springbrook Hills to see my dad, and I met some amazing people who reminded me of who I am. They reminded me of what I really wanted to accomplish and offer to kids like you. So I went back to my roots. Literally." His eyes are on mine now, no longer scanning the crowd. Those warm depths holding me captive, holding me still.

"When I came back, I had planned to create a new store with a few campsites at Sunshine Falls Park. We had the plans set up, and we would have started building on Monday. But things changed, and I got some sense knocked into me." The breath is stopped again in my lungs as a tiny, golden kernel of hope takes over the dark sadness that's blanketed me for a week.

"So instead of a store to sell things, we're building a camp for kids who want to learn more and connect with the great outdoors. We're creating a space for kids to go and have the best summer ever. We'll have everything from hiking to fire building to archery and horseback riding lessons. Crafts and s'mores and fishing. All the things that will make the most memorable summer for the kids in our community. In this community, I grew up in."

My heart is melting, the water from the ice flooding my eyes, knowing what this means. Knowing that Hunter overcame whatever was haunting him, is following his dream and using his very first failure to create success. Not just for him, but for the kids.

Knowing that he's using my dream to do it. My idea, my wildest daydream, Hunter is making happen.

"The best part is that we'll be offering scholarships and subsidized tuition for kids who can't afford a camp like this normally. We want to give everyone who is interested the chance to attend, to give your parents a bit of a break, and allow you to connect with nature and your friends."

Tears begin to fall.

This was my dream.

The dream I told him shyly in the safe cover of night, embarrassed that my dreams were too big, too unachievable.

Embarrassed to tell this successful businessman about my little idea.

He's giving these kids what I would have killed for. He's giving these kids the chance to thrive where they might have failed. A small warm, weathered hand grabs onto mine.

Mags. My eyes finally break from Hunter. Looking at her, I see the love and warmth, and pride that is always in there, but that invisible layer of worry and sadness I've always seen has lifted.

"So I'll be here for a bit to talk to any of you who have questions, but I'll also be leaving some pamphlets for you to take home, take a look at with your parents and decide if it's something you'd like to do next summer. We'll also be having a shorter winter session during winter break.

"But before you head out, make sure you go over to that big truck and grab a backpack with some fun Camp Sunshine gear in it." My head whips over to see Autumn, Steve, and the kids standing on the bed of a truck filled with bright yellow backpacks, waving at the bleachers. Zoo, my ass. The tears flow in earnest now, unstoppable and free.

"Alright, you hooligans. You all can get up and go. Grab a bag, go play in the fields, and talk to Mr. Hutchins. We'll have a snack at three!" Maggie says from the mic. I didn't even realize she had left my side, I was so lost in Hunter.

For the next 20 minutes, my ass stays planted in the bleachers trying to process everything. Kids are milling around, reading the pamphlets, chatting with Hunter. He's in his element, joking with the kids, laughing, and encouraging. Talking about this new program that I had no idea existed. How long has he been working on this? What happened to the new Beaten Path location?

As the kids peter out, off to different activities, Hunter walks my way with purpose, a small, nervous smile playing on his lips.

"Hey," he says, sitting next to me.

"Hi." The panic and shock still haven't worn off. The confusion and the hope are so near to the surface.

"What do you think?"

"About what?" I ask because at this point, I have pretty much no idea what's going on. Hunter barks out a laugh, warming my soul. God, I've missed this man.

"Everything." Turning to me, he pushes a lock of my long dark hair that's fallen out of my bun behind my ear.

"I'm so confused." My voice is soft and quiet. He laughs again, this time a small, gentle chuckle.

"Can you come with me?"

"Come where?"

His rough, calloused hand grabs mine. "Just come with me. I have so much to tell you. We have so much to talk about."

"Do we?" I seem unable to string together enough words to create a full sentence.

"Oh, yes, baby. We really do." For the first time since he ended us, a hopeful smile comes to my lips. That spark of hope turns into a warm ember in my belly, heating me through.

"Go, get on," Maggie says, coming up behind us on the bleachers. "You two get out of here before it gets too nuts with snack time." Without another word, Hunter stands and grabs my hand. He leans over to kiss Maggie's cheek and then leads me down the bleacher and through the field, where I spot his truck in the gravel lot. Each step reverberates through my body, confirming this is not a dream my hungover mind brewed up. But just to confirm...

"Is this a hungover dream?" I mumble under my breath, rocks crunching under my worn sneakers as we walk hand in hand to his Bronco.

"No, baby, this is very much real." He waves at Autumn in the now-empty truck bed, who smiles big at me. I try not to flip her off for lying to me. Hunter opens the passenger door, helping me into his truck.

Hunter hops in, turning the key in the ignition. "Just trust me, okay, Han?" he asks, looking into my eyes before he backs up, taking off down the road.

THIRTY-SEVEN
-HANNAH-

It takes a few minutes to figure out where we're headed, but when it clicks, I remember this is the way to Sunshine Falls, where we went on our first date. Where he's... opening a camp. A camp that is everything I've ever dreamed of in my wildest imagination. We all have our own crazy *if I win the lottery* dreams, and this has always been mine.

"Hunter, what is going on?" My voice shakes as the words tumble out. In all honesty, the stress and fear, and hope flooding me are too much, overwhelming my system. If I let the hope take over, let it consume me, let that small ember burn through me, and this all crashes down, it will take everything I am with it.

"Please, trust me, baby. I know I don't deserve it, but give me a few minutes. That's all I'm asking."

He grabs my hand again as he looks away from the road quickly in an attempt to reassure me. His tan hand looks so huge, holding my tiny one on the worn fabric of the bench seat. Breathing in deeply, my eyes divert to the window again, watching the suburbs turn into forests and woods.

As we approach, the simple, empty road that was here last time has transformed into a home for construction vehicles. Men in hard hats wander around. Hunter reaches to the floor and grabs a pass he pops on his dashboard. The workers wave him through easily.

The Bronco navigates through bumps and turns until we reach the same lot we were in a few weeks ago. It looks different now, though—a tent has tables with workers hanging out, looking at papers. Trucks are parked all over. Some work trucks, and some construction vehicles. A few trailers are parked seemingly strategically throughout. Hunter parks before walking around the truck. He opens my door, leans in, and unbuckles me before taking my hand to help me out.

There's purpose in his steps as he leads me through the parking lot, waving at a few of the men, and tipping his chin at others. He never stops, never says a word. We walk in silence through the woods, the same path we took last time, and I know where we're headed.

The hike isn't calming or peaceful this time. Emotions are churning, making me a nervous wreck. Sweat is building on my palms, made even more embarrassing since Hunter's hand is still securely tucked in mine. Occasionally my eyes slide to watch him, but his gaze remains fixed straight ahead and determined. Unlike me, though, he looks at peace. If I didn't feel so confused, I'd be shocked to see the foreign look on his handsome face.

Eventually, we step into the clearing.

On the small area of grass void of water or trees is a picnic blanket, a small basket beside it. Finally, his hand is out of mine as he walks over to the basket sitting on the blue and white blanket. He's reaching in and pulling things out—glasses, wrapped sandwiches, salads, cookies. Wiping my sweaty hands on the back of my jeans, I stay standing, nearly lightheaded at the vision in front of me.

"Come sit, baby." Complying, I sit gently on the blanket, in the furthest corner from him.

"Hunter, what is going on?" I ask, losing grip on my patience and any sense of bravery or sanity.

"I fucked up." His eyes are pointed directly at mine, solemn and full of regret.

"Hunter, I—"

"Give me this, okay? Let me tell you everything. Once I'm done, if you want to, I'll walk you back to the Bronco and drop you off at Autumn's." I hesitate but nod my agreement.

"Ten years ago, I trusted a woman and made the biggest mistake of my career. For years, I used that mistake as a reason to distance myself from everyone. From my father and sister, from my nieces. From friends. From women. I used it as a justification for not creating relationships, and for focusing on nothing but my business.

"For years, I set out with the intention of building Beaten Path to the point where I could afford to transform the Sunshine Falls location into something profitable. Something I could bring back to my dad and show him that his faith in me was worth it.

"I came home to be with my dad, of course, but more, it was to oversee the project here in Springbrook Hills. We were finally working on building a store here, as you know. It wasn't my original vision. Not even close. It wasn't going to benefit the community or help people. But it was going to be profitable, and it was going to grow our bottom line. And then, the day I arrived back in town, I walk into my sister's house to see a gorgeous woman with kind eyes and a killer fucking body singing *Bohemian Rhapsody* with my family. Everything changed, Hannah. I didn't know it then, but from that moment on, my life has been forever changed."

My breath hitches, catching in my chest as that ember burns, catching fire to the broken shards he left in me a week ago. All of it becoming tinder for something bigger, something more. Something beautiful.

"Since that day, I've been distracted. Distracted from deadlines and work, but also distracted from what I thought was my end goal. Distracted from feeling like I have something to prove. Distracted by the loneliness and the misery I've created for myself. I think it was here, that first time I brought you here, that I fell in love with you."

Hunter reaches over and grabs my hand again, and this time, I don't care if they're sweaty. Tears are filling my eyes again, and that fire is shining through me now.

"You're so beautiful, Hannah. Not just your body and your eyes and your gorgeous hair. But inside. You've been let down so many times by people who were supposed to love and support you, and you haven't let that change you, you haven't let that tear you apart. You trust everyone, and work to give them your whole soul, not just the pieces that you can give while keeping yourself safe.

"After I fucked everything up, I realized that's what I was doing. I was giving everyone just enough of myself to keep my walls up, protect my heart, and keep myself safe. Never have I been able to or even wanted to give someone a chance. But then you came in and showed me if I did, if I was brave like you and opened up, I could have it all." He pauses, and I watch his Adam's apple bob with a swallow.

"When Dad was rushed to the hospital, it was the first eye-opener of many over the last few weeks. I had this vision of seeing him after this project was underway, but things kept happening, delaying the start. I think it was a sign, some higher-up power telling me it was all wrong. But at the time, all I knew was the project was having issues, and it was like deja vu. Another woman coming in and distracting me from the plan.

"It was when I talked to Dad that it all clicked. He helped me see what a fucking idiot I was being. How far I'd been pulled from my original vision. I wanted to help people, you know? Years ago, I wanted to help kids who were like me, overwhelmed and feeling lost. And somehow, it turned into this monster out of my control.

"The day I talked to Dad, I called everyone and canceled everything. The start date was moved back while I worked with Tanner, and he helped me dream up a new plan. We needed emergency meetings with the town to get it approved, but they saw my vision and what it would bring to the community. We were able to break ground today with the modifications.

"Maggie helped me plan everything, what would be needed. I

signed on as a primary owner of the Center. While Camp Sunshine is technically a separate entity, it will run concurrently with the Center's summer program. Offering subsidized summer childcare and summer camp experience to the kids. We're bringing on licensed guidance counselors, teachers, and therapists as the counselors to help the kids who really need the help, need this experience to save them."

Tears are flowing as I remember telling him my vision. My vision that he is bringing to life.

"How did you manage that in two weeks? Hasn't this been in the works for months?" I ask, trying to play out the timeline in my mind.

"Turns out, when things are meant to be and work, it goes smoothly. I've barely slept for two weeks trying to fix this, but the town rushed the approvals when I told them about the community benefits. Had Maggie vouch for me. Everything else fell into place."

"Hunter, I—" I try to talk, to tell him what this means to me, what *he* means to me, but he doesn't let me.

"A few more things, okay?" I nod, agreeing because as much as I want to talk, I'm eager to listen. "I know you accepted the position officially, but I don't think you read your contract all the way through. In there is a bit about working at an off-site summer camp." He's right. I didn't read it at all, trusting Maggie implicitly. Like she probably knew I would. That sneaky woman. A smile peaks through my teary face, knowing this was his plan all along. That this wasn't some kind of impulsive decision.

"I need you. I need you to help build this vision, to create a program that will help these kids, help them heal, and grow. I need you to be my right hand, my moral compass. Your heart is so huge, and this was your vision, Hannah. I need you to help me make it happen.

"But even more, I need you to make me whole. God, I fucked up so badly, Hannah. I should have listened to you about Dad. Should have listened to you about *us*. I knew all along I was falling, and it scared the shit out of me. When I wasn't letting my mind get in the way, I could see it, see a life together. See you mothering our kids, see you growing old with me. See you baking me oatmeal raisin cookies and driving me insane every day. I see you collapsing on the couch with me after we get our kids to bed, and then you waking up next to me, cranky and sleepy. See you growing old with me, keeping me in line. Hannah, I fell in love with you in this spot. I fell for you hard without ever even realizing it. I fell for you and took you down with me, and then I let you fall, forgetting I was supposed to catch you and keep you safe."

I'm sobbing now, the hope burning through my skin. It's no longer plain hope but joy and passion and excitement for this beautiful future he's painting for us.

"Hannah Marie Keller, I love you. I love you more than I ever thought possible. You've opened my eyes to things I didn't want to admit were missing from my life. You fit in my family like a puzzle piece. You make me so damn happy, and you're kind and generous and sweet and sassy. You're a beast in the morning, and you make me so fucking hard I can't think of much else when you're nearby." He smiles at me with a wink, and I let out a giggle.

"You're beautiful, which I know you know, but I promise to tell you until I die. You're a great friend and an amazing nanny. You give to everyone you meet. I'm not asking you to give me forever—I know I have a lot to prove, and I have so much to make up for. I know you don't want forever until you can trust it, and I'm here to tell you I'll work for that trust every single day until I have it. All I'm asking is for the chance to prove that to you."

Since we broke up, I've felt a painful, gaping hole inside of me that I feared would never mend. A missing piece that should not have been there after only a few weeks. But now I realize it was a hole that had been there my entire life. A hole in my soul caused by my parents neglecting me, and by a lifetime of men not living up to my expectations. Hunter had filled that, if only for a short while. And when he left, knowing what I felt like whole broke me.

Could I give him the chance to break me again? The chance to give me a taste of feeling whole and complete, only for him to decide I was a distraction and not worth it?

"What about New York?" I ask, knowing he isn't planning to be here forever. He has a life out of Springbrook Hills, and if I agree, that's just another hurdle we'll have to jump.

"Condo's for sale." The words come quickly, with no hesitation.

"What?"

"Selling it. Moving home."

"You're going to stay at Autumn's?" I ask, kind of confused because I know that Steve and Autumn have loved having him there, but not indefinitely.

"I bought my dad's house from him. Well, I'm in the process, it's probably going to take another month to finalize. Then we're renovating the Mother-in-Law's cottage out back so he can be close once he's in full remission. I think I know someone who can help me with that." He smiles at me, and I can't help but smile back.

"But... your work. It's in the city, right? Your office?"

"I'm fixing my priorities. The office isn't too far for a day or two if they need me. Gina will still be there, and most of my work is online meetings, anyway. I'll have an office at the new house. But I need to be here. For Dad, for the new camp. But mostly, baby, for you."

My shoulders droop in relief, like all the pressure that's been on them has lifted. Smiling at him through a new flood of tears, I ask, "So you're staying here?"

"I'm staying here, baby."

"To... be with me?" I ask hesitantly.

"To be with you, Hannah." He's closer to me now, and I'm unsure how that happened. But his hand is curling around my neck into my hair, and his forehead is pressing to mine. Hunter's eyes, those warm, brown eyes that make me feel safe, are looking right into mine, telling me... telling me everything. That he's being honest. That he's missed me. That he wants to try this out. That he's sorry. That...

"And you love me?" I ask, my voice barely a whisper of breath over the water falling behind us.

"And I love you, Hannah," he whispers back, his lips gently brushing mine as he does. Breath fanning past my lips, tempting me.

"I love you, Hunter," I whisper, moving my head the tiny millimeter needed to lock our lips. To seal the deal. To give this man my heart and hope he takes care of it. The kiss is unlike any we've shared—it's soft and sweet with no urgency, as if confessing everything has taken the restraints from us.

But then my lips open gently, letting his tongue inside. And something snaps in me. I've missed this man, missed his lips and his body, and what both can do to me. My hands creep behind his neck, tangling in his overlong hair and pulling him closer to me as a small moan escapes my mouth. Our tongues dance and teeth clash, frantic to get closer, like the time apart has put a barrier between us only skin on skin can crumble.

His hands trail down my sides as he guides me to the ground, so he's propped above me, and I'm lying on the soft blanket. As we kiss, breath mingling and hands exploring, my heart is floating with happiness and relief. Joy is shining through me, so bright I'm sure Hunter can see it on my skin.

My hands trail down, then back up under his shirt, exploring the skin of his back, pulling him close to me. Without even trying, he's positioned himself, so his growing length is right against my clit, causing me to mewl and push my hips up, needing more friction.

"Fuck, I've missed you," he mutters against my neck, licking and sucking in a way that has me sure I'll need coverup tomorrow.

"God, me too," I agree, moaning loudly as his hand creeps up my shirt and bra, grazing a nipple.

"Shhh, we're not alone this time," he says, a chuckle in his voice. "Should I get you off in the woods again? Make you come with all the men working not far from here?" His mouth is next to my ear, his fingers now pinching my tight bud. The hussy in me is screaming *YES!* because it feels like it's been forever since his hands have been on my skin. But the realistic human in me knows we live in a tiny town, and I can't handle that kind of embarrassment.

"Hunter, we—" Another moan pulls from my lips as he moves his hand to my other nipple, tugging gently. This morning's decision to go with a thin bralette was a sound one.

"Shh, don't worry, baby, I'll take care of you." He's kissing me again, making me forget my protests, and we kiss and writhe on the blanket, desperate to be closer, to make our reconciliation real and final. A bolt of pleasure jumps right to my pussy with his voice, dripping in sex and want.

"Okay," I say, accepting his offer because, really, what else can I say as he grinds himself into me *just the right way,* so I'm panting and desperate.

"CRRRK!" A sound screeches from not too far away, and we stop, freezing with him on top of me, his hand up my shirt.

"What was that?" I whisper, terrified that we're going to be murdered in the woods, right after I finally get the love of my life. It's like a bad horror movie.

"CRRRK, over," a voice and a static sound say, making me realize it's someone with a walkie-talkie not far off from us. Hunter sits up, pulling his hand from my shirt and I do the same, straightening the material.

"Who is that?" I whisper, humiliated and embarrassed.

"Probably one of the men," Hunter says, smiling. He thinks this is funny!

"This is not funny!" I whisper yell at him, smacking his shoulder. He pulls me closer, hugging me against him.

"Oh, it's funny, trust me." I want to argue. I really do. But I'm in Hunter's arms after thinking we were done for good, so instead, my body melts into his.

"What is it about this place?" I ask, settling in his lap with my arms around his neck. Looking around, I see the same tall trees as last time, and the same beautiful waterfall, but it feels different—no, changed—somehow.

Lighter, freer.

Or maybe that's just us.

"I think it's just you. I feel the same no matter where we are." He pinches my ass, making me squeal, followed by an embarrassingly girly giggle as I slap his chest.

"You're such a guy."

"Would you rather I be a girl?"

"No, but you don't have to think about sex all the time," I say.

"Uh, baby, yes, I do. Have you seen you?" he asks, grabbing a handful of my ass and making me laugh. My smile turns solemn when I think of how good this feels. Goofing with him, being with him. "What's wrong?" His hand pushes my hair from my face, another insignificant gesture I've missed.

"Just missed this. Missed you," I mutter into his shirt, pushing the tears back. His sigh can be felt through his chest as he tugs out my hair tie, combing through my hair with his fingers. God, that feels so nice.

"I fucked up," he says. My face snuggles deeper into his chest. We sit in silence for a bit, and I'm thankful the worker seems to have walked away. "Okay, so we've got two options. Spend the afternoon here, eat this lunch I packed, or bring it back to my place and eat it there after I fuck you until you can't move." My core clenches in tandem with my arms around him, making him chuckle.

"Your place?" I ask, looking up at him, unsure where that is.

"My dad's house. I bought it, remember? It's not ready, still has all the old furniture and decorations, but fuck if I wouldn't want to fuck you in my childhood bed." He growls this last part, nipping my lip. Okay, why does that sound so hot?

"Your place," I say quickly, which makes him laugh.

THIRTY-EIGHT
-HANNAH-

The old Hutchins place is a large brick colonial with white trim and black shutters. I've been here a few times when Autumn dragged me on holidays and always loved the house. It sits on an acre of bright green, well-tended grass with the most perfect cobblestone walkway. It's picture-perfect.

We walk hand in hand up the walkway, the picnic basket in Hunter's other hand, and it's like I'm in a dream. The mere thought that Hunter has bought this place from Ron with the intention to... what?

Live here?

Be with me?

Build a life in his hometown?

It seems surreal. My heart is suffering from major whiplash.

As we enter, he places the picnic basket on the island in the kitchen as we pass it before pulling me up the grand wooden staircase. He's tugging me, speeding me up like he can't wait to get where we're going. His impatience makes me smile and draws a quiver from my nether regions.

"In a rush, big boy?" He stops at my words, turning to me, a step above, and dips to press his lips to mine.

"It's been forever since I've been inside of you. Fuck yeah, I'm in a rush," he says when he releases me. I throw my head back in a startled laugh, but Hunter isn't playing around. Instead, he lifts me, cradling me in his arms like a new bride as he scales the last few steps.

A foot kicks in a door right off the stairs, and he was not kidding—this really is his childhood bedroom. The walls are covered in band posters and an orange and black Springbrook Hills High pennant. On the mahogany desk in the corner, I see a picture of Hunter, Tanner, Luna's brother, Zander, and Tony in football uniforms, smiling at the camera, young and handsome.

"You were a hottie when you were a kid."

"And now?" He crawls up my body after placing me gently on the bed. A smile plays on my lips.

"Are you fishing for compliments, Mr. Hutchins?" God, I feel giddy, a lightness in my soul that I'm not sure I've ever experienced.

"Oh, no, I don't need to go fishing for them. I just need to get you all hot and bothered and you start handing them out on your own." I laugh, but also, it's the truth.

"Hmm, so why don't you get on to that, yeah?" My lips are pressed against his, breath mingling with his as my hand creeps up into his hair. Instead of answering, his mouth is on mine, devouring me in the most beautiful, gentle way.

Unlike any other time we've been together, this feels unhurried and at ease. Like Hunter coming to terms with himself, coming back to me, admitting his feelings lifted something.

If I had allowed myself to daydream about this, about us being together again after everything happened, I would have imagined frantic lust, hands and teeth and a lack of restraint. This is anything but.

My hands slowly explore his body, relearning the curves and muscles, his flat stomach and hard back. Slowly, I inch his shirt up before he helps me out, crossing his arms behind his head to grab the back and pull it off.

His callused hand dips under the staff tee and cami I still have on, tugging it over my head. Leaving me in a thin, grey sports bra and a pair of soft, athletic shorts. Shoes and socks were removed sometime earlier, but all I can think about now is his thumbs inching towards my nipples, hard and peeking through the thin cotton.

His eyes are on his thumb as it softly, so soft it's a ghost of a touch, grazes the peak and a quiet, desperate moan escapes my lips. "Hunter."

Meeting my gaze, he looks at me with a satisfied smirk, sensing my need. Instead of sliding off the fabric as I hoped, he leans down, places his mouth over the thin cotton and sucks, mouth pulling fabric and skin into his mouth with fierceness. My back bows off the bed as a low moan creeps out of my chest. His teeth nip before he stares at his handiwork, the light grey turning dark in a wet circle.

"Hunter, take it off, I want to feel you." I buck my hips to try and get some kind of friction. But he shakes his head and repeats the sweet torture on the other side, making me crazy with need. When he pulls back once more, I decide I've had it. With some kind of inner strength I didn't know I had, my hips bucking and rolling over him until I'm straddling him and tear off my bra.

Looking down, I expect to see shock, but a smile on his lips tells me he probably let that happen, let me take control and get what I wanted.

Something tells me that Hunter will always and forever give me whatever I want. The thought brings butterflies to my belly as I lean down, pressing my naked chest to his, and every thought, every emotion, and lingering sadness that'd plagued me the last two weeks melts away at the utter rightness of having Hunter's body pressed against mine.

I know he feels it too when his hands immediately start to graze my bare back, groaning not with pleasure or withheld lust but with relief.

"God, I missed you, Hannah. Fucking missed this so bad. Was hollow for weeks, a damn zombie." His words hit me hard with the knowledge that he was in the same space I was. They fuel me, fuel my need to be with him, to be as close as we can.

"I need you, Hunter," I say, tugging at my shorts. The movement is jerky, frantic as the need overpowers me. No more games, no more teasing.

"Yes." His hands help me remove my shorts and then his own, rolling once again until I'm on my back, Hunter hovering above me. His forearms hold him above me so as not to crush me, but I'd take it. I'd take his entire weight on me so long as it held the knowledge of us, that this was right and this was forever.

Quickly, his hand travels down my body, grazing the side of my breast and my ribs before going to my thigh and in, up to my slit.

"Ready for me," he groans aloud, and I mimic the sound, the feel of his thick finger running through my wet and grazing my clit unbearably softly..

"Yes, Hunter, now." My legs come up to circle his hips, bringing him right where I need him. The hand already between my legs guides him in, the thick head stretching me deliciously. It's so right. It's so perfect, and has been since that first time.

Leaving just the head filling me, he takes his arm back to rest beside my head, both hands cradling the top of my head as he holds my eyes. "I love you so much, Hannah," he says. The words create a tidal of emotion in me, and even though I want him, need him in me to satisfy this need and hunger, if that's all I had, this moment, I would be fine.

"I love you, Hunter," I say, my voice so soft and the words coming out gravely with emotion. His eyes shine with joy and love, and relief as his lips come down to mine, and he pushes into me, filling me, completing me.

His mouth absorbs the cry that falls from my lips, my eyes drifting shut as he continues to thrust into me hard, then soft, fast, then slow, no consistency within the movements. He's as overtaken by this as I am, completely arrested by what's happening, by the feelings, the emotions.

Slowly, the pressure builds within me, his thick length sliding in and out of me, his pelvic bone grinding deliciously against my clit with each forward thrust. His breaths are heavy, colliding with my own in a storm between us, our lips now grazing each other but no longer able to kiss or do more than stare at each other.

It's like for the first time in my life, I'm home.

Pleasure starts to bloom in my belly, my lower spine tingling with the nearness of my orgasm when I call to him. "Hunter, I'm close." The words come out frantic, almost scared. This release will consume me, and change me. Never will I be the same after this, and I know it for certain.

"I know, baby, me too, let go." His voice is strained, eyes still on my own. And just like that, like my body needed permission from his tongue, my whole body clenches, and my world explodes, leaving Hunter at the center of it once and for all as he follows me over the edge.

Hours later, we're in bed eating our picnic lunch, now a picnic dinner. The sheet is pulled up over my naked chest and covers Hunter's hips, but I keep getting the most distracting glimpses of hipbones and a happy trail. My tongue comes out absentmindedly to trace my bottom lip as I stare.

"Stop it, or we're never going to eat," he says, and I raise an eyebrow, reminding him without words that he's, well, *eaten* quite a bit since we've gotten here. He laughs, throwing a bag of chips at me, which I open and start munching. All the emotion and physical exertion have me starving.

"So, tell me everything. What happened?" I ask around a mouthful of chips, not even caring about manners. "What is going on with the house? And the camp? Are you really selling the condo?" Nerves flutter in my belly, eager for what his answer will be and how it will impact me. Impact us.

"As I told you—I talked to my dad. He clarified a lot of things, but mostly that I'm an idiot who needed to figure out my priorities. I've spent ten years trying to make up for something but lost myself in the process." He unwraps a sandwich, handing me half. "So I got to work and restructured my entire business, scrapped the retail location, and planned out the camp in a few days. My business partner wanted to murder me for a bit, but I think he sees the vision now."

"Business partner?"

"Jonathan. You'll meet him at some point and probably hate him, but he's a good guy." A noncommital sound leaves my lips, not sure how I feel about a partner I'll 'probably hate.'

"And the house?" I ask. His living situation can make or break just about everything. I don't want to force him to leave his life in the city, but I also know that I'll never leave Springbrook Hills. There's too much rooting me here.

"It's mine. I'll be remodeling the whole thing to suit our needs better, but until the master bedroom looks nothing like my dad's room, meaning I'll never be able to fuck you in there without being creeped the fuck out, I'll be staying in here." My sandwich gets caught in my throat, and he pats my back to help me out. When I can breathe again, I face him.

"*Our* needs?"

"Me and you, baby. Autumn said she's fine with you living here and working for her. It was practically her idea. It's only two blocks, so it's not far if they need you last minute." He says it like it's no big deal. "But this way, we won't be staying in your tiny ass bed."

"I'm sorry, what? Don't you have to, I don't know, *ask* someone to move in with you before you make plans and talk to her employer about it?"

"Well, for normal people, probably. But have you met Autumn? She was the one who brought it up. Not me."

God, the Hutchins children are going to be the death of me. "You guys are insane."

"You don't want to move in here?" It's hard to tell if he's offended or amused by me.

"I... I don't know? This is all going super fast. This morning I thought we were done forever, and I'd never find anyone else and live the life of a shrew. Nannying for Rosie's kids until I die, which, to be honest, is a terrifying thought because Rosie is a nut job, and can you imagine kids of Rosie's?" I'm rambling, a fun habit I have when I'm nervous. Hunter laughs, pulling me into him by my neck and smacking a wet kiss on my lips, immediately calming my fears. "I mean, I guess I could move in here. If you asked nicely."

"Look, I don't expect you to move in tomorrow. But I've fucked this up enough already to know I want you in my life. And not just for the summer, Hannah. I'm not gonna freak you out and ask for more than you're willing to agree to right now, but I think you know where my head is at." He's right not to push because I am completely freaking out internally.

"I see that look. Calm down. We're working on this one day at a time. The first is getting this house in shape and making a spot for Dad. I'll need your help because I hate decorating and your cottage looks amazing. But please, spare me the lace and flowers." A smile comes to my lips, chasing off my anxiety a bit. "And then from there, we can figure it out. Even if it's switching beds for a few weeks. Or months. But please, not years, because I'm getting old, and I don't want to be an old dad."

Annnnd there goes my anxiety again.

"Dad?" I say and freeze, chip in my fingers, pausing right before my mouth.

"Eventually." Jesus Christ, who is this man.

"Who are you?"

"I'm yours, baby," he says softly, taking the chip from my fingers and eating it before pulling me into his lap. "I realized a lot of things about myself since you've been gone. But most importantly, I've realized that I want to do whatever it takes to make your dreams come true."

His lips brush against mine.

"If that means taking it slow, we'll take it slow. If that means calling Rosie tonight and telling her she'll be getting her flower girl on this weekend, I'll make it happen. What I'm saying is that I love you."

My eyes go hazy as tears fill them.

"I love you, and I know in my gut that I want to be with you. I want to grow old with you and run through the sprinklers with our kids in the summer. And I want to take family camping vacations and teach our kids how to fish. And I want to fill up your passport with stamps. I want to take care of you, the same way you take care of everyone else in your life. To stand alongside you as we build up the camp, so kids have more opportunities. I want to make your dreams come true, Hannah."

I'm crying now, full, body-wracking sobs escaping my mouth at his beautiful words.

I'd lost faith. I'd lost faith that I would find this, find a man who wants me for me, wants to take care of me. Lost faith that my person was out there, willing to take a risk on me, who was broken in my own way. But then he came into my world, shook it like a snow globe, and showed me the possibilities life had for me.

"Okay," I whisper through my tears.

"Okay?"

"Okay. I want that all too. Not right away. We should date first. And eventually, one day, I want you to ask me for real. So Rosie will have to wait. But I want the whole shebang. The wedding, the party, all of it. I don't want that to distract me from the new camp." Hunter laughs, then brushes one of my tears away with a finger.

"You're the greatest distraction ever, Hannah Marie Keller." He says, his hand going behind my head to twine in my hair. He pulls my mouth to his, kissing me, placing the seal on everything he's said. His lips tell me everything his heart feels, and I hope mine do the same, telling him what my clumsy words can't.

And not long after, we're rolling around in a bed of crushed chips, once again distracted by each other.

THIRTY-NINE
-HANNAH-
3 MONTHS LATER

"No, no, no! These are for the bake sale!" I shout, slapping hands with my spatula as I'm transferring cookies from the baking sheet to the cooling rack. This seems to be a common trend when the Hutchins men are around. Two sets of identical eyes look back at me, both faces stuffed with cookie.

"F'orry 'annah," Ron says around his chocolate chip one. He's a liar. He's not sorry at all. Hunter stands there smiling and chewing, not even trying to act ashamed, the ass.

"No more!" I say, waving the pretty, light blue spatula I got when I moved in as if it's going to deter them. This is why I double just about every single baking recipe these days.

"What bake sale is it this time?" Hunter asks, leaning back against his kitchen island after stealing another cookie. Correction: *our* kitchen island. It's been exactly two weeks since officially moving into Hunter's house and out of the cottage. After three months of him begging and pleading with me to do so, I caved in. Okay, fine, there was no begging from Mr. Hutchins, but there was some carefully crafted conniving, some of which included my friends. Some of which included his bed and his mouth. I shiver just thinking about it.

"The Center," I say quickly, turning my back to him nearly immediately.

"What does the Center need?"

"Nothing big." In the last few months, any time Hunter hears we need something at the Center, the crazy man just... goes and buys it. He says it's a tax write-off, a donation, blah blah blah, but it's getting excessive. And since we're a small, under-funded non-profit, we pretty much *always* need something.

"What is it, Hannah?" He asks again.

"Honey, seriously, it's nothing. Let us handle this one." Instead of answering, Hunter digs into his pocket, pulling out his phone. Unlocking the screen, he swipes a few times before lifting the sleek device to his ear, eyes on me.

"Mags, Hunter. Yeah, yeah, Hannah's good. She's baking up a storm, though. What does the Center need now?"

Goddammit. I swear, introducing the two of them was a huge mistake. Since officially becoming an 'us' he meets with her at least twice a week, sometimes *without me*, grabbing coffee at Rise and Grind to brainstorm and bitch about me. I know this last part because Sadie is a good friend and rats on them.

It's like opening the camp and finally utilizing the Sunshine Falls location opened him up to realize his true passion: helping kids. And while I love that about him and I adore that it helps *my* kids, it can be a bit much.

"Hunter! Stop it!" I jump towards him, reaching for his phone hand, but he simply puts up an arm, using his hand on my chest to keep me back. Ron is laughing outright, taking pleasure in my frustration. I swear, the whole damn Hutchins-Sutter family loves to see it.

"Ahh, got it. Can you send a note to Gina, and let her know what you need? We have that account for you guys now, so you can go directly through her with any requests."

"Hunter!"

"Okay, yup, I'll tell her. Love you too, Mags, bye." God, I want to be so mad at him, but hearing him tell Mags he loves her, the woman who saved me in more ways than one, melts me a bit.

"What the hell, Hunter?" My hands are on my hips, a full-on rage brewing. He smiles the special smile he saves for when he finds me cute. Then he pulls me into his body with hands on my waist.

"New sports equipment and uniforms for the rec basketball team will not break me, baby." God, I love it when he calls me baby in that soft, smooth voice. The problem is, he *knows* that and uses it against me.

"You can't pay for everything, Hunter."

"I'm not. Beaten Path is. This summer, we did fantastically and with winter sports and the holiday season coming up, Q4 is looking just as great. We need to move some more money into donations and charity, or else tax season will kill us." We both know this is bullshit. Hunter is an amazing entrepreneur, and he has an amazing team backing him. They could easily find other ways to allocate that money and offset increased taxes.

"You know what I mean. Plus, the kids were excited to raise the money."

"That's a lie. Last week Sara told me that no one was signing up for your bake sale and you were going to do them all yourself." What a freaking little tattle tale.

"So you knew about this last week?" I look up at him.

"What?" He looks like a deer in headlights. "Uh, no, just came down and saw..." I lean back in his arms to look him in the face, seeing the truth before slapping his chest.

"Oh, my God! You waited until I baked all the cookies before you said anything, didn't you!?" With that, Ron busts out laughing again,

It's great to hear it, too. Last week, after two months in the clinical trial and a month of monitoring, we got the glorious news that Ron was officially in full remission. He's been living in the Mother-in-Law suite out back after Hunter renovated it to fit his needs. The day we found out, late at night in our bed together, Hunter broke down crying in relief and happiness, an emotion that he trusted only me with.

"You shut up." I whip my head to the traitor.

"Hush, babe, it's not a big deal." Hunter is still laughing as he reaches for another cookie.

"Not a big deal!? I've spent the last three hours baking seven dozen cookies! I have enough dough for five more!"

"Perfect, we'll have cookies for days and dough for fresh cookies later." He presses his mouth to mine, chocolate and brown sugar and vanilla on his lips, and I find it impossible not to melt into him.

"I hate you," I mumble against his lips.

"No, you don't, you love me."

"I would have just made you cookies if you asked," I grumble, walking out of his arms to start cleaning up.

"Yeah, but this way, I get a variety. Is that oatmeal raisin?" he asks, excitement flooding his voice when he eyes a pile hiding in the corner.

"Maybe," I say, running to block the plate with my body. "Maybe I made them and hid the good ones for you, but now I'm second-guessing my kindness."

Hunter comes over to me, wrapping an arm around my waist and using the other under my chin to tip my head up to look at him. "You're my dream woman, you know that?" And again, I melt, because what else are you supposed to do when the hottest guy on planet earth does that?

"You're still a jerk. But I love you." My toes roll up, raising me to reach his lips for a quick brush that sends shivers down my spine.

"Uncle Hunter! Are the cookies done?" Glaring up at him, I see Rosie from over Hunter's shoulder bounding in, glittery pink bike helmet on.

"Are you kidding me?" Hunter smiles, kissing me again before reaching behind me for one of his gross oatmeal raisin cookies.

"Yup, come get 'em," he says to his niece, who is followed by her dad and Sara. My glare intensifies as Ron just laughs.

"Yeah, come get some of these oatmeal raisin cookies," I say, grabbing the plate and running towards the girls, laughing.

"No way! Those are mine!" Hunter yells, coming after me to rescue his cookies.

"Why do I always forget how exhausting they are?" Hunter's finger draws shapes on my exposed hip above my pajama shorts as we lay on the couch.

"I don't know, we've been having them over on Fridays for months now."

Saturday mornings are usually lazy and slow once the kids leave. Every Friday night, they stay at our house for a sleepover while Autumn and Steve go out. I try my best to pack in a full night of crazy fun, and by the morning, we're usually both drained.

"They're fun, though."

"The best." Autumn picked them up about an hour ago, but the mess they left in their wake is waiting for us.

"Soon, they'll call you Aunt Hannah," he whispers in my ear.

"Hmm, you have to ask me first." He says this often, and each time it warms me all over.

"How many?" Hunter asks, creeping his hand up the soft, oversized Beaten Path t-shirt I'm wearing, his thumb brushing just under where my belly button is. The same tee he gave me months ago.

"Hmm?" His devilish hands are distracting me from our conversation.

"How many?" His breath creeps along my neck and leaving a path of goosebumps behind.

"How many what?" My voice is breathy, ready for him already. Always.

"How many kids?" he says, and my world stops turning. Of course, I want kids, obviously with Hunter. He knows that. But we've never talked about it.

"What?"

"When it's time. How many do you want? I think three sounds fun, but then we'll be outnumbered. Two is a blast, but I always wanted a brother as a kid." His thumb is still playing lightly with my skin, but now his other hand is playing with my hand. Rotating a thumb at the base of my left ring finger, like he's seeing something that's not yet there.

"How many... kids? Three?" A shocked hope courses through my body.

"Not now. But soon. Soon I'm gonna ask you a question and put something right here." He pinches my finger now, right where an engagement ring would sit. "And then Rosie will be a flower girl." A small smile hits my lips as his hit my neck with a light kiss. "And then sometime after that, I'm gonna talk you into letting me put a baby in you and building a family." A tear slides down my cheek, seeing it all laid out in front of me. So simple, so beautiful. It's all I ever wanted.

"Like you'd have to talk me into it," I whisper.

"Hmm," he says, lips running up and down my neck.

"I thought I'd be scared." My voice is rough with unshed tears. "I thought when the day came for me to choose, I'd be scared to make the wrong decision. I don't feel scared, Hunter." The words coming out of my lips are whisper quiet, and I'm not even sure he can hear them.

"I'll work my whole life to prove your trust in me is worth it."

"I love you, Hunter."

"I love you, Hannah." His hand slowly, so slowly, trails down my belly, into my shorts, touching the very tip of his middle finger to my wet. My breath hitches at the unexpected jolt it sends through me. The calloused finger circles gently, round and round, until I'm squirming, panting, needing more.

"Hunter." I arch my ass into his hard crotch, knowing there's nothing beneath those sweatpants, and the thought of so little material between us has my pulse pounding.

"Yeah, baby?" he asks, casually, like he's just lying next to me and I need a crossword answer.

"Want you," I whisper, grinding back against him again, aching for him. This gentle, lazy Saturday mood is overcoming me with need, my heart full and my body ready.

"Mmmm," He says, using his other hand to ease down my loose shorts to mid-thigh. The hand curls in on my thigh, playing with my entrance while the other hand continues to play with me, tease me.

"Hunter."

"I know baby, be patient," he says, sinking one finger in, but only to the second knuckle, barely giving me anything. A moan, low and soft, falls from my lips, filled with needing, wanting, *craving* him. He pumps that finger in, slow and agonizing, gentle and sweet.

Once more, I grind my ass onto him, feeling him achingly hard behind me, knowing that with my shorts down, there's now a single layer keeping him from me. The groan he let loose comes from his chest, vibrating straight to my clit. I'm close already, this lazy love-making is exactly what I need.

Suddenly his hand is fumbling with the waistband of his sweats, pulling them down with the hand that was inside me, just far enough to release himself. He quickly lines his hard cock up with my entrance as I tip my ass back, and he pushes in, making both of us groan in appreciation.

"Every damn time. So fucking good," he murmurs into my hair, thrusting into me, driving me insane. From this angle, each thrust has the tip of him brushing my g spot, making the breath in my throat catch each time.

"God, Hunter, I need..." My hand pats behind me, trying to find his hand. Once I do, I drag it up my belly to my breast, placing his thick callused hand on top and forcing him to squeeze.

"So perfect, baby," he grunts. He's as close as I am, waiting for me to fall so he can follow. Leaving his hand, which is now pinching my nipple perfectly, I trail down my front, teasing before I spread my fingers over my pussy, feeling where he's entering me, the wetness that I'm leaking, and my swollen clit begging for release.

"Yeah baby, do it, make yourself come," he groans in my ear, nipping it before sucking the spot behind it that drives me insane. Pressing three fingers onto my clit and rubbing hard, I instantly fall apart around him, moaning his name and arching my back, urging him in further. Seconds later, he slams in one last time, and I can feel him coming in me, pulsing with each spurt he releases.

We stay like that, Hunter still in me, his come leaking from me as we catch our breath. He eventually moves my hair from my neck in a move I've come to love almost as much as the man himself.

"When I ask, will you say yes?" he says quietly, sounding winded and nervous and excited all at once.

"What do you think?" I tease, running my hand up his tanned forearm draped across my belly. He stays quiet, contemplating. "Of course, Hunter," I whisper, taking his hand in mine and squeezing.

"Good," he whispers once more, squeezing back.

NEXT IN THE SPRINGBROOK HILLS SERIES

The Protector
-luna-

Coffee in hand, I head to the bar, ready to take on the day. Well, the night. I make it an effort to get to the bar at 12, but usually unlock the door closer to one, which is why I always tell my employees to get there at 1:30 for prep,

By two we'll be open, which is later than the pub just outside of town that serves food and has a more low-key atmosphere, but it works for us.

Most days, I stop at Sadie's grabbing a coffee and gossip since our jobs run on the exact opposite schedule. My apartment is right above my bar, so the commute, in theory, shouldn't be long, but I rarely stay there for more than sleep, instead choosing to use it as a crash pad in between long nights at the bar, visits with friends, and running errands.

This morning over our coffee, she told me that Hunter asked Sadie for details on a ring.

A ring!

While we weren't in the same year at Springbrook Hills High, we're a pretty close trio. If anyone deserves the Prince Charming, sweep-you-off-your-feet thing, it's Hannah.

As I ponder this, a smile on my face as I step in any extra-crunchy leaves I see lining the paths, my phone chirps with a text. With one hand, I reach in to dig it out of my slouchy tote bag. The thing is adorable and huge, but it's always a disastrous black hole. I bet if I gave it to Hannah she'd have it orderly in no time with some fancy bag organizer, but that's not my style.

I'm the "go with the flow, rock-and-roll, hippie princess girl" to Hannah's Mary Poppins.

Grabbing onto the sleek black glitter case, I pull it out victoriously, looping the strap back on my shoulder as I stare at the screen. Immediately, ice fills my veins at yet another blocked number on my phone screen with the words *Time for games is over* flashing on the screen.

Unfortunately, this has been happening for weeks. Unknown numbers, texting, random notes in my mailbox, calls with no answer. The message is usually something vague, like the first note that just said, "hello gorgeous" on it.

Those messages were at the beginning when he seemed kind of like a sweet, shy guy. Back then, I would respond and we'd chat a bit, but it would end as soon as I asked who it was.

But they started getting... creepy in the last couple of weeks. First, it was a screenshot of my online dating profile that Sadie set up asking me what I was planning for it. Then it was a picture of me on an *actual* date, taken from behind a corner. Each text has gotten more and more unsettling, but I didn't want to make a big deal out of it.

The thing is, I run a bar. I've met and come into contact with my fair share of creeps. I've had to call the authorities a few times when my eagle eyes caught an unsavory character with ill intentions. More than a couple have yelled threats and obscenities as my security dragged them out or as the police took them in for the night.

But this feels... different. It feels ominous and greasy, dangerous even. Common sense tells me I should have brought it to someone long before now. Unfortunately, my alpha female "Yes We Can" attitude sometimes bites me in the ass, like right now. Plus, when your brother and the man you've been avoiding for ten years are both officers, you avoid it at all costs.

Stopping on the sidewalk, I stare at the screen, watching the typing bubble pop up. *Other men are not for you,* the next text reads, followed by a grainy shot of me smiling at a guy who bumped into me at Rise and Grind. The man had bumped into me, apologizing for almost spilling my drink, then complimented my shirt. He was also so not my type and moved on quickly.

As much as I don't want to admit it, I'm starting to think it's time to let an actual professional handle this. But that means I'd probably have to talk to... nope. What am I thinking? It's probably some lonely loser doing this for attention. No reason to waste precious town resources. Right?

Pulling up all of my bravery and borrowing some false bravado that Sadie is known for, I close the messaging app and throw my phone back in my bag, head high as I walk towards my baby, Full Moon Cafe.

I opened her up nearly four years ago now, taking out loans right out of school and buying up the old bar in my hometown with big hopes and dreams. I spent an entire year and acquired so many IOUs to friends and family as I built her up, renovated, designed, and curated the perfect space to grab a drink and listen to a local band.

Nothing makes me happier than turning this corner and seeing the big black and purple sign in a funky font with the phases of the moon on it reading my bar's name. Except, this time when I turn the corner, I'm forced to slow down when I see a group of people standing out front, whispering. It's too early for customers to be out front, and I'm not late, so it wouldn't be employees waiting to be let in.

But as the bar's front window comes into sight, I notice the bright red words on the front of the glass windows.

FUCK YOU WHORE

The words are sprayed across the windows in dripping spray paint. As I walk closer in a daze, I feel the blood drain from my face, clear by my immediate light-headedness. I'm forced to grab onto a metal bench beside me to stop the world from spinning. When my phone beeps again, I pull it out to look.

Like my art? It says in the same text conversation as before. The world around me spins, nausea roiling in my stomach. Why is this happening to me? Who is this?

"Oh, God, Luna! I'm so sorry! I called the police a few minutes ago, they should be here any minute!" It's Daisy, the sweet, young bartender that's been working for me for about a year. Her blue eyes are wide with fear and worry.

I should comfort her. I

'm her boss, and she's young, not even 22. But all I can do is put a hand to my knees while I hold the chilled metal bench and try to force air into my lungs. My breaths are shallow, coming in short pants as I hyperventilate. Focusing on a small ant that's walking across the sidewalk carrying a large crumb of something, I try to get it together.

"Luna! Luna! Are you okay? Luna!" Daisy's hand is on my back, but I swat her away, standing and trying not to sway as the bar comes back into focus, the crude letters sending another wave of nausea through me. "Come, sit down," she says, guiding me to sit on the bench.

What should I be doing right now?

Should I be crying? Or yelling? How does someone react to something like this?

These are the kinds of things I always wonder about when something bad happens. How does a normal person react? If I passed out right now, would it be weird? If I started screaming, is that normal?

What feels like years flies by, but common sense says it was only seconds before my brain snaps into shape. All emotions are pushed into a vault that I lock, holding onto the key to reopen and release later when no one is around, preferably when I have a bottle of wine nearby. Instead, I pull out my boss lady hat, securing it, and taking action.

Immediately, my mind makes a list of whom to call. I'll need to call Dan over at the glass company—now I see one pane has been shattered. The insurance company should cover this, so they'll need a call as well. And my brother, I'll have him bring his power washer. I wonder if that can blast off spray paint. Maybe Susan at the paint shop knows a good way to get that paint off, too.

But then, my moment of clarity ends as Daisy sighs in relief, "Oh, thank God, the police are here."

"What?" I say, panic rising as I look at her.

"I also called Garden State Security when I came. They just arrived. It looks like it's..." I can assumer she tells me who has arrived her voice is already a drone in the background, my mind turning all outside noise to static.

Because I know who it's going to be that shows up. With a day like today, luck like mine, it can only be one person.

And looking to my left, I see the man I've been avoiding for years relatively successfully: Tony fucking Garrison.

DON'T MISS LUNA AND TONY'S STORY IN THE PROTECTOR

Out now in the Kindle Store and on Kindle Unlimited

He was her first love.

Luna Davidson has been in love with Tony since she was ten years old. As her older brother's best friend, he was always off-limits, but that doesn't mean she didn't try. But years after he turned her down, she's found herself needing his help, whether she wants it or not.

She's his best friend's little sister.

When he learns that Luna has had someone stalking her for months, he's furious that she didn't tell anyone. As a bodyguard for Garden State Security, it's his job to protect. But can he use this as an excuse to find out what really happened all those years ago?

Can Luna overcome her own insecurities to see what's right in front of her? Can Tony figure out who is stalking her before it goes too far?

WANT A DELETED SCENE?

When Hunter leaves town for work, he finally makes good on his

promise to listen to her over the p

hone. But there's a twist Hannah doesn't know about, yet!

I've written a special deleted scene ONLY for my readers—join my newsletter and grab your copy!

Get yours for free here!

WANT MORE SPRINGBROOK HILLS?

Out now in the Kindle Store and on Kindle Unlimited

He was her first love.

Luna Davidson has been in love with Tony since she was ten years old. As her older brother's best friend, he was always off-limits, but that doesn't mean she didn't try. But years after he turned her down, she's found herself needing his help, whether she wants it or not.

She's his best friend's little sister.

When he learns that Luna has had someone stalking her for months, he's furious that she didn't tell anyone. As a bodyguard with Garden State Security, it's his job to serve and protect. But can he use this as an excuse to find out what really happened all those years ago?

Can Luna overcome her own insecurities to see what's right in front of her? Can Tony figure out who is stalking her before it goes too far?

Out now in the Kindle Store and on Kindle Unlimited

She was always the fill-in.

Jordan Daniels always knew she had a brother and sister her mom left behind. Heck, her mom never let her forget she didn't live up to their standards. But when she disappears from the limelight after her country star boyfriend proposes, the only place she knows to go to is to the town her mother fled and the family who doesn't know she exists.

He won't fall for another wild child.

Tanner Coleman was left in the dust once before when his high school sweetheart ran off to follow a rockstar around the world. He loves his roots, runs the family business, and will never leave Springbrook Hills. But when Jordan, with her lifetime spent traveling the world and mysterious history comes to work for him, he can't help but feel drawn to her.

Can Jordan open up to him about her past and stay in one place? Can Tanner trust his heart with her, or will she just hurt him like his ex?

WANT THE CHANCE TO WIN KINDLE STICKERS AND SIGNED COPIES?

Leave an honest review on Amazon or Goodreads and send the link to reviewteam@authormorganelizabeth.com and you'll be entered to win a signed copy of one of Morgan Elizabeth's books and a pack of bookish stickers!

Each email is an entry (you can send one email with your Goodreads review and another with your Kindle review for two entries per book) and two winners will be chosen at the beginning of each month!

ABOUT THE AUTHOR

Morgan is a born and raised Jersey girl, living there with her two boys, toddler daughter, and mechanic husband. She's addicted to iced espresso, barbecue chips, and Starburst jellybeans. She usually has headphones on, listening to some spicy audiobook or Taylor Swift. There is rarely an in between.

Writing has been her calling for as long as she can remember. There's a framed 'page one' of a book she wrote at seven hanging in her childhood home to prove the point. Her entire life she's crafted stories in her mind, begging to be released but it wasn't until recently she finally gave them the reigns.

I'm so grateful you've agreed to take this journey with me.

Stay up to date via TikTok and Instagram

Stay up to date with future stories, get sneak peeks and bonus chapters by joining the Reader Group on Facebook!

ALSO BY MORGAN ELIZABETH

The Springbrook Hills Series

The Distraction

The Protector

The Substitution

The Connection

The Playlist

Holiday Standalone, interconnected with SBH:

Tis the Season for Revenge

The Ocean View Series

The Ex Files

Walking Red Flag

Bittersweet

The Mastermind Duet

Ivory Tower

Diamond Fortress

Printed in Great Britain
by Amazon